Unnatural

Unnatural

AN ARCHANGEL ACADEMY NOVEL

michael griffo

KENSINGTON PUBLISHING CORP.
www.kensingtonbooks.com

K TEEN BOOKS are published by

Kensington Publishing Corp.
119 West 40th Street
New York, NY 10018

ISBN-13: 978-0-7582-5338-5
ISBN-10: 0-7582-5338-9

First Kensington Trade Paperback Printing: March 2011
10 9 8 7 6 5 4 3 2 1

Printed in the United States of America

For my parents

Acknowledgments

I'm enormously grateful to my agent, Evan Marshall, for his support, honesty, and willingness to take a chance on an unknown writer. I am equally indebted to my editor, John Scognamiglio, for his insight, vision, and enthusiastic encouragement. I can't imagine my work or my career being in better hands.

And special thanks to Linda, Lori, Jim, and Joan for giving me a quiet place to write when I couldn't find some quiet on my own.

Unnatural

one drop
two drops
three drops
four

floodgates open
the waters pour

cool and
warm and
clear and
red

am I alive?
or am I dead?

prologue

Outside, the earth was wet.

The rain had finally stopped, but it had poured hard and long during the night, the sudden storm catching the land unprepared for such a prolonged onslaught. From Michael's bedroom window he could see the dirt road that led up to his house had flooded and the passageway that could lead him to another place, any place away from here, was broken, unusable. Today would not be the day he would be set free.

Ever since Michael was old enough to understand there was a world outside of his home, his school, his entire town, he had fantasized about leaving it all behind. Setting foot on the dirt path that began a few inches below his front steps and walking, walking, walking until the dirt road brought him somewhere else, somewhere that for him was better. He didn't know where that place was, he didn't know what it looked like; he only knew, he felt, that it existed.

Or was it all just foolish hope? Peering down from his second-floor window at the rain-drenched earth below, at the muddy river separating his home from everything else, he wondered if he was wrong. Was his dream of escape just that, a dream and nothing more? Would this be his view for all time? A harsh, unaccepting land that, despite living here for thirteen of his sixteen years, made him feel like an intruder. Leave! He could hear the wind command, *This place is not for you.* But go where?

On the front lawn he saw a meadowlark, smaller than typical but still robust-looking, drink from the weather-beaten birdbath that overflowed with fresh rainwater. Drinking, drinking, drinking as if its thirst could not be quenched. It stopped and surveyed the area, singing its familiar melodious tune, *da-da-DAH-da, da-da-da,* and pausing only when it caught Michael's stare. *Switch places with me,* Michael thought. *Let me rest on the brink of another flight, and you sit here and wait.*

And where would you go? the meadowlark asked. *You know nothing of the world beyond this dirt.*

Nothing now, but I'm willing to learn. The lark blinked, its yellow feathers bristling slightly, *but I'm not willing to forget everything that I know. Da-da-DAH-da, da-da-da.*

How wonderful would it be to forget everything? Forget that the mornings did not bring with them the promise of excitement, but just another day. Forget that the evenings did not bring with them the anticipation of adventure, but just darkness. Forget it all and start fresh, start over.

The meadowlark was walking along the ledge of the birdbath, interrupting the stagnant water this time with its feet instead of its beak, looking just as impatient as it did wise. You can never start over. The new life you may create is filled with memories of the old one. The new person you may become retains the essence of who you were.

No, Michael thought, *I want to escape all this. I want to escape who I am!*

Humans, such a foolish species, the lark thought. *Da-da-DAH-da da-da-da.* You can never escape your true self and you'll never be able to escape this world until you accept that.

Michael watched the meadowlark fly away, perhaps with a destination in mind, perhaps just willing to follow the current—regardless, out of view, gone. And Michael remained. The water in the birdbath still rippled with the lark's memory, retaining what was once there, proof that there had been a visitor. Michael wondered if he would leave behind any proof that he was here when he left, if he ever left. Not that he cared if anyone remembered his presence, but simply to leave behind proof that he had existed before he began to live.

He turned his back to the window, the meadowlark's memory and song, the flooded earth—none of that truly belonged to him anyway—and he gazed upon his room. For now, this sanctuary was all he had. He was grateful for it, grateful to have some place to wait until the waters receded and his path could lead him away from here.

But that would not happen today. Today his world, as wrong as it was, would have to do.

chapter 1

Before the Beginning

Like a snake slithering out of the brush, a bead of sweat emerged from his wavy, unkempt brown hair. Alone, but determined, it slowly slid down the right side of his forehead, less than an inch from his hazel-colored eye, then gaining momentum, it glided over his sharp, tanned cheekbone. Now the bead grew into a streak, a line of perspiration, half the length of his face. He turned his head faintly to the left and the streak picked up more speed and raced toward his mouth, zigzagging slightly but effortlessly as it traveled over the stubble on his cheek and stopping only when it landed at the corner of his mouth. He didn't move. The streak grew into a bubble, a mixture of water and salt, and hung there nestled between his lips until his tongue, in one quick, fluid movement, flicked it away. Then it was gone. All that remained as proof that it had once existed was the wet stain of perspiration that ran from his forehead to his mouth. That and Michael's memory.

Sitting next to his grandpa in the front seat of his beat-up '98 Ford Ranger, Michael had been watching R.J. in the rearview mirror as he pumped gas. He was still watching him, actually; he couldn't help it. His viewing choices were his grandpa's unwelcoming face, the flat dirt road, the dilapidated Highway 50 gas station, the cloudless blue sky, or R.J. Without hesitation, his eyes had found the gas station attendant, as they always did when he accompanied his grandpa on Saturday mornings to fill up the tank on their way to the recycling center. Today, the last Saturday morning in August and a particularly hot one, found R.J. more languid than usual.

He pressed his lean body against the Ranger, his left arm raised overhead and resting on the side of the truck so that if Michael inched forward a bit in his seat, he could see the hairs of R.J.'s armpits jutting out from underneath his loose, well-worn T-shirt. Michael inhaled deeply, the smell of gasoline filling him, and his eyes followed that smell to the pump that R.J. held in his right hand. Michael's eyes moved from the pump to R.J.'s long index finger wrapped around the pump's trigger and then traveled along the vein that lay just underneath R.J.'s skin. The vein, large and pronounced, started at his knuckle, spread to his wrist, and then moved along the length of his arm until it ended at the crease of his elbow. His arm, flexed as he pumped the gas, looked strong, and Michael wondered what it would feel like. Would it feel like his own arm or like something completely different? Something much better.

Absentmindedly, Michael touched his forearm; it was smooth and hot. He traced his own much smaller vein with his finger and he could feel his pulse, rapid, restless, new, and he wondered if beneath R.J.'s lazy demeanor his pulse was just as quick. Or was Michael the only one who felt speed underneath his skin?

The click of the gas pump ended all speculation. Michael shot a quick glance to his grandpa, who was staring out at the land, busy smoking his third Camel in an hour, since his grandmother refused to allow him to smoke inside the house. As always his mind, like Michael's, was elsewhere.

Michael heard the snap as R.J. returned the nozzle to its cradle, the quick tick-tick-tick as he closed the gas cap, and the slam as he shut the cover of the gas lid. And just as he turned to look out his window, hoping to catch a whiff of R.J.'s scent as he walked around the car to collect the cash from his grandpa like he always did, R.J. decided to change the rules. He squatted down next to Michael's window and peered into the truck.

"That'll be twenty-seven fifty," R.J. said in his usual low hum.

This was a surprise. Underneath his skin he felt his pulse increase, but Michael had learned not to show the outside world what was happening inside him and so his expression remained calm. Just another bored teenager sitting in a truck with his grandpa on a hot August Saturday morning. But he was much more than bored; R.J.'s face ignited curiosity.

Unable to turn away, Michael soaked it all in. Up close, Michael could see that there were a few more beads of sweat on R.J.'s forehead, lingering there, not yet ready to take the trip down his face. While Michael's grandpa reached into his front pocket to pull out his cash, R.J. rested his chin on his forearm and closed his eyes. His eyelashes were like a girl's, long, delicate, with a beautiful upcurl to them. Michael had the urge to run his finger through them as if they were strings of a harp. Like most of his urges, he repressed it.

How many freckles were on his slender nose? Six, eight . . . before Michael could finish counting, R.J. brushed his cheek against his arm, wiping away any telltale signs of perspiration that had remained, and looked up directly into Michael's eyes. His mouth formed a smile and then words, "Hot today, ain't it?"

Keep looking bored, Michael thought, *uninterested, so no one will suspect.* "Yeah," Michael said, nodding his head.

"Gonna be a scorcher today," Michael's grandpa said, "but ya can't trust those weathermen to know nothin'."

R.J.'s face retained its expression, no change whatsoever. Was R.J. suppressing what he really felt too, or did he agree with Michael's grandpa? "Can't really trust anybody," R.J. said. "Can ya, Mike?"

That sounded odd to Michael's ears; nobody called him Mike. He wasn't a Mike, it didn't fit, but maybe it could be the name that only R.J. used. That would be okay. Michael cleared his throat and then replied, "Guess not."

"Here." Michael's grandpa thrust some bills in front of Michael, and R.J. reached out to grab them. A beat later, Michael reached forward to grab the money and pass it along to R.J., but he was too late. Or maybe he was right on time? His fingers brushed against R.J.'s forearm and he discovered that R.J.'s skin was just as smooth as his, but much hotter and firmer than his own. Michael mumbled "sorry," but he was drowned out by his grandpa's command, "That's twenty-eight there, Rudolph; credit me fifty cents next time."

Rudolph. Michael's grandpa was the only one who called him by his real name. Sounded more inappropriate than calling Michael *Mike.* But Mike and Rudolph? That had an exciting sound to it. Michael didn't see R.J.'s patronizing smile; he kept his gaze down at the fingers that had recently touched his skin, but he did hear him. "Will do, sir." He didn't look back up until he heard the motor running and heard his grandpa shift the car into drive. He turned to catch one more glimpse of R.J.'s face, but he had stood up and all Michael could see was his hand stuffing the cash into the frayed pocket of his jeans. And then there was a breeze.

R.J.'s T-shirt lifted and for a moment his hip flank, sharply defined and smooth, was exposed. Michael thought it looked like a small hill on an otherwise flat plain where he could rest his head, maybe dream a little. As the truck pulled away, Michael looked through the rearview mirror, but the breeze had died and R.J.'s T-shirt covered that interesting piece of flesh. Later that night, Michael would remember it, though, because no matter how hard he tried, he just knew it was something he wouldn't be able to forget.

After Michael helped his grandpa bring the cans and bottles to the recycling center, there were other errands to run. Had to pick up a new fog light at Sears that he would later be forced to watch his grandpa install in his mother's car because she turned a corner too sharply and busted hers; then they had to drive over to the Home Depot to get a new toilet chain that Grandpa would watch Michael install in the downstairs bathroom; and of course it wouldn't be Saturday if his grandpa didn't play the Nebraska Lottery.

"Up to a hundred seventy million this week," the redheaded cashier informed them.

"If I win, you and me'll bust outta here," Grandpa said.

"My bags are already packed!" the redheaded cashier chortled. Even though the cashier was roughly forty years younger than his grandpa and still what locals would call fine-lookin', Michael had no doubt that if his grandpa came back next week waving a winning lottery ticket, she would hop in the Ranger to drive off with him to parts unknown. Weeping Water was not the kind of town that instilled loyalty in its residents, unless they had nowhere else to go.

But Michael did have some place he could go. He had started his life somewhere else, he was born someplace far, far from this town, where he could be living right now. But his mother had put an end to all of that. Why?! Why had she ruined everything? No. No sense blaming her now; the damage had already been done. He would just spend the rest of the day imagining how far from here he would travel if he were lucky enough to win the lottery.

When all the dinner dishes were washed and put away and his grandparents were sitting in their own separate chairs in front of the television, he finishing an after-dinner beer, she finishing yet another knitting project, Michael sat on his bed rereading *A Separate Peace,* one of his favorite novels, some music that he vaguely recognized filling the space of his room. Before he finished chapter one, his mother knocked on his door to ask the same question she'd been asking all summer long.

"Heya, honey, aren't ya going out tonight?"

Grace Howard had once been a beautiful woman. So beautiful that she won a series of beauty pageants culminating in Miss Nebraska, which meant that she could fly to Atlantic City to participate in the Miss America contest. Pretty big stuff for any town desperate for some notoriety, incredibly huge stuff for a town like Weeping Water. She didn't crack the top ten, but she did catch the eye of a young college student on vacation from England. Against the vehement protests of her parents, Grace nixed a return to Nebraska and instead flew to England with Vaughan. She had never done anything so spontaneous or rebellious in her entire life. Three months after the contest, she and Vaughan Howard got married on his family's estate in Canterbury, roughly an hour southeast of London. Vaughan was her winning lottery ticket. Until she decided to rip it up into little pieces and return home, dragging her crying toddler with her.

"No, I need to finish this before school on Monday," Michael lied with just a glance in his mother's direction.

"But it's the last weekend before school starts back up."

Don't remind me, Michael thought. "I know, that's why I have to finish."

His mother was in his room now, which meant that either she wanted to discuss something or she was incredibly bored and had exhausted all conversation with her parents. "Can't believe you're a sophomore already; my little guy's gettin' to be a man." She was standing in front of the oak bookshelf, looking at the spines of all the books Michael had read and would most likely read again. They were his escape. It didn't take a genius to figure that out. "I hated to read when I was your age; still can't concentrate long enough to get through a magazine article."

From behind, Michael's mother still looked youthful. Her brown hair was full and fell an inch or two below her shoulders, her arms were taut and hadn't yet gotten flabby, and her hips still held their curve. It's when she turned to face Michael that he saw age had crept into her face prematurely. Michael knew that a thirty-seven-year-old woman shouldn't look like that.

"You know Darlene's daughter?"

"Who?"

"Darlene Garrison. Michael, sometimes . . ." Now she was fiddling with something on his desk. "Sometimes I don't think you pay attention to anything except these books of yours. Darlene owns the beauty parlor A Cut Above; she does my hair. Her daughter, Jeralyn, is in your grade."

Michael had no idea who Jeralyn Garrison was, so he lied again. "Oh yeah, I think so."

"Where'd you get this?" His mother held up a Union Jack bumper sticker.

"I found it at the Sears auto store when I was there with Grandpa. He told me I couldn't put the British flag on his Ranger. I told him I had no intention of doing that; I bought it 'cause I liked it."

Michael saw the familiar glaze come over his mother's eyes. He remained silent because he knew that if he kept on talking, if he asked her a direct question even, she wouldn't hear him. She was in the room, but her mind wasn't. Her heart might not be in the room either, but his mother rarely talked about what lay in her heart, so it was hard to tell about that. When she placed the bumper sticker gently back on his desk and turned to face him, he was compelled to speak despite knowing it might be futile.

"Do you ever miss London?"

Grace looked at her son. *He doesn't look a thing like me, does he? I don't have blond hair, my skin isn't so pale, my eyes aren't green. If I hadn't been there when the doctor pulled him out from inside of me, I would never believe this person was my flesh and blood. But he was, he is,* she thought. *In some ways, he's all I'll ever be able to truly call my own.*

"No," she lied. "I told you before, it's a crowded, loud city. Dirty, no space to breathe, no clean air. I can't believe you remember it; you were only three when we left."

"I don't really have memories, but impressions. I don't know, I just get the feeling that I would like it."

He doesn't even sound like me, Grace thought. *He never does. He says things that just don't make sense, that make me question why I ever became a parent, why I ever wasted my life raising him.* "You mean you just get the feeling that you'd like it better than here."

And the change had begun. Michael saw his mother's lips press against each other to form a smile that meant to convey anything but joy, her head tilt to the right, and her eyes fill with disbelief. Their roles had reversed. She was the emotionally reactive teenager and he was the insightful parent. Experience had taught him this conversation would not be any different from any other conversation he'd ever had with his mother about London or what their life was like before she brought him to this place, the place where she grew up, or what their

life could be like if they moved back. Nothing important would be disclosed, nothing important would be
shared between mother and son. And so he just went
back to reading.

His mother paced the width of the room, once,
twice. She hated when Michael asked about London.
For her it was another lifetime ago, a mistake. No, not
a mistake entirely. *What should I call it?* she thought.
She couldn't come up with a word. As always, the
mention of London and her past made her fidgety, confused. The only thing she was certain of was that it
was part of her past and that's where it should remain.
Yes, it should remain buried and silent. Because when
she thought of London, all she thought of was him,
Michael's father. The man she ran away with and the
man she eventually ran from. The man she once loved
and would always love. The man she never wanted to
see again. "Do me one favor," Grace said before leaving her son alone. "When you get married, be a better
husband than your father was."

A cold sensation of fear trickled down Michael's neck
and found its resting place on his heart. It squeezed, it
constricted, until Michael could hardly breathe and had
to consciously put down his book and gasp, gasp for a
breath that should have come easily. But his mother saw
to it that it didn't. She had to mention marriage and becoming a husband, didn't she? If Michael didn't know
better, he'd think his mother was punishing him for bringing up London. And maybe she was. Lately she had been

acting so erratically he had no idea what she was thinking. All he knew was that whenever his mother, or anyone for that matter, insinuated that he should get married
and become a husband, he panicked. It just felt wrong.
The only thing that made him feel worse was that, to
everyone else, it felt perfectly right.

Just as his breathing returned to normal, he heard the
medicine cabinet open, which could mean only one
thing: His mother needed some comfort. Maybe it was
the white pill; perhaps tonight it would be the blue pill.
It didn't matter. Michael didn't have to see into the
bathroom to know that his mother was taking a pill to
calm her nerves. A pill before bedtime was the only
thing that seemed to help her these days. That and a
nice glass of white wine.

*What happened to the mother who used to help me
with my homework after dinner? Explain to me how to
figure out percentages and the differences among the
three branches of government. When did she stop wanting to help me and start wanting to create me in her
image?* Now Michael was pacing his room, back and
forth, trying to figure out why his mother was no longer
on his side, pacing, pacing, pacing, until he forced himself to stop moving. He gripped the windowsill and
looked out into the night. The moonlight allowed him
to see only a few yards of the dirt road; the rest was hidden in darkness, out of his reach once again. *Why do I
hate it here so much?!* Maybe, just maybe, it had to do
with what was taking place downstairs.

"Again with the wine," Michael's grandfather snick-
ered.

"Should I drink whiskey?" Grace asked. "Would that
make you happy? Oh, that's right, there's nothing that
would make you happy."

"Don't you talk to me like that!"

"And don't you dare tell me what to do!"

That was different. Michael's mother didn't usually
talk back to her father. Guess the pills and the wine
weren't working as quickly to calm her as they usually
did.

"Maybe if you weren't drinking all the time, you'd be
able to straighten out that son of yours."

"You leave him out of this," Grace said, much quieter. *Ah, now the pills are kicking in.* "He's a good boy."

"He ain't no boy!" his grandfather shouted. "He's
like that fairy husband of yours!"

"He's nothing like Vaughan!"

"Is too! A sissy boy and he ain't gonnna 'mount to
nothin'! Mark my words!"

"You shut your mouth, Daddy! Shut it! Michael is
not . . . like *that*. He's perfectly normal!"

But Michael knew his mother was wrong. He wasn't
normal. His grandfather didn't have to come right out
and say it; Michael knew what he was. He stared at his
reflection in the window and he could see it in his own
eyes. What he saw made him disgusted, scared, but yes,
just a little excited even though he knew what he was
seeing wasn't right. Tomorrow at church he would pray

that it would all go away, that he would be able to change who he was, but tonight . . . tonight he would lock his bedroom door, block out the sounds coming from downstairs, and think about R.J. And he would convince himself that it was the most natural thing in the world.

chapter 2

Not a word was spoken during the half-hour drive to church. It would be optimistic to think that Michael, his mother, and his grandparents were all engaged in private meditation, but the truth is, they had nothing to say to one another. At least nothing that would be appropriate to say en route to God's house.

They took Grace's gray Ford Taurus, complete with its new fog light, but Michael's grandpa drove because Grace, who sat in the back with Michael, was too tired to drive. Hungover was more like it, but no one contradicted her. Why point out the obvious? So the only sounds that filled up the emptiness were the whir of the air conditioner, the crunch of the tires on the dirt road, and then the softer hum when they merged onto the highway. And of course the sounds that filled Michael's head.

He turned to look at his mother, silent now, eyes closed, trying to sleep, summoning the strength to make it through another sermon perhaps, and heard the words she shouted to his grandpa last night: "He's perfectly normal!" It wasn't the first time he'd heard her say that or words just like it; they often argued about him when he wasn't in the room and he imagined that their arguments were louder and their words more tactless when they knew he wasn't in the house and there was no chance of his overhearing. Yes, the words bothered him, but worse was the sound of his mother's voice, hopeful, a bit defiant, but mostly desperate because she knew even as she spoke the words that they weren't the truth.

Michael wasn't perfectly normal. And the older he got, the more of a problem it was becoming. But if only his mother supported him, maybe it wouldn't have to be such a problem. Maybe he could handle everyone else's criticisms and unkind comments if he knew she didn't view him as such an incredible disappointment. Wasn't his mother supposed to love him unconditionally? Wasn't she supposed to defend him without letting her own doubts and fears emerge? Time and time again his mother failed him and she only succeeded in making him realize that he was on this earth by himself. He hated the feeling, but lately he was forced to admit that it was liberating. At least he knew where he stood.

"I'll try to get that radio fixed this week," Grandpa said. Now that they were in the openness of the church parking lot and not the confined space of the car, it was easier to speak.

Walking up the wooden steps of the church, he felt each plank bend and creak with his weight as if the steps were acting as guardians deciding if they should allow him entry or break in half and swallow him whole. He smiled to himself. *How ironic; that's how I already feel, swallowed up by the earth, silenced.* He watched his mother and grandma smile and nod at the other parishioners. Occasionally his grandma would clasp another old woman's hand, not out of affection really, but just a desire to connect to someone, anyone, but they too were silent. Only Grandpa made noise.

Whether welcoming men who looked as tired and weary as he did with a gruff hello or slapping someone on the back vigorously, his grandpa was heard. In the company of his kindred spirits he was simply unable to restrain his innate rowdy behavior even while clad in his iron-pressed Sunday clothes. Michael envied such freedom. To be able to act upon your instinct—now, that would truly be liberating. Unfortunately, his instinct was frowned upon by the church, so when he saw R.J. bound up the steps with some girl, some girl who wasn't even pretty, he didn't rush to him and slap him on his back or shake his soft, firm hand; he resolutely followed his family inside.

A few minutes later when all the pews were filled with bodies, either eager or resigned to spend the next hour in reflection, Michael looked around at his family, the congregation, at the people who inhabited his world, and he was overcome with a feeling of loneliness. He just didn't belong. It struck him like a nail through the palm; he knew it in his mind, he felt it in his body, his soul . . . no, he didn't want to contemplate his soul, not here, not surrounded by these strangers; he didn't want to open his soul up to inspection and risk contamination by others.

Where was R.J.? He scoured the pews in front of him and couldn't find his face. Bending down as if he needed to scratch his leg, he looked quickly behind him and there he was, next to her. Why was she giggling in church? And why did she look so ugly when she laughed? Michael looked at R.J. and he wasn't laughing, but he was definitely smiling. And definitely not looking at him.

He gripped the back of the pew in front of him with both hands until his knuckles were white. In the distance he could hear Father Charles reciting something, a prayer, some words, and he tried to remember that, despite what those around him thought, even he was welcome in this house. He felt his eyes begin to water. No, he wouldn't cry, not here, not now. Why was he acting like this? It was hardly his first time in church; isolation among this group was not a new sensation. Maybe he couldn't pretend anymore. Maybe he couldn't pretend that being different didn't matter. Everyone has their breaking point. And that's when he saw his mother reach hers.

The tears that Michael refused to shed poured quietly down his mother's face, without fanfare, without a desire to be seen, just a part of her that could no longer remain locked away. Her face, however, was unburdened by sadness; on the contrary, it looked blank, which only confused Michael more. He had often seen his mother cry, after she had had too much to drink, when the paramedics carted her off once, twice, to a place where she could rest, a place where she didn't want to go. But those times her tears were accompanied by shouts, screams, a face contorted with anger and fear; these tears were different, they were alone. His mother was crying, but it was as if she were discarding her tears because she had learned she had no use for them; tears no longer made a difference.

The Lord's Prayer was being recited around them, and Michael wished he could stare straight ahead and mutter the words, but he couldn't do anything but stare at his mother. What was happening to her? And for that matter to him? And why was she leaving?

Grace had grabbed her purse and was now awkwardly stepping in front of Michael and then the rest of the people in their pew until she reached the aisle. The voices continued speaking "as we forgive those who trespass against us," but all heads turned to see Grace genuflect deeply and cross herself before turning and walking out of the church.

Michael looked at his grandma and he wasn't sure what he saw in her eyes. Was it compassion, was it indifference? He could never tell with her. His grandpa's story was much easier to interpret. In his eyes he saw disgust.

Following the same path his mother just took, Michael made his way toward the aisle. He didn't stop to genuflect but simply turned and swiftly walked away from the altar and toward the huge wooden church doors. He was so focused on getting outside to find out what was going on with his mother, he didn't even pause when he saw R.J. ignore the girl next to him and look in his direction. No time for him now. His grandma started to make the same journey, but her husband, not taking his eyes off Father Charles, placed his hand firmly on top of hers, and she did what she always did; she gave in to his command.

Outside he saw his mother sitting on the church steps; her body looked tiny but, in an odd way, strong. Her back was straight, her head turned up to look at the dark, ominous clouds that had settled overhead, as if she were saying one final good-bye before the steps broke in two and the earth swallowed her up forever. *No, take me,* Michael thought. *She belongs here, I don't.*

By the time he sat down next to her, the raindrops started to fall. She was still looking up at the clouds, so he couldn't tell if her face was streaked with tears or rain; he also couldn't tell what she was feeling or thinking since her face was still a blank mask. In that moment Michael felt closer to his mother than he had in years; he too understood the need to conceal what was going on underneath the skin, keep all your emotions and desires secret. Could it be that they weren't that different? Could it be that she understood? No.

"Michael," his mother said, her eyes unblinking in the rain. "I want you to get married right on these steps so you can have a good start in life." She had no idea. "If only I had gotten married here, standing on this solid wood instead of foreign soil, maybe my marriage would have been built upon a stronger foundation, maybe I wouldn't have broken my vows. And maybe I wouldn't have disappointed so many people."

She closed her eyes and tilted her head back, allowing the rain to cascade down her face and through her hair, and finally she displayed some emotion. She smiled. Her sins were being washed away. Swept off her skin by the rain to be absorbed by the church steps. And if that didn't do the trick, there was always a pill.

Without looking into her purse, she found the pill she needed, the one that would help. She opened her mouth and collected the rain. Michael watched, amazed by the primitive yet efficient gesture, as his mother waited until a little puddle was created in her throat and then she popped the pill into her mouth. She swallowed both the rain and the pill, like they were the blood and body of

28

Christ. Sitting next to his mother, witness to her own private mass, Michael felt the stab of truth in his gut: He could not rely on her to protect or defend him. She was too engaged in her own struggle for survival. And even though he felt a certain amount of empathy for his mother, he noted with more than a small degree of sadness that what he felt even more for her was disappointment.

Lying in his bed later that night, *A Separate Peace* folded against his chest, he dreamed, not of disappointment, but of satisfaction. For some reason, Phineas looked just like R.J. and had an accent, British, Irish. Michael couldn't place it, but he liked the way it sounded; the rhythm and the lilt were comforting. Phineas was telling him that he could jump from the tree, that the fall wouldn't hurt him, and even though he was high, very high above the grassy knoll, Michael trusted him. Arms outstretched, chest inflated, Michael leapt into the air and for a few brief seconds he floated without concern, without fear, with only the certainty that love could bring. He knew that neither Phineas nor R.J. would lie to him, he knew that his landing would be soft. What he didn't expect was that his landing would be wet.

Instead of touching down on the ground, Michael plunged through the surface of water. He didn't know if he fell through a lake, an ocean, a pool; he only knew he felt water, cold but exhilarating, engulf him tenderly. He could feel every inch of his body, every pore, submit to its power and it felt wonderful, it felt natural, and when Phineas reached his hand out to him, Michael instinctively reached his hand out to grab hold. When Phineas pulled Michael close to him and his face morphed into R.J.'s, Michael didn't pull away but allowed the older boy's strength to embrace him. Here in his dream, underwater, Michael could finally admit this was where he wanted to be, in another boy's arms, looking directly into eyes that were like his, eyes that in real life, that on land, had not yet been found.

R.J.'s hazel eyes beckoned Michael to come closer, and so he did. He saw in them understanding and beauty and peace and he longed for all those qualities to permeate his soul, and so he came even closer to R.J. until their faces were separated by only a thin strip of water. Their mouths opened and breathed; here they were not restricted by nature, here they could breathe, here they could do anything they wanted. And what they wanted to do, what Michael wanted to do most of all, was to become one with R.J., give himself up entirely to him so he wouldn't feel so alone. He felt the heat within his body ignite against the cold water and his mouth searched R.J.'s. He wanted to kiss him, fully and powerfully, and he knew that R.J. wanted to do the same thing.

But what R.J. did was scream.

Shrieking loudly, R.J. pulled away, pushed Michael from him so he tumbled backward, stumbling in the water's current. Shrieking as if he were in agony. How could Michael think he wanted to do something so disgusting as to kiss another boy? How could Michael think that he would want to do something so vile? R.J. was shrieking so loudly, the vibrations made the water start to churn; it came alive, spinning like a whirlpool that threatened to swallow Michael whole. Deep, guttural screeching that caught in Michael's ears and wouldn't let go. Now the sound was higher, a shrill piercing that pushed Michael through the water's surface and left him gasping for air. That's when he realized the screams were not coming from his dream, but from downstairs.

Startled, Michael shot up in bed, his book falling to the floor. "Noooooo!!!" His eyes darted around his bedroom; he couldn't see much as the room was lit up only by the moonlight peering through his window, but even still he knew that he was alone. R.J. and Phineas were gone; they were no longer beside him. The voice, however, hadn't left. "Let go! Get him off of me!" He recognized that voice because he had heard it scream many times before. It was his mother's.

He reached the top of the stairs just in time to see two men grab his mother from both sides, each one holding a different arm. They made sure to grab her by the forearms, not far below her elbow, but far above her bloody wrists. Michael wondered why they hadn't worn protective gloves if they were concerned with getting their hands bloodstained, since this wasn't the first time they had been called to this house for such an emergency.

The woman who writhed and wriggled between the two men looked nothing like the woman who had sat on the church steps earlier that day. Michael reminded himself that his mother could go from tranquil to frenzied in much shorter time and had previously done so; this should be no surprise. But of course it was. This woman was still his mother.

"Go back to your room!" his grandpa shouted as Michael was halfway down the stairs. "We don't need you down here!" Frozen, Michael couldn't move. He wasn't ignoring his grandpa's directive; he just for the moment couldn't follow it. There was too much going on.

A third man entered the house, holding a syringe, and when Grace saw this, her tearless eyes grew more wild and fearful, her movements quicker and more convulsive. She knew what was coming. She knew the needle of the syringe would be jabbed into her skin, its liquid would be unleashed into her bloodstream, and she would lose control. She would wake up somewhere unfamiliar knowing, when her mind cleared, that once again she was a disappointment to those around her.

Michael too was disappointed with those around him. In the corner of the room he saw his grandma fumbling through a rosary, looking helpless and, Michael couldn't believe he felt this, pathetic. She couldn't even find the strength to look at her daughter but instead gazed at the rosary beads as if they had some power. The only power they had was the ability to make her ignore her daughter's true problems, stare at the white beads, not at the white jacket that the men were now putting on his mother. A white straitjacket that, unfortunately, was a perfect fit.

He was also disappointed with his grandpa, which he loathed to admit was not so unusual. The old man told the paramedics that he wouldn't be riding with them in the ambulance and that he wouldn't be following in his car, either. He wasn't going to the hospital this time; somebody had to wash out the blood from the rug before it left a stain.

"I'll go," Michael heard himself say.

"I told you to git upstairs!" his grandpa shouted back.

One of the paramedics said that his mother was in good hands, that she would be asleep for hours, so he should do as his grandfather said. Funny how a stranger was kinder to him than his own flesh and blood. Funnier still was how mean his grandpa could really be. "You're the main reason she's like this anyway! 'Bout time you faced up to it!"

He didn't have to look at the other people in the room; he knew they had involuntarily cast their eyes away from him, their faces a mixture of shock and compassion. Michael was young, but he wasn't stupid. He also wasn't strong when it came to defending himself against his grandpa, so he didn't deny what he'd said, he didn't yell back. He accepted his words and felt their anger and frustration saturate his skin.

"Someone from the hospital will call you," one of the men said to no one in particular. Michael looked at his mother, her face serene, already asleep. He wondered if she was content. Had she gotten what she wanted? Was it her plan to be taken from this house, taken violently because she didn't have the strength to leave peacefully? He might never know. She had tried this before but of course had never given a full explanation as to why, at least not to her family. Perhaps her doctor, the psychiatrist, had a better understanding of why she harmed herself, but if he did know, he never felt obliged or compelled to share it with those closest to her. Her family was forced to guess.

As they wheeled her out on the stretcher, Michael noticed that the bleeding had stopped. That was a good sign. The cuts wouldn't be so deep this time. She would stay in the hospital for a few days, recover, and then come home to resume her place in the family. No one would mention this night, and this disturbance while not forgotten would go unspoken.

One last look. His mother was sleeping now, her eyes closed, her expression blank but soft. The pain, wherever it came from, was sleeping now too. A sheet covered the straitjacket, so as she was wheeled away, if Michael wanted to, he could forget it was there; he could imagine that she was simply being taken to the hospital for routine surgery. Remove a gallbladder or an appendix. Something that wouldn't return to destroy the fragile foundation this family was built upon.

He left his grandparents to their beer and rosary and went back up to his room. From his window he saw the ambulance drive away, down the dirt road and into the night. Despite everything, he couldn't help but think how lucky his mother was. At least she, for a time, was elsewhere.

chapter 3

First day back to school was never a happy time for Michael. First day back to school when your mother was in the hospital under psychiatric evaluation made the day even worse.

Last year when Michael entered Weeping Water High School he thought things might improve from his grammar school and junior high days; he might find someone, anyone, who shared his desire for knowledge. He thought his new classmates might be a little smarter, might be a bit more interested in actually learning about world history or English literature and not just in figuring out the easiest way to cut class without getting caught. No such luck.

The majority of kids at Two W mainly fell into two camps—the jocks and cheerleaders who thought life should be spent on the football field, and the slackers who preferred to watch life speed by them. The only thing the two camps had in common was a desire to learn the least amount of studying they would have to do to produce a report card full of average grades.

Of course Michael wasn't an anomaly; there were other kids in school who wanted to learn, who wanted to learn as much as possible in order to get accepted into a good college so they could have the kind of life and career that the Weeping Water public school system on its own couldn't provide. Problem was that none of those kids wanted to be Michael's friend.

In a small town, word travels fast, and before he had even put in one full day as a freshman, the entire student body knew that Michael Howard was the kid whose mother was in and out of psychiatric care and who was kind of weird himself. It didn't matter that Michael was an excellent student, salutatorian of his junior high class. Not a star athlete but definitely not the most uncoordinated kid in gym class. He just didn't fit in.

The whispers had begun about Michael well before his teen years. As a young boy it was noted that his diction was too refined; he didn't sound like somebody who was brought up in Nebraska. His vocabulary was much too vast. "Nobody from around here uses words like that," people would say. "Do you think he dyes his hair? No boy's hair is that blond all by itself." And then there was his attitude.

Michael knew that part of the reason he didn't have any friends and was ostracized by his peers was because everyone thought he considered himself better than everyone else. It didn't matter that he never once voiced this opinion, it didn't matter that this wasn't how he felt; all that mattered was that one group of kids interpreted Michael's timidity and intelligence as arrogance and they then shared their assumptions with another group of kids and soon Michael had earned a reputation of being an egotistical jerk. An unjust reputation, but one he didn't have the strength to fight.

"Heard your mother's back in her own padded cell."

He didn't need to turn around; he knew without looking who made that remark. Mauro Dorigo had been taunting Michael since third grade, from the first day Mauro moved here from New York. Michael tried ignoring him, he tried tattling on him, he tried running from him, but Mauro ran faster, and when he caught up with him, he surprised him with a roundhouse punch that gave Michael his first black eye.

Mauro was a tough kid who grew up on the streets of the Lower East Side. The only way he knew how to take care of himself was with his fists, and the best way he knew to make sure no one messed with him was to mess with somebody else first. So on his first day at his new school in Nebraska, he searched the school yard for the weakest-looking kid and stopped when he cast his eyes on Michael. He had nothing against Michael at the time; it was just that he had that scared look about him, almost like he was waiting for someone to pounce. Mauro was more than willing.

Seven years later, not much had changed. Mauro was still more overweight than muscular, but he had the advantage because fear still clung to Michael. Fear that at any moment someone was going to attack, physically or verbally. That someone was usually Mauro.

"I hear they're going to name the loony bin after her, she's spent so much time in there."

Now a group had gathered and some kids laughed, others whispered. He knew they knew what had happened to his mother; everyone always found out, so there was no sense in denying it.

"Yes, it's going to be called the Grace Ann Howard Wing," Michael said. "The ribbon-cutting ceremony is scheduled for next week; you should put it on your calendar."

When he turned to walk away he caught a glimpse of some of the kids' startled faces; they looked impressed. Yes, they definitely were impressed with Michael's comeback. He knew he shouldn't joke about his mother's condition, but what else was he going to do? Mauro was right. By the end of the year, his mother would be making another trip to the mental ward; might as well own up to it. But Mauro always had to have the last word.

"So, Howard! I guess that makes you a gaytard!" The kids who seconds ago were impressed with Michael's wit switched allegiance and were once again back on

Mauro's side. "If your mother's crazy, you must be a re-
tarded homo!"

Fire erupted in Michael's cheeks and he felt his mouth
go completely dry. Laughter boxed his ears and he
briefly thought he was going to faint right there in the
corridor. But somehow he kept walking, walking, walking; he just needed to get to the end of the hallway so he
could turn the corner and escape. Once he could get
away from the laughter, away from the words, he would
be fine.

He rounded the corner and took a deep breath. He
pushed his way through the crowd of students and
ducked into the first room that looked empty, chemistry
lab, and leaned against the teacher's desk. *They're just
words,* he told himself, *they don't matter.* But he knew
that wasn't completely true. The words themselves were
only part of the problem; the worst part was what the
words conveyed. They told everyone that Michael was
someone who should be ridiculed, someone who should
be singled out because he was . . . sick and repulsive. He
had heard those words all his life, but each time was like
the first, a jagged knife cutting through innocence. He
simply didn't know how much longer he could take it.

"Are you all right, Mr. Howard?"

Once again he didn't have to turn around to know
who was speaking. It was Mrs. Clyde, the head of the
science department. "Yes, I . . ." Michael started, but
when he tried to finish his sentence he didn't know what
to say. Should he tell her the truth? *I just needed a place*

to hide for a few minutes. Or *I was running away be-cause the school bully was calling me names again.* "Yes, I'm fine." Those were the words that finally came out of his mouth and although he knew someone as perceptive and savvy as Mrs. Clyde would not believe them, they would have to do. The first day of school was definitely getting off to a bad start. And it was only going to get worse.

"I don't think they teach soccer in gaytard school."

Michael ignored the comment, but here on the soccer field, there was no hallway for him to turn into, no empty room for him to hide in. He was exposed. He had two choices—he could act as if he didn't hear Mauro's comment or he could confront him. Without hesitation he chose the former. Which only meant that Mauro would continue to goad him.

Gym class was only forty minutes, Michael reminded himself. Mauro would shortly grow tired of teasing him and move on to somebody else. He just had to deal with it for a little while longer. In the meantime maybe he could impress some of his classmates with his newfound agility as he did earlier with his impromptu wit. The esteem hadn't lasted very long, but perhaps he was a better athlete than a comedian.

This past summer, Michael grew three inches and as a result lost ten pounds. He was five feet ten and a lean 170 pounds. He didn't have a six-pack and he wasn't incredibly muscular, but he had spent many summer mornings running before the sun grew too strong, so he had built up his stamina and, most exciting, he was learning how to use his body. He knew he could make an impression if he was just given the chance.

He had to wait a while, but sure enough, with only ten minutes left to go in class, Michael got his opportunity. With the score tied, Jay Rogers, one of the best athletes in the school, had driven the ball forty yards down the field on his own. He was ten yards from the goal, but there were too many players from the other team blocking him, so he couldn't make a clean shot. His go-to guy, Bobby Z, couldn't shake the kid who was tailing him, and the only other teammate in the free and clear was Michael.

Kicking the ball from one foot to the other, Jay hesitated. He didn't want to pass it on to Michael; he wasn't reliable. And he wanted to score one more goal so he could win the first game of the new school year. But the field didn't change; the only one who remained open was Michael and so he had no choice.

When Michael saw Jay bring his right foot back and whack the ball in his direction, he couldn't believe it, but it was unmistakable. The best player in school had just passed the ball to him. That's when he decided to do something just as unbelievable; he decided to attack. Running toward the spinning ball, he deflected it off his right foot to slow it down and then kicked it farther toward the goal with his left. He ran after it and caught up with the ball just in time to spin around so his back was in front of some Spanish kid he didn't recognize. He paused for a moment, kicking the ball from one foot to the other to try and confuse the kid so he could move past him. Jay and the rest of the team were in shock. Michael Howard was actually playing soccer really well.

Michael could feel his heart beating so fast and loudly he thought it was going to crash through his chest. He concentrated entirely on the soccer ball, deliberately ignoring the screams from his classmates. Honestly, he didn't know if they were cheering for him or insulting him and he didn't care. He was doing this for himself. He had to prove that he could fit in, at least for a few minutes during one gym class; that's all he was asking.

Shifting his weight to the left and then quickly to the right, he faked out the Spanish kid and suddenly found himself a few feet in front of the goalie. Mauro didn't even bother to protect his net. He was laughing hysterically and saying something that Michael refused to hear. He reared his right leg and brought it back, determined to give the ball the hardest wallop he could muster. But he failed. His foot missed the ball completely and he came crashing down on the grass, his left hip first and then the rest of his body.

People were shouting, some were laughing, and Michael had the impulse to roll over and bury his face in the grass. But even if he did, he would still be able to hear them. "Keep that move for the Special Olympics, gaytard!" Mauro accented his comment by slamming the ball on the grass inches from Michael's head. Then the bully proved his own agility by doubling over with laughter and high-fiving somebody at the same time.

Before Mauro could continue his victory dance, Mr. Alfano, the gym teacher, pushed his way through the crowd and grabbed Mauro by the shirttail. "Enough, Dorigo!" Strutting off the field, surrounded by his cronies, Mauro shouted at Michael once more, "That'll teach ya to try to pass for one of us, gay boy!"

Mr. Alfano, immune to such insults on the sports field, didn't even chastise Mauro for using such hateful language. He merely extended his hand to Michael, completely expecting him to grab hold and pull himself up. But Mauro's last comment, shouted so that every single person in class could hear, had paralyzed him. *Why won't the earth just swallow me? Let me disappear so I don't have to look at all these faces.* They all agreed with Mauro, Michael could just tell; they all knew.

Leaning in close to Michael, Mr. Alfano whispered to him, "You've gotta stand up for yourself, Michael; otherwise it's only going to get worse." He looked into his teacher's face and he saw something he had never seen before. Mr. Alfano looked at Michael with respect. There was no pity in his face, there really wasn't even compassion, just respect from one person to another. Michael reached out and grabbed his hand; with the other he pressed on the grass and pushed himself up. "Good job," Mr. Alfano said, then turned to the rest of the class. "Shower up."

On the walk back to the locker room, Michael kept

his head down. There may have been one or two faces in the group that smiled at him or shrugged their shoulders as if to say, *It's no big deal,* but he didn't see them. He concentrated on putting one foot in front of the other.

As usual, he waited until almost all the boys were done in the shower before he entered. Thankfully, Mauro had already showered and left so he didn't have to deal with him. He had enough to deal with in here. Being naked in the large, open shower stall was a dangerous place for Michael to be, so he did his best to make sure he was there with as few people as possible. He stood beneath the showerhead, trying not to think about the stupid thing he did in gym. He tried not to think about the stupid thing his mother did last night; he tried not to think about the stupid things both of them would do in the days to come. He just bowed his head, eyes closed, and prayed that no one would notice him.

He wanted to shout, scream as loud as he could, but instead he scrubbed his head vigorously with the greenish liquid that passed as shampoo. He had set out to impress his classmates—once unconsciously and once purposefully—and had failed miserably on both tries. At least no one else seemed to gang up on him. For the moment, Mauro was still acting solo, so the day could not possibly get any worse.

Rinsing the soap off of his body, he turned slightly and saw the Spanish kid staring at him. He recognized that stare immediately. It was the way he stared at R.J.

Abruptly, Michael turned his back to him just as he had done on the field and adjusted the nozzle so more cold water would pour over the front of his body, just in case. He couldn't help but feel a bit ecstatic. Could he have found someone who was like him? A part of him, a very strong part, wanted to turn around and see if the kid was still looking, see if he was still interested. All he had to do was turn his head slightly. But wait, wait, wait. Suddenly his brain clicked in and he recognized that this could be a trick, nothing more than a setup. That had to be it, he was sure of it. Nobody was like him.

No, he couldn't risk it. No matter how desperately he wanted to connect with someone else, he wasn't willing to take the gamble, not after he had made such a fool of himself just a few minutes before. *Do not give in, do not make things worse.* Determined, he shut his eyes and let the cold water cool him, waiting for the adrenaline to stop pumping through his veins and praying for a distraction. He didn't have to wait very long.

"Howard! Get over to the principal's office," Mr. Alfano yelled into the shower room. "Your grandfather's here."

Dried and completely dressed, Michael sat on the bench in front of his locker, head down, holding his backpack between his legs. One after the other he mentally ticked off all the reasons his grandpa would come to pick him up at school. None of them were good. This was the first time it had ever happened, so there wasn't any precedent; Michael had nothing to compare it to except what he conjured up with his own imagination. And after what took place in his house last night and what had taken place there on other similar nights, his imagination brought him to a dark place. It had to have something to do with his mother, he thought; there would be no other reason he would come to the school, absolutely none.

He was so engrossed in trying to come up with another reason that he didn't notice Tomás, the Spanish kid, half dressed, give him the barest of waves as Michael left the locker room. At this moment he had forgotten the kid even existed. When he made the left at the end of the hallway and saw the glassed-in principal's office at the other end of the corridor, his pace quickened. A few steps later and it picked up even more and as he was walking he thought that maybe this had something to do with his grandma; that would make sense. Maybe she had been dwelling on thoughts of her daughter all day and could no longer take the strain and needed to go to the emergency room. Grandpa was here to pick him up so he could go visit her. But the second he entered Mr. Garret's office, he knew he was wrong. This was definitely about his mother.

What an odd place to hear about your mother's death, Michael thought, in the principal's office. This was supposed to be the place where you got into trouble or where you confessed to a misdeed or racked your brains trying to come up with a fake, but believable, alibi. It was not where you heard life-altering news. And yet this was where Michael's grandpa decided to tell him that his mother would not be coming home from the hospital this time. In fact, she would never be coming home because she had finally succeeded.

On the drive home, his grandpa went into more detail than he had in front of Mr. Garret. "She killed herself. Gotta say it out loud, she's a suicide; everybody else is gonna be sayin' it, so we might as well be the first." Michael stared straight ahead and watched white line after white line disappear underneath the truck. He couldn't say a word and he definitely couldn't look at the man who was matter-of-factly telling him this news. Grandpa rambled on and explained that she pretended she didn't want to be alone, that she wanted one of the guards to stay with her at all times, but then there was a fight down the hall—one of the other patients was having an episode—and the guard left her, but only for a few minutes. It was all the time she needed. When he left the room, she took the razor blade she had found earlier—must have found it in the bathroom or the infirmary, Grandpa said; the hospital was still investigating that—and sliced her wrists, this time making sure she cut deep and severed the veins. She was already unconscious when the guard returned, and by the time they got her to the emergency room, she had bled to death.

That was it, Michael thought. *I no longer have a mother.* Michael turned to look out the window and coughed loudly to stifle a laugh. Didn't he just say something about the day not being able to get any worse? He should have already realized in his short life that no matter how terrible things are, they can always get worse. But if they were so horrible, if this news was so devastating, where were the tears?

Michael got out of the truck before his grandpa turned off the engine and he walked past his grandma, who was sitting at the kitchen table, holding but not sipping a cup of coffee. Ignoring her, he went straight to his sanctuary. Sitting on his bed he waited for the tears to come, but nothing. He waited for pain to constrict his heart, but he was oddly numb. What the hell was wrong with him? He had just found out that his mother was dead and instead of reacting in some way, any way, he felt nothing.

Maybe it's because he hadn't felt like he had a mother for quite some time now; that could be it, he thought. That's right, tell the truth, don't make her out to be anything more special than what she was. For the past several years she had been preoccupied with her own demons, unable to focus her attention beyond herself and on her son, and when she did turn the spotlight onto Michael, it was only to remind him that he needed to make her proud, he needed to do things that she wanted to do, things that she had forgotten to do. Or worse, he had to do things that she had screwed up in order to somehow make amends for her messed-up life.

She didn't look at her son and tell him that she would

support him no matter what path he took. She didn't see him for who he was or try to understand him or attempt to comfort him when he was in pain. She had left him alone to fend for himself years ago. So he should be used to her absence. Should be.

Michael opened his bedroom door, knowing that he was expected to go downstairs and talk to his grandparents, but he didn't hear anything. If he was going to be a part of silence, it might as well be his own. So he closed his door on them.

Standing in front of the mirror in his bedroom, he looked at his face, searching for a trace of his mother. There was nothing there. His complexion was lighter, his nose smaller, his cheekbones sharper, his chin more pronounced. Blond hair, green eyes, not brown hair, brown eyes. Were her eyes brown? Maybe; he couldn't remember.

But even though they had differences on the surface, deep inside they were similar. Michael was forced to admit that. They both carried fear with them wherever they went, an unspoken terror. Michael didn't understand the burden that his mother struggled with, but he knew there was something that lived deep inside her that to her was very real and, based upon her last act of rebellion, insurmountable. Michael blinked and then looked into his own eyes and realized he could very well wind up the same way.

Gotta say it out loud, his grandpa said. Gotta stand up for yourself, Mr. Alfano said. The words formed in his brain but got caught in his throat. *Try again.* No use. He pursed his lips as his chest tightened and he clenched his fists. Swiping the air, his fist stopped inches from the glass. *Just say the words, get it out, don't be like your mother.* "I'm gay."

He relaxed. His mind, his heart, his entire body, grateful. For unlike his mother's, his burden, while not completely erased, had definitely been lessened.

chapter 4

The voice belonged to a little boy. Michael couldn't see
him, but the voice was everywhere; it surrounded him.
The boy was reciting a poem in a singsong voice. "One
drop, two drops, three drops, four." Drops of what?
Water, probably, but maybe sweat? Blood? The voice
continued. "Floodgates open, the waters pour." Yes,
water. Of course, that's why they came here, to the
ocean, to feel the waves, rough, tall, and imposing,
crash on the beach to create giant arcs of spray and long
horizontal lines of bubbly foam. Michael thought it
looked strong, majestic, exactly the way he felt. There
was not a boat or a cloud in view. He turned around
and he could see that no one was on the beach except

them. The voice was gone, it had done its job, it had led them here. Now the ocean was theirs and they were going to take it.

Michael walked into the water, the foam mingling with his feet, then a little farther, his ankles submerged. He turned to the dark-haired boy and beckoned him to join him. His companion looked nothing like R.J. or Phineas; he resembled Tomás—yes, that was the kid's name—in that his body was muscular, but his skin was much, much paler. His name didn't matter. He was beautiful and he wanted to swim next to Michael.

Together they ran into the ocean and at mere seconds apart dove into the crest of a wave just before it was about to collapse. They emerged next to each other as if even underwater with their eyes closed, they couldn't be separated. Their bodies now embraced, the sun making their skin glisten, drops of water desperately hanging on to their smiling faces, unwilling to let go and return to the ocean. It was so much better to be a part of them than to be watching from the sidelines.

Michael looked into this nameless boy's eyes and he allowed his fingers the freedom to caress his scalp, feel the curve. He had never done anything like that before and it felt wonderful. What felt even better was when he wrapped his right ankle around the boy's left calf, entwining their legs so that their bodies were pushed even closer together. The boy mimicked Michael's actions so his fingers cradled Michael's head and his other leg intertwined with Michael's. They were wrapped together, floating beyond the waves in the calmer part of the ocean, completely alone. The only thing left for them to do was to kiss.

Tilting his head gently to the right, Michael felt their noses touch. The boy's hand moved from the back of his head until his fingers found Michael's ear. *That feels good,* he thought, and so he did the same thing. Then tentatively, their lips met. Unsure, in unfamiliar territory, they remained there for a moment, motionless. And then their instinct directed them and their lips moved, they kissed softly, tenderly, and Michael almost cried because it felt like the most natural, the most normal thing in the world. Until he saw his mother.

Grace was on the beach staring at them, the straitjacket unbuckled and hanging loose from her shoulders. Underneath she wore a white hospital gown and she was dripping wet. Her hair, her clothes, soaked. But soaked in blood.

The boy stood in front of Michael, trying to cover his face from this apparition, but it was no use. Even if he closed his eyes, he could still see her blood-drenched body. Instead, Michael found the strength to stand in front of the boy to protect him, shield him from this grotesque vision. His mother raised her arms, and the blood from her wrists spilled out into the ocean, staining its beauty with her infection. A stream of her blood traveled toward Michael and when it reached him, when his mother's blood touched his body, he could feel its warmth. But it was hardly comforting. "Leave me alone!" Michael shouted.

Astonished by her son's cruelty, Grace fell to her

knees, the blood discoloring the sand, and she let her
wrists, outstretched, fall upon her thighs, and she stared
at them. "But I'm so ashamed." Her voice was just a
whisper, but Michael heard her clearly. And then she
looked at her son. "Just like you."

Michael splashed cold water on his face. *Shake it off,
it was only a dream. You don't have anything to be
ashamed of.* If that was the truth, then why did Michael
avoid looking at himself in the mirror?

On his way back to his bedroom he paused. He recognized that voice instantly even though he only heard
it once or twice a year on the phone on Christmas and a
few days after his birthday had passed. He assumed his
father would make the trip from London or from whatever country he happened to be working in this week,
but he never imagined he would make the trip so
quickly. Michael thought he would have a few more
days to prepare for this reunion, so he took a moment
to collect himself before descending the stairs. He didn't
feel guilty about making his father wait. Why should
he? This would be the first time Vaughan Howard had
ever set foot on Nebraskan soil.

Several times during his childhood, Michael's father
promised to come visit him, but each time something
more pressing arose. Usually something to do with
work that prohibited him from flying out to see his son.
At first Michael was upset, but like so many children of
divorced parents, Michael had grown accustomed to his
father's empty promises and knew that each proclama-

tion, no matter how passionate or sincere, would be dismissed. He learned quickly that he was not an important aspect in his father's life. And so he made the same adjustment.

That's not how Vaughan intended it to be, however. He had intended to be a very good father, but it was evident shortly after Michael's birth that Grace would not allow it. She was obsessed with being the sole parent and convinced that she was the only one who could provide for Michael and comfort him. When Vaughan tried to play his part, when he tried to take over his share of the responsibilities, Grace grew even more unstable. She claimed he didn't know how to handle a child. He didn't know how to bathe him or feed him or rock him to sleep. He played too roughly, he sang lullabies too loudly, he did nothing right, and soon Vaughan, even though he knew she was wrong, decided it wasn't worth the effort to prove her accusations false.

Unfortunately, Grace wasn't entirely wrong. There were things in Vaughan's past that she did not discover until after she became pregnant that made her question her husband's ability to be a good father, things that he would have preferred be kept secret. And there were things that she knew he wanted to do with his future that made her certain he would not be an acceptable parent. So although she loved him, she took her son and fled London to return to her hometown, to a place that she believed would be their safe haven.

After Grace and Michael left, Vaughan selfishly thought he would remarry and have another baby, but that never came to pass and Michael remained his only child. For years he settled in the knowledge that he simply brought another human being into this world and did not steer or navigate him through life. Now all that had changed. Grace had taken his son away from him and now Grace was giving him back. For many reasons, he was overjoyed.

Blunt as always, Grandpa made the announcement before Michael could even introduce himself to his father. "Your father's come to take you back home."

The first thing Michael noticed was how youthful he looked in comparison to his mother. His eyes were bright and alert despite being as black as midnight, and his skin was smooth and flushed where his mother's was lined and ashen. Looking at Vaughan, it was clear to Michael that none of the demons that ravaged his mother's beauty ever visited his father.

When Michael spoke, the only word that came out of his mouth was "hello."

"Hullo, son," Vaughan said, his British accent sounding out of place amid the Midwestern décor. "It's so good to see you."

Before Michael could brace himself, Vaughan hugged him. It felt awkward. Michael could feel his father's hesitation, his arms filled with insecurity, and to make matters worse, Michael didn't have much experience in making physical connections, so he hugged him back with the same lack of confidence. But when his father stepped back, Michael peered into his face once again and some of the anxiety he felt was soothed; he really did resemble his father. And the similarity served as some kind of anchor.

"You want something to drink?" Grandpa asked. "A beer?"

Michael glanced at the clock. Five A.M. Even though it was still dark outside, he didn't think a beer was an appropriate beverage for this time of day. Neither did Vaughan. "No, thank you."

His grandma cleared her throat. "I can heat up some coffee."

The way his father looked at his grandma, Michael could tell that he didn't want any coffee, but there was something about the way she spoke, something in her voice that made Vaughan accept. "That would be lovely."

Watching his grandma scuttle around the kitchen, turning on the stove, pulling coffee cups and saucers from the cabinets, he realized his father agreed in order to give her something to do. It was an act of kindness and in this house that was rare. Perhaps this man, this absentee father, really could be his salvation.

"What do you mean you're taking me home?" Michael asked.

It was Vaughan's turn to clear his throat. "Well, I was just telling your grandparents that in light of the situation, it might be best for you to get away from here. It's difficult for the elderly to raise a teenager."

"With all due respect to ya," Grandpa interrupted, "I already told ya we ain't elderly."

"I'm sorry," Vaughan said, turning to face him directly. "My words are a bit different; they don't have the same meaning. Forgive me." Grandpa had no idea how to respond to a gentleman's apology, so he furrowed his brow and shrugged his shoulders. "But, Michael," Vaughan continued. "Well, you are my son."

And where were you for the past thirteen years? Michael wanted to ask. *Why did you wait until my mother's death to swoop in here like a vulture to peck at what she left behind? Why did you let me fester in this place where I never belonged?!* But Michael just nodded.

"And so I thought it best . . . oh, thank you," Vaughan said, accepting the coffee from his ex-mother-in-law. "No cream; this is fine. Thank you." Michael's grandma smiled and sat back down at the kitchen table. "Your grandparents and I believe that it would be in your best interest if you came back with me to London." The rain had stopped, the pathway was finally dry. "There's an excellent school that has an opening. Archangel Academy. It has an outstanding curriculum. . . ."

"Yes," Michael said without hesitation. He didn't see his grandma's eyes water or hear his grandpa mumble "figured that." All he knew was that this man, this stranger who was his father, had thrown him a lifeline and he wasn't going to hesitate, he wasn't going to dwell on past actions or question his motives. He was simply going to hold on to it and allow it to pull him away from here. He knew that if he didn't grab on to this opportunity, his life would be as miserable as his mother's and possibly with the same outcome. "Yes, I'll go with you."

Vaughan smiled, honestly, happily. He searched for a spot to rest his coffee and bent over to place it on an end table and then he hugged his son again, this time without feeling awkward, without worrying if the gesture would be reciprocated. And it was. Michael hugged him back and held his father tightly. He pushed away the memories that had latched on to his mind. Vaughan forgetting to send him a birthday card or Michael overhearing his mother arguing with his father because he canceled—at the last minute—a trip he and Michael were supposed to take. Those were petty and they were in the past. His father held him now with the promise of a future. And then his father left, explaining that he needed to catch an early flight back to Europe and, in a quieter voice, that he didn't feel Grace would want him at her funeral. No one disagreed with him. Even still, before escaping into the early morning darkness, he informed them that he would pay for all of the funeral expenses and would arrange for Michael to fly to London in a few days. No one should worry about a thing. Michael for one didn't. He was saved.

Watching the casket lowered into the ground, Michael hoped that his mother was now saved too. Saved from more decades of unhappiness and dread, saved from the knowledge that she was ridiculed by her neighbors, from any more pain that she could inflict upon herself. And saved even though she committed what the church considered a mortal sin.

Michael had sat through endless sermons and homilies in his life; he had listened to priests speak passionately about heaven, berate their parishioners for not leading lives worthy of entering heaven, and yet he still wasn't convinced such a place existed. Now watching his mother's body encased in an expensive, elaborately designed coffin that Vaughan had picked out and paid for, he wondered what was to become of her. Was she to be swallowed up by the earth and remain in this place for all eternity? Or had her soul already left her to travel the world silently, invisibly, to all the places she had never journeyed to when she was alive? What a waste if that was true, he thought. How could she have wasted her life—and his—by staying locked in this stupid town and refusing to venture anywhere else? He wasn't going to make the same mistake his mother did. He was determined to live.

But at the same time, he was quite unexpectedly bothered by his grandparents' willingness to let him leave Weeping Water. He didn't really get along with either of them. His grandpa was caustic, his grandma voiceless, but they were, for better or worse, his world. And yet when Vaughan announced that he was taking Michael to London immediately since the school year had only just begun, neither grandparent had put up a fight. It was as if they were both relieved not to be duty bound to their daughter's offspring.

He knew it was complicated and he didn't blame them entirely; he wanted to leave this place more so than anyone. It just would have made him feel better if they had protested the tiniest bit. But when Vaughan finished his pitch by saying, "And you know as well as I do that Michael doesn't belong here," they both nodded their heads in agreement. So his fate was sealed without hesitation or hindrance. Michael tried to rally the anger to condemn his grandparents, but he couldn't. *It just confirms what I've always believed,* he told himself.

A few days later Michael went to Two W for the last time, to clean out his locker and return all his schoolbooks to the principal. His father had already made the necessary preparations for Michael to enroll in his new school; in fact, he would be flying to London later that night. He looked at the few mementos he had stuck to the back of the locker door and left them alone; there wasn't anything he wanted to take with him. In a few hours this school and this town would be part of his past and he knew that if he ever returned, it would not be willingly.

"So, gaytard! Heard you're going to an all-boys school in England." Mauro had come to bid him farewell. "You must be creaming in your pants."

Michael slammed his locker shut. He didn't think about the choice, he just made it. "Shut up, Mauro."

"Ooh, the gaytard finally talks back!" Despite his surprise, Mauro laughed and so did the group of kids who had gathered to watch the final round between Michael and his nemesis. In a strange way, he took power from his mother's last action. Was she a coward, was she brave? It wasn't for Michael to decide, but she had made a decision and that gave Michael strength. He could not allow Mauro to have the last word, not this last time, so he decided to follow in her footsteps and do something.

"I said shut the fuck up!"

Eyes widened, Mauro was truly shocked, but in no way scared, and when he spoke again, he took a few steps closer to Michael. "And who, Miss Gaytard, is gonna make me?"

Again Michael followed gut instinct and not thought. He dropped the pile of books he had been holding, turned to face Mauro, and shouted, "Me!" as he pushed him back against the lockers. Using the element of surprise, Michael pushed him again, this time harder so Mauro's books tumbled to the floor and he lost his footing. It was then that he saw something he had never seen in Mauro's face, a tinge of fear. "Me! The gaytard's gonna shut you up!" Michael shouted.

Before the words stopped echoing down the hallway Michael threw a punch at Mauro's face with such force that he bounced into the lockers. It didn't matter that the punch only clipped Mauro on the chin, it didn't matter that the only reason Mauro didn't pounce on top of Michael was because one of the janitors pulled his arms behind his back; all that mattered was that Michael fought back. He faced a demon, this bully, and he didn't cower.

Shaking a bit and red-faced, Michael saw that the crowd of students was looking at him differently. So this was what it was like not to be looked at like a fool, not to stand alone. It wasn't the exit he had planned, but it met with his approval. He wasn't the only one who felt that way. "Better late than never," Mr. Alfano said, stooping down to help Michael pick up his books, smiling with that same look of respect he had given him the day before. "Good luck to you, Michael."

"Thank you, sir." But to the rest of the students, the ones who until that day had made his life miserable, who didn't take a moment to reach out to him, he said good riddance. He had planned on being equally cavalier with his grandma, but when the moment arrived, he couldn't be that disrespectful.

His grandpa had already shaken his hand roughly, told him to stay out of trouble, and was now waiting in the airport bar having a beer and so Michael sat among the other travelers with only his grandma as companion. "I will miss you and Grandpa," Michael said, trying to sound convincing. "It's just that . . . well, Archangel Academy really is a much better school and, you know, he is my father."

True to her nature, his grandma remained silent. Michael never could figure out if she was a woman of so few words because she had little to say or because she had learned as a young woman that no one listened to her when she spoke. Ah, well, another mystery that would stay unsolved. She did, however, place her hand in his and together they sat in silence until it was announced that his plane was ready to depart.

Michael turned to her and he thought she would break tradition and offer some words of love and wisdom that she had failed to say all the time he had been living with her, but instead she hugged him tightly, and when she pulled back, she placed a folded envelope in his hand. "This is for you" was all she could say before the lump in her throat interfered with her speech. Michael stood there and watched the short, gray-haired woman, wearing clothes that she made herself, clutch her pocketbook and walk slowly away. He knew it would be the last time he would ever lay eyes on her.

He couldn't wait any longer. He had wanted to read his grandma's letter when they were flying over the Atlantic Ocean, but that wouldn't be for another hour. Thousands of miles above Kentucky or Pennsylvania or some landlocked state, his curiosity proved stronger than his discipline and he pulled the envelope out from his backpack, where he had stuffed it upon boarding the plane. Before he opened it, though, he knew it wasn't from his grandma. He recognized the handwriting as his mother's.

He waited for his hands to stop trembling and then he used his index finger as a letter opener to break the seal. There was only one page, one page of his mother's scribbled handwriting, dated the day she killed herself.

Dear Michael,

  I don't have much time left, but I have to say good-bye. I know I wasn't a very good mother, not the kind I had hoped I would be. I had so many dreams for our family, but somehow—well, I can't explain away my

actions, why I did the things I did, and none
of that really matters now anyway. All that
matters is that you know that I love you and
everything I did was to protect you. I know
you hate it here and you feel like you don't
belong and in many ways I feel the same way.
That's why I know you're going to leave.
When I'm gone your father will want to take
you back home with him and I know you
won't be able to resist his invitation. Just like
I couldn't. All I can do is beg you to be
careful. Yes, England is an exciting country,
like none you've ever seen, but remember not
everything is what it seems. And neither are
people. I can't blame you for wanting the
adventure of a new life, and nothing I write
will make you want to stay in this town, but
just remember that no matter where you go,
you can't run from who you truly are.
Your mother

Tears fell onto the paper without warning. Michael
turned to face the window, shielding his face from the
other passengers. Even in death his mother was a mystery to him. What did her letter mean? *Protect me from*
what? Warn me about England? My father? Michael
didn't understand. *I can't run from myself?* So she knew.
She knew and she never said anything. Why would she
waste her time writing something like that minutes before she put an end to her own miserable life when she

never took a moment while she was alive to say, *Yes, Michael, I'm as unhappy in this place as you are* or *I understand what you're going through?* Her letter, like her life, made no sense. So Michael chose to ignore it.

Just as he crumbled up the letter into a tiny ball, the pilot announced that they were now flying over the Atlantic Ocean. Finally, he was going to be separated from his past. He wasn't running from anything, but moving toward something greater. Michael brushed away his tears; he didn't need them any longer. He didn't need to feel sorry for himself or conceal his truth and he definitely didn't need his mother or her insane instructions. Because on the other side of the water, his life was about to begin.

chapter 5

The Beginning

Outside, the earth was new.

The moment Michael stepped off the plane, he knew his life had changed. He was not in Weeping Water, Nebraska, any longer and try as he might he couldn't conceal the smile on his face. It stayed there even when he saw the text on his cell phone from his father's assistant advising him that Vaughan was called away to Istanbul for an emergency meeting, so his father's driver would be picking Michael up to take him directly to Archangel Academy. That was a change in plan. But his own driver? Istanbul? He had definitely entered a world in which the town of Weeping Water didn't exist.

His smile remained even when he had a flashback to

when he was seven or eight and his father had promised he would visit so the two of them could spend the week together, just them, fishing, camping, doing the type of father-and-son stuff that Michael had seen fathers and sons do on television and in the movies. But as Michael lay in his bed, dressed in his fishing outfit so he wouldn't have to waste time getting dressed in the morning, Vaughan called to cancel. Loose business ends needed to be tied up. For a moment, standing alone in the airport, time halted and Michael was that little boy again, disappointed but determined not to show his true feelings. "That's all right, Dad, I understand," Michael said back then alone in his bedroom before crying himself to sleep. And that's what he said now.

Now, however, there weren't any tears and his disappointment didn't sting as sharply. His father was a busy man, his calendar ever-changing, and Michael understood that. He knew that very soon they'd have their own moments together and they would be worth the wait. For now he would be content to know that his father wanted him back in his life, as hectic and unpredictable as that life might be. In the meantime, he needed to find his chauffeur.

Among the crowd of people in the airport, there was a very tall man holding a sign with the name Howard printed on it. Michael would have recognized him as his father's driver even if he weren't holding his last name in his hands. Dressed cap to boots in black, most of it leather, the man possessed the austere quality needed to be an employee of Howard Industries.

"You must be my driver," Michael said.

"Follow me," the driver responded. "Your bags are already in the car."

Even though the man's black-framed sunglasses prohibited Michael from seeing his eyes, he was sure they weren't smiling. This man was all business. But Michael didn't care; he was thousands of miles away from a life he never felt accustomed to and about to start what even his mother called the adventure of a new life. Despite the knowledge that he was on his own for the first time in his life, he could feel little bolts of energy pulse through his veins. He looked around at the faces passing by him—tourists, businessmen, employees. Could they tell? Could they tell that Michael was happier and more excited than he had ever been in his entire life? He knew he shouldn't feel this way; only a few short days ago he had buried his mother, only a few short hours ago he had said good-bye to his grandparents for what could be a very long time, but the difference in his spirit couldn't be denied. He felt as if he were back where he belonged. And on his way to where he was destined to be, in grand style.

The interior of the car, all black like the driver's outfit, was plush and luxurious. Michael sank into the seat; the leather was soft and slightly heated and he felt the warmth penetrate and calm his anxious body. The sound of violins, Mozart maybe, drifted into the space from some hidden speakers, unhurried and soft. There was a smell vaguely like cinnamon, but definitely crisp, autumnal. He closed his eyes, and the memory of his grandfather's Ranger faded easily.

The car wasn't quite a limousine, but a sedan with a smoky gray glass partition that separated the backseat from the front so Michael could see the driver but couldn't converse with him without pressing the red intercom button on the door panel. Not that Michael was in the mood to chat; he was too busy looking out the window, watching the city transform into the countryside. Skyscrapers became oak trees, concrete pavement a rolling green landscape. His life was changing right before his very eyes.

Several hours later, they sped past a sign that welcomed them to Eden, a small town of Cumbria County in the northwestern part of England. Michael pressed a button, and the dark-tinted mirror descended, giving him a better view of the surroundings. Outside, the land looked untouched and the few buildings worn and weather-beaten, as if they were built centuries ago, which Michael figured they most likely were. After a few miles during which time no buildings interrupted the grasslands, they made a right turn onto an even narrower road. "Almost there," the driver announced. *Almost there.* Those two words were both comforting and uncomfortable and made Michael's heart leap and his stomach lurch. In a few minutes he would reach his destination here in what could easily be labeled the middle of nowhere. He closed his eyes and asked God, "Please let it be worthy." When he opened them, he saw that God had not denied his request.

Stepping onto the cobblestone path, Michael could feel the past detach from him and float away on the breeze. As he stood on the uneven walkway, he felt, for the first time in his short life, grounded and as if he had returned home. It was a wonderful, welcoming feeling. And, Michael had to admit, odd. He had never been here before, he had never even heard of Eden or Archangel Academy until his father told him about the school a few days ago, and yet, yet somehow, he knew this was the place he had been dreaming about. This was where he had longed to come when he had longed for something new, something better. He took a deep breath and savored the moment because he had learned, in his short life, that such extraordinary feelings were not ordinary.

He looked around and was awed by the sight of nature at its purest. The grass was so many different shades of green, all of it growing wild and free. Clusters of purple and yellow flowers populated the brush, some large, some small, but all radiant in their color. Trees with thick, gnarled trunks rose high overhead and their branches sprayed out dense with leaves that rustled in the wind, their sound mingled with birdsong. Weeping Water, in comparison, looked like a desert of dry, flat land.

The only artificial element among the scenery was the impressive entrance gate, the top of which had the name Archangel Academy spelled out in an arc made up of twisted pieces of metal. Very tall, but only about thirty yards in length, the gate was decorative and not practical; it wouldn't keep trespassers out, but simply announced to all the school's presence. Michael couldn't believe that beyond the gate the buildings he saw in the distance comprised one of the most elite boarding schools in the world. From where he stood, they looked like the buildings he saw on the sides of the main road, abandoned stone houses belonging to the past and not part of an institution of higher learning. The metal, the stone, even the wild nature created a strong, masculine appearance. But the look was neutralized by the smell of lavender on the wind, wistful and feminine. All boys were welcome here. Michael stood in front of the gate and gave it a push. *Archangel* separated from *Academy* and the gate easily opened.

"We can drive to the main office," the driver said from the car.

"I'd rather walk," Michael replied.

He followed the cobbled path for a little over half a mile until it stopped at a building that looked as old as it had from the gate. Inside the greeting room, the driver was already waiting for him, standing in a corner, Michael's bags placed around the driver's feet. The room's walls were painted a deep forest green to mimic the surroundings and were barren except for a huge rectangular mirror, wider than it was high, that hung on the wall directly in front of the door. The thick frame was dark brown oak decorated with carvings of angels—not cherubs, but guardians, warriors—the seven archangels that gave the school its name.

On the top of the frame, in the left-hand corner, was

the angel Gabriel, foreboding but gentle, making his presence known by holding his celebrated horn to his lips. In the right-hand corner was Raphael in mid-flight, his rippling robes in perfect balance with the strength of his muscular arms. On the side of the frame underneath Gabriel was Uriel, his fiery sword pointing toward the center of the mirror, and below Raphael was Sariel, floating an inch above a crest of bones.

Ramiel lived in the bottom left-hand corner, behind a cloud of thunder, and in the opposite corner was Zachariel, whose face was framed by the sun. Finally, Michael's eyes rested upon the largest carving, which lay in the bottom center of the frame, the one of his namesake. Michael the archangel was depicted in the traditional image, wings outstretched, sword raised to heaven, his foot pressing down mercilessly on Satan's neck, his exquisitely carved expression triumphant and a bit vainglorious. Michael knew that feeling. He could feel his own private demons squirming under his feet and so he pressed down firmer to remind them who was in power. He liked it here.

His feeling was revealed by his reflection in the mirror. He noticed that he stood a bit taller. His shoulders weren't slumped forward and his expression was more relaxed, his brow not so furrowed. He was off to a good start. But then something caught his eye. His reflection, while crisp and certain, was different from the driver's. Only a portion of the stalwart driver could be seen in the mirror, but in it he appeared smaller, hunched, and a bit hazy. Maybe it was the angle, or all that black.

Michael was about to take another look when the door at the far left corner of the room opened and the headmaster, Mr. Hawksbry, emerged. All thoughts of the driver and his distorted reflection instantly disappeared.

Alistair Hawksbry was a man who commanded attention. At six-two and two hundred fifteen pounds, he wasn't quite as tall or as powerfully built as the driver, but he exuded the type of physical ease that made his bulk seem standard instead of imposing. He was comfortable in his own skin, which at forty-seven wasn't unusual. What was unusual was his youthful countenance. His face was still unlined, save one deep cleft on his left cheek that developed into a dimple when he smiled.

"Michael Howard," Mr. Hawksbry said, his accent precise without sounding affected. "I'm Alistair Hawksbry, headmaster. Welcome to Archangel Academy."

Mr. Hawksbry's handshake was firm. "Thank you, sir," Michael replied. "I'm very happy to be here."

"We're very pleased that your father has decided to instill us with the care of your education. I know the American public school systems are quite good, but I think you'll find our curriculum to be, shall we say, greatly varied and our study more intense." And then he added almost as an afterthought, "And we're very sorry for your loss."

What? Oh yes. Michael hadn't thought about his mother in hours. "Thank you, sir."

"Why don't you leave your bags here and the staff will bring them up to your room?"

The driver cleared his throat and announced his departure. "Good luck to you." Maybe Alistair hadn't seen him or maybe he was just startled by his sudden pronouncement; whatever the reason, Michael was sure he saw him flinch. The driver touched the brim of his cap with his gloved hand and was about to turn on his heel and leave when Michael instinctively extended his hand to him; already he was adopting a more formal British custom. After a moment's hesitation, the driver shook Michael's hand and Michael tried not to wince. If he didn't know any better, he would have thought the driver was trying to crush the bones in his hand, but he didn't seem to display any effort. Given such a powerful grip, Michael wondered if he doubled as his father's bodyguard.

When Alistair nodded good-bye to the driver, it was more like a nervous tic. Only when he and Michael were strolling on the grounds of the academy on their way to his dorm room did he resume his relaxed demeanor. Michael just assumed the headmaster had grown more adept at talking to students than to adults. One of the by-products of his job.

The campus was a sprawling hundred acres with twenty-two buildings, all made of stone, all no taller than three stories high, collectively giving the appearance of a small provincial village. And an isolated one. "The front gate doesn't seem very secure," Michael said.

"For decoration only," Mr. Hawksbry replied. "We have an electronic system that surrounds the entire campus. Since we knew you were arriving today, it was turned off, but once your driver is on the other side of the gate, it'll be turned on again, I assure you."

The headmaster then pointed out some landmarks, the three libraries, the many halls where classes were taught, each named after a different saint; the theatre, which housed both a traditional proscenium arch stage for mainstage productions and a smaller black box studio space for more experimental theatre; the infirmary; and the several dormitories.

Michael's dorm, named after St. Peter, was located next to Archangel Cathedral, which was the one architectural exception and towered high above the rest of the campus's buildings. Erected sometime in the fifteenth century in the Gothic style by a group of monks, it was, Mr. Hawskbry explained, the centerpiece of the academy, which was later built around it. Looking at the church, Michael understood why the academy's founders would want to build their school around such an amazing structure.

There were no steps leading into the entrance, only wildflowers, dirt, and then an arched doorway about two stories high, adorned with carvings similar to those on the frame of the mirror in the greeting room. Above the door was where more majesty lay. Two flying buttresses flanked the sides of the center pointed arch, which was made up of an intricate lattice of wood in front of a huge circle of yellow stained glass. Even though the sky was cloudy, with only a portion of the sun able to shine through and hit the cathedral, the effect was still magnificent. The yellow glass in the sun's light glowed radiantly, splintering through the latticework to create beacons of light that sprang out from the face of the church into the air and onto all those who walked by. Again, Michael felt worlds away from Weeping Water.

When Mr. Hawskbry spoke, he startled Michael, who was staring intently at the rays of light. "It's beautiful, isn't it? The perfect combination of man and nature."

Yes, Michael thought, a perfect combination.

Just as they were about to enter St. Peter's Dormitory, Michael noticed a group of boys in the distance in a rush, either coming or going to a class. He felt a familiar tingle in his stomach as he watched them race by, their white long-sleeved shirts turned up at the sleeves, pieces of cloth untucked from their navy blue pants, their gold and navy blue ties flying in the wind. And their hair, soft, unruly, free. He forced himself to glance away from them and saw that Mr. Hawksbury was staring at him.

"Don't worry. Your father ordered you several uniforms. They should be hanging in your closet."

When he walked into the dormitory, Michael felt a bit of melancholy waft over him. It was just as beautiful as it was on the outside and he was so grateful that he was in this building and not at Two W, but the only reason he was here was because his mother killed herself. Why was she so desperate? Why was she so afraid to live? His eyes burned a bit and he blinked away the tears. No, not here, not ever again, because tears weren't going to change anything.

"This is your room." They were on the second floor in front of a door just off the stairs. Before Mr. Hawksbry could knock, the door opened and standing there was a boy roughly Michael's age wearing a neater version of the school uniform. "Ciaran Eaves," the headmaster said, "may I introduce you to your new dorm mate, Michael Howard, from America."

"Welcome to the Double A, mate," Ciaran said, extending his hand.

"Thank you." Michael grabbed his hand and was grateful that the tingling in his stomach didn't return. He was also hopeful that the only thing the Double A had in common with the Two W was a similar abbreviation.

The headmaster did a quick survey of the room to ensure that Michael's bags had been delivered and his uniforms were indeed hanging in his closet. Once satisfied, he took two pieces of paper out of his jacket pocket, giving one to each boy. "Michael, this is your class schedule. Today, Ciaran will show you around, but tomorrow you'll be on your own. Most of our professors detest tardiness. It might be in your best interest to draw a map so you don't get lost on your first day." Michael could tell this was the headmaster's attempt at a joke, but he felt the slow coil of terror rise from the pit of his stomach. After Mr. Hawksbry left and the boys were alone, the feeling remained.

Happily, Michael noted this feeling was different from the other rumbling. Standing here alone with Ciaran, it was not curiosity and desire that were awakening deep within him, but rather, unfortunately, fear. It was as if one of the stones from the building had just fallen onto his skull. *I'm in a new school, in a foreign country that I haven't been in since I was a toddler, sharing a room with a complete stranger,* Michael reminded himself. *This is absolutely nerve-racking.* Luckily, Ciaran was a calming presence.

Although they were the same age, Ciaran carried himself with more maturity than Michael. Not only did he look like the tall, lean English lad who populates a Jane Austen novel, he sounded like one too; his accent was clipped but his tone friendly. Even the pronunciation of his name, *Keer-in,* accent on the first syllable, sounded as if it came from the pages of a nineteenth-century story. He simply evoked the reserve of a young man who had spent his life in a boarding school where etiquette and poise were held in high regard. "Nebraska must suddenly seem very far away," Ciaran remarked.

Michael looked confused. "You say that like it's a bad thing." And suddenly the fear was gone and they were just two boys laughing instead of strangers forced to share the same room.

"This is where I spend most of my time." Ciaran pointed to St. Albert's Library for math and science. "I'm on the premed track, at least for now."

"You've already decided that you want to be a doctor?" Michael remarked. "Impressive."

Ciaran wished everyone shared his supportive point of view. "My mum calls it narrow-minded. She'd prefer I follow in her footsteps and become a barrister." Ciaran shrugged. "Who knows?"

"I think it's good that you have direction; you have a head start over most of us," Michael said, knowing he wasn't sure what career path he wanted to follow. "Have you decided on what kind of doctor you'd like to be?"

A red robin flew by them, chirping loudly. "Hematologist," Ciaran said.

"What's that?" Michael replied.

"Blood disorders."

"Really? That's specific."

"Hence the reason my mum thinks I'm narrow-minded."

Ciaran must have heard something in Michael's silence. "I'm sorry, mate. Here I am prattling on about my mum and, well . . ."

"That's okay," Michael assured him and it really was. He wasn't silent because he was thinking of his mother again; he was silent because he was thinking that in a few short months these grounds were going to be familiar to him. These buildings, his schedule, the bends in the grass, soon they would all be his routine.

Glancing at Michael's class schedule, Ciaran led them to St. Joshua's Library, which housed the liberal arts collection. "St. Joshua is the patron saint of literature and reading. Looks like you'll be spending a great deal of time in here." The building looked just the same as all the others with the exception that it was lined in white roses. Flowers of all kinds grew near the other buildings, but none of them seemed to be growing as deliberately as these, in such formal rows. "No one can really figure it out," Ciaran offered. "They pop up every year, from what we're told. Quite beautiful actually. They go untouched except for the night of the annual Archangel Festival when some of the blokes pluck them to use as a cheap corsage."

Ciaran explained that the Archangel Festival takes place in early November to celebrate Archangel Day and is one of the few times that Double A and St. Anne's officially commingle. "St. Anne's is the girls school in a gated community on the other side of the campus," Ciaran said, bending down to more closely inspect one of the roses. "You know, if you go for that sort of thing."

Did Michael hear that right? If you go for that sort of thing? He was pretty sure he was referring to girls and not gated communities, but not sure enough of himself to ask for clarification. Instead, he made a mental note: He and Ciaran may have different intellectual pursuits, but they might have other interests in common after all.

At dinner that night in the main dining room of St. Martha's, one of the two common halls where students from all the dorms could meet, he discovered he had practically nothing in common with Fritz Ulrich. Fritz was one of Ciaran's friends who lived down the hall from him in St. Peter's. Fritz was exotic-looking, the result of a mixed heritage. His father was German, but his mother was from Ethiopia, which meant he was very tall and muscular with fine, dark brown hair, skin the color of espresso, and eyes the color of light russet. He was loud, opinionated, and pompous, everything Michael was not. He also found Americans very boring. "So do I," Michael said nervously. While his comment made Ciaran and Penry Poltke, Fritz's dorm mate, laugh, it failed to amuse Fritz.

"And that," Fritz declared, "is a perfect example of why."

After Fritz left the table to join a crowd of boys who were equally as loud as he was, Penry, a genial, red-headed kid from Wales, informed Michael, "Don't worry 'bout Fritz none. He looks bloody dangerous, but he's harmless." That comment stayed with Michael while he and Ciaran were walking back to St. Peter's, not because it made Michael think of Fritz, but because it made him think of his mother. In her letter she told him that things aren't always as they seem. And neither are people.

At the entrance to their dorm, Michael told Ciaran, "I think I'm going to do a walk-through of my classes before I turn in."

"Good idea. If you're not back in an hour I'll send out the cavalry."

There were only a few exterior lights sprinkled

throughout the campus, but there was a full moon, so there was enough moonlight to help Michael navigate the unfamiliar territory. Just as he was at the halfway point of his run-through, his father called.

"Hello!"

Vaughan was calling from his factory in Istanbul, the larger of his two factories in Turkey, so the cell phone reception was patchy at best. "Hullo, Michael, how was your day?"

"Good," Michael said, then realized that he should elaborate. He brought his father up to date and said he was looking forward to his first full day of classes tomorrow.

"That's my boy! I knew you wouldn't mind going directly to school," Vaughan shouted, but the rest was indecipherable. Michael wasn't sure if his father could hear him, but he shouted "thank you" into the phone and he meant it. After he lost the connection, Michael realized that this was probably the longest conversation he had ever had with his father and took it as a sign of good things to come.

Once he completed walking through his class schedule, getting lost only once, he headed back to St. Peter's. Before he checked in for the night, however, he was once again drawn to the cathedral. It dazzled just as it did during the day. The moonlight, like the earlier sunshine, bounced off the yellow stained glass, creating a mesmerizing display of silvery moonbeams. He was so engrossed with the exhibition of light, he didn't notice one drop, two drops, three drops, more as the rain began to fall. He also didn't notice the boy staring at him. But once he did, he couldn't turn away.

A few yards from him was the most beautiful face he had ever seen. The boy was a student, maybe a year older. He couldn't tell. But despite the distance, he could tell he had a manliness about him that Michael had yet to possess. As the raindrops started to fall with increased speed, Michael blinked the wetness from his eyes so he could see more clearly. The boy's face was extremely masculine, with a strong jaw and high, sculpted cheekbones, no longer a boy's face but not entirely a man's. Regardless of his age, the boy's face was rugged, fierce, but with blue eyes so shimmery, almost the color of the silver moonbeams that danced above his head, that it gave him a much softer glow. Who in the world was this?

Thunder roared overhead as if to announce the introduction of one to the other and the rain fell down harder, but neither boy moved. Michael lowered his gaze and saw that the body too looked strong. Underneath his wet T-shirt, his chest and biceps curved and his skin looked so pale, it was like white marble. Without touching the skin, Michael knew how it would feel, like cool water over rock-hard stone. Michael blinked again and when he opened his eyes he saw that the boy was looking directly at him, unsmiling but inviting. It was unnerving, though not in a frightening way, and Michael was completely calm and fascinated by every detail of this boy, his arms hanging loose, easily, at his side, his hair, jet black, thick, and straight, lifted slightly by the wind. But when he noticed that this boy, this apparition, this miracle, was still staring back at him through the raindrops, Michael could feel his heart pound within his chest. *This is it,* Michael thought, *this is the thing I've been waiting for, something good.* And then things got better still as Michael watched the boy start to move toward him.

Even if Michael wanted to run away from him or run toward him, he couldn't; he was incapable. He wasn't going anywhere. He watched as this handsome stranger walked, walked, walked over to him in a few relaxed strides and stopped to stand directly in front of him. How could someone who looked so strong and, yes, brutal move with such a fluid grace? Michael had no answers. He was just grateful that this stranger, bathed in moonlight, washed in rain, allowed the first few seconds of their meeting to play out in silence so he could catch his breath.

"My name is Ronan," the stranger said, in an accent much less refined than Ciaran's. Michael could feel breath escape from his lips, but not words. It was only when he remembered something else from his mother's letter could he speak. *No matter where you go, you can't run from who you truly are.*

"I'm Michael."

Neither one of them extended a hand to the other and yet they both felt completely connected. It was as if they both understood that a handshake was not for them; they were destined for a different kind of connection, something more intense, better.

"I've never seen you before," Ronan whispered gruffly.

"I'm new," Michael told him. "Just arrived today."

"Well, then," Ronan said, pausing to stare deeper into Michael's eyes, "this is my lucky day."

Michael had no response. This was the stuff of dreams, the kind of stuff that he made up as he was falling asleep or seconds after waking. Wait, could it be? This boy looked just like the boy from his dreams, from the ocean. No, that wasn't possible. This was real, this was better than any dream because in spite of what he dreamt in the past, he never fully allowed himself to believe that another teenage boy would speak to him like this; no matter how much he wanted it to happen, he always felt it was wrong. But make no mistake, Ronan was speaking to Michael in the way he dreamed someone would, softly, romantically, and with heartfelt interest. Yes, Ronan had spoken only a few words to him, but he sensed that he wanted to say so much more. As did Michael. But further conversation would have to wait for another time.

"It's getting late," Ronan said, not taking his eyes off of Michael. "I should be getting back to my dorm."

"I'm here at St. Peter's," Michael offered, not really knowing why.

"I'm in St. Florian's." That's why. Now Michael knew where Ronan lived.

Michael pushed his feet into the ground a bit more

firmly and resisted the urge to run. "It was very nice meeting you, Ronan."

"You too." But Michael almost missed his reply; he was too busy staring at the raindrops falling from Ronan's nose, onto his lips, his chin. Regaining his focus, Michael replied, "I'll see you tomorrow."

"Yes," Ronan answered, his mouth forming a wet smile. "You will."

And that, Michael thought as he closed the door to St. Peter's, was how it began. Before the door completely closed, he stole one more glance but couldn't find Ronan anywhere. Was he an apparition? No, no, that was absurd; he was real even though the encounter had an air of the unreal to it. Ronan was flesh and blood and, best of all, perfect.

Dried, dressed, and ready for bed, his first night in his new home, Michael's head swam with images of the day. It was a whirlwind. The rain was still pounding the earth outside, hitting the window next to his bed, reminding him of Ronan. He looked across the room and saw Ciaran about to get into his own bed and he could no longer keep this stranger to himself.

"Ciaran?"

"Yes."

"Do you know someone named Ronan?"

Did Ciaran's body stiffen? It was dark in the room, so Michael couldn't tell, but he was certain that his body language meant he recognized the name. "Why do you ask?"

"I met him in front of the cathedral. He seems . . ." Michael couldn't finish the sentence because he really didn't know how to put his feelings into words. This was all very new to him, and Ronan seemed unlike every other boy, man, person he had ever met. Even though he had been in his presence only for a few minutes—they hadn't even touched—the impression Ronan made, like his beautiful face, was incredibly strong.

"Yes, he does make . . . quite an impact."

So Ciaran does know him. I knew it. Not that that meant anything. Double A wasn't that large a school. "So I wasn't just imagining things," Michael said, hoping it didn't sound as dumb to Ciaran as it did to him.

"No, you didn't imagine a thing." Ciaran rolled over onto his side, his face turned away from Michael's. "His name is Ronan Glynn-Rowley," Ciaran said quietly. "He's my half brother."

chapter 6

When Michael woke up, Ciaran was already gone. Sitting up in bed, the room half-lit by the morning sun, he could see that Ciaran's bed was made, his backpack, which had been propped up against his dresser the night before, no longer there. He leaned forward and saw that the bathroom door was open, the room dark. He was certain he was alone.

Michael threw the covers off to the side, and when his feet hit the floor, he saw the note next to the lamp on his dresser. *I had an early lab. Meet me at ten in front of St. Joshua's. C.* Michael wasn't sure what this meeting would be about, but he hoped it would have something to do with Ronan.

He couldn't believe the boy he met last night in the rain was his dorm mate's half brother. How incredibly perfect. Michael had wanted to question Ciaran further about their relationship; in fact, he wanted to hear every single detail Ciaran could offer about Ronan, but he got the sense that, at least for the time being, Ciaran had said all he wished to on the matter. Just because they were related didn't mean they were close or that they even liked each other. Michael should understand that better than anyone. So instead of pursuing the topic, Michael lay awake in bed most of the night and made up his own stories. He imagined that Ronan and Ciaran had the same father but different mothers and grew up in separate parts of Great Britain and were reunited only when they attended the same school. Then he imagined they had the same mother, who raised them side by side on a rambling estate or who brought them with her while she traveled the world. No matter what the scenario, each one ended in the same way, with Ronan introducing Michael to his new family. *This is Michael,* Ronan would say, terrifically happy but with a trace of shyness in his voice. His parents would welcome Michael into their lives graciously and Ciaran would embrace him with a warm hug and whisper something in his ear. What did he say? He could never clearly make out Ciaran's words, so he made up his own: *Welcome to the family.*

In the shower Michael closed his eyes and imagined that the water was rainfall. He pictured himself outside, naked, concealed by the overhanging branches of one of the sprawling trees. Facing him, his back leaning against the tree, wearing the academy's uniform, sheltered from the rain, was Ronan.

Like hundreds of tiny streams, the warm currents slid down Michael's face, his arms, zigzagged across his stomach, curled around his legs while Michael kept his eyes closed and visualized Ronan watching the water crisscross his body. He sighed involuntarily, thinking what it would be like to be examined like that, so thoroughly and completely scrutinized. The vision was almost too intense. He pressed his hand against the porcelain to steady himself. This was better than anything he had ever imagined before, better than R.J. and all the other boys, because they were just faces, bodies, people he would never really connect with, boys he would never really know. But with Ronan, there was a sliver of possibility.

When he finally opened his eyes, he stood motionless and waited for his breathing to return to normal. The water poured down over him and washed away the soap that he had lathered all over his body. He turned off the water, grabbed a towel off the rack, and buried his face in it. Smiling into the softness, the image of Ronan fully dressed, leaning against the tree and staring at him, just would not go away.

His uniform fit perfectly. His father had managed to pick out all the right sizes, and there was something about the regimented look of the outfit that suited

Michael, much more so than the jeans and T-shirts he wore every day at Two W. Already, that part of his life seemed so far away. He looked into the mirror and searched for traces of Nebraska. It appeared that his past had been stripped from him. The only time it crept in was when he made his tie. A memory enveloped him, his grandpa standing behind him, both hands holding the two ends of a tie, folding, wrapping underneath, pulling fabric between fabric, creating a knot, all the while instructing Michael, teaching him how a man ties his tie. Michael couldn't remember what event they were attending that called for him to dress so formally, but he could remember, very clearly, the smell of nicotine on his grandpa's fingertips and the pride in his voice. "You're gonna drive them girls crazy today, Michael, just you wait 'n see." No matter how nice Grandpa tried to be, Michael thought, he always ruined everything.

Before the eight o'clock bell rang to announce the start of the day, Michael was already sitting in his seat in his world history class, notebook open, pen out, and amazed by his new surroundings. This classroom was a combination of old-world style and modern technology and was a vast improvement over the ones at Two W. There, everything looked out-of-date despite the fact that the school was only three decades old. The walls were institutional gray, the carpet a shade darker and stained, the blackboards the same as the ones used in nursery schools, and the technical resources rudimentary. Here, the walls were made of the same large stones seen on the exterior of the buildings, and the floor was thick planks of wood that gave the room an antiquated feel, but the technology was cutting edge. In the front of the classroom, in place of a blackboard, there was a large flat-screen television, probably sixty inches, built into the wall and flanked by two narrow Smartboards; and a wireless laptop was sitting atop a mahogany podium. Michael presumed the teacher typed on it to display text that was then transferred onto the screen. The only accessory the classroom seemed to lack was Ronan.

Michael's eyes kept darting to the front door every time another student entered just in case Ronan happened to begin his day with world history as well. No such luck. He did, however, notice Penry, whose face, upon seeing Michael, brightened, and whose walk quickened so he could grab the empty seat next to him.

"Welcome to *Wind Up the Willows*," Penry said.

Confused, Michael replied, "This isn't world history?"

Penry laughed, which for him came quite naturally. "It is, mate. Willows is the professor."

"Oh. Is he tough?" Michael asked.

"You know *The Wind in the Willows*, don't you?" Michael was familiar with the classic story. "Well, Old Man Willows is not only filled with hot air, but he's also got a bug up his arse." Penry laughed again. "Takes this whole world history thing very seriously, you know. Just do your reading and you'll be fine."

Penry's laughter was contagious; unable to resist, Michael found himself laughing along with him. Yesterday Ciaran, today Penry. It felt good to share a laugh with someone. He could count on his left hand the times he shared a laugh or a joke with someone at Two W. How remarkable that he could feel so lonely at a school where he knew almost all the students since childhood, and yet here on his first day in a brand-new school, where he knew only a handful of students for less than twenty-four hours, he already felt like part of the group. Even when Mr. Willows, looking as old and dour as Penry implied, made him stand up and introduce himself to the class, he felt more at ease than when he had to read aloud at Two W. He hoped it wasn't simply beginner's luck.

Halfway through British literature, his second class of the day and another class that he shared with Penry, Michael hardly felt like a beginner. It was a strange feeling. He had assumed there would be more of a learning curve, a longer period of adjustment, but no. Two classes in and he felt like he had attended Double A for years. Sure, his journey had only just begun, but already he liked the energy, the pace, the more advanced level of teaching. He also had to admit that he liked being in a classroom made up exclusively of boys.

Surprisingly, he wasn't distracted. If anything, he was more focused on the subject matter because although he found many of the boys attractive, he also found them smart and inquisitive. Unlike most of the boys and even the girls back at Two W, these students, from what he could tell so far, wanted to learn, respected education, and were interested in expanding their already impressive minds. Michael was thrilled to be a part of their company; he too wanted to absorb as much information as he could. But he was still a teenager, and try as he might to reel in his thoughts, his mind did stray. While he listened and took notes during Professor McLaren's lesson about morality among the different social classes as played out in *Middlemarch,* he kept glancing at the clock above the door, almost willing the hands to reach ten o'clock so he could race to St. Joshua's during his free period to meet Ciaran and talk about Ronan. Finally the time had come.

"I've got bio for the next two hours," Penry announced. "Save me a seat at lunch."

"Of course," Michael replied. Saving a seat at lunch for a classmate. That would be another first.

Making a left out of the building, Michael walked until he reached St. Jerome's, where all of the foreign language classes took place, then made a right. Although the buildings looked as if they were placed haphazardly, they were actually sectioned off into groups of four and categorized by subject matter. Michael didn't have the whole campus memorized, but before he left his room that morning, he made sure he knew the route from British lit to St. Joshua's Library. He wanted to get there as quickly as possible.

Even though it was September, there was already a

chill in the air—this was northern England after all—
but Michael could feel heat fill his cheeks and flame out
to his ears and he felt beads of sweat form on the palms
of his hands. He wasn't flushed because he was walking
quickly; it was because of what he saw in the distance.
In front of St. Joshua's he saw Ciaran, and standing
next to him was Ronan.

There he was. He wasn't merely a dream, he was a
person. Involuntarily, Michael's face broke into a smile.
How odd that he just couldn't hide his true emotions; he
had gotten so good at doing that back home. But here
and now, he reminded himself, he had to. He couldn't
risk everything by walking up to Ronan with a beaming
grin, smiling as if their meeting last night was anything
more than unexpected. As if it was the beginning of
something. But it was. It was and Michael knew it. Even
though he had no proof, no logic as backup, he knew
that last night underneath the moon and the rain, in
front of the cathedral, something had begun. However,
today in the sunlight he had to at least try to act as if
last night was mere happenstance.

Despite his conviction to act casual, he felt his pace
quicken and so he forced himself to slow down. Mustn't
look too eager. His slower strides also allowed him to
take in the view for a few more seconds and he had to
admit it was a captivating one. The two boys looked
nothing alike, Michael remarked to himself, with Ciaran
tall and lean, and Ronan shorter and more muscular.
But beyond the physical dissimilarities, there was some-

thing else that separated the two, an intangible quality, almost like a class difference. Ciaran and Ronan may have been half brothers, but to Michael they just didn't look as if they were part of the same family. And by the way they stood next to each other, bodies facing in separate directions, not speaking, he got the distinct impression they both wished they weren't.

As nonchalantly as possible, Michael wiped his right palm against his leg to dry it off in case Ronan wanted to shake his hand today. He didn't want their first touch to be sweaty. But Michael didn't have to worry because when Ciaran muttered, "I think you two already know each other," Ronan nodded slightly but kept his hands in his pockets. Somewhat more verbal, Michael was able to add a "yes" to his nod.

The three of them sat in the anteroom to the main library. It wasn't a large room but one where conversation was allowed. In front of them was a bay of windows that allowed the light to illuminate and heat the room, and to their left was a large fireplace, unlit at the moment. Its size meant it would be a great help during the winter months when the room would need more than sunlight to create warmth. Above the fireplace in a beveled gold frame was a huge painting of a monk, Brother Dahey, according to the small inscription, who Michael presumed was one of the founders of Archangel Academy or at least a prominent person in its history. He was dressed in a simple brown robe, his red hair cut short in the unflattering style adopted by monks in the fifteenth century, and while his expression was serious, it was oddly alluring. But there was something wrong with the painting. The monk's eyes were incredibly black, not typical for a redhead, yet that wasn't completely it. Then Michael realized he didn't see any rosary beads hanging from his waist or around his neck. Despite attending mass regularly on Sundays, Michael didn't know a great deal about religion, but he thought monks were supposed to adorn themselves with rosary beads or at least a crucifix. Wasn't that the whole point of their existence? And wasn't the whole point of his being here to get to know Ronan better? Ecumenical ponderings would have to wait until another time because Michael needed to concentrate on making a good impression.

He and Ciaran shared a small sofa made of velvet in a pattern of brown and gold paisley while Ronan sat to their right in a wing-backed olive green leather chair. Michael noticed that Ronan's hair, now dry and set off against the green material, looked fuller and more luxuriant than it did the night before. Unfortunately, he also noticed that Ronan looked terribly uncomfortable, sitting hunched forward, his hands clasped, head down. This was a mistake.

Ciaran shouldn't have arranged this meeting without talking to him first. *At least give me the chance to prepare,* Michael thought. What was he thinking? Yes, what exactly was Ciaran thinking? Maybe Michael was wrong; maybe Ciaran wasn't like him and he wasn't gay and he didn't understand when he spoke to him about

Ronan. Maybe it was only wishful thinking on Michael's part, an incorrect assumption that Ciaran was like him. That had to be it. Ciaran probably thought he was simply introducing Michael to another friend, someone like Penry. It was not as if Michael said anything specific about Ronan the night before; he merely asked if Ciaran knew him. And now the three of them were sitting in silence. Until Ciaran realized he would have to begin the proceedings.

"I thought this would be a good place for the two of you to officially meet," Ciaran announced. "This library is Ronan's favorite place on campus and you seem to share his passion for literature."

Without moving his head, Ronan raised his eyes and spoke in a voice hardly more than a whisper. "You like books?"

Find your voice, Michael told himself. "Yeah." *Make it stronger.* "Yes, I really do like to read."

Ronan lifted his head and turned to look at Michael. It wasn't a dream; he was real. "What else do you like?"

What? Think, Michael, think. This isn't a trick question. Just think of something and answer him. "The usual stuff." *Oh, a brilliant response,* he thought, *brilliantly stupid.* "Movies and stuff . . . you know."

Ronan didn't know, but it didn't matter because he wasn't focused on Michael's words, but on his hair, how blond it was, like sunlight. Ronan spoke without thinking. "Yeah, me too." *Me too what? What did I just agree to? Oh yes, movies.* Sure, movies were nice, but not as nice as Michael's hair.

Ronan's comment mattered even less to Michael because he was too busy staring at Ronan's arms. His sleeves were rolled up to the elbows, exposing his forearms, and Michael loved the slanted strands of jet-black hair on top of unblemished, pure white flesh, such a stark contrast.

"And sports."

What?! Did Michael just say that he liked sports? "Really?" Ronan wasn't expecting that. "Any chance you like rugby?"

"Um, well, you know," Michael stammered. "I don't really know much about rugby."

"Oh, right," Ronan said. "America."

"Yeah, America. You know, we Americans aren't really what you'd call your typical rugby fans," Michael said. "But it looks cool."

"Oh yes, yes, it is." *That was smart, Ronan; like he's going to know anything about rugby.* "Football?"

"What?" This time Michael didn't hear him because he was desperately trying to think of a topic that had nothing to do with sports.

"Do you like American football?" *Oh, Ronan, what are you saying? As if American football is any better a topic of conversation than rugby.*

"It's okay." *You brought up the subject,* Michael reminded himself, *so pick a sport, any sport that you can say more than a few words about.* "Tennis! I like tennis," Michael declared, feeling very relieved and even a little bit triumphant.

"Oh yes," Ronan said. "Tennis is good."

"Yes. Yes, it is."

Neither of them knows a bloody thing about sports, Ciaran silently fumed. *I wish they would shut up and quit rambling. This was a dumb idea, bringing these two together. What was I thinking?*

After a pause that bordered on awkward, Ronan asked, "So you're enjoying Double A?"

Finally, something I can answer easily. "Yes. Even though, you know, it's only day two, I'm really enjoying it. Very much."

So am I, Ronan thought. *But what on earth am I doing? He's so beautiful, so innocent. So unlike me. No, don't think about that, not now. There's enough time for that later. Just try and enjoy this. Enjoy him.* "That's good. It's a great school."

"Yes, much better than my old one."

"In America?"

"Yes, Nebraska."

"Never been there."

"Not a place most people visit."

"Yeah, guess so."

"Yeah."

He couldn't remain silent any longer. The words poured out of Ciaran like a waterfall. "So imagine my surprise when my dorm mate told me he met my half brother on such a dark and stormy night. Why, it's like the plot of one of those prim and proper romantic novels you're so fond of, Ronan."

Before Ronan spoke, he reminded himself that Ciaran was just jealous. *Don't let him get to you, not in front of Michael.* "Ciaran doesn't get Jane Austen."

"And you do?" Michael blurted out. *Oh no, did that sound as insulting as I think it did?* Ronan wasn't insulted; he was amused. He sat back and unclasped his hands, placing them on the arms of the chair. He smirked slightly. "Don't I look like the typical Austen fan?"

"No, I must say that you don't." It felt good to say what was on his mind. Ronan may have been telling the truth, but he looked like a rugby player or a soccer player or a player of any type of sport, but not a devotee of nineteenth-century fiction.

"Well, I cannot tell a lie. I like her," Ronan said. "And she's kind of hot."

Michael laughed and Ronan loved the way his green eyes glistened in the light. And how he kept laughing even when he spoke. "Yeah, in that nineteenth-century-spinstery sort of way."

Fighting to keep a serious expression, Ronan stood up for one of his literary idols. "Do not mock my Jane."

"Nope, not mocking. I'm a fan myself."

"Oh, really?" Ronan asked. "First you mock her, now you're a fan?"

"I'll have you know I've read all her books. Is she your favorite?"

"One of."

"So who tops the list, then?"

A faint shade of pink started to slither up the curve of

Ronan's ears. "I guess if I have to pick one, it would be Oscar Wilde."

Michael hadn't read all of Oscar Wilde's books, but he knew enough about the author to know that if he was Ronan's favorite, there was an extremely good chance that Ronan liked boys just as much as Michael did. When Michael answered, he tried not to reveal too much of his delight in deducing this little bit of information. "He's cool. Do you, um, have a favorite book of his?"

Ronan paused. He felt as if he were going to share a deeply guarded secret and even though he was nervous, something told him he could trust Michael. "*The Picture of Dorian Gray.*"

Michael had read that book, quickly and only in his bedroom, and had delighted in its every word. He imagined Ronan reading the book in his bed, one soft light illuminating the words on the page, his heart beating a bit faster than normal as the tale of eternal youth, beauty, and forbidden love unfolded line after line. Maybe they could reread the book together and talk about how lucky Dorian was to be so handsome and so admired. "That's probably his best," Michael offered.

Ronan tilted his head, his hair falling across his forehead. "Definitely his most popular and mainstream."

"Mainstream?" Michael couldn't see his grandparents or his mother relating to the story. "You think?"

"Down deep, everyone feels like an outcast."

Ciaran fidgeted in his seat, not sure how much more he could listen to. He had a vague understanding of what the novel was about, but no interest in hearing it discussed and analyzed. In fact, he hated when Ronan prattled on about literature in general, finding it to be self-indulgent and boring.

Michael completely disagreed even if he didn't completely understand Ronan's comment. "Everyone? An outcast?"

Don't ramble, Ronan, don't give too much away. "Wilde was part of . . ." *Choose the right word, Ronan.* "A minority. And so he was able to look at life from a different viewpoint. He understood that each of us in some way carries shame." Ronan glanced at Michael's eyes but couldn't hold his gaze, and looked away. "Shame put there by another person, society, to make us feel like an outsider, someone who doesn't belong." When Ronan found the courage to look back, he saw that Michael had never taken his eyes off of him.

It's like he understands exactly what I'm thinking, what I'm feeling. This was such a new feeling for Michael, to be in direct connection with one other person, that he had forgotten that sitting next to him was the boy who made this whole conversation possible.

Odd man out. Ciaran hated the feeling, hated being once again in this position. *It's always the same when it comes to Ronan, though, isn't it,* he thought. His brother always had time to talk to someone else and never to him. He wanted to blame Michael, but he knew he couldn't. He wanted to blame Ronan, but he knew that would be useless. So he blamed himself. *You should've kept your mouth shut and never called Ronan this*

*morning to tell him that Michael had asked about him
in that voice, that tone that said exactly what was in his
heart. And when Ronan demanded in the guise of a
whispered request, "You must bring him to me," I
should've said, "No, go find him yourself." Why can't I
resist him? Ever. But enough. Enough is enough.*

"Whilst I find this dialogue scintillating, an organic
chem lab awaits," Ciaran said, standing up. "And please
note that the scientist was able to wedge the word
'whilst' into his farewell."

Michael started to stand up, but halfway through his
motion realized how awkward he must look and
quickly sat back down. He caught Ronan's bemused
look. "I'll, um, see you at lunch, Ciaran. Okay?" Ciaran
didn't stop to answer Michael but kept walking until he
was outside. The mixture of sunshine and wind was refreshing and he paused for a moment to allow it to revive him. A breeze flew through him and he got a chill;
he knew he shouldn't have told Michael he was related
to Ronan. Some things are best unsaid. But he consoled
himself with the knowledge that he did not introduce
them. They met on their own with no interference from
him, so whatever happened between them, and Ciaran
knew in his heart that something would definitely happen between them, Michael could never accuse him of
setting things into motion.

Ronan was watching Ciaran through the window.
"My brother prefers the company of a laboratory over a
library."

Michael was still having a hard time conceiving these

two as brothers. "I can't believe you two are half brothers."

"Brother, half brother, same thing, isn't it?" Ronan traced the stubble on his chin with his fingers. "Still bound by blood."

"I'm an only child," Michael offered. "I wouldn't really know."

He is so easy to talk to. "Sometimes I feel like an only child."

"You and Ciaran didn't grow up together?" Michael asked.

"Oh no," Ronan said, his gaze not meeting Michael's. "Our childhoods couldn't have been any more different." Michael used every ounce of restraint not to respond immediately but to let Ronan offer whatever information he chose. It's not that he didn't want to know everything there was to know about him; he simply wanted to appear interested and not obsessed. Thankfully, after a moment or two of silence, Ronan explained. "We have the same mother, but Ciaran was raised by his father in London. Well, really by his father's employees, nannies and such; his father travels a lot. Bit too busy sometimes to be a full-time parent."

"That's too bad. And you?"

"Edwige raised me in Ireland."

"That's a cool name, Edwige. Sounds beautiful."

Ronan laughed. "It means 'war.' " His laughter was like a rock hitting the surface of a lake, unexpected with a loud thump and then with smaller echoes cascading out after it. "Which is exactly what she had with Ciaran's father."

"A war?"

"Let's just say that our mum raised me as if I didn't have a brother."

"Wait a second," Michael said. "Ciaran mentioned his mother to me; he made it sound as if she was a part of his life."

Ronan shrugged and shifted in his chair, leaning his body to the right and crossing his legs. A feminine gesture, but on him it looked anything but. "Trust me, Michael, he wasn't talking about Edwige. He must have been referring to his dad's new wife. Can't remember her name, but from what I remember, she has less interest in being a parent than his father. The bloke's very much on his own."

At a different time, Michael would have cared to hear more about Ciaran's non-relationship with his parents, but Ronan had just called him by his first name. *Michael,* when spoken with an Irish brogue, sounded like a question. There was a lilt to it, an air of expectancy as if something should come after it. He liked the way it sounded and especially how it sounded flowing from Ronan's lips. But what came after it was not what Michael wanted to hear.

"What's your mum like?"

What was my mother like? Michael thought. Sadly, he didn't know. Complicated, depressed, dead. "She passed away," Michael said. "Recently."

Ronan's blue eyes filled with genuine regret. "I'm sorry."

"That's all right," Michael said. And he meant it. "I can't run away from it. It can be difficult, but I have my dad. And her death, you know, is what brought me here, so in a weird way I'm grateful."

Ronan stood up. *No,* Michael thought, *why did I have to say something so stupid? Grateful; that was absurd. Ronan can't possibly understand what I meant by it; no wonder he wants to leave.* But he thought wrong. "Take a walk with me, Michael." It took Michael a second to realize that it wasn't a question but a command. Once he understood the difference, he obeyed without hesitation.

Outside, walking side by side, Michael could feel the space between them, like a magnet pulling them together yet not allowing them to touch. This was good, for now. At least they were walking together in the same direction. Now he just had to think of something to say. Silence was good, but only in brief snippets.

"So, um . . . where in Ireland did you grow up?"

"Oh . . . a little place you've never heard of," Ronan said, pausing to stare down at his shoes, at the grass. "Inishtrahull Island."

"Inish . . . what?"

Ronan laughed, then overenunciated. "Inish . . . tra . . . hull Is . . . land."

It sounded like music, albeit an unknown melody. "You're right, I've never heard of it."

Ronan finally looked in Michael's direction. "Not

many have. It's in Northern Ireland, not where they had the Troubles, in Belfast, although it does have its own violent history."

Something about the sunlight and the crisp breeze made Michael feel relaxed. "C'mon, don't leave me hanging. Sounds more interesting than Willows's lecture about the Crusades."

There was Ronan's smile again, reluctant, boyish. *I just can't resist this bloke, can I?* Resigned, Ronan continued. "Well, if you must know, Inishtrahull Island translates to Island of the Bloody Beach."

"No joke?"

Ronan stopped under a huge oak tree and pulled a piece of bark from the trunk.

"No, I wouldn't joke about a thing like that."

The wind stirred the leaves as Michael spoke. "Of course not, no, I mean, that's . . . that's a really interesting translation, Ronan."

Ronan felt that his name spoken with an American accent sounded the way it was meant to sound, harsher, more grounded and less melodic. He liked it. Leaning back against the tree, he tilted his head and closed his eyes. He should resist, he should walk away without looking back, but he couldn't. He was where he wanted to be.

And exactly where Michael had dreamed he would be. *It's happening again. As unbelievable as it sounds, I've seen him do this before,* he thought, *in my dream. How is this possible?*

"According to folklore, the island got its name because a group of men got into a vicious, bloody battle with some Scots from Islay over a woman." Ronan opened his eyes suddenly. "A woman, can you imagine that?" Michael couldn't. "A man can be happy with any woman," Ronan said, reaching up overhead to pull on one of the branches and pluck off a leaf. "As long as he doesn't fall in love with her." He let go and the branch shot back up, bouncing a bit before settling into place. Ronan stared at the leaf for a few seconds, inspecting it, rubbing it between his fingers. "At least that's what Wilde said." Then he brushed it against Michael's nose before letting it fall, carefree, to the ground. Michael felt his knees buckle and thought he would follow the leaf, but he pushed the soles of his feet firmer into the soft ground. Firmer still until he felt, once again, in control of his body. What was happening was absolutely unreal. This handsome boy was flirting with him; he was certain about it. Under this tree, on this campus, with students coming and going all around them, he was flirting with him. There was absolutely no doubt about it. Ronan was just like him. Now, if only Michael knew how to flirt back.

"Oh! Weeping Water has some folklore of its own too you know."

"That's where you're from?"

"Well, I'm originally from London," Michael explained.

"Really?" Ronan said. "Keeping secrets, I see."

Flustered, Michael tried to explain. "No, not at all,

it's just that . . . well, I didn't have a typical upbringing either. I, um, moved with my mother to Weeping Water, Nebraska, when I was three." Michael reached up to grab a leaf for himself, but when he pulled, the leaf proved too strong and wouldn't break off. He tugged harder while trying to continue his story. "We moved in with my grandparents." Finally, Michael gave up and let go of the branch but used a bit too much force, so instead of it bobbing gently back into place the way it did when Ronan released it from his grip, it bounced hard, hitting Michael on top of the head. "Ow!"

Hurt and embarrassed, Michael grabbed his head, knowing he looked like a klutz. Ronan thought he looked cute. "Are you okay?" When he reached over to try and soothe Michael's head, Michael flinched and ducked a few inches. *Oh God, what am I doing?* Ronan was very impressed with himself that he didn't laugh. He wanted to, but he could tell that Michael didn't find his slapstick as humorous as he did. Instead Ronan put his arms behind his back and crossed his ankles. "So tell me about this legend."

The sun was shining directly into Michael's eyes, so he took a step closer to Ronan, just a step and for practical reasons, but maybe it would look like he was finally flirting back. Better late than never. "Well, um, the 'Ballad of Weeping Water' is a poem that tells of a fight between these two Indian tribes. It was so bloody that all the squaws from both tribes wept for days," Michael said. "Their tears formed a stream, which was named

Weeping Water, and that's, well, that's how the town got its name."

Ronan didn't move, but his eyes studied Michael. *God, he's beautiful. Could he think the same thing about me? Should he?* Ronan didn't know. All he knew was, now that Michael was standing so close to him, so close that he could smell the freshness on his skin, it was starting to drive him crazy. "I like it."

He likes it. Maybe I'm not such a fool. Then again, just because he likes the story doesn't mean he likes me. "We both seem to come from a bloody heritage."

It looked like a shadow passed over Ronan's face. Might be sadness, might just be the rustling leaves blocking out the sun for a moment. "I prefer to look at it as if water plays an important part in both our histories."

"I hadn't thought of that. I guess you are like Oscar Wilde."

"An outcast?" *Oh, Ronan, come on, he didn't mean that.*

"No, no, I meant that you look at life from a different viewpoint."

Another shadow. "Of course. I guess I am, then."

Before Michael could make another observation, the bell rang signaling the end of third period. The boys had three minutes to make it to their next class, and Michael had theology, which was far on the other side of campus. It was Ronan's turn to sit through Old Man Willows's take on world history, so his class was much closer. "I, uh, better go," Michael said. "Don't want to be late on my first day." Unable to think of anything else to say, he nodded, looked at the ground, and then started off toward his next class until he heard his name.

"Michael." Michael turned around quickly just as Ronan took a step toward him. And for the first time the boys touched. Only their hands, Ronan's left in Michael's right, but it was electric. Ronan's hand felt just as Michael knew it would, like cool water over rock-hard stone. And Ronan loved how Michael's hand was warm and smooth and softer than his. They were so pleasantly and unexpectedly surprised, they held on to each other for a few seconds after they became self-conscious. But even when they let go, they were still connected. So many thoughts were swirling in their heads, neither of them could speak; they could hardly think.

Finally, breathless and hoarse, Ronan told Michael good-bye, and just as Michael turned away, he was compelled to add "for now." Happily, Michael nodded yes in response before running across campus to get to his next class. Ronan watched him go, sure that he had said the wrong thing, but confident that if he had to repeat his actions, he would say the same words all over again.

The simple truth was that both boys felt their relationship was inevitable, but neither of them knew what truly awaited them.

They also didn't know that they were being watched.

In the distance, two people were staring at them, both disturbed by what they saw. Ciaran, from the other side of the library, and, hiding behind a tree, a strange, dark-haired girl that neither of them knew but whose main purpose today was to observe.

chapter 7

The two boys had no way of knowing it, but they were
both having the same dream.

The only sound that could be heard was their breathing, heavy and quick, as they treaded water in the middle of the lake, above them glorious sunshine, below
them miles of cool and even cooler water. But Michael
and Ronan didn't care to look at what was above or
what was below; they both looked straight ahead into
each other's eyes, trying to gauge the other person's next
move.

They were playing a game they had just made up. A
game whose sole point was to give them an excuse to
roughhouse in the lake and feel the nakedness of their

bodies, arm clashing against arm, leg against leg. Ronan brought from the shore a stone, perfectly round and white, that they would take turns throwing up into the air between them. They would remain still, eyes fixed on each other, not watching the stone rise, pause, and begin its descent. They would move only when they heard the stone hit the water's surface. Then the game would begin.

Diving into the lake, each boy would try to grab the stone first and emerge into the sunlight, hand over head, clasping their treasure. Sometimes Michael would find the stone, other times it would be Ronan, but no matter who would wrap his fingers around the prize first, the other would use his fingers to try and pry it free so he could claim victory.

If it was solely a test of strength, Ronan would win every time. His body was bulkier, his muscles more pronounced, his advantage unfair. But in the lake it wasn't only strength that mattered. Michael was agile and could move and flip around with a bit more ease. Plus, Ronan absolutely loved the way Michael looked when he won. His blond hair plastered down around his face to bring focus to his delicate features, his green eyes sparkling in the sunshine, his full lips forming a wide, happy smile to reveal teeth so white and straight. So incredibly straight. Ronan smiled back at him, but deep within his mind, even in his dream, he thought, *What am I doing with him? He's so innocent, and I haven't been for quite some time.*

While Ronan tossed in his sleep, Michael lay still. He

wanted to play this game forever; he wanted to feel Ronan's power on top of him as he struggled to keep the stone in his hand. He wanted to feel his powerful chest press against his back, Ronan's cheek with a bare hint of stubble graze against his face, and his hands, those magnificently strong hands, cover his own, smooth and hard on top of his knuckles. Plus, Michael absolutely loved the way Ronan looked when he won. His rugged face brightened like a young boy's; his eyes filled with surprise as if each win was his first, his arm stretched high overhead creating a deep dimple in his shoulder blade. Ronan could have the stone; he could win every game. Michael just hoped he would never want to stop playing. And then Ronan broke the rules.

He threw the stone up between them, but before it fell, Ronan shouted something to Michael, something he couldn't quite hear, and dove through the water. What was he doing? He couldn't have a head start, that wasn't part of the rules, Michael thought. But he saw through the blue ripples of water that Ronan was diving deeper and deeper into the lake.

Michael dove in next, the white stone swirling near him, now forgotten, its use finished, and he began to swim after Ronan, deeper and deeper until the blueness of the water had turned from pale to dark. But Ronan was nowhere to be found. Michael felt his heartbeat increase as he looked wide-eyed to the left, the right, but still could not bring Ronan into his vision. Where was he? Where had he gone? *No, our game isn't over,* Michael thought, *not yet. It's only just begun.*

Feeling his chest tighten, Michael brought his knees up, then pushed down to propel himself back up toward and through the water's surface. Gasping, he gulped air back into his lungs, spinning around to see if Ronan had emerged in a different part of the lake. No, he was alone. As alone as he was back in Weeping Water, as alone as he had been for the first sixteen years of his life. It wasn't fair. Why should he meet someone who held the promise of companionship, of escape, of possibly a future, only to have that person taken away from him in a split second? Treading water, his legs growing weary, Michael acknowledged with a full heart that life could sometimes be cruel. Then he quickly learned it could also offer hope.

He felt the placid water next to him turn into a current, then a wave, as something shot past him from underneath into the sky above. It was Ronan. His entire body, his entire naked body, free from the confines of the lake, glistening in the sun, was airborne. Michael was astounded by the sight. Pieces of porcelain-colored flesh, midnight black hair slicked back, droplets of water falling from curved muscle, Ronan looked like a god, and Michael thought he looked at him with godly passion.

Now Michael stirred in his bed, his sleeping mind consumed with new and fantastic thoughts, while Ronan lay still. But in their dream they switched roles. Splashing back down, Ronan's face was euphoric; he embraced Michael roughly and held him close, their bodies melding into one. Michael held on tightly, a bit

afraid to journey into this new territory, but fully aware
that Ronan would lead him to his destiny. And Ronan
was fully aware that without Michael next to him, his
destiny would not be worth reaching.

Ronan unfurled his clasped hand and showed Michael
the white stone. Always playing games, Michael thought.
But no, the time for games had come to an end. Ronan
tossed the stone up and behind him because they no
longer needed an excuse to touch each other, to give in
to the urge to feel each other's body. They were alive
and they wanted each other. It was that simple. And
nothing and no one would make them feel ashamed of
their desires.

Ronan kissed Michael deeply and then pulled back
and repeated what he said to Michael before he dove
deep into the water's hidden area. "I can't wait to show
you all my secrets."

Finally, both boys awoke bathed in a mixture of joy
and fear.

St. Sebastian's Gym was the largest building on the
entire campus. It housed a basketball court, an indoor
track, a weight room, a gymnastics annex, locker rooms
complete with sauna and steam room, and, on the far
end of the building, an Olympic-size swimming pool.
The pool was lined with a series of windows just as in
St. Joshua's Library, but these were larger, floor to ceiling, and overlooked the unpopulated forest that belonged to Double A. Long ago the students had given
the woods a mysterious name: The Forest of No Return.

Just an attempt to be funny, somewhat grand, they had no idea that truth lay behind that name. The trees were so tall and so close together you couldn't see more than a few feet into their depth and there were large patches within the body of The Forest that held no sunlight, no opening to the sky. Looking out the window, Michael felt as if he were standing at the entrance to the unknown. It was the same feeling he got when he looked to his right to stare at Ronan.

They smiled at each other but turned quickly away, if only for practical reasons. Every boy in class was wearing the same bathing suit, a skimpy navy blue Speedo with two gold *A*s on either side of their hips. While their suits were perfect for the game of water polo they were about to play, they were not the best for concealing their excitement upon seeing each other. Luckily, they only had to distract themselves for a minute before Mr. Blakeley blew his whistle, which meant the kids could jump into the pool's, thankfully, cold water.

Actually they were playing a cross between water polo and volleyball since the pool was only three feet deep. Fritz was the captain of his team, which included Michael, Ciaran, and several other students Michael didn't yet know. Ronan and Penry were part of the opposing team, led by a slender Japanese boy he hadn't met but had heard Ronan call Nakano. He was one of the few kids wearing protective eyewear, goggles made of bright yellow plastic. His hair was cut razor short, but still maintained its deep black color. Michael thought he looked like a bumblebee. After Nakano served the ball with a swift, aggressive punch accompanied by a loud grunt, Michael changed his mind. Nakano looked like a hostile bumblebee.

"Hey, Nebraska!" Fritz shouted. "You might want to try to return the serve next time."

Michael heard the words in his head. *Shut up, Mauro!* But this wasn't Mauro, this wasn't Two W, this was new, his new life, and Fritz was just ragging on him. It was no big deal. He had heard Fritz taunt some other guys so it wasn't like he was zeroing in on Michael. At least not for now. Still, he had to figure out a way to veer Fritz's comments in another direction or say something that would combat them directly. What did Mr. Alfano say? "Stand up for yourself; otherwise it's only going to get worse." He agreed with Mr. Alfano, but for the moment he decided it was best to keep quiet.

He was uncomfortable as it was in gym class, He needed to focus all his energy on playing the game and not trying to come up with a clever retort. Michael looked over at Fritz and shrugged his shoulders, missing Ronan glare at Nakano. Ronan's glare spoke volumes and as a result Nakano's next serve wasn't nearly as powerful. Surprised, Michael almost forgot to react, but at the last second, he clasped his hands together, right thumb into left palm, and was able to bounce the volleyball off his forearms and into the air. Ciaran lunged forward and spiked it over the net. One, nothing.

"Like that?" Michael asked Fritz. It was a bit cocky, but Michael couldn't help himself.

Neither could Fritz, not when it came to competition.

"That's one score, Nebraska. The game hasn't even started."

One score was better than none. Michael felt some of the fear that had been suffocating him for so long being released, breath by breath, and replaced with a feeling that resembled happiness. Sad that at sixteen he was only just beginning to be happy; but no, ignore that, ignore the past and look forward, straight ahead at Ronan. Right into the eyes of his future.

What kind of future can I possibly offer him? Ronan tried to push the thought out of his head, but he was so preoccupied with it, he swung and completely missed the ball when Penry lobbed it right to him. It plopped into the water a few inches to his left. "You're a bit off your game, aren't you, mate?" Penry asked, and followed up with his trademark laugh. Just as Ronan arched his thick black eyebrows and shrugged his strong shoulders, Nakano remarked in a low voice, "And onto someone else's." Michael couldn't quite catch what he said, but he saw Nakano's head tilt slightly in his direction. He was definitely talking about him.

The rest of the game seemed to fly by. Fritz shouted some more and a few times aimed his voice at someone other than Michael, Penry made a couple of excellent saves, and Ciaran proved to be the most graceful player in the water, lunging effortlessly to and fro and never once missing the ball when it came to him. It was quite an unexpected display of athleticism and Michael was impressed. Not as impressed as he was with Ronan's skill in the pool, but he had already spent the morning dreaming about Ronan's aquatic prowess, so nothing he did in person was really that much of a surprise. Except when he pushed Nakano harshly into the net.

Immediately, Mr. Blakeley blew his whistle and yelled "foul" partly so everyone would remember who was in charge and partly to prevent the boys from upgrading their push into a scuffle. For a moment, only the water could be heard splashing into the sides of the pool as Nakano and Ronan stared at each other, no one, including them, sure of what would happen next. "Gentlemen," Mr. Blakeley said, "shake hands."

It was hard to tell what Nakano was truly feeling; his eyes were blurred by his goggles, but he stood as if he was ready to pounce. Head tilted slightly forward, fists clenched, his long, lean muscles seemingly on notice. In contrast, Ronan looked calm; he had regained his composure and watched Nakano, waiting for him to make a move. He looked as if he could wait all day. "I said shake hands!" Suddenly, Ronan reached out his right hand, steady and strong. Nakano now had no choice, so begrudgingly he extended his arm and the two boys shook hands. But the whole scene unsettled Michael. He did feel a surge of pride, knowing that Ronan was the first to concede, but there was also a tinge of anxiety. What caused the incident in the first place? And why did Michael have the strong suspicion that it started because of him?

It was clear that something had happened between Nakano and Ronan, but no one could agree on just what that was. Later on in the locker room while they were changing, Penry whispered to Michael that he thought Nakano hip-checked Roman to throw him off balance, you know, just for fun, and Ronan took it the wrong way. "He can be a bit brash, that one." But Michael heard two other boys, their heads together, tying their shoes, mumble something about Nakano not knowing when to give up. What did they mean by that? And why did it make Michael feel unsettled? And why was Fritz staring at him?

"Well, Nebraska," Fritz said, loud enough so everyone in the locker room turned around. "You didn't suck."

That was a relief. Maybe Fritz wouldn't turn into a Mauro after all. "No, Howard, you didn't. You played rather well, actually." Michael turned to face Mr. Blakeley. Although he was several years younger than Mr. Alfano, he wasn't as worked out. Physically, he looked more like a proponent of yoga than of weight lifting. However, their eyes shared the same kindness, the same desire to see their students succeed in and out of the classroom. "You swim as well as you play water polo?"

Hmmm. "Well, since this is the first time I've ever played water polo," Michael said, feeling more confident with every syllable, "I'd have to say my swimming has got to be much better."

"Let's put it to the test. Swim team tryouts are Saturday morning," Mr. Blakeley advised. "Be there."

Really? Michael thought. A teacher was suggesting that he join a sport. How else was his life going to change? *It's only going to continue to change if I let it,* Michael thought, so he decided to do something impulsive for the first time in his life. "Okay, I'll be there."

"I think Blakeley wants you to try out just so he can see you in your Speedo again." Michael blushed before he turned around. He couldn't believe Ronan had just said that. "It was quite a sight."

Michael opened his mouth to speak but couldn't form one word. He glanced around him to see if anyone else had heard Ronan, and while it looked like they hadn't, he couldn't be sure. He couldn't be sure of anything anymore. "You're quite a sight yourself," he mumbled.

"What did you say, Michael?" Ronan teased. "I didn't quite catch that."

Now Michael laughed, and it felt so good. "If you're having trouble hearing me, Irishman, I suggest you clean the potatoes out of your ears."

Ronan's mouth dropped and Michael thought for a moment that he had insulted him. He knew the Irish were sensitive about their culture and perhaps he shouldn't joke about it. But then a roar of laughter burst out of Ronan that surprised Michael. What surprised him more was when Ronan reached out and clasped him on the shoulder. Michael discovered in that moment that an unnecessary touch is just as exciting as an unexpected one. Unnecessary or unexpected, both aroused suspicion.

"Looks like Ronan's made himself a new friend," Fritz observed.

This wasn't news to Nakano and he had to control every muscle in his body not to lash out at Fritz for stating the obvious. "Looks like you'll need a new date for the festival." Nakano ignored Fritz's comment and even the boy entirely and stared at Michael and Ronan. It was a good thing that Nakano had replaced his goggles with dark-tinted glasses because one look into his black eyes and his secret would be revealed. He was consumed with a white-hot rage.

The second-largest building on campus was St. Martha's, where all the students had their meals. It was cavernous and consisted mainly of one extremely large dining hall filled with rows of long rectangular tables, each lined with ten chairs apiece. The chairs were upscale folding chairs, cushioned, and made of heavy-duty plastic in a silver color designed to look like metal. They were modern utilitarian and completely out of place with most of the décor in the rest of the school, but they were efficient since their sole purpose was to temporarily house hundreds of hungry boys.

Michael sat across from Ronan, but the distance between them would have been less if Michael were sitting back at the lunchroom in Two W. On the way from gym to lunch, something else happened between Nakano and Ronan, something else that Michael didn't fully understand but was determined to figure out.

While Penry informed Michael that he and his girlfriend, Imogene, had just this morning decided to date each other exclusively, Nakano and Ronan fell to the back of the crowd. With one ear listening to Penry gush about how Imogene was his first real girlfriend and how she thought she needed to lose five more pounds, but how Penry thought she was perfect just the way she was, Michael used his other ear to try and pick up Nakano and Ronan's conversation. Unfortunately, he could only pick up a word or two. *Never, forget it, don't interfere.* Fortunately, between those words and the stern tone of Ronan's voice, he knew the conversation was not a pleasant one. By the grave expression Ronan now wore on his face, Michael was convinced it could definitely be categorized as unpleasant.

"Your eyes bothering you again, Nakano?" Penry asked. Nakano's sunglasses reminded Michael of the ones his driver wore and he wondered if they were considered trendy here in England. "Chlorine turns my eyes red," Nakano said. "I keep forgetting to take my contacts out."

Penry regaled them with a story about how Imogene had to be rushed to the emergency room once because she couldn't see out of her left eye after wearing her contacts for a whole week. She was fine now and there was no permanent damage.

"Are you sure about that?" Nakano asked, fiddling with his mashed potatoes.

"Oh yes," Penry confirmed. "Right as rain."

"Then if she can see, why the hell is she still with you?" A few of the guys at the table laughed, including Penry. It was kind of funny, but Nakano's face remained serious. Michael got the distinct impression that he hadn't been trying to make a joke; he was just being mean-spirited. Fritz might be obnoxious and loud, but Nakano appeared to have a bit of a nasty edge to him. *Maybe that's why Ronan pushed him; maybe he said something spiteful about me,* Michael thought. Ronan could have been defending him. But if Nakano did say something against him, something that made Ronan respond physically, why was he sitting next to him now? Granted they weren't having a friendly conversation, but they weren't arguing and they weren't completely ignoring each other either.

"You trying out for water polo on Saturday?" Nakano asked. Although he looked straight ahead, it was clear that his comment was directed to the person to his right.

"I'm the captain," Ronan said.

"Was," Nakano corrected, raking his fork through a pile of creamed spinach.

Ronan stared at his food. "And will be again," he seethed. He got up so suddenly, everyone at the table was startled, even Ronan himself. He didn't move, he didn't look at anyone. It was as if his action took even him by surprise and he didn't know how to follow it up. He pressed his left index finger into the table so hard that the white flesh turned deep red, and then mumbled to no one in particular, "Excuse me."

Helpless, Michael watched Ronan walk away from the table, from him, and down the aisle. He felt all the energy in his body will him to get up, to go after Ronan, but he stayed in his seat. Something within him told him not now, he needs to be alone. Nakano's inner voice was telling him something completely different. "Guess I have to make things right with my mate," he announced.

As he got up, Nakano looked directly at Michael, his sunglasses slipping down just a bit on his nose. Michael shivered as a ribbon of cold fear shimmered down his spine and tied a knot around his breath. Nakamo's eyes weren't just black, they were filled with blackness. Cavernous, they were like tunnels that lured toward something he couldn't quite identify. Michael wasn't sure if *evil* was the right word, but that's what came to his mind. For an instant, Michael wasn't surrounded by a hundred other boys in St. Martha's; for an instant, it was just him and Nakano, and he was afraid. It didn't make any sense, but there was something wrong with the boy who stared at him, something terribly wrong. And then the feeling was gone. Nakano pushed his glasses back into place and Michael's fear disappeared. As he watched Nakano walk out of the lunchroom, Michael wondered what had taken hold of him and why he wasn't the one leaving in search of Ronan.

"Boys!" Fritz declared. "Sometimes I just don't understand 'em." With that announcement he and a few others got up from the table and left, leaving Michael between Penry and Ciaran. Michael tried to catch Ciaran's eye, but it was as if he were deliberately avoiding him. *He knows something,* Michael thought. *He knows what's going on between them.* As if he could read his mind, Ciaran turned to Michael. "If you want to know their history, ask Ronan. I've already done enough."

Gathering his books quickly, Ciaran got up to leave. He didn't mean to snap at Michael and he would spend the rest of the day feeling guilty about it, but there was very little he could say. He couldn't be honest with Michael, only Ronan could, and he found it wearisome to lie, so he kept silent. Michael would find out the truth soon anyway; the way he and Ronan kept staring at each other, it was inevitable. And inevitably, Ciaran would be there to pick up the damaged pieces once the truth was revealed. But for now he had to leave.

"Another lab?" Michael asked.

Ciaran nodded. He looked at Michael and made himself smile. "I'll see you back home." It wasn't Michael's fault. Ciaran's problems were here long before Michael arrived, so he shouldn't take them out on him. "I have an English quiz tomorrow; maybe you could help me study?"

"Sure," Michael said. "Of course."

Both boys felt the urge to say more. Michael hadn't yet thanked him for arranging the meeting with Ronan the other day, and Ciaran wanted to warn him about any future meetings, but both remained silent, instinctively knowing that the other really didn't want to hear what they had to say. They didn't have to worry about finding the right thing to say or even being heard, because suddenly Penry made enough noise for the both of them.

"Imogene!"

Everyone looked at the front of the hall, near the kitchen entrance, to see a rare sight at Archangel Academy. Standing next to the headmaster was a girl. And not just any girl. It was Penry's girlfriend.

"What the devil is she doing here?" Penry cried out,

looking quite shocked, but very delighted. " 'Scuse me, mates, I have to see my girl. "

Imogene Minx was a sophomore at St. Anne's, the all-girls school on the outskirts of campus, but Michael thought she looked more like a pop star or someone you would see on TV. She had a look about her that demanded attention. Of course she wore the mandatory uniform, which for the girls was a navy, white, and gold plaid vest and pleated skirt, which could rise no more than a half inch above the knee; navy blue stockings and tie; and a white long-sleeved shirt with a Peter Pan collar.

On the upper left side of the vest, over their hearts, the girls each wore an oval patch of St. Anne, her hands folded in prayer, her white robe bright against a golden yellow backdrop. Each girl had to hand-sew the patch on herself in front of the headmistress, Sister Mary Elizabeth, as a ritual before being allowed to attend class. No words would be spoken between the headmistress and each student until they submitted their handiwork for inspection, at which time Sister Mary Elizabeth would say, "Welcome." It didn't matter if the effort was perfect or flawed; all who tried were accepted. The sewing was more an offering than a test.

Now it looked as if Mr. Hawksbry's patience would be tested as he stood between Penry and Imogene. Her lips were the same red color as Penry's hair, but that's really all they had in common. Where Penry was almost always brimming over with enthusiasm and movement, Imogene was calm and still. She held a small stack of books that she rested on her right hip, which was slim and hadn't yet developed a womanly curve, and a black bag hung from her left shoulder, adorned with a large gold *A,* presumably for St. Anne's. But it was her hair that caught Michael's attention. She wore it in a severe style, bangs high and straight across her forehead and the rest no longer than her chin, cut the same length all the way around. The color was beyond dark, so black that in places where the light hit it, it looked blue. And even from where Michael stood, he could see her eyes were the same color, round and open, as if she didn't want to miss anything of her surroundings. But right now, all she was looking at was Penry.

Michael and Ciaran walked by them just in time to hear Imogene announce that she was interviewing Mr. Hawksbry for her school paper and he was kind enough to let her grab lunch here instead of walking all the way back to the cafeteria at St. Anne's.

"Mr. Hawksbry," Imogene said, "you're a scholar and a gentleman."

The headmaster coughed, uncomfortable being on the other end of such a pointed compliment on school grounds, and for no other reason than to change the subject, he put his hand on Michael's shoulder, preventing him from walking any farther away.

"I don't presume you've met our newest student," he said, turning Michael to face Imogene. "This is Michael Howard all the way from the Midwest. America, that is, and specifically Nebraska."

Up close, she looked even more severe, but despite

her look, she wasn't at all aloof. She seemed to possess the same friendly quality Penry did; she just wasn't as loud. "It's a pleasure, Michael. I've been to the States a few times, actually. I've relatives in California, Los Angeles."

"Nebraska is pretty far from L.A.," Michael said. "In every sense of the word."

Mr. Hawskbry's eyes brightened and he snapped his fingers. "I have an idea. Perhaps you could arrange to do a story on Michael."

"That's brilliant!" Penry shouted. "New bloke on campus and all that."

Imogene thought about it for a minute. She was obviously the type of girl who didn't like to be told what to do. "I'll consider it. I'll present it to our editor and see if we have room."

"It's a right smart idea, Ims," Penry said. "You know it is."

Imogene smiled at Penry, making him become quite self-conscious in front of the headmaster, who not so self-consciously glanced at his watch. "Next period is about to begin; time to carry on."

"See you later, Ims," Penry said. Imogene's smile softened her look. She didn't say anything but merely winked at him. She was trying to appear cool, but she was definitely infatuated. It was fun to see the two of them in each other's presence, and Michael hoped he would see more of them as a couple. Then just as she was about to enter the kitchen, she turned around, her hair swaying a bit so that a strand of hair caught the crease of her mouth. "Michael," Imogene said, "I'll be in touch." Looked like he would be getting his wish.

After school, walking aimlessly across campus, Michael couldn't get the image of Penry and Imogene out of his head. Had Michael met Imogene first, he would never have imagined she would go for a guy like Penry, but sometimes opposites attract. All that mattered was that they looked happy together. He wondered if he and Ronan were going to be happy. Or better yet, would there ever really be a Michael and Ronan? Today had started out with such great promise. Ronan was flirty, attentive, but then Nakano ruined everything. As Michael wandered in front of St. Florian's Dorm he saw that Nakano was still at work.

He stopped in his tracks as he saw Ronan and Nakano at the side of the building in the shade of a huge oak tree. They were covered by late afternoon shadows, but Michael could see enough to know that they were having an argument. To be exact, a one-sided argument. Nakano was whispering loudly. None of his words reached Michael, but his arms were moving up and down, a finger poking the air to accentuate a point, a hand forming a fist. It was clear he was angry. But Ronan just stood and listened, his eyes never leaving Nakano's face. Then he raised his hands and reached out, looking as if he was going to grab the sides of Nakano's head.

Instinctively, Nakano raised his hands inside Ronan's arms and deflected them, making them swing out to the side and away from his face. Instead of growing angrier, reacting more physically, both boys settled down. Michael could feel the knot in his stomach grow tighter as he watched Ronan reach his hands up to Nakano's face, slowly, and gently take off his sunglasses. They stood facing each other—they didn't speak, they didn't move—until finally Ronan hugged Nakano. Michael couldn't tell if it was a friendly hug or a tender one. He didn't care; they were hugging. This morning Ronan was shoving him in the pool and now he was hugging him; it just didn't make sense. Devastated, Michael wanted to scream or hide or return to Weeping Water, where at least he knew he would never be happy. Here he thought he could be and briefly he was, but already it was over. Everything he thought was possible was destroyed in that one embrace.

Just as Michael turned to run from the scene, Nakano turned his head and saw him. His eyes, two black dead holes, showed absolutely no emotion, but his mouth formed a victorious smile.

chapter 8

Michael was hardly interested in trigonometric functions, but today he hung on every word that came out of Father Fazio's mouth. He wasn't fascinated by what his teacher was saying, nor did he fully grasp the importance of learning about right angles, but if he focused on each word of the lesson, he wouldn't have to think about Ronan. Or about Ronan and Nakano hugging in the shadowlight. Or about how Michael and Ronan had ended even before they truly began. He needed to occupy his mind with something else, anything, so he tried to push everything else from his mind and just concentrate on what his teacher said. It wasn't working.

There were several reasons why: Father Fazio, one of the few priests who taught at the academy, spoke in a monotonous drone that lulled students to sleep. Michael didn't like math, so even during the most interesting or easy-to-follow lessons, his mind had a tendency to stray. But mainly it wasn't working because Ronan was sitting two seats behind him to his left and had been trying to get his attention ever since he walked into the room.

Ronan was already seated when Michael entered a few seconds before the last bell and looked relieved when he saw him. Michael, on the other hand, looked startled. He knew Ronan would be in class, but he had avoided seeing him all day, so this was their first encounter and it made his stomach flip. Earlier in the day, he ignored his text messages and rebuffed his request to meet at St. Joshua's, claiming he needed to catch up on some reading. But when he entered the room, the magnetic pull between the two boys was in full force and Michael's eyes immediately found Ronan's.

Briefly, Michael forgot about his odd behavior and the hug and he only saw Ronan, handsome and muscular and staring right at him, but then it came back to him in a flash and he realized no matter how hard he wanted to erase what had happened, he couldn't. Head down, Michael walked to his seat and gave Ronan the barest of nods and a quick half smile before sitting down and facing the front of the classroom.

If this were British literature, Michael could lose himself in the lecture, or if Father Fazio looked more like Professor McLaren, good-looking and tanned instead of portly and pasty, Michael's mind could wander in a different direction, but every few minutes, no matter how hard he tried to pay attention to the mathematical drivel about sine and cosine, his mind always wound up at Ronan's doorstep.

Finally, he gave in and for the last ten minutes of class, he ignored everything his teacher said and thought about Ronan. Replaying in his mind Ronan pushing Nakano, whispering to Nakano, hugging Nakano, over and over again. Out of the corner of his eye, Michael could see Ronan try to smile at him. *He's acting like nothing happened.* Maybe nothing did happen, Michael told himself. No, no, he saw it with his own eyes.

Why won't he look at me? Ronan knew he had acted strangely yesterday, but he didn't think he deserved the silent treatment. There were some things that Michael didn't understand just yet, might never understand, but he had to know how he felt about him. He had never been so obvious in all his life. He had never before taken such a chance on exposing himself, but the moment he saw Michael's beautiful face outside the cathedral, he knew the time had come. Their time had come, but now it appeared as if their time was already over. What in the world was going on?

Before the bell stopped ringing, Michael was already at the door. Ronan had to push past some students just to catch up to him. He wasn't letting him get away, not after the risks he had already taken.

"Michael," Ronan called out. "Wait up." Instinct lost and Michael obeyed. "Hi."

"Hi." *Don't look into his blue eyes,* Michael told himself. *Don't look at how shimmery they are and don't give him the satisfaction.*

"Is something wrong?"

All around them, boys hurried past, laughed, shouted, but the space between the two of them was silent. There was so much they both wanted to say to each other, but how to begin? How could Michael say what was really in his heart when he hardly understood it himself? He had lived such a sheltered life in Nebraska, so alone and lonely, that the first time he met a boy who he thought was interested in him, a boy that stirred within him a real passion, he made a fool of himself. He created a world that didn't exist. He built a relationship based on a few conversations because he was so desperate to connect with someone else. It didn't matter that in his heart and his mind he felt the connection was real. It didn't matter that he felt a peace he had never known. It was all fake.

Michael shook his head. "No, why?"

This wasn't how it was supposed to be, Ronan thought. This boy was supposed to be his salvation. He had lived long enough, lived through enough to know the difference between finding someone who would be a fun mate and finding someone who would change your life forever. Michael was supposed to be the latter. He was supposed to be the one who would make his life, as unnatural as it was, feel normal. No, much more than that—feel astonishing and worth living. Why was he acting like this? Like none of that was true when Ronan knew, fully and completely, that it was.

"You're, um . . ." Ronan suddenly became aware that they weren't alone but in a crowded hallway. "Could we go somewhere and talk?"

Yes, Michael thought, *let's go somewhere where it's just the two of us.* Nobody else, no other students, no teachers, no Nakano. "No." Michael didn't mean to sound so blunt, but it actually felt good to be direct. "No, we can't."

This was new for Ronan, this feeling of defeat. But he was a survivor and he wasn't going to give in so easily. "What about after class?"

His strong defense fading, Michael knew he had to break free from Ronan's presence. There was something about him, something about his eyes, his cool smell, like mist on a lake, that he just couldn't fight. "Maybe." *No, stand up for yourself, have some respect.* "Probably not; I've got a lot of reading to do."

He's lying, I know it. I don't know why, but I just know it. "More reading?" Ronan asked.

"Yes," Michael said softly. "More reading."

If only I hadn't seen the two of them together, Michael thought, the anger building within him. *If only I didn't know that the boy in front of me, who held such hope yesterday, was the bearer of such misery today, then I could smile and flirt, or try to flirt, and say "Of course we could meet after class; there isn't anything else I'd rather do."* And there wasn't anything else

Michael wanted to do, but to spend hours in Ronan's company, but that wasn't going to happen. It was that simple.

"Bye," Michael said. As he walked past Ronan, their shoulders brushed against each other. Despite his resolve, he could feel the excitement grow within him, in the pit of his stomach, such a strong sensation that now would just lie there with the rest of his anger and his frustration.

"Wait!" Michael stopped, but didn't turn around. He felt that if he did, he would do something stupid like start to cry or yell and he couldn't do either, not here, and there was no reason to, there was nothing between Ronan and Michael now except a few conversations and a magical meeting under the stars and in a rainstorm. That was it. That was all. "This is for you."

Ronan handed Michael a piece of paper, actually more like parchment, folded up. When Michael took it, he made sure not to touch Ronan's fingers either accidently or on purpose. There was no reason to touch him any longer. There might be a need, but there was no longer a reason.

"What is it?" Michael asked, trying to sound uninterested.

Kiss him, Ronan heard himself say silently. Kiss him and make him understand that there was a reason they met, there was a reason he came to this particular school out of all the schools in the world and they happened to be in the same place at the same time that first night. There are no coincidences. Ronan knew that;

Michael had to learn. But he kept all that information to himself. "Just something I drew. I thought you might like it."

"Oh, thanks." Michael slipped the paper between some pages of his geometry textbook. He couldn't look at it now; in fact, he couldn't bear another second looking at Ronan's face. "I have to go." This time when he turned and walked away, he didn't turn back even though he knew Ronan stood there waiting for him to do so. The strength of his conviction surprised them both.

The rest of the day was a blur, a cyclone of thoughts and impressions and feelings most all of which had to do with Ronan, but some featuring Mauro and even Michael's mother. He wondered if she was happy wherever she was. But if she was never happy on earth, could she ever be happy off of it? During theology, his last class of the day, Michael wondered if he should ask Professor Joubert if a soul could find happiness by way of suicide, but somehow he didn't think it would be appropriate since they were only just beginning to study the basics of the New Testament.

Michael did find it strange that his theology class was taught by a layman while his math class was taught by a priest. Seemed counterintuitive to him. In fact, he thought more of the teachers would be priests, given the school's name, but even though many priests and monks lived on the property, most of the teachers were from the secular world. It actually didn't matter; just by the names of the buildings and the artwork each one housed, spirituality, if not organized religion, permeated every inch of the campus. He liked this subtle approach and found it more effective in sparking his interest than the way he grew up, which was being forced to attend church every Sunday to listen to a fire-and-brimstone sermon. Maybe if he remained quiet and listened to the lessons the school had to offer, he would learn if his mother could ever find happiness.

While he would have to wait to find out if his mother's quest for happiness was successful, he would no longer have to wait for his father's return. When class was over, he noticed Headmaster Hawksbry standing outside the door next to his father's driver.

"Howard," the headmaster said, his fingers nervously tapping his thigh. "Looks like you'll miss out on Mexican fiesta night. Your father has requested that you join him for dinner."

It was hardly warm today, but there were tiny beads of sweat on the headmaster's forehead. Little bubbles of fear, Michael thought. *Why does he look so nervous? Maybe he doesn't like to break the rules?* Penry did tell him that while he was a "right fair mate," he was a strict rules man who liked to follow the book to the letter, and according to what Michael had been told, new students weren't allowed to leave the campus during the week.

"Is that allowed?"

Mr. Hawksbry took out a crisp, white handkerchief from his inside jacket pocket and dabbed at the sweat. "Technically, no, but due to your circumstances we, um, felt it appropriate to allow this brief reunion. Your father's assistant said he is only in London for a few days."

London was about three hours away. "I'm going to London?"

Now he used the handkerchief to cover his mouth when he coughed. "No, no, he's staying at a hotel here in Eden for the night. Your driver has strict instructions to bring you back here before eleven."

The driver didn't respond in any way; he just stood, hands clasped in front of him, and stared straight ahead. At least Michael thought he stared straight ahead. He was still wearing his sunglasses, so Michael couldn't really tell. The same ones Nakano wore, quite fancy with thicker-than-usual arms. They were most definitely part of a British trend.

When he looked back at the headmaster, he knew that this time he wasn't imagining things. Alistair Hawksbry was definitely nervous in the presence of his father's driver. Michael didn't really understand why, but he was sure of it. Could be the driver's silence. He wasn't the most chatty of chaps, which was the way Michael thought a Brit might describe him, and Mr. Hawksbry's career was all about communicating. Weird, but maybe he just didn't trust people who only spoke as little as humanly possible.

Luckily, the drive to the hotel was short, because during the entire ride Michael thought about Ronan. He kept thinking about how blissful it would be to have him sit next to him en route to meeting his father for the first time. The cool smell of Ronan mixing in with the crisp smell of cinnamon that wafted throughout the car, the two of them holding hands, sinking into the luxuriousness of the leather, the only sounds the soft violins and their breathing. They would steal a few kisses before having to leave their sanctuary, certain in the knowledge that Michael's father would approve of his son's choice. But none of that was going to happen now. When Michael got out of the car, he got out alone.

Vaughan was staying at the Eden Arms, a small boutique hotel that was little more than a bed-and-breakfast. It was also the only hotel in town, which was to be expected because, besides Archangel Academy, Eden was mostly made up of residential houses and a smattering of small businesses. It was mainly a picturesque snapshot of English countryside that Michael found so much more pleasing than the dreary flatness of Weeping Water.

"Son!" Vaughan exclaimed. "The uniform suits you."

This time when father and son hugged, it was a bit more relaxed, partially because they were prepared this time and partially because they wanted their relationship to forge ahead and grow. Neither wanted to go back to the way things were before.

"So Hawksbry tells me you've impressed all your professors," Vaughan said, sipping a glass of red wine.

"Well . . . I don't know," Michael said, unused to such flattery from his father.

"Don't be modest. It isn't becoming on us Howards," Vaughan said with a loud laugh.

Michael took a large sip of his soda and decided to be

honest. "I really like my classes a lot, so I guess my enthusiasm shows."

"More than enthusiasm, son. Hawksbry tells me you're already at the top of the list academically."

Could that be true? "Really? I just got there."

"Believe me, first impressions are all that matter. If you don't grab them in the first meeting, you've lost them forever," Vaughan declared. "Sounds like you grabbed them so hard they're never going to want to let go."

It was difficult to be in his father's presence without the specter of his mother. He had heard so many things about him from her, either directly or indirectly, that he had created a persona of the man without ever meeting him. He got the feeling that his version was quite different from the one who stood before him now, but he realized only time would tell whose version was more accurate. One thing he would learn to get used to was that his father was full of surprises.

Just as Michael glanced over to the small dining nook and saw that there were three place settings and not two, there was a knock on the door.

"Right on time," Vaughan announced.

For some reason Michael felt uneasy. Wasn't this just supposed to be a reunion between father and son? "Is someone else coming?"

Vaughan opened the door. "Brania, come in. I'm so glad you could make it."

The girl who entered the room was stunning. At only sixteen years old, Brania O'Keefe was already a young woman, beautiful, confident, and poised. Even though Michael didn't grasp her beauty on an emotional level, he understood it intellectually. This was the type of woman men fought over. The kind of woman who would have ignited a bloody battle between the Inishtrahull islanders and the inhabitants of Islay. He saw her beauty; it just didn't make him feel anything.

Vaughan, however, was quite taken with the girl and it was easy to see why. She didn't really look like a girl. Her deep auburn hair was parted at the side and cascaded effortlessly down the sides of her face. Her skin was the color of alabaster. Michael thought it looked like the feminine version of Ronan's, and in fact her eyes were the same shimmery blue. Her body was a multitude of curves, shoulders, breasts, hips, and contained none of the straight lines that Imogene possessed. Here was a woman who just happened to be sixteen.

"Mr. Howard, thank you so much for inviting me," Brania said. "It was very thoughtful."

"Nonsense," Vaughan said, erasing the thought with a wave of his hand. "When your father told me he had to cancel our meeting and you got caught in the cross fire, there was no way I could leave you to fend for yourself."

"He's very grateful as well and he told me to tell you that whatever terms you want on the deal, consider them done."

Vaughan smiled like a man who had gotten exactly what he wanted. "Your father is an honorable businessman."

Michael had a jolt. This was what Ciaran must have felt like when he was speaking with Ronan at St. Joshua's—a third wheel, unnecessary. He would have to remember to apologize. But first it was his father's turn. "Forgive me for my lack of manners. Brania O'Keefe, this is my son, Michael Howard."

"Hello," Brania said. "And welcome back."

Michael realized his father must have told her that he was born in England but grew up across the pond, as the natives say. "Thank you, it feels good to be home."

What didn't feel good was Brania's hand. Yes, hers was soft and delicate, but Michael much preferred the strength of Ronan's grip and how his hand almost covered his own.

"May I freshen up before dinner, please?" Brania asked.

"Of course, dear, right in there," Vaughan said, pointing to the door past the kitchen.

She could spend an hour in the bathroom freshening up and he still wouldn't find her as attractive as Ronan. Funny, he thought, he'd been here for less than a week and already he was able to admit more about himself than ever before. He liked acquiring this self-knowledge. It made him feel more in control of himself. He was amazed at how suddenly that control could be stolen away.

"Brania is the daughter of the wealthiest real estate mogul and land developer in Great Britain," Vaughan whispered. "And the girl I'd like you to marry."

Even after they had begun eating their first course, a

thick tomato soup, Michael was still reeling from his father's comment. Marry? Was his father insane? First of all, he was only sixteen, and even if he was inclined to marry, which he wasn't, a wedding date wouldn't be set for another five, maybe ten years. It was a bit premature to tell your sixteen-year-old son you want him to marry a girl he just met, a girl whose company he had been in for less than an hour, especially when your son had no intention of ever marrying a girl. Michael would have thought it was hysterically funny if he hadn't caught the undercurrent of seriousness in his father's voice. He truly wanted Michael to marry Brania. Well, that wasn't going to happen, so Michael told himself to just get through the dinner and this whole evening could be forgotten.

Once he made the decision never to see Brania again or discuss the topic with his father, he was able to relax a bit more. Until they were just about to eat their steaks and Vaughan's cell phone rang.

"Excuse me, you two, this is Tokyo. Problem with an overnight delivery at the factory; shouldn't take too long."

In spite of the rumbling in his stomach, Michael took a large bite of steak. If he was chewing, he couldn't talk.

"I think it's sweet," Brania said.

So much for not talking. "The problem in Tokyo?" Michael said, trying not to speak with his mouth full.

Brania smiled a bit condescendingly. "No, silly, our fathers trying to set us up. It's sweet. A bit old-fashioned, but sweet nonetheless, don't you think?" Brania's tone of voice matched her smile. She was definitely a girl who was reared in a lofty circle. Her actions, however, were a bit more primitive. Peering at Michael, she used her tongue to flick a drop of blood that clung to her fork, swallowing it as if it were a thick piece of meat. *Please, God, don't let her be flirting with me,* Michael prayed. When Ronan did it, he was nervous, but also excited. Now he was just downright unnerved.

He swallowed hard and felt the unchewed piece of steak travel down his throat with difficulty. "I don't think that's what they're trying to do."

Brania smirked haughtily and let her fork fall onto her plate, disrupting the air with a noisy clang. "Don't be a child. We both know what they're doing. Do you have a girlfriend?"

"No."

"A boyfriend?"

Taken aback, Michael scoffed at such a suggestion. "No! Of course not."

Folding her napkin precisely and placing it over her uneaten steak, Brania had her answer. "You really should learn not to give yourself away so easily."

Where was that control I was just feeling? Michael thought. *And how dare she say these things to me? Who does she think she is?* "I . . . I don't know what you think you know."

"Have you ever been with a girl?" Brania asked, interrupting and ignoring Michael's comment.

"Yes. I mean, well, no, not exactly." Michael hemmed

and hawed. Why was his mouth suddenly so incredibly dry? "It's really, um, it's really not any of your business."

Again that condescending smile. Michael couldn't tell if she liked him or thought he was the stupidest creature on the face of the earth. She rested her chin in the palm of her hand and would have looked bored if not for the determination in her eyes. "May I give you some advice?" Michael didn't answer because he knew Brania wasn't asking for permission. "Don't make any decisions regarding your gender preference until you've tested them both out. There are only two, so it really shouldn't take you very long."

When Vaughan returned to the table, he either didn't see Michael's shocked expression or he ignored it. "Situation Tokyo under control," Vaughan announced. "Ready for dessert?"

At precisely ten thirty Vaughan's cell phone rang again. This time it wasn't a business emergency, just the driver announcing that it was time for him to drive Michael back to the academy. "It was a pleasure meeting you both," Brania said before leaving to go to her room, which was located on the first floor of the hotel. "I hope to see more of you, Michael."

Although Michael told her that he hoped they could too, he didn't mean it. What he didn't know was that Brania was the type of privileged girl who always got everything she wanted.

Beaming, Vaughan gripped Michael by the shoulders

and smiled. "You've made me so proud tonight, son." Michael felt uneasy. The only reason he made him feel proud was because he didn't tell him exactly what he thought about his ludicrous ideas about marriage. "You'd make me even happier if you invited Brania to that Archangel Festival they have at your school," Vaughan said.

"Um, maybe, I'll, um, think about it," Michael mumbled.

"Good man."

Michael had no intention of thinking about Brania, marriage, or taking her to the festival. All he wanted to do was get back to school, to the place where he felt he belonged.

The countryside was invisible in the darkness. Michael looked out the window but couldn't see a thing. He grabbed one of his books that he left in the car, thinking he should use his time wisely to catch up on some homework and not ponder what to do about Ronan or his father or even Brania. But he wouldn't get any work done. When he opened his geometry book, a piece of paper fell out, the paper Ronan had given him after class. Heart beating faster, he slowly opened up the folded parchment and saw that it was a drawing, a quick sketch that Ronan must have done while Father Fazio was rambling on about triangles. The tears fell before Michael even felt them gather, dropping off his cheeks and onto the paper below. He was looking at a drawing of himself. It wasn't an exact likeness; it really wasn't even that good, but it was drawn by Ronan's hand. It was Michael's face with his green eyes and his blond hair, contained within a picture frame. Underneath the drawing were the words *The Picture of Michael Howard*. Next to them he had written *Forever beautiful, Forever mine.*

Ronan was Oscar Wilde and Michael, his very own creation.

chapter 9

Ronan had a bad feeling. He woke up knowing that something was wrong and that something terrible was about to happen. He wished he could ignore it; he wished he could convince himself that his mind was being manipulated by something other than instinct, but long ago he had learned to trust his intuition. Especially when it sensed danger.

To make matters worse, he knew that at the center of his apprehension was Michael. Ronan shivered. *It's already started. I've already drawn him into a world where he is unsafe, into a world that he will never comprehend and that will disgust him. It's a world that I be-*

long to, and sometimes, not always, but sometimes, it even makes me wish I had never been created.

Maybe I shouldn't have glanced his way in the moonlight, Ronan thought. *Maybe I should have just kept walking, alone, the way I was meant to live. No. No! That is not how my life was meant to be; none of us were meant to live like that.* He reminded himself what his mother had always told him: "Our people may be different, Ronan, but we were meant to live, and the only way we know how to live is to love."

Ronan looked at his reflection in the mirror. Despite the anxiety and fear that were growing deep within him, he couldn't help but feel blessed that he was to be able to see his true image. He was grateful his eyes were a beautiful shade of blue and not the deep, empty black that so many others possessed. Thankful that his face, strong and chiseled, was capable of his feeling the sun's light anywhere in the world without fearing that his flesh would burn beyond repair. Yes, he was lucky, lucky that he wasn't one of Them. But would that matter to Michael? Would he understand the difference or would he just think he was a monster?

Part of him was convinced that Michael would accept him for who he was and want to spend the rest of eternity with him, but the other part, the one that housed his insecurities, wasn't fully certain. And yet just the thought of Michael, just the idea that the two of them could become a couple, could grow close and inseparable, made Ronan smile. A lazy and effortless smile formed on his face. The more he thought about Michael, the more the smile grew, and here in his bedroom, alone, unworried that anyone would see him, he allowed the full truth of who he was to be revealed in the mirror.

His skin became almost translucent, like the surface of a blue-clear lake, and his eyes widened just slightly and emitted a shine, a crisp beacon of light that could illuminate darkness. Then two of his upper teeth, the canines, on opposite sides of his mouth, started to grow in length and slowly descend, transforming into razor-sharp fangs until they curved over his bottom lip and pressed into the skin underneath. These fangs, so primitive, so like an animal's, somehow made Ronan look even more human because his true self was no longer hidden, but exposed. His breathing deepened, his fangs pressed down even harder onto his lip but never cut the now bright red flesh, and Ronan had to grab on to his dresser to steady himself. He stared at his reflection and was both proud and ashamed. This beautiful thing was him.

But what would Michael feel if Ronan ever found the courage to display his true likeness in front of him? Would he be proud to become his boyfriend? Or would he be ashamed? Ashamed to even know his type existed. Ronan overwhelmed by doubt, his fangs retracted and disappeared. His skin, his eyes, returned to their more common form. To look at him now, he seemed like any other sixteen-year-old boy, normal, human. But that was so far from the truth, and now riddled with uncertainty, Ronan had to turn away. He couldn't bear to look at himself any longer. It was time anyway to move on, to see if his intuition was correct. It was time to find Michael and make sure he was safe.

Nakano had a good feeling. Ronan and Michael were never going to be a couple, thanks to him. He hadn't planned on it, he hadn't planned on Michael seeing him alone with Ronan in the shadows, but sometimes accidents happen. And accidents aren't always bad things. Michael saw them together and he instinctively understood that they were meant to be, that Nakano was the one whom Ronan was supposed to spend eternity with, not some asinine kid from Nebraska, of all places. No, Michael was an interruption, a tangent, and now Ronan and Nakano were back together where they belonged.

Well, Nakano reminded himself, they were on their way back together. But it was only a matter of time before Ronan came to his senses and realized he could never have a relationship with Michael, a complete outsider, and that he and Nakano should continue where they left off. *What was Ronan thinking?* Nakano thought. If Nakano had difficulty accepting Ronan for who he was, for who his people were, how in the world could Michael? It was never going to happen and Ronan knew that. He was just mesmerized by this boy, by his blondness, his newness, that was all. It was only a matter of time before everything was once again the way it should be.

Oh, how he wanted to rip his sunglasses off right here

in Latin class. How he wanted to show everyone the depths of his power, his incredible strength, but he knew he couldn't; he knew he had to conceal his truth. *That's all right,* he thought, *it won't always be like this.* Someday, someday very soon, he and Ronan would be together, like inseparable lovers, traveling to the remotest parts of the globe, and they'd be able to reveal their true selves to the world. What a wonderful day that would be. But what a wonderful day today was too. And Nakano just knew it was going to get even better.

Ciaran had a sinking feeling. He felt his heart plummet the moment he caught Michael staring at Nakano. Sitting in the back of class, he knew in an instant that Michael had found out about Ronan and Nakano's past. It was evident by Michael's glare, his scowl. He tried to pretend that he was concentrating on Professor Volman's lesson, but he hadn't written a note, not a word, for the past fifteen minutes. All he did was stare at Nakano, and his expression didn't waver and it wasn't kind. It was that of one scorned, one absolutely and thoroughly ticked off. How Michael had found out that Nakano was Ronan's ex-boyfriend, Ciaran didn't know, but he knew just by looking at him that he had acquired that information and he was not at all pleased by the knowledge. And Ciaran wasn't pleased by the knowledge that he would try to set things right.

"He knows about you and Nakano," Ciaran said. The moment Ciaran saw Ronan between classes, he told him. He knew he would eventually tell him. Why act as if he were going to keep this information to himself? Why not just get it out in the open as quickly as possible and spare himself hours, it not days, of anguish contemplating exactly when and precisely how to convey the news to Ronan, when in the end the result was going to be the same. If anything, Ciaran was practical.

Slowly, disbelief crept into Ronan's face. "Why did you tell him?"

And this is how I'm repaid. "I didn't say I told him," Ciaran said, hurt, but unfortunately not surprised by Ronan's immediate reaction. "You really think I'd do such a thing?"

Disbelief was replaced by guilt. "No. I'm sorry," Ronan said quietly. "How? Are you sure?"

"I don't know how he found out, but he definitely knows," Ciaran replied. "If Michael had a wooden stake, Nakano would be ashes by now."

What did he just say? "You think this is funny?"

"I think this is a mess, a mess that you created, and a mess that's going to bring us all down."

"What are you talking about?"

Ciaran looked at Ronan; he couldn't believe that someone like him could sometimes be so innocent. "Do you really think that Michael is going to want to become a part of your life when he finds out exactly what you are? Do you think that he's going to remain quiet like I have?"

Ronan looked at Ciaran; he couldn't believe that

someone like him could sometimes be so resentful. "I think that this really doesn't concern you, so you shouldn't bloody worry about it."

"Well, I do worry. As much as I'm sure you'd like to forget, I am your brother. I may not be treated like it, but I am a part of this family," Ciaran said, fighting to keep his voice low among the mid-class traffic. "So you can all push me aside, ignore me, and it won't change a thing. I know everything and I haven't said a word. I doubt you'll be able to say the same thing about Michael when he finds out."

Ciaran turned to run, but Ronan grabbed him by the arm. *God, his hands are so strong.* "You're wrong," Ronan said. "Michael's different; there's something about him, there's a reason he came here and into my life. I can just feel it."

He didn't want to, but Ciaran shook his arm free of Ronan's grasp. "And you're willing to risk everything on a feeling?"

It was useless to lie to Ciaran, so Ronan told the truth. "Yes."

It's not what Ciaran wanted to hear, but it's what he knew Ronan would say. He knew this was how it was going to play out the second he saw Michael glare at Nakano; this would be the domino effect, this was how things were going to end up, with him walking away by himself yet again, and Ronan running off in pursuit of some absurd romantic notion. Ciaran may have been logical and thought-out, but he didn't know everything, because Ronan didn't run off after Michael, he went to find Nakano.

The area behind St. Martha's was usually secluded. The only activity took place in the early morning when either a truck came to deliver food to the main building or another truck came to take garbage away from the three large Dumpsters made of steel and always sealed shut so none of the animals who lived and roamed on the campus would be attracted to the smell of decaying food. So except for the early morning hours, it was a desolate place. Except for now.

Sitting on the ground with his back against the cold steel, Nakano could smell death inches away. He loved it. He loved taking a deep breath and letting the rottenness fill his body; he loved allowing something to penetrate him that humans found so incredibly repulsive. It gave him power. He was so much better than all of them, and one of these days they were going to understand just how superior he was. Until then he would be satisfied knowing that Ronan thought he was special. And he did. Just look at how he stared at him.

Several feet away, directly across from Nakano, almost hidden by some wild bushes, Ronan stood. And yes, he was staring, but no, he was not happy. "What did you do?" Ronan asked.

"I knew you'd find me here," Nakano said. "It's our special place."

Ronan didn't move a muscle, but suddenly he was standing in front of Nakano, towering over him. His shoulders square, the thick vein in his neck twitching every other second, Ronan looked down at him. "I asked you a question." Ronan gave Nakano exactly three seconds to reply and when he didn't, he reached out his hand and then Nakano was standing. Actually, he was floating a few inches off the ground and Ronan was holding him by his shirt collar. Nakano's feet dangled, unable to find a flat surface. He looked as helpless as a pup being carried by the scruff of the neck by its mother, but Ronan wasn't holding Nakano gently, he wasn't carrying his newborn to a safe place; he was clutching Nakano's clothing, even some flesh, and pressing him against the rough surface of the Dumpster because he was angry, betrayed. He raised Nakano an inch higher and with his left hand he pressed into his shoulder, pushing most of his weight into him until Nakano winced. "Tell me," Ronan growled, "what did you do?"

It was hard for Nakano to form words in this position, but he managed to squeak one out. "Nothing." Ronan pushed into him harder. Now his full weight was pressing against Nakano and in response the Dumpster creaked loudly as if awakening from a long, unbothered slumber, and rose a few inches from the ground. Nakano found more words, all of which sounded breathless and desperate when finally spoken. "I didn't do anything." Unfortunately, Ronan didn't believe him.

He let go of Nakano and for a split second Nakano thought it was over—this was just one of those rough games Ronan liked to play—but he was wrong. Ronan was repositioning himself. Before Nakano could slide

even an inch down the side of the Dumpster, and before
the Dumpster could fall even the slightest bit back down
to earth, Ronan grabbed Nakano by the throat with his
right hand and with his left pulled Nakano's wrist down
toward his thigh and twisted. Again he pressed his
weight on top of him and repeated his question, this
time his words containing more force. "What did you
do?"

The Dumpster groaned against the weight and the
unfamiliar position, rising just a bit higher. Nakano was
afraid they would tip over. He tried to struggle beneath
Ronan, he tried to break free, but he knew from past experience that his attempts would be futile. Ronan was
stronger. Usually that fact filled him with excitement
and desire, but right here, pinned against the side of the
Dumpster, diagonal, Nakano was filled with fear.

"Get . . . off . . . me!" Nakano cried, gasping for air.

Ronan hadn't even broken into a sweat. "Not until
you tell me what you said to Michael."

A red robin perched on the end of the Dumpster. Curious and small, it looked at Nakano and chirped.
Once. Once more, and then as quickly as it arrived, it
flew away. *Yes, fly away,* Nakano thought, *and I'll follow.* One last attempt. Nakano pushed all his strength
against Ronan, which was formidable, and the Dumpster slammed down onto the ground, small clouds of
brown dust rising like little mushrooms, then evaporating into the air. "I didn't say anything to him," Nakano
spat before turning to run. But he didn't get far at all.
Before he reached the edge of the Dumpster, Ronan had

grabbed him from behind, Ronan's right arm wedged underneath his chin, his left arm holding on to Nakano's wrist and bending it backward so his hand was in the middle of his shoulder blades. Involuntarily, Nakano squealed out in pain. "I'll break it, Kano," Ronan whispered in his ear. "I'll break it right off. You know I can."

Nakano writhed against Ronan's chest, his legs flailing until Ronan twisted his arm just a bit more and the pain became too great. "I didn't say anything. He saw us!"

Ronan released his grip but didn't let go. "Where?"

His breathing rough, Nakano replied as succinctly as possible. "Outside St. Florian's, under the tree."

Michael must have seen us talking, Ronan realized. He must have seen me reach out and embrace Nakano. But he doesn't understand. He doesn't understand that I was consoling him because I feel sorry for him. I pity Nakano because he can't have the kind of life that I do and because, as harsh as it sounds, I will never love him the way he loves me. "You saw him?"

Nakano let his hands rest on Ronan's arms, which still held him under his chin. So strong and warm, how many afternoons did they spend in the secrecy of The Forest of No Return like this, lying on the cool earth, Ronan's arm around Nakano? Those days could not be over forever; they just couldn't be. "Yes," he answered defiantly. "And he ran off because he knew what he saw."

Ronan spun Nakano around so they faced each other

and then, unable to control his fury, he slammed him back into the Dumpster. Over the echo of steel, Ronan asked, "Why didn't you tell me?"

Too incensed to lie, Nakano spoke the truth, at least as he saw it. "Because it's better this way," Nakano said. "It's better that it's over before it even begins. Michael isn't worthy of you. He wouldn't even stay and fight for you once he thought you were with someone else, someone who is perfect for you!"

The rage Ronan was feeling quite unexpectedly turned to laughter. "You? You're perfect for me?" If anyone happened to witness Ronan just at this moment, they would never have imagined that mere seconds before, he had been capable of breaking Nakano into pieces. He was laughing hysterically, which was only making Nakano even more furious.

"Do not laugh at me!"

"Then don't say stupid things! You know as well as I do that you're not perfect for me. You've told me so yourself."

"I never said that," Nakano protested.

A little bit of the rage was returning and Ronan glowered. "How many times have you told me that I'm different? How many times have you reminded me that even though your race despises me, you personally understand that I cannot be judged for what I am?" Ronan hissed. "And now you tell me that you're perfect for me? What am I supposed to do but laugh?"

Nakano slammed his fist into the Dumpster, denting

it slightly, but not even bruising his knuckle. He was angry because once again he was not only battling Ronan, he was battling himself. His heart was speaking a language his mind didn't fully comprehend. "I know what I said, I know what our races believe, but I also know you and me and I know that we are perfect together."

Now Ronan saw Nakano for what he was. A sad little boy who was trying to think for himself, but not yet capable. "You don't mean that, not really. You only think we're perfect for each other because you think I might be able to find happiness with someone else," Ronan explained. "Until Michael arrived, you were ignoring me."

"That's not true!"

"I told you yesterday, Kano, what we had was wonderful; it really was very sweet, but it's over," Ronan said as kindly as he could. "It's part of our past and it's not going to be repeated, so you need to accept that and stop interfering in my life."

The hell with you, Ronan! "Because you think some kid, some dumbass American, can replace me?!"

Don't take the bait, Ronan, don't let him goad you on like this. "I looked into your eyes yesterday. I looked into the very essence of who you are and I didn't turn away. Doesn't that prove that I still care about you?"

"Oh, and you think I should thank you for that?"

Suddenly, Ronan was tired. Tired of this conversation, tired of the endless battle, and tired of Nakano.

"No, but it would be nice if you could just be happy for me." Now Ronan looked at Nakano with pity and disgust. "But I guess that's too much to ask from your kind."

Just as Ronan was about to turn the corner of St. Martha's and be out of his view, Nakano couldn't suppress the desire to have the final say. "When you tell Michael what you really are, let me know if he hopes you're happy!"

Those words were echoing in Ronan's ears when he knocked on Michael's door. Even though he knew he wasn't going to reveal his true self to Michael—he wasn't going to expose every secret—he was still nervous. He was going to try to explain that Nakano meant nothing to him and that, well, he thought, and maybe he completely made it all up in his head, but he thought that Michael had wanted to get to know him better too. He thought that the two of them could just spend some time together to learn more about each other. When the door opened and it was Ciaran, Ronan was more than a little relieved.

"Is Michael home?"

"Well, hello to you too. Yes, Ronan, thank you, I'm fine," Ciaran said sarcastically.

Ronan lowered his head, duly chastised. *Sometimes I just can't win with this one,* he thought. "Sorry, how are you?"

"Does it even matter?" Ciaran opened the door wider as a means to invite Ronan into his room without actually having to ask him to come in. It also enabled him to see that Michael was sitting on his bed going over some Latin homework.

"Michael."

How could one simple word make him feel so good? Michael didn't understand it, but when Ronan said his name, he got the same feeling he did the first time he heard him say it. Like he was hearing a new language, a word that up until now had been unknown, like Ronan was asking him so many important questions just by saying his name, in that one word, there was so much potential, so much possibility. And then Michael remembered what he had seen.

"Hi, Ronan," Michael said in a flat tone, and then returned to his Latin homework. His eyes couldn't even focus on the foreign words, *cruor, cruorem;* his head was swimming with thoughts about the boy who was standing in his doorway. He had so much he wanted to say to Ronan, he didn't know how to begin, but he definitely wasn't going to say anything in Ciaran's presence. He couldn't, but thanks to Ronan that obstacle was about to be removed.

"Ciaran," Ronan said. "Could you please give us some time alone?"

Don't be surprised, Ciaran; this is what you knew would happen. You knew Ronan would track Michael down like prey and you know that in five minutes Ronan will explain everything away, explain that Nakano is part of his past, ancient history, and he and Michael will begin their new life together while you get to watch everything from the sidelines. Do you like watching Ronan live his life? Do you enjoy seeing him constantly move farther and farther away from where you're standing? From where you're stuck? You only have yourself to blame, Ciaran; you could've kept your mouth shut. Unfortunately, Ciaran knew certain things about himself. The first was, he would spend his life trying to help Ronan in whatever way he could. And the second was, no matter what Ronan asked him to do, he would comply. "Of course," Ciaran said. "Fritz said he needed some help with his chem lab."

It didn't even occur to Michael to protest, to tell Ronan that they had nothing to talk about because although he was afraid to have this conversation with Ronan, he wanted to share his space. What he didn't want to do was appear interested and so he desperately fought the urge to look up and continued to stare at his textbook. He even went so far as to copy some more words down from his textbook. *Vivo in profundum.* He had no idea what he was writing; the words weren't from today's lesson. But at least he was doing something other than acknowledge Ronan, so that made him feel good.

Ciaran gathered his books and tossed them in his backpack. Before he opened the door, he looked over at Michael just as Michael could no longer fake indifference and looked up from his books. He noticed something in Ciaran's face that he hadn't seen in quite some time; it was the same look he would see in his mother's face when he would catch her staring at him. It was a look of concern. Yet again, Michael felt remorse. When he saw his mother looking at him like that, it made him furious, but now seeing Ciaran wear the same expression, it gave him comfort. Having your mother constantly worry about you could be suffocating, but having a friend watch your back was different; it was nice. "Have a good chat, boys," Ciaran said, closing the door behind him. And then Ronan and Michael were alone.

Now that there were no barriers to overcome, the boys were finding it difficult to start a conversation. They smiled and nodded; Michael wrote down a few more words—*procul nox noctis*—and Ronan surveyed the room. He had been here countless times before to return notes that he borrowed from Ciaran or a textbook; on a few occasions, he even came by just to hang out and visit, but this time was different. He wasn't here to see Ciaran; he was here to see Michael and confess, in part, the truth about his past. But he had no idea how to begin, so he started to walk around the room aimlessly.

Michael was neater than he was; he liked that. His clothes weren't thrown in a pile and his sneakers weren't left where he kicked them off. His books too were stacked neatly on his desk; a few already had Post-its coming out of them to remind him of an important page or passage at a later date. His surroundings were as well kept as he was. Even sitting on his bed doing homework in a baby blue T-shirt and navy track pants, he didn't look like he just rummaged through his laundry bin to pick out something to wear; he looked like he stepped out of the pages of a magazine. His feet, bare, looked so smooth, the arch so perfect. *Oh, he's so handsome; please make him believe me. Please make things go back to the way they were just a few days ago when everything was on the brink of a new beginning.*

They caught each other's stare at the same time.

Ronan said, "Is this your mum?" at the same time Michael said, "How are you?"

"Sorry, you first," Ronan said.

"No, that's okay," Michael replied. "Yes, um, that's me and my mother at a fair back home."

The picture was old, but it was Michael's favorite. He and his mother had gone to the Nebraska State Fair in Grand Island when he was ten years old, just the two of them. Grandpa had wanted to go, but his mother, sensing her son needed a break from his grandpa's company, told him that she wanted a mother-son day and so they drove the fifty miles alone singing along to the radio, talking about nothing in particular, at least nothing important that Michael could remember. At the fair they ate too much junk food, rode the roller coaster three times in a row, and his mother won him a stuffed panda in the water balloon race. But what he cherished most about that day was how much they laughed. Easy and often. They laughed more that day than they ever did before or since. It was as if that one day was a reprieve from his mother's worry, her nervousness, her hovering. If only, if only every day could have been so joyful.

Ronan was holding the picture in his hands, his thumb absentmindedly caressing Michael's face. "You both look happy."

Michael couldn't help imagine how Ronan's thumb would feel if it touched his cheek, his lips. "Yes, we were," Michael said, and then added quietly, "That day anyway."

Ronan placed the picture back on the shelf as if he were hanging a painting in a museum, with too much attention and special care. It was simply a tactic to avoid the real reason he was here. But no matter that he was just as nervous, Michael wasn't going to allow him to stall any longer. "So what do you want to talk about?"

"I think you know." *Oh, that's good, Ronan, accuse him.*

"I'm not a mind reader." *Terrific, Michael, be arrogant; that's a great way to start a conversation.*

They said "I'm sorry" at the same time. Michael closed his books—it was useless to pretend that he was actually studying—and looked at Ronan. He was about to speak when Ronan began. "I think you may have seen something the other day that, um, looks different from where you were looking at it from, different from, um, what it really was."

Michael tried, but couldn't follow Ronan's words. "What?"

Be direct, Ronan, just be direct; that's always the best way. "Nakano and I weren't hugging."

Oh, really? "Could've fooled me."

"Well, yeah, we were hugging," Ronan started, "but we weren't *hugging*."

"Oh, of course, now I get it." *Great, Michael, so much for not being arrogant.*

"I'm sorry, Michael. What I'm trying to say is, I was saying good-bye to Nakano. He's my ex." *Say the word, Ronan, just say it and get it out there so there's no confusion and you don't have to wonder if Michael is interested in you as a friend or as something more than that.*

"He's my ex-boyfriend."

He is gay. Thank God. Wait a second, why am I relieved? He just told me he was hugging his ex-boyfriend. I shouldn't be grateful about that. "It didn't look like a good-bye hug to me."

He didn't make a comment about my having an ex-boyfriend. I was right. Okay, one hurdle behind me. Behind us. "That's what it was. I'm not going to lie to you. Nakano still has some feelings for me. I don't think they're honest feelings."

"And what exactly is that supposed to mean?"

"I think he's just jealous of you."

Don't smile, Michael, this whole thing is not supposed to make you happy. "Me? Why would he be jealous of me?" *Oh, wow, I actually made Ronan blush. He looks like he just ran a mile; his cheeks are all blotchy. And just adorable.*

"Because, Michael," Ronan whispered hesitantly, "I like you."

Don't say a word, Michael, let the moment seep in.

This is what you've been waiting for, this is what you've been waiting for him to say.

"And, well, he isn't going out with anyone right now, so you know, he sees me and you . . . not that there is a me and you, but he knows that I, um, would like there, maybe, to be, and he started acting weird and saying things, and I told him that what he and I had, which was over a year ago, by the way, was over and he had to forget that anything would ever start up again. So even if there is no me and you, there isn't going to be a me and him." Michael wanted to toss his Latin textbook to the floor and jump up and down on his bed, but he sat still and didn't say a word. "I'm going to try to stop rambling now. But I'm not really sure if I can stop, so it might be best if you could say something." Michael loved how he looked right now, more boy than man. "Please?"

Michael looked at Ronan's face, and for the first time he looked at him not as a stranger, not as someone he just met, not as someone he could dream about, but as someone he was going to have a relationship with, someone who was going to become his boyfriend. "I like you too."

A smile ignited Ronan's face. He couldn't conceal it even though other thoughts were filling up his mind, thoughts that caused him concern and worry, but for now he was going to push them away, squelch their sound, and concentrate on what Michael just said. "Really?"

"Yes, Ronan," Michael replied, thrilled that he had

the power to bring Ronan such obvious pleasure. "Really."

"Blimey! That's good," Ronan said, sitting on Michael's bed. "That's really good."

"It is good," Michael said, his eyes darting all over his room, not confident enough to just settle on Ronan's face. "Really, um, really good."

Good for now, until he finds out everything, Ronan thought. *No, please, please don't make me think of all that; just allow me a bit of time, some happiness.* "I think I liked you, Michael, from the moment I laid eyes on you."

Find the courage, Michael; just look him right in the eye and tell him. "I know. That's how I felt the first time I saw you outside the cathedral. Ever since then . . ." *Don't say too much. Oh, why not? Just tell him.* "Ever since that night, you're all I can think about." There, it was in the open. It felt invigorating not to keep secrets hidden. They reached out and their hands found each other.

"Oh," Michael said. "I didn't thank you."

Ronan's thumb stroked the softness of Michael's hand. *It's not my cheek,* Michael thought, *but it's a start.* "For the drawing that you made. The Picture of Michael Howard."

Ronan held Michael's hand tighter, his cheeks getting back some of the rosy glow they had lost. "Oh, well, I'm not a very good artist."

"I think it's beautiful."

This was absolutely effortless, Michael thought. All

the years spent worrying and being frightened that he would never be able to just sit with another boy and hold his hand and talk to him were washed away. Because here he was. And here was Ronan. And they were together, sitting, smiling at each other, their fingers intertwined, knowing what they wanted to do next. Unfortunately, that would have to wait, for at that moment, there was a knock at the door.

"Knock knock, is anybody home?"

It was Brania.

And just like that, Ronan's bad feeling returned.

chapter 10

At the same time, Michael and Ronan asked the same question, "What are you doing here?" And then two seconds later, they both let go of the other's hand.

"You know her?" Ronan asked Michael.

"Um, yeah," Michael said, then added incredulously, "You know her too?"

Ronan looked at Brania, who had already come into the room, closed the door behind her, and was sitting with them on the bed. She clearly didn't need an invitation to make herself at home.

"Of course Ronan knows me," Brania said. "We're childhood friends."

Michael wasn't sure what disappointed him more,

that pronouncement or the fact that he and Ronan were
no longer holding hands. When their dinner date—so
thoughtfully arranged by his father—had ended, he
thought that was the last he would see of this girl, but
now here she was, unexpected and unrequested, sitting
on his bed, next to the boy whose hand he wanted to
hold and whose mouth he longed to kiss. Why in the
world was she here? And if this was the way Ronan re-
acted when he saw a childhood friend, Michael didn't
want to know what he looked like when he saw an
enemy.

When Ronan spoke again, Michael noticed that his
voice was lower, more serious. He sounded the same
way he did when he was outside St. Joshua's standing
next to Ciaran. "How do you know her?"

"We met at my father's hotel for dinner," Michael explained. "Our fathers are business associates."

"Such a tiny, tiny world," Brania said. "Isn't it, Ronan?"

If possible, Ronan's voice sounded even more serious
when he spoke again. "What are you doing here?" But
what concerned Michael more was his expression; it
was grave. To look at him, it appeared that there was
bad blood between these two, but one look at Brania
dispelled that theory. She looked relaxed and downright
playful. Stretched out on Michael's bed, she lay on her
side, her slender neck resting in the palm of her right
hand, her left knee bent so she looked very much like a
fully dressed centerfold. "Now, is that any way to make
a lady feel welcome?"

Before Ronan answered he stood up, almost as if he were backing away from her. "Is that any way to answer a question?" Michael was confused. Ronan's voice was confrontational, harsh, and yet his body language was hesitant, uneasy.

Brania's body language was anything but. Smiling, quite seductively, she rolled over onto her back with her knees bent so her skirt fell and covered only a few inches of her thigh. It was funny, Michael thought, millions of guys, teenaged and several years older, would kill to have a girl as beautiful as Brania lounge on their bed, half exposed, but he just wanted her to leave so he could be alone with Ronan. He was not going to get his wish.

Brania closed her eyes and moved her hands fluidly in the air as if following the current of some unheard music. Her slim, manicured hands floated and curled to the silent rhythm as her knees rubbed together softly. What was she doing? And why was she doing it in his bed? Michael thought, "Um, Brania?"

"Sshh," she replied softly, not opening her eyes and holding up her index finger as if that gesture alone would stifle any further queries. And it did. Michael remained silent and watched her as she listened to her imaginary music. He didn't feel any longing whatsoever to touch her, but she was absolutely compelling to watch. He glanced over at Ronan to try and get a sense of what he thought of the whole scene, but Ronan was acting as if Michael weren't even in the room. He was standing in the corner, his back against the wall, eyes riveted on this strange girl. And there was something about the way Ronan looked at her that frightened him. His teeth were clenched, his brow furrowed, and Michael felt the same rush of sudden fear as he had sitting across from Nakano at the lunchroom table. He couldn't explain it then and he couldn't explain it now. The two boys looked nothing alike, the situations were completely different, but both times Michael was consumed with the same irrational feeling. And once again the feeling ended as quickly as it arose.

"Song's over," she announced, sitting back up and smiling at them both. "Now, did someone ask me a question?"

It was apparent by the way Ronan still looked that he wasn't going to be able to speak, so Michael spoke for them. "We were, um, just wondering why you're here?"

She ran a hand through her luxuriant hair, making it bounce a little. "I had such a wonderful time with you at dinner, I just wanted to say hi. How do you like it here at Archangel, Michael?" She reached out and a few of her sharp, red-painted fingernails touched Michael's arm, scraping his skin. He didn't mean to react so abruptly, but he did, standing up and crossing his arms across his chest.

Maintain some control, Michael. This girl is teasing you, trying to get the upper hand; it's what girls do. Michael uncrossed his arms and placed them on his hips, trying to adopt a more relaxed pose, but he felt and knew he looked just as uncomfortable. "We kind of had this conversation the other night at my father's hotel?"

Now Brania repositioned herself and sat cross-legged on Michael's bed as if she were about to practice yoga. Did she ever sit still? Michael couldn't believe this girl who was behaving so oddly was the same well-mannered guest at his father's hotel. If he didn't know any better, he'd think it was her evil twin or something. "Michael, you know as well as I do that what took place in your father's hotel room was polite talk designed to put your father at ease, to make him feel relieved that he'd made the right decision to bring you halfway across the world to a place you no longer remembered, before your mother's body was even cold in the earth. So I'd like to know the truth: Are you enjoying your life here at Archangel Academy?"

Michael didn't feel a wave of fear when he looked at this girl, but now, stripped of her manners and showing her true personality, he didn't like her. No matter how beautiful she might look on the outside, Michael found her to be ugly. "I told my father the truth," Michael said. "I love being here. Now, if that's all you came to ask, I think you should go."

His words didn't faze Brania one bit; if anything, they amused her. She leaned back on her elbows and laughed. "Oh, don't get all excited. I know I interrupted a little tête-à-tête between the two of you, but there's time for that later," Brania said. "Ronan here has all the time in the world. Don't you, Ronan?"

Ronan moved to stand next to Michael. He didn't touch him, but just having him closer made Michael feel better. It was as if they were presenting a united front against this intruder. Ronan also didn't answer Brania's question, but rather stated another fact about her. "Brania has always been inappropriate, ever since we were children."

Propelled by a memory, Brania jumped off the bed, stood in front of both boys, and clasped their hands. So much for keeping the intruder at bay. "Oh, remember Nanny Long?" Brania exclaimed. "She was quite pretty but had the most horrid teeth, even by British standards, and Daddy arranged for her to be a mail order bride of sorts. So this academic from Edinburgh comes to dinner presumably to whisk Nanny Long off to get married. But all throughout dinner and even dessert afterward, she was so dour that I finally demanded that she smile. The academic, whatever his name was, agreed with me, so finally Nanny Long did, and before tea was served, the academic was on his way back to Scotland, and Nanny Long was jilted before she ever took one step toward the altar." Finished with her presentation, Brania sat back down. "Daddy was so angry with me! But he got over it."

How could she be so malicious? "Whatever happened to your nanny?" Michael had to ask.

Without a hint of sadness, Brania explained, "Oh, she died the following year. So you see, the marriage would have been a waste of time." Smiling, she turned to Ronan. "I miss those days, Ronan; we had such fun."

Ronan wasn't smiling. The way Michael saw it, he was amazed that he was still breathing. He really looked as if he had been holding his breath ever since Brania burst into the room. "I don't understand, Brania," Michael said. "How did you know where to find me? How did you even get onto campus?" He then had an absolutely horrific thought. "You don't go to St. Anne's, do you?"

"You're so inquisitive," Brania said. "I like that." She got up and started to walk around the room, her arms clasped behind her as if she were inspecting for cleanliness. "No, I don't attend St. Anne's; I have private tutors." Even though Michael had already decided Brania wasn't the type of girl he'd want to be friends with, it was hard not to appreciate her physical attributes. Especially in her current outfit. Tight-fitting emerald green V-neck sweater, black miniskirt, and black knee-high socks. To finish off the look, she was wearing patent leather Mary Janes with three-inch heels. It was as if the classic beauty he had dinner with had a sexed-up makeover. What was happening? He actually was becoming distracted by her looks, and then to illustrate his point, he suddenly realized she was still talking.

"But my father owns this land that the academy calls home, so I can pretty much come and go as I please and, you know, get whatever information I want. So I called up Hawksbry and asked what dorm you're staying in and Alistair told me St. Peter's." When she finished walking, she wound up right next to Michael. "And here I am."

The same odd fear crept up Michael's back. What was wrong with him? This was a girl, yes, a possibly crazy girl, but hardly dangerous. If that was true, then why was Ronan staring at her as if she were going to pull out a butcher knife from under her skirt? Michael was starting to feel caged; the room was large, but it definitely couldn't hold the three of them much longer. Brania was thinking the same thing. "Let's go for a walk."

Outside, Michael breathed a bit easier. Maybe it was because the September air felt so cool and refreshing or because the moonlight created just enough light to keep the sky a deep shade of blue instead of an impenetrable black. Michael couldn't tell; he just took a moment to look up and gaze at the stars flickering above, and even though he and Ronan were walking with Brania between them, he knew the stars were giving the two of them their blessings. To his amazement, Michael wasn't as annoyed as he'd thought he'd be having to share the night with Brania because he knew he and Ronan would spend so many nights walking together underneath this star-filled sky. Once, of course, they got rid of this girl.

"Have you met Ronan's mother yet, Michael?"

"No, but, um, I hope to," Michael said cautiously. "Soon."

"Well, prepare yourself," Brania replied. "She's a mother who's not necessarily . . . motherly."

Yes, Michael was surprised by Brania's rude comment, but he was even more surprised by Ronan's silence; he didn't say anything in his mother's defense. "And just pray that Ronan doesn't take after his mother," Brania continued. "Edwige has a history of running through men, you know."

This time, Ronan did defend his mother. "Brania's still angry because my mother dumped her father after we all lived together for a year."

"You lived together?" Michael asked.

Brania looked thoroughly annoyed. "Didn't you hear me speak of Nanny Long? She was nanny to both Ronan and me." She fiddled with the neckline of her sweater, running a finger underneath the material, down toward the cleft between her breasts. "Didn't they teach you in Nebraska that it's rude not to pay attention?"

Michael ignored Brania's criticism and her cleavage. He couldn't get over the fact that Ronan and Brania were more than just childhood friends, they were practically siblings. First Ronan is half brothers with Ciaran; now he's almost half siblings with Brania. She was right; the world is such a tiny place.

"If she had only been honest with my father when you two moved in, and told him that she had no intention of claiming another husband," Brania said, "his heart wouldn't have been broken." Somewhere in the distance an owl hooted, three times, breaking the awkward silence that followed Brania's statement. Unfortunately, the owl remained silent following Brania's next statement. "So I must be frank, Ronan. I don't approve of you trying to lure Michael to your side of the sexual fence. I'm quite certain our friend here is undecided when it comes to choosing what gender he'd like to cuddle up with, and seeing that you, like your mother, have enough boys to play with, I think you should leave him for me."

Both Ronan and Michael stopped walking at the same time. Brania continued on for a few more steps until she realized she was walking alone and then turned to face the would-be paramours. "Did I say something untoward?"

When Michael spoke, he wasn't just responding to Brania's outrageous comment, he was responding to his father, his grandpa, his mother, his classmates back at Two W, everyone who questioned who he was and whoever made him feel that who he was wasn't adequate or normal and that he needed to be something that was more palatable for them. Perhaps it was because he knew that Ronan was by his side, figuratively and literally, that gave him the strength to speak his mind; perhaps it was because, ever since coming here to Double A, he had found a self-respect that he had long ago forgotten existed. It didn't matter; the only thing that mattered was that he found the courage to give his words life.

"I am not being lured anywhere, Brania, and for you to insinuate that I am means that you haven't been paying attention to me. I'm gay. You may not like that, but frankly I don't care. And this may hurt your feelings, but given the choice of spending time with Ronan or with you, I choose Ronan." Michael took a quick breath and continued. "As far as you implying that

Ronan is going to use me until somebody better shows up, well, that's just your own jealousy talking and not the truth. In fact, as of tonight I'm Ronan's boyfriend."

Once he heard that last sentence come out of his mouth, he prayed that he hadn't made a fool of himself.

Ronan looked at Michael at first with shock and then with pride. "Yes, he is."

This is all working out perfectly, Brania thought. *These two fools don't suspect a thing. Just keep playing the game, honey; remember you're supposed to be dejected.* "Well . . . I guess this shows me," Brania said, feigning gloom and then spite. "Let me ask you. Does your father know all about this aspect of your life?"

How interesting, Michael thought. *Even the mention of my father doesn't make me reconsider what I just said.* "No, Brania, he doesn't. I may not have the guts to tell my father just yet—I hardly know the man—but I will. And just so you know, if you have the urge to run and tell him, feel free. I won't deny it."

Oh, sweet, stupid Michael, I couldn't have said it better myself. "Well, *bra* to the *vo,*" Brania shouted, clapping her hands in applause. "Looks like Mikey's got himself a man, and I am woman enough to step aside." Brania shrugged her shoulders and smiled. "I hope you don't hold it against me, Michael. I would really like for all of us to be friends."

There was something about Brania that reminded Michael of his mother. Nothing physical, nothing specific really; it was just her nature because she, like his mother, was quixotic, unpredictable. One minute Brania was writhing on his bed, then giddily sharing a childhood memory, then making bitchy comments, and now acting as if they were on the threshold of becoming best friends. His head was spinning; he couldn't keep up with her mood swings. However, he did know for certain that he didn't want to be her friend. Luckily, reinforcements had just arrived and he was spared having to respond to her request.

"Penry!" Michael shouted. He was thrilled to see his friend and just as unthrilled to see who he was walking with. "Nakano. Hi." Michael literally bit his tongue because although he wanted to, for some reason he felt weird asking Nakano why he was wearing his sunglasses after sundown. Brania felt no such discomfort.

"If you're trying to create an air of mystery, Nakano, you've failed. The sunglasses make you look like an idiot."

Hopefully, these two knew each other, because even though Michael did not like Nakano, Brania's statement was still embarrassing. By Nakano's response Michael understood immediately that the two shared some sort of history. "Thanks, Bran. I have an eye infection, and sunglasses are a lot more attractive than oozing puss."

"Well said, Kano. It's good to know the Double A is still churning out eloquent students," Brania mocked.

Penry didn't care about Nakano's contagion or Brania's sarcasm; he had more important plans for the evening. "Mates, I'd love to stay and chat, really I would," Penry said quickly, "but Imogene is waiting for me. She's got a fifteen-minute choir break and we're going to spend it snogging. Cheers!" They all laughed as they watched Penry race off toward St. Anne's.

"How queer," Brania said. "A boy lusting after a girl."

"Shut up, Brania," Nakano said. Only Ronan noticed Brania's skin grow even paler, and he knew that later, when the two of them were alone, she would make Nakano regret his comment. Michael only noticed that, while he didn't like Nakano, he had to admit that he did approve of how he handled Brania. He also approved of how simply, yet efficiently, Ronan handled their exit.

"It's getting late. We should be heading back," Ronan announced. "Do you have a car or something, Brania?"

"Such a gentleman. My driver is waiting for me at the front gate. And no, I don't need an escort; I know my way around, and since Penry's run off into the arms of his girlfriend, I think I'll be quite safe."

Again an owl hooted to fill the silence. Michael imagined an owl perched somewhere on a branch, acting as a lookout whose sole purpose was to create sound when there was none. "Brania, no hard feelings?" Michael extended his hand to her and she, after only the slightest hesitation, took it. He didn't want to be her friend, he didn't want her to think that this cordial expression was anything more than manners, but he was feeling magnanimous. After all, he was leaving with his boyfriend. Which was of course the last bit of information Brania felt the need to publicize.

"None at all, Michael," Brania said. "You and your boyfriend have a lovely evening." This time, there was no owl's hoot to invade the silence, only Nakano's sharpened breathing. Large intake of breath through his nose, strong push outward. "Oh, sorry, Kano, haven't you heard? Your ex has moved on with the pretty blond American." So Brania seemed to know quite a bit about Ronan and Nakano. She might not be hiding a butcher knife, but she was definitely dangerous.

Nakano still hadn't controlled his breathing, but he was able to speak. "No, but that's really great news." By the tone of Nakano's voice, it hardly sounded great; it sounded as if he had just announced the death of everyone on campus. But Michael figured that was to be expected. He had no idea what it felt like to lose a boyfriend; he hoped he never would. He wanted this to last with Ronan forever. Yes, yes, that's a dumb comment, he knew that, but he didn't care. He'd only had a boyfriend, his first, for about five minutes, so he wasn't going to waste time thinking about how he would feel when the relationship was over. He just wanted to leave this place and go back to his dorm room with Ronan and pick up where they left off. Thankfully, Ronan wanted to do the same thing.

"Thank you," Ronan said to Nakano. "But like I said, we have to go."

Ronan shoved his hands into his pockets and turned, Michael followed, and the two of them walked back to his dorm, their bodies illuminated by the moonlight. Each wanted to hold the other's hand, but it didn't feel right. They knew they were being watched and they wanted to touch each other in public when they were ready, not because they felt they had to impress.

Fingers splayed out at his side, nostrils flaring, Nakano moved toward Ronan and Michael, intent on following them, but never made it past the first step. "Don't move," Brania commanded, then added in an unyielding tone, "Come with me. I have something to show you."

Like a dog on a leash, Nakano followed Brania all the way to the edge of The Forest of No Return. His typical obstinate and uncooperative nature suppressed, Nakano didn't ask where they were ultimately going to wind up, he didn't ask what Brania wanted him to see, and he didn't ask why it was so important that he see it tonight. He did what she said; he had no choice.

Although she was wearing heels, she had no problem navigating the rough ground of The Forest. She knew what holes to step over, what loose rocks to move around, when exactly to bend underneath a low-hanging branch. She had been here before.

When they reached the clearing, her car was waiting for them. The black sedan looked incredibly inappropriate here in the middle of The Forest, almost completely surrounded by immensely tall trees and no obvious path visible, but here it was. And standing next to the sedan, his hands folded in front of him, was Vaughan's driver.

"Hello, Jeremiah," Brania said.

"Ms. O'Keefe," Jeremiah said, nodding his head slightly.

Nakano couldn't keep silent any longer. "You brought me here to see a car?"

Brania turned to look at Nakano, more curious than

angry that he spoke. "Did I say you could speak?" Behind his sunglasses Nakano rolled his eyes, tilted his head, and let out a little sigh. However, he made no verbal response, which was not good enough for Brania. When she spoke, it was slowly and deliberately. "I said, did I say you could speak?" Everyone remained silent. "Answer me."

Finally, boldness was replaced with submission. Nakano may have secretly wanted to, but he didn't dare, rile Brania. "No, you didn't. I'm sorry."

Pleased, Brania continued. "Now tell me, Kano, why aren't you wearing your contacts?"

"They don't fit me right; they hurt."

"I understand," Brania said in a surprisingly gentle tone that would've been appropriate for a kindergarten teacher. "But you must understand that they're necessary. Your sunglasses, while quite flattering to the shape of your face, are conspicuous. And we don't, at this moment in time, want to draw any attention to ourselves. Jeremiah can get away with them because they look like part of his uniform, but on you, people ask questions. Do you understand that?"

Nakano swallowed a nasty comeback. "Yes, Brania. I understand."

"Good, because I have a gift." She kept smiling at Nakano, but snapped her fingers at Jeremiah. "Trunk, please."

Before Jeremiah could move, his cell phone rang. It wasn't a standard ring, but the ending to *Nessun dorma,* the famous aria from the opera *Turandot.* The music swelled in the air, wrapping around the trees and the leaves and rising toward the stars. Brania closed her eyes and seemed entranced, as if she wanted to immerse herself within each note. "Don't answer it." Jeremiah wanted to, but he, like Nakano, didn't dare betray Brania's order. When he saw the caller's name written on the phone, however, he grew concerned enough to speak.

"It's Vaughan."

The spell was broken, the music contaminated. Brania opened her eyes to look at Jeremiah, taken aback that he would interrupt her reverie. "I said don't answer it." She then asked no one in particular, "Why is no one doing as I say?"

Jeremiah wasn't as confident in this girl's company as he'd like to be. Unconsciously, but nervously, he bit his bottom lip until the tender skin broke. A small slit, horizontal and deep, but producing no blood. "But . . . but he's expecting me to pick him up."

Leaves crunched underneath Brania's shoes as she took a step toward Jeremiah. He wasn't worth making the full trip to walk right up to him; however, one step should create the illusion she was after. "And whom, may I ask, do you work for? Vaughan or my father?" It worked. Jeremiah didn't hesitate but turned off his cell phone and returned it to the inside pocket of his jacket. Then, following the tilt of Brania's head, he continued on to the trunk and opened it. The trunk light shone on a plain cardboard box that had some symbols written on it in black marker.

Nakano peered into the trunk and read the symbols on the box, which were written in his native language. "Contacts. Are they new?"

"New and improved," Brania corrected. "Straight from the factory."

Brania reached in and, with one hand, ripped open the box without breaking a nail. She pulled out two smaller boxes and gave them to Nakano. "Wear these. And please, for all our sakes, do try to fit in."

His usual sarcasm was replaced with sincerity. "I will. Thank you."

She touched his face; his skin was as smooth as a girl's. "Long ago, my father made it so we would all be protected. You shouldn't act so surprised when an act of kindness befalls you."

If Brania was acting like the caring mother, Nakano took on the role of the petulant child. "Is that why you stopped me from going after them? I could've taken Michael right in front of Ronan! Now it might be too late."

Brania's soft touch turned into a firm grip and for the second time that day, someone stronger, someone much more powerful, grabbed him by the throat. She held him tightly and brought his bewildered face close to hers. Nakano held the two small boxes between them in a desperate attempt to create some distance between himself and this odd, odd creature. "Ronan will not take Michael tonight. He's not thoughtless and impulsive like you. He will need time to gain Michael's trust." Brania yanked Nakano and brought him closer to her so when she spoke, her lips touched his ear. Shaking, Nakano dropped the boxes and could do nothing but listen. "So what you will do, what your only job will be, is to watch them, and just before Ronan is about to transform Michael, you will sweep him away from Ronan and forever change their destiny."

"Oh" was all Nakano could say.

"Yes. Oh," Brania scoffed. "And when we own Michael, we'll have the leverage we need to make Ronan turn his back on his heritage and become one of us." She released Nakano's throat from her grip. He stumbled back and coughed, then bent down to pick up the boxes he had dropped. Brania looked down at him with what could only be described as a mother's disgust. "And don't you ever tell me to shut up again."

In between coughs, Nakano was loath to concede that the plan Brania spelled out was perfect. He wasn't happy being reprimanded, but he couldn't think about that right now; all he could think about was the hunger growing within him. He looked up at Brania like a poor, homeless child. "But, Brania, I'm so hungry."

This was the part Brania loved to play the most. Yes, the bitchy schemer was fun; yes, the woman in charge had its kicks; but being the one who could grant gifts and miracles, that's the role she loved the most. She extended her hand to Nakano and he took it, rising up to stand and face her. Once again she caressed his face; he was after all just a child. "And that's why I brought you a feast."

Next to the box in the trunk was a blanket. Brania

lifted the blanket with the flair of a magician and tossed it to the side. She watched approvingly as it floated and undulated to the ground. Presentation was so important. Then she stepped out of the way to reveal what lay underneath the blanket. It was a body. The body of Alistair Hawksbry, naked and unconscious, and full of precious, warm blood.

Nakano ripped off his sunglasses and the two black holes that were his eyes couldn't believe what he was seeing. It was the headmaster. This was being inconspicuous?! Nakano didn't care about the consequences right now; he was overwhelmed. The headmaster smelled so ripe and pungent and Nakano could hear his blood pumping through his veins, still strong and compelling. Jeremiah scooped up the body and tossed it at Nakano's feet.

Brania smiled at her minion. "What are you waiting for? Dig in."

chapter 11

The first bite into flesh still held a thrill for Nakano. And when Alistair's blood, thick and flavorful, filled his mouth, he felt dizzy.

As the headmaster groaned, awakened slightly by the intrusion, Nakano dug his fangs deeper into his neck, making the connection between the two even more solid. With his right hand he cradled Alistair's skull and with his left he pressed into his shoulder, one hand gentle, the other firm, creating a balance. Tender and rough. He was giving Alistair incredible pleasure even as he was taking life from him.

Underneath Nakano, Alistair's muscular body rose

and fell into a slow rhythm. His eyes quivered but remained closed, and escaping from his mouth were a series of sighs, soft and involuntary, making it clear that although he was being violated, it was not at all an unpleasant experience. And that made Nakano's head spin even more. He was a mere student, only a sophomore, and yet here he was, bringing such joy to the headmaster. God, how he loved being a vampire. He had such force, such liberty to do as he chose, take what he wanted, and, when he was so inclined, give unparalleled ecstasy to those inferior humans around him. But what he had yet to grasp was that even vampires need to understand limitation.

"Enough, Nakano," Brania said.

Nakano didn't hear her. He was trying to figure out what spice he tasted in Alistair's blood. Was it curry? No, it wasn't that sharp. It might be coriander, but no, he couldn't place it. Well, whatever it was, Alistair's blood definitely had zest.

"I said *enough*." This time Brania grabbed Nakano by the shoulder and yanked him back, his fangs letting go of the headmaster's flesh reluctantly. He looked at Brania, his lips still smeared with warm blood. "Why did you do that?"

Looking at him, Brania tried to remember what it was like for a young vampire, when every sensation was new and overwhelming and almost unable to resist. When every feeding felt not only like the first, but as if it would be the last as well. She tried to remember so she could find patience. "Because others are hungry too."

Nakano's eyes followed Brania's as she looked over at Jeremiah.

"Oh," Nakano said, "sorry." Then he extended his tongue, longer and more flexible now than when he was mortal, and licked from one end of his lip to the other. First the top lip, then the bottom, until no blood was left. Cumin! Yes, that was the spice. Satisfied, he stepped back so Jeremiah could take his turn, but before the driver could plunge his own fangs into the headmaster, Brania placed a hand on his shoulder. "Remember, we don't want to drain him." Jeremiah nodded and understood. He wasn't the brightest vampire on the face of the earth, but he took orders relatively well. And Brania liked to reward those who behaved, so just as his fangs were about to enter the still-gaping holes that Nakano had created, she added, "Just yet."

A cold wind passed by and Alistair's body trembled. Jeremiah ignored the movement and continued feeding, but Brania placed a hand on Alistair's thigh to soothe him. After a moment, his body was calm and warm, and when Jeremiah released him from his grip, Alistair looked like he was merely taking a nap in the woods. Brania smiled and marveled to herself: Looks could be so deceiving.

She was sure that when people, men especially, looked at her, they had no idea what they were truly looking at. They thought she was just a girl, mature for her age, curvy, but still a girl. She was also certain that when Michael looked at Ronan, he thought he was looking at another sixteen-year-old boy, nothing more.

How she wished she could see the expression on his face when he learned the truth.

A cold wind flew through her, taking with it all thoughts of Michael and Ronan. It was a reminder that she still had work to do. "Put him back in the trunk, Jeremiah," she ordered. "My father wishes to speak with him."

"Your father?" Once again he unconsciously bit his lip, but this time he was full, so blood oozed from the pierced flesh, Alistair's still-warm blood, which Jeremiah immediately flicked with his tongue. Mustn't waste a drop of the red ambrosia.

As Jeremiah resolutely carried out his task, Brania took the opportunity to cast an even stronger spell over Nakano. "Thank you, Kano," she said sweetly.

He was startled. His mind was just beginning to calm after the frenzy that always followed a feeding and he had no idea why she was thanking him. "Uh, of course," he muttered, trying to sound convincing, but was then compelled to ask, "For what?"

Her moist, ample lips formed a smile, no teeth exposed, no fangs revealed, just her lips meeting and curving upward, making her cheeks plump and her eyes twinkle. She knew that while Nakano preferred the intimacy of boys, he wouldn't be able to resist the intimacy that she now offered him, because his looks were also deceiving. He presented an outward persona of fire and arrogance, but his hidden truth was that he was simply a lonely kid. "For obeying and trusting me," she replied. "You can always count on me, Kano."

She really is so compassionate, Nakano thought, *so maternal. Hell of a lot more than my own mother ever was.* "I know that, Brania," Nakano said. "And that means the world to me."

Hiding her arrogance with yet another smile, this time less full and more wistful, Brania embraced Nakano and told him to go home and rest. "You may be a child of immortality, but you're still a student at Archangel Academy." And then she threw her head back and roared, "And I am quite the poet!" She was still laughing sitting alone in the backseat of the car as Jeremiah drove away, but if she wasn't so preoccupied she would have been able to read Nakano's mind, and then her laughter surely would have stopped. The instant she was out of sight, he forgot about her empathy, her motherly thoughtfulness, and saw her simply as yet another person to whom he had to answer, yet another person who wanted to control him. "Someday, Brania, I'll be the one giving the orders," Nakano told himself. "And you, and Jeremiah, and even your father, will do as I say." And then because he didn't have decades upon decades of practice like Brania did, he was unable to hide his own arrogance, so he yelled after the car as it sped out of the forest, "I swear to it on my blackened soul!"

At that moment, another gust of wind ripped through Ronan. This one was sudden and much stronger; maybe a storm was brewing, maybe just a warning. Either way, Ronan didn't hear a word Michael was saying as they walked toward his dorm, not because he wasn't interested; he just couldn't concentrate. In the back of his mind he knew that Brania and Nakano were up to something and it was as if the wind were trying to tell him he was right, even trying to offer him a clue. He was grateful, but he didn't really need the wind's help; he knew the moment they met Nakano that somehow he and Brania were working together. Brania was sly, but Ronan was savvy, and he noticed her expression change ever so slightly and felt her temperature rise by a degree or two when they bumped into Nakano and Penry. He knew Penry meant nothing to her, but Nakano—they were linked and for some reason that thought frightened him. So even though he didn't want to leave them together to roam the campus freely at night, his first priority was to get Michael away from them and back here, to the safety of St. Peter's.

The building itself didn't offer foolproof protection—although the golden frieze over the front door depicting a series of crucifixes and chalices would definitely deter a vampire who was out to kill from entering—there was an inhabitant of the building who would never give Nakano or Brania permission to enter their dorm after dark. Ciaran knew better. Ronan didn't have to ask him to refuse them entry; Ciaran just knew it was not a wise thing to do.

"I'm sorry," Ronan said, "I didn't hear what you said." Ronan hoped that Michael would think he didn't hear him because Ciaran was listening to the radio while taking a shower and the mixture of music and the loud hum of water pumping through the pipes drowned out his words.

"You see, I'm right," Michael said.

"About what?" Ronan asked.

"Ever since Brania showed up, you've been preoccupied." Michael sat on his bed and unlaced his sneakers. *He doesn't just kick them off and toss them into a corner like I do,* Ronan thought. "It's almost like you're afraid of her."

He's too perceptive, Ronan thought as he tried to come up with a diversion to steer the topic of conversation away from Brania and toward another, less complicated subject. "Are you seriously putting your sneakers back into their shoe box?"

Michael looked perplexed. "Don't you go avoiding my question by pointing out my quirks."

"That's no quirk, Michael, that's downright queer." The word hadn't even made contact with the air before Ronan's cheeks turned red; by the time it hit the ground, Michael's jaw dropped in delightful surprise.

"Well," Michael said, "if the sneaker fits." He shrugged his shoulders and tossed the shoe box into his closet. Correction, he placed the box on top of a stack of other boxes and then closed the closet door. Both boys couldn't help but laugh, and Ronan was glad he was able to change the subject. But Michael wasn't finished talking about Ronan's sort-of half sibling. "So is there a specific reason you don't like her or just her general nature?"

He's not going to let this go, so think of something,

Ronan, give him an answer. "We've just never gotten along."

By Michael's expression, Ronan knew that wasn't a good enough answer. "Really? She seems to genuinely like you," Michael said. "Though it is hard to know when she's being genuine. She was acting like a completely different person tonight than when I first met her. I'm not sure which one is the real Brania."

I hope to God you never meet the real Brania. "It's complicated," Ronan started. "We were like family for a while and then our parents separated."

"Because your mother didn't want to get married?"

Ronan didn't like talking about his mother, but he had to put an end to this topic, so he felt he had little choice. "My mother . . . she never loved Brania's father and, trust me, he wasn't heartbroken when she left him. He never loved her, either." Ronan stopped himself to make sure he wasn't revealing too much.

Sounds like Ronan's mother might be as complicated as mine. "So why did you guys live with them in the first place?"

Ronan noticed another photo he hadn't seen earlier. It was of a handsome man holding a young boy, no more than a year old, in his arms. The photo captured the boy in mid-swing. They were in the country somewhere, in the middle of a wheat field maybe, or just a field of sunburnt grass. It could have been Nebraska, it could have been the English countryside. Ronan couldn't tell. He could tell, however, that the man looked very much like Michael and had straight, very blond hair and the same high cheekbones. Ronan assumed it was his father. *This is what Michael will look like if he grows older, if he ages. If I let him. Did he just say something?* "What?"

Michael repeated his question and this time Ronan fixed his gaze onto Michael himself and not onto the image of what he could look like if he had a normal future. "Contrary to what Mr. Wilde wrote, women *are* geniuses and much more than just the decorative sex," Ronan said, and then explained further. "My mother was skint broke, she had no money, we had no place to live, so she convinced Brania's father that she loved him and that we should live together as one big happy family. Worked fine for a while until my mother received an inheritance and we no longer needed assistance to survive. So we moved on."

Just like we did, Michael thought. Grace got tired of the man she was living with just like Edwige got tired of hers. "Sounds like our mothers really do have a lot in common."

By this time, they were both sitting on Michael's bed facing each other, the way they were before being interrupted. "Don't get me wrong, Michael. What my mother did wasn't right, but she's my mother, she's all I have. I can't really condemn her, can I?"

Michael thought about all the things his mother did, especially her last successful act, and although he was angry with her often and he didn't approve of her actions, he realized he didn't condemn her; he couldn't find it within himself to judge her that harshly. "No, you can't."

"So I know that when Brania starts in on my mother, what she's really doing is protecting her . . . father, but it still doesn't make it any easier to hear. And you know something?" Ronan said, exhaling a long breath. "I just think she's a right balmy lass."

"Does that mean you think she's crazy?"

"Certifiable."

They shared another laugh and instinctively they each reached out to grab the other's hand. Michael stopped laughing, but the smile never left his face as he examined Ronan's hands with his own. His fingers were blunt, some of the nails chewed off, just like his, and underneath he had some rough patches, calluses that felt deliciously manly. He couldn't wait to know what it would feel like to have those hands touch his face, his arms, the small of his back. But for now the back of his hands would have to do. They were so lost in each other's smiles and each other's touch that they didn't notice Ciaran standing in the bathroom doorway, watching them.

"I don't mean to spoil the moment, but I have to get to bed?"

"So early, mate?" Ronan asked. "It's not even ten."

"Early lab in the morning," Ciaran replied.

"You and those labs, Ciaran," Ronan grumbled. "You shouldn't spend so much time looking through that microscope of yours. There's a whole wide world out there."

Thank you, Ronan, I had no idea I was missing out on anything, but it's good to know I am. When Ciaran spoke out loud, he tried to add a bit less sarcasm to his words. "I'll try to remember that."

"I don't know how you do it, Ciaran," Michael said. "I have one biology lab and I barely know what I'm doing. I just don't have the brain for it."

Ciaran softened. He really did like Michael and wished they could be better friends. It's just that with Ronan in the picture, he wasn't sure that was possible. "Well, you know, everyone has their strong suit. You boys seem to be able to lose yourself in literature; for me, I'd prefer a test tube and a specimen of blood." Michael didn't see both Ronan's and Ciaran's face turn white. "Or, you know, bacteria," Ciaran added quickly.

"I should go," Ronan declared abruptly, jumping off the bed. Michael followed, a bit more slowly.

"I'll walk you downstairs."

Before Ciaran rolled over in bed, Ronan saw his face. He wasn't mad exactly. Put out was more like it. This was his home, and his space was being invaded. *Oh, that's not it, Ronan; you know it's because he's alone. He looks at you and sees you with Michael while he's spending another night by himself and he's envious, plain and simple. Don't flaunt it in his face. Maybe what you could do is try to be a better brother.* "No, that's okay," Ronan said. "I know my way out."

The right words didn't come to Michael's brain quickly enough, so he heard himself utter something totally trite. "Okay, sure. I'll see you tomorrow."

And yet another night has passed without me knowing what it feels like to kiss him. But at least it wasn't a night without hope.

Standing on the other side of the doorway, the door partially closed, Ronan couldn't see Ciaran and so he could speak more freely. Even still he whispered, "I'm glad we cleared the air, Michael." Michael smiled. "Me too." And then Michael told every muscle in his body to relax because no matter how badly he wanted to, he was not going to pounce on Ronan in the hallway with Ciaran as witness. Later on, he would dream about doing that minus Ciaran's presence, but for now he simply said, "Good night."

"Good night." Ronan then pushed the door open. "Good night, Ciaran. Um, maybe we can meet at St. Joshua's during break tomorrow and hang out."

Don't be cynical, Ciaran. He's not just asking to look good in front of Michael; he wants to spend time with you. "Okay, I'll see you there."

One final smile and then he was gone. Ciaran almost laughed out loud at the irony. This time he was the one satisfied with the evening's outcome and Michael was left feeling disappointed.

But there was another boy who was feeling even more satisfied than Ciaran because his evening didn't end with just one kiss, but with several. Penry had just ended his first make-out session.

"For someone who claims not to have any experience in boy-meets-girl relationships, you're a pretty good kisser," Imogene declared.

A bit more self-conscious now that the kissing had stopped and he had to do something else with his mouth, such as talk, Penry paused a moment before speaking. "Well, I think it's because I have such a great partner."

"Are you trying to say that I must be the one with experience?"

Does she really mean that? Penry was confused. *She always says these things with such a straight face, I never know if she's joking or not, and I have a feeling that I should be able to figure this kind of stuff out. She's just a girl after all. Ah, maybe Pop is right; girls just aren't supposed to be figured out. He's always saying that Mum's a mystery to him.* "No, Ims, I like kissing you."

Imogene's smile told Penry that she was just teasing. It also told him that she liked to tease him and that for as long as they would date, she would continue to tease him. All of which made him smile right back at her. And shake his head because he just never thought he, Penry Poltke, self-described nerd, bookworm, and all-around geek, would actually have a girlfriend as sassy as Imogene Minx. Life held so many surprises.

"And I like kissing you too, my little PP," she said.

Oh, not again! "You really have to stop calling me that," Penry insisted.

Imogene was shocked. "Why?! You're my little PP."

His father was right; girls were an absolute mystery. Maybe Ronan and the others were the smart ones; boys were so much easier to figure out. "Do you have any idea what that sounds like? 'My little PP'?"

What was he getting so upset about? Imogene thought. *Don't boys like it when their girlfriends make up cute little nicknames?* "It means you're my boyfriend and I'm your girlfriend and I get to call you something special, but more unique than honey or baby."

How was he going to make her understand without being vulgar? "A nickname is sensational, Ims, but not one that reminds people of, you know . . ." And then even though they were alone and outside, he added in a whisper, "Doing number one."

Now Imogene was thoroughly confused. "Number one?" Then suddenly the gender gap was mended and she understood. "You mean like going to the bathroom? Tinkling!"

"Yes!"

Her mother was right; boys were an absolute mystery and practically a different species. "That is thoroughly disgusting and you should get your head out of the gutter," Imogene demanded. "Or at least out of the toilet." But she couldn't stay mad for more than a second because once she thought about it, she realized Penry was right. "My little PP" was not a really great nickname. So much for trying to be original. "What if I called you Pens?" she suggested. "Kind of like how you call me Ims."

Penry smiled at his girlfriend and was even brave enough to give her one more unexpected kiss. "I like the sound of that." But that would be the last kiss of the night they would share because if Imogene didn't get back to practice in thirty seconds, she was going to be screamed at by Sister Christopher, the music teacher, in front of the entire choir. And since Sister Christopher had an operatic soprano voice, when she screamed, it was like a banshee's screech. "I'll see you tomorrow," Penry told her just as the door to the music room closed shut behind her. But before the door closed, there was another gust of wind and Imogene's scent was carried off into the night air until it reached Nakano. When he caught a whiff of the young girl, the hunger that he thought was fulfilled returned with a vengeance.

He couldn't identify what girl was giving off such a tantalizing scent; he just knew it was the smell of fresh, virgin blood. Blood that he had to taste. He told himself he would just take a small swallow, maybe two, nothing more; he couldn't let this girl, whoever she was, get away.

He began to sprint toward this new aroma just as Michael told himself that he couldn't let Ronan get away, not again. Mumbling an excuse to a half-asleep Ciaran, lying that he must have dropped something on the front steps, Michael left the dorm and walked into the night. Without really thinking, he started jogging in the direction of St. Florian's, or where he thought St. Florian's was. He didn't know that part of the campus very well and soon he realized that he was walking in the direction of St. Sebastian's near The Forest of No Return.

Breathing hard thanks to the unexpected chill in the air, Michael stopped to catch his breath and try to figure out where Ronan's dorm was in relation to the gym. First he thought it was south, but after a few steps, he corrected himself and realized it was west. Or was it?

"How can I possibly be lost?" Michael asked himself.

The question Nakano asked himself was "How can I possibly be so lucky?"

About twenty yards away, right at the ridge of The Forest, Nakano saw Michael standing bent over, his hands on his knees, a bit winded from running in the cold night. He could hear his heart pounding, the smell of his blood puncturing the air. It wasn't as sweet as the unidentified girl's, but Nakano was drawn to it. Michael's blood was even more alluring. All he had to do was walk up to him—he wouldn't even have to run, just say hello—and ask him what he was doing out so late. Start a casual conversation and then when Michael least expected it, he would bare his fangs and stab his flesh and let his warmth cascade down his throat, the warmth that Ronan had yet to feel. Nakano felt his own head pound just thinking about it, just thinking about taking this fool away from Ronan. Somewhere in the depths of his mind, he knew Brania wouldn't be pleased by his taking action so soon and against her wishes, but he didn't care. He wasn't thinking with his brain any longer; an opportunity had presented itself and Nakano was not about to let it pass by.

Looking around, Michael didn't see Nakano quickly hide behind an oak tree; he didn't see anything, nothing that would help give him back his sense of direction. Not that it mattered, because suddenly he was very tired and felt the need to rest before he could continue on. He entered The Forest, causing Nakano to stifle a shout of victory. "Could this be any more perfect?" he asked himself. Michael sat on the ground and leaned against a thick tree trunk, his head nestling into a groove in the bark, and closed his eyes. He didn't see the fog swiftly envelop him, but Nakano did.

Nakano watched in amazement as the crisp, clear night changed in an instant. It didn't make sense. The fog, dark gray and dense, seemed to originate from where Michael sat and then spread out like an oil spill or a fire, quickly and randomly, until it reached a few inches in front of Nakano. "What the hell is going on?!" He flailed his arms in front of himself to try and swipe the fog away, but that was no use. It was more substantial than air; it didn't thin out when he passed his arms through it. He stepped into the fog, but that only made matters worse, which made even less sense to him. Usually it's easier to see within a fog than from outside of it, but this was different. He was inside, part of the mist, and yet he still couldn't see his hand in front of his face, let alone where Michael was resting.

Blindly he took a few steps but crashed face-first into a tree. Furious, he pushed at it and could hear its roots tear apart from the ground below, but he couldn't see his accomplishment; all he saw was blackness. "Michael, where are you!?" he called out. Nothing. He cried out again, but it was as if the fog even blocked his words, as if they were being swallowed up by cement the moment they came out of his mouth. *Something's wrong,* he thought. And then he stopped moving entirely, fear gripping his small frame. *It has to be Brania. She has to know what I'm doing and she's making me stop.*

Once that seed was planted, all thoughts of devouring Michael and destroying the connection between him and Ronan were gone. All he wanted to do was get out of the fog and back into the security of the night. He felt the uprooted tree and turned around, arms out in front of him, as he slowly, deliberately placed one foot in front of the other and started to walk back toward the night to escape the fog. He stopped only when his hands touched a body.

Nakano felt powerful again. Even though he couldn't see Michael, he felt him and then he grabbed him so his back was pressing in against his chest, and his hand was covering his mouth. Not that Michael's screams would be heard; the fog made sure of that. Nakano howled with laughter. The very trick Brania used to try and protect Michael would ensure his eternal enslavement. Before he unleashed his blood-hungry fangs, he made a silent apology. "Forgive me, Brania, for I am about to sin." Then he allowed his fangs to penetrate the flesh they so desperately craved.

One delightful bite and the ripe blood passed from victim to predator. Nakano wanted to feed, feed, feed until there was no more blood, but even in his wild state, he knew he couldn't; his trophy needed to remain alive. Forcing himself to stop, he released his hold and let his fangs slowly slide out of the abused flesh. Delirious, Nakano stumbled forward, falling to the ground, and finally emerged from the dark fog. Underneath the moon's glow he knelt and turned his prey over to make sure he was still breathing.

He was stunned to see that his prey was Penry.

chapter 12

High above the ground the meadowlark rested on a narrow branch and watched Michael. It was impressed. The boy had traveled quite far, he had a much farther distance to go, but he'd begun, and beginning was always the most difficult. Thirsty, the lark dipped its beak into a dewdrop that clung to a leaf and drank, drank, drank until the drop was gone and the leaf dry. It sang a few notes, *da-da-DAH-da, da-da-da,* sang again, and waited until Michael was no longer alone. When the lark saw the other boy kneel down next to him, it knew it could carry on with its own journey. Michael would be safe and so it flew off, its yellow feathers nearly lost in the morning sunshine.

The first thing Ronan did was look at Michael's neck, first one side, then the other. They were both unscarred, just smooth, heavenly flesh, and Ronan felt great relief. He bowed his head to murmur "thank you," holding back tears. But when he lifted his head and looked again at Michael's face, he felt an urge overcome him. *No! Please, God, no!* Against his will, his fangs descended and his eyes brightened and only one thought consumed him, the thought that in seconds he would taste Michael's blood. Valiantly he fought the feeling, tried to shake it off, but he couldn't, and he knew why: He was too close to his Day of Feeding. Unlike Nakano, Brania, and the others like them, Ronan and his kind had to feed only once a month. One glorious and fulfilling monthly feeding. Because it was less frequent, it was almost ceremonial, but it was still about need, and definitely about hunger. And right now, looking at Michael, asleep and dangerously handsome, Ronan was hungry.

He turned Michael's face to the side to fully reveal his neck. Ronan could almost see through the skin, into the vein, and to his blood underneath, alive and flowing. He bent forward and the smell, a mixture of Michael's skin and blood, was enthralling. Ronan closed his eyes and breathed in deeper. He bent lower still and traced the vein with the tips of his fangs, lazily, back and forth, just connecting with the skin. Then he let them travel across Michael's jaw, over the curvature of his lips, to the height of his cheekbones. The desire to feed had never been this strong and it frightened Ronan; he thought it might consume him. He felt his fangs vibrate, a sign that they were ready, and all he wanted to do was devour Michael right here, right now, with The Forest and sun as the only witnesses. But then Michael opened his eyes.

The sunlight was so strong, Michael had to blink. He thought he saw an animal and by instinct he clawed at the earth, clutching at the grass frantically, and started to scramble to his feet to get away from the thing. It grabbed him at the ankle, it felt like a hand, and then it took hold of his wrist. No. No! He twisted violently but couldn't break free. What *was* this thing?! He collected a mouthful of fear and let out a scream, hoping it might frighten the animal, but no, its grip only tightened. Finally, he looked into its eyes. "Ronan?!"

Michael quickly took in his surroundings and, perplexed, saw that he was outside, near The Forest. Off in the distance he could see the windows of St. Sebastian's. Panting and confused, he took a moment to realize he wasn't being attacked by some wild animal, he was being held by his boyfriend. Confusion quickly turned to happiness. "Ronan, what's going on?"

Hesitant, Ronan clutched his mouth with his hand and was relieved not to feel his fangs protruding over his lips. It did make sense that they appeared of their own volition; his Day of Feeding was tomorrow morning, but it was a close call. He wasn't yet ready to reveal himself to Michael and he knew that before he did, he would have to explain certain things to him. His kind weren't the vampires of common legend; their history was more complicated. But for now he felt the need to keep things simple. "I found you out here asleep."

"Asleep?" Michael asked in disbelief.

Ronan nodded his head. "I went to your dorm this morning and no one was there, then I checked St. Martha's. I thought you might be having breakfast."

Michael shook his head. "No, the last thing I remember, I went out looking for you last night after you left."

"What?" Ronan didn't mean to sound so harsh, but it was fear speaking. He knew that it was dangerous for Michael to walk the grounds at night without protection. In a much softer voice he asked, "You were looking for me?"

Michael let out a breath and started slowly, hoping he wouldn't sound like an obsessed teenager. "Well, I didn't like the way we left things last night. Not that anything bad happened. I just, well, I was hoping that it would have had a different ending."

So was I, Michael, Ronan wanted to say, but instead he tried to make a joke. "Like you falling asleep in the woods?"

How could something like this have happened, Michael thought, *and why do I feel so wonderful? It doesn't feel like I spent the night on the cold, hard earth.* "I have no idea how this happened. I remember losing my way a bit: It was foggy last night. And then getting really, really tired. I came here to rest for a minute and the next thing, I opened my eyes and there you were." Michael was beaming. Part of his euphoria could be attributed to the fact that he was now holding Ronan's hand.

Neither boy realized it until after it happened, but while they were talking, their hands once again found each other and they were sitting with their legs intertwined. The magnet had pulled them together and they were unable to resist. "And here we are," Ronan observed.

Curious to see how things were progressing, the meadowlark flew by for one more look, singing its signature tune, and Michael got a flash of memory. He remembered words, maybe from a dream, or a book: "You can never escape your true self and you'll never be able to escape this world until you accept that." Right now Michael knew that he couldn't escape his true self and, in fact, he didn't want to. There was only thing Michael wanted to do. "This is how I wanted last night to end."

Michael covered Ronan's hands tightly with both of his, and looked deep within his beautiful blue eyes. He had no idea where he was finding the courage; he only knew that he had spent much too long thinking and dreaming, and now it was time for him to act. He leaned into Ronan closer until he could feel his breath on his lips, until their noses touched, and until, finally, so did their lips.

Ronan ached. A part of him wanted desperately to push Michael away and run from this place, but he couldn't, not after feeling this sweet boy's mouth against his. It was gentle and soft, filled with love, and just a touch of nervousness. Ronan responded by pressing his lips a bit more forcefully against Michael's so he would know that he too wanted this connection as much as Michael did. Their kiss grew and became fuller and held the promise of much more passion yet to come. But they had time for all of that, they had time for passion. Right now was just a beginning. And it was perfect. Their kiss ended, but neither boy pulled away. Their foreheads, warmed by the sun and their emotions, remained connected. Ronan slid his face to the right so their cheeks rested upon each other and whispered into Michael's ear, "And what a perfect way for our morning to begin."

Lost in such intense feelings, Michael had no words. His first kiss could not have been any better. Gently they embraced. The boy he had dreamed about, an idyllic setting, a dead body nearby. What?! Over Ronan's shoulder, Michael could see a body sprawled out on the ground, facedown, and not moving. His body tensed and he pulled away. His face must have turned white because Ronan started asking him what was wrong. All Michael could do was point in the body's direction.

Ronan wished he was surprised, but he wasn't. *I was right,* he told himself, *something bad has happened.* Now, looking down at the lifeless body, he had proof and when he turned the body over, he gasped, "It's Penry!"

"Oh no!" Michael cried. "Is he dead?"

Before Ronan checked for a pulse, he tilted Penry's head to the side and saw two small holes on his neck, encrusted with dried blood that was now more black than red. Quickly, Ronan turned Penry's head to the other side so Michael wouldn't see the markings, and felt for a pulse. "No, he's just unconscious," Ronan said. "Go get Dr. MacCleery. I don't want to move him in case he's broken any bones." Michael didn't move. "Go! And find Hawksbry too."

This is insane, Michael thought. *That could be me.* Penry was only a few yards away from where Michael had slept during the night and yet he was fine, he felt invigorated, even before kissing Ronan, which now seemed hours ago. All through the night he slept, never once waking, while Penry had been attacked and left for dead. He literally shook his head to try and rid his mind of such thoughts and ran off to the infirmary, shouting, "I'll be right back!"

When Michael was gone, when Ronan was alone with Penry, his body once again took control and began to act on its own. He saw his hand turn Penry's head to expose his wounds and when the smell of blood wafted up and through him, Ronan became light-headed. His fangs reappeared and his eyes shone with the kind of determination only brought on by an insatiable hunger. He would feed a day early. It wasn't proper, but he just couldn't resist.

He placed his hand over Penry's face, he didn't want to see the boy when he plunged his fangs into his neck, but just as he bent his head, he heard a twig break. Ronan froze. Who was watching? Who was interrupting his feeding? He prayed it wasn't Michael and cursed his own lack of self-discipline. When he looked up, cautiously, he saw it wasn't Michael but Nakano.

His black eyes taunted Ronan to finish what he most certainly started. But once again Nakano failed in an attempt to destroy because seeing Nakano's sinister glare was exactly what Ronan needed to bring him back to reality and help him regain control of his body. One of the cardinal rules of his people was that you don't attack a fellow student, especially on Archangel land. He was furious with himself that he came so close to breaking that rule. But now wasn't the time for self-loathing; he had to help his friend.

Ronan buried his face in Penry's neck, but instead of reopening the two gashes with his own sharp fangs, he licked the wounds with his tongue, which was as long and as flexible as Nakano's. That was one trait they did share, but it was becoming clearer to Ronan that they had little else in common. If Nakano had his way, Penry would have bled to death, and the whole school, all of Eden in fact, would know that they were more than myth, that they were real. Ronan couldn't let that happen, not just yet.

The cuts started to fade—Ronan's body could heal as effectively as it could kill—and in seconds Penry's neck once again resembled Michael's, smooth and untouched. Ronan looked up, but Nakano was gone. The fear, however, that he instilled in Ronan remained. Why would he do such a thing? So reckless and brazen. Was this what he and Brania were planning? To begin attacking the students one by one? Possible, but their strategy made absolutely no sense to Ronan. He knew how they operated and how they thought; he knew that they could be vile and duplicitous, and so he knew that if they were going to start attacking students, the first one on the list would be Michael. But Michael was only a few yards away and he was unharmed. There could be only three explanations why: He was placed there as a warning, he was somehow being protected, or he was just plain lucky. Ronan didn't like any of those scenarios since none of them allowed him to control the situation. And if he couldn't be in control, he couldn't ensure Michael's safety. No one could. But matters of Michael's safety would have to be put on hold for the time being because Penry was in far more immediate danger.

The archway to the infirmary was decorated in the same way as the mirror frame in the academy greeting room, with the seven archangels that gave the academy its name. But here they were larger and chiseled out of stone instead of carved out of wood, so while their appearance was still otherworldly, it was also more lifelike. Gabriel, Raphael, Uriel, Sariel on top of a cluster of bones, Ramiel, Zachariel in front of the sun, and, of course, Michael, slayer of Satan. At the apex of the archway they were joined by St. Luke, patron saint of doctors, his arms outstretched to the sides, inviting the archangels to join him in his mission to heal the sick. To his right was a small calf lying on a hearth, its side split open dripping stone droplets of blood as a sacrifice to God. As he passed under the arch carrying Penry in his arms, Ronan wondered how many humans had been sacrificed for his kind and if Penry would be the next. He also wondered if St. Luke would have the slightest clue how to cure a vampire bite, but doubted the saint or even the archangels possessed that knowledge. His only hope was that Dr. MacCleery wouldn't need those skills today.

"Lay him on the stretcher, Ronan," the doctor ordered and then whisked Penry into a separate room, the door closing after him.

Ronan and Michael were left alone in the infirmary's waiting room with Mrs. Radcliff, the school nurse, who definitely had no such knowledge of anything beyond rudimentary medicine. Despite what she knew about Penry, she simply assumed he passed out after a night of drinking. Archangel wasn't known for its rowdiness. In fact, in the almost thirty years that she had worked at the academy, she could only remember three students who had a fondness for alcohol. None of them lasted very long despite the large checks their parents wrote to keep them enrolled. Hawksbry felt the school had a reputation to uphold and refused to compromise that reputation no matter how large the financial gift. The way she stared at Michael and Ronan, it looked as if she thought she had uncovered three more and assumed they all drank the night away. Luckily, Penry had an alibi, who showed up just in time to save all their reputations.

"Thanks for calling me, Michael," Imogene announced

upon entering the room, followed by a girl whom neither boy recognized. "Is Penry going to be okay?" Imogene asked.

"Well, that depends," Mrs. Radcliff said, looking up
from her paperwork to gauge Imogene's reaction to her
question. "How much did he have to drink last night?"

"He wasn't drinking!" Imogene said. "He was with
me while I was on a break from choir practice."

The nurse eyed both Imogene and her girlfriend,
whose name she couldn't place, and her instinct, honed
by decades of listening to teenagers lie, told her that
Imogene was telling the truth. Her statement corrobo-
rated what she already knew of the boy; he was a good
student, a poor athlete, but not a drinker or someone
who took drugs. She took off her eyeglasses, held together by a fake-crystal beaded chain that she wore
around her neck, and laid them on her formidable
breasts. She looked matronly and could be empathetic
when necessary, but most often she knew the students
preferred she be honest. "He doesn't have any broken
bones or even any bruises, but it looks like he tripped on
his way home and possibly suffered a concussion."

"That's not that serious, right?" Imogene asked.

"As long as he wakes up, it shouldn't be," Mrs. Radcliff said as unemotionally as she could.

Ronan didn't contradict the false diagnosis, but he
knew better. He knew that as long as Nakano hadn't
taken too much blood from Penry, he would be fine. But
if Nakano took too much, past the point a human body

needed to survive, no amount of science or medicine was going to keep Penry alive. Ronan just couldn't be sure how far Nakano went, how much of Penry's blood now flowed through Nakano's body. Penry was still breathing when he found him, which was a promising sign, but Ronan was concerned that he was still unconscious. Imogene was more than concerned, she was quite scared. "Why won't he wake up?"

Mrs. Radcliff couldn't help but smile at the girl. Her personal experience with young love was a distant memory, but thanks to the students, she was reminded of it constantly. "Dr. MacCleery will be able to explain everything once he's done examining him."

Her girlfriend gave her hand a gentle squeeze and said softly, "Give the doctor a chance to do his thing."

Ronan almost laughed; there was nothing for the doctor to do. He himself had healed Penry's external wounds, but whatever damage Nakano did to Penry internally was already done. It was up to Penry now. Not having the same insight, Mrs. Radcliff offered some hope. "He's probably a little anemic, that's all."

The rest of her words were lost among the onslaught of questions that arose when Lochlan MacCleery came out of the examining room. Unfazed, he did what he always did when faced with a group of concerned and very loud students; he took off his thick glasses, rubbed them with his shirttail, which was always untucked, put his glasses back on, and spoke at a volume louder than the crowd's. "So who found the boy?"

Michael raised his hand. "I did."

He must be the American, MacCleery thought. "You're not in class, son."

"Sorry."

Ronan cleared his throat. "Actually, we found him together."

Should I be surprised? Lochlan ran a hand through his thick bush of grayish-brown hair and massaged his scalp a few times the way he always did when he was searching for the right thing to say. Seven years as resident doctor and he still loved his cushy job, he loved living out here in Eden's countryside, he even loved dealing with the students on a daily basis. He never had kids of his own; his wife died before they even contemplated trying, so he always figured this was God's way of making things up to him. Until he met Ronan.

Something wasn't right with the boy. He had no idea what; maybe it was because he just looked too darned perfect. Lochlan had never been good-looking, so he readily admitted that he could simply be feeling some latent jealousy; he wasn't above such pettiness. However, he couldn't shake his suspicions. The way Ronan was looking at him right now, head cocked to the side, voice a bit too steady, yes, he was hiding something, but what? "I've run some initial tests and I haven't found anything to make me concerned. He's probably anemic and fainted."

"That's what I told them," Mrs. Radcliff announced proudly.

"Did you notice anything unusual when you found him, Ronan?" the doctor asked.

He suspects; he always has. He has no idea what's behind his suspicions, but he can tell there's something different about me. Ronan shrugged his shoulders casually. "No. We were just walking and we saw him lying on the ground."

"Facedown," Michael interjected, feeling the need to be helpful. "We turned him over. I hope that was okay?"

"Perfectly fine, son, perfectly fine," the doctor said. "Has anyone informed Hawksbry?"

"I called his office, but his secretary told me he hadn't come in yet," Mrs. Radcliff explained.

MacCleery looked at his watch and frowned. "He must've slept in for the first time since I've known him."

Imogene couldn't take it anymore. Why were they all just jabbering when her boyfriend was lying in there dying, or worse, in excruciating pain? "Nothing's perfectly fine! It won't be perfectly fine until Penry opens his eyes and wakes up."

Lochlan suppressed a laugh. This girl was definitely going to give Penry major headaches. A great deal of amusement as well, but headaches nonetheless. "Are you Imogene?"

"Yes."

"Penry's been asking about you."

Stunned, Imogene fought the impulse to thwack the doctor across the side of the head. "He's talking?! Why didn't you say so?!"

"Because it's quite early, lass, and my bedside manner doesn't click in until I've had my morning coffee," the doctor said wearily, his Scottish brogue deliberately more pronounced. "Would you like to see him?"

Wiping away a few tears, Imogene told the doctor that, yes, she would definitely like to see Penry. "Wait for me," she told her girlfriend before leaving.

"Of course."

The doctor gave Penry's chart to Mrs. Radcliff and told her that he should be fine, but he wanted him to spend the morning resting before he resumed classes. Just before he went in search of his morning coffee, he turned to Ronan. "If you remember anything you think might be important, why don't you stop by."

Michael answered for both of them. "Of course, sir, definitely."

"I should check in on the lovebirds; don't want Penry getting overexcited," Mrs. Radcliff said, exiting the room and leaving Ronan and Michael alone with Imogene's friend.

"I'm Phaedra."

"Hi, I'm Michael and this is Ronan."

Ronan smiled and nodded his head. "You go to St. Anne's?"

"Yes, just transferred from New York."

A fellow American. Michael surprised himself by getting excited. He wasn't homesick for Weeping Water, but here, surrounded by so many accents and students of obvious non-American descent, it was nice to meet someone from the same part of the world. Not that Nebraska and New York had much in common, but they were still on the same continent. "Me too. Well, I'm from Nebraska."

"Never heard of it," Phaedra said with a laugh. "Actually that's not that far from the truth. My parents are terrible urban snobs and would be mortified to know that they spent all this money to send me to an exclusive boarding school just so I could hobnob with a country bumpkin. And I mean that in the nicest possible way."

Michael smiled. "Well, you can rest easy; my father is from London and rather sophisticated, so you can say I'm only half country bumpkin."

Interesting, Ronan thought; for the first time since he found Penry, he felt calm. Nakano's foolish actions, Dr. MacCleery's pointed comments, the concern he felt about Michael, all of that dissipated when he looked at this girl. Her eyes were extraordinary. Gray-blue, cold-looking like an icicle, but somehow they were warm and inviting. However, she wasn't telling the whole truth. Ronan could sense that. "You're not a native New Yorker, are you?"

Phaedra turned to look at Ronan, her dark brown hair, curly and more free-flowing than unkempt, swayed a bit, but her eyes remained clear, precise. "You got me. I was actually born in Mykonos while my parents were attending my grandmother's funeral. I'm named after her. Phaedra Antonides."

"I thought I detected a slight accent," Ronan said.

Her brown eyebrows, not nearly as perfectly plucked as Brania's, rose about an inch. "I'm impressed. No one usually picks up on that."

No humans anyway, Ronan thought. "I have a really good ear."

Regardless of where she was from, Michael liked her too. She didn't calm him as she did Ronan, but he felt that she was a breath of fresh air. "Well, Phaedra Antonides, I'm Michael Howard and this is Ronan Glynn-Rowley. It's a pleasure to meet you and if I may be so bold, I predict that we're all going to be great friends."

"I find nothing bold about that statement at all, Michael," Phaedra said, smiling. "I find it to be quite accurate."

Ronan wanted to question Phaedra further about Mykonos and New York, not that he didn't believe her, but he felt drawn to her, compelled almost. He usually didn't find girls that interesting and worth the effort of getting to know, but this one seemed different. Phaedra seemed sincere. However, before any more questions could be asked, Imogene came out of the examining room, her cheeks streaked with tears. "My boyfriend's going to be all right!"

Standing in the doorway, Mrs. Radcliff didn't even bother to try and quiet the group when they started to cheer. She knew trying to control a bunch of screaming teenagers was a pointless task. Instead, she said a quick prayer thanking God that yet another child would recover and then told the kids they had three minutes to say good-bye to Penry before they had to let him rest.

"But I feel fine," Penry protested.

"Doctor's orders, Pens," Imogene overruled.

Ronan was thankful Penry was all right. He looked a bit pale and was more lethargic than he would admit, but Nakano didn't cause any permanent damage. At some point he would have to confront Nakano, make him understand that what he did was unacceptable and hope that he could talk some sense into him. But he feared he wouldn't listen. Brania was Nakano's master, not Ronan, so there was only so much he could do. But for today, he had obviously done enough.

"Thanks, Ronan," Penry said.

All heads turned to stare at Ronan, who was caught off guard. "For what?"

A little color dotted Penry's cheeks. "For, um, finding me and, um, carrying me from The Forest. Thank you."

"No problem, mate."

"You too, Michael." Then Penry added with a sly wink, "Guess I'm lucky that you two were out having a . . . morning stroll."

In response Imogene giggled, Ronan blushed, Michael started to make up some excuse, and Mrs. Radcliff announced that their time was up. Only Phaedra remained silent.

"Take good notes in history, Michael," Penry said. "You know Willows isn't going to let me get out of tomorrow's test." It looked like Penry would fully recover.

Ronan was a different story. Try as he might, he couldn't move past the morning's events. He tried to remind himself that Michael was unharmed and Penry had survived, but he knew he didn't have the full story. He wasn't prepared to speak with Nakano, so he avoided him all morning. One altercation with his ex-boyfriend per week was more than enough, so he remained true to his word and met with Ciaran at St. Joshua's. Two minutes into the conversation and Ciaran wished he had reneged.

"Ronan, is it possible that this is all just coincidence and not worth further speculation?"

"I would like it to be nothing more, but Penry's neck," Ronan whispered. "He was bitten."

It wasn't that Ciaran wasn't concerned; Penry was one of his best friends. He just knew that one bite wasn't deadly. If it was followed up by another, well, then, yes, things could become more serious, but for the moment, as far as Ciaran was concerned, there was nothing to worry about. Still, he couldn't hold his tongue. "You know as well as I do that Nakano's a loose cannon. I told you that when you started dating him, but as usual, you didn't want to listen to me then." Ronan felt his patience growing thin. He didn't need to be reprimanded, he needed advice. "So isn't it at all remotely possible that he bumped into Penry and just couldn't resist him?"

Why was his half brother so incredibly dense sometimes? "Yes, of course it's *possible,* but it's never happened before. Nakano knows the rules. We all do, and we all know the consequences. Aren't you at all concerned? Aren't you frightened?"

He wasn't, not at all, but Ciaran wasn't going to reveal why, so he lied. "Of course I'm frightened, but worrying isn't going to change anything." Ciaran traced the looping paisley pattern on the couch with his finger. "Do I need to remind you that I'm virtually powerless against you . . . *people?*"

"Do not lump me in with Them!" A few heads raised, but not Ciaran's. He had anticipated Ronan's outburst, so he remained focused on the couch. "I am nothing like Kano and his kind," Ronan said in a much more civilized tone.

Looking up, Ciaran lied again. "Sorry, I didn't mean that. I just don't know what to tell you. Unless you want to expose yourself and tell Michael the truth, there really isn't any way you can protect him, not one hundred percent."

Suddenly, Ronan reached out and grabbed Ciaran's hand. He did it so quickly, for a second Ciaran didn't comprehend how unusual an act it was. "Promise me, Ciaran, promise me that you'll watch over Michael and help me keep him safe."

All thoughts of provoking or antagonizing Ronan vanished as pride swelled Ciaran's heart. This was all he wanted, to feel needed and connected, to be part of a family. He looked at his brother's pleading face. He needed him, needed his help, and of course he would have it. "I will do everything humanly possible," Ciaran said. "But you, Brother, you'll have to take care of the rest."

Once again Ciaran said something borderline inappropriate, but this was different. Ciaran was actually displaying a sense of humor, and it calmed Ronan. First

Phaedra and now Ciaran. It was an odd sensation, one second to be concerned and aware of imminent danger, and the next to be peaceful and mindful that help was nearby. He had a feeling this was all Michael's doing. Ever since they met, his life had changed. He didn't say the words out loud because he wasn't sure if Ciaran was ready to hear them, but he knew that Michael was his salvation.

And Michael felt the same way about Ronan. He never imagined from that first meeting in the rain that he would come to feel so brave and self-assured, or at least more brave and self-assured than scared and lost. So when he saw Ronan after school heading over to St. Sebastian's for a swim before tomorrow's tryouts, he called out his name in a strong voice that was uncolored by shame. "Ronan."

Stopping in his tracks, Ronan turned around to greet Michael and felt some butterflies fluttering in his stomach, mainly because Michael looked perfectly poised. His voice matched his appearance. "Ronan Glynn-Rowley, would you like to make it official and go out on a date with me?"

A strong wind blew past them and the butterflies were swept away. Ronan had so many reasons to say no, so many reasons to ignore what had taken place between them, their first meeting, their kiss, and to tell Michael that despite his previous declarations, he wasn't ready to have another boyfriend or he just didn't want to complicate his life by dating a classmate. But all of that would be a lie. The truth was, he wanted to spend every waking moment with Michael and he wanted to make their relationship official. And so he said yes.

"Excellent," Michael said. "Tomorrow night, then. I'll pick you up at seven."

Ronan couldn't wait for tomorrow night to come. "I'll be waiting."

He wouldn't be the only one. In the distance, Phaedra stared at them, observing their actions the same way she had when she first saw them outside St. Joshua's. But this time, she was even more alarmed than before.

chapter 13

Michael and Ronan were both swimming in the water. They just happened to be roughly 252 miles apart. Michael was on his third lap in the pool in St. Sebastian's while Ronan was swimming in the ocean off Inishtrahull Island. They were separated, yes, but only by distance; they each swam with the same powerful determination. They had goals to achieve.

Michael was determined to make the swim team. He didn't really care about impressing Mr. Blakeley or Fritz, who just this morning expressed doubts that the American had the stamina to make the team, or any of his fellow students. He wanted to impress himself. Prove that the awkward, self-conscious Michael from Weeping Water was nothing more than a distant memory. Ronan, on the other hand, had to feed.

Earlier this morning, he had followed the scent of death to an elderly man living alone in a cottage in the town next to Eden. When Ronan arrived, the man, very tall and thin, was lying on top of an old, stained quilt, barely conscious and having difficulty breathing. Small puddles of sweat gathered in the folds of his neck, and his hands, wrinkled and speckled with liver spots, shook. He never opened his eyes, not even when he spoke. "Hurry up," the old man groused. "Don't have much time left."

His final words were barely spoken before Ronan began draining the blood from the old man. Gulp after gulp of blood, slightly bitter, flooded Ronan's throat, slid down to his stomach, and spread out to his limbs. His brain was throbbing with the infusion, his entire body starting to glow. Finally the old man's hands stopped shaking and went limp at his sides, his suffering and his life mercifully ended. Ronan, however, felt incredibly alive. The blood that in the old man's veins was diseased and no longer able to sustain life thrived in Ronan's body. But his feeding wasn't over.

Moving faster than the human eye could see, his feet hardly touching the ground, Ronan raced from the cottage to the beach at Inishtrahull Island. Stripped naked, fangs bared, eyes like two beacons of light, he took a moment to look out at the water. *This is my world,* he thought. *Every last drop of it is mine.* He took a deep breath of the fresh sea air and then plunged into the ocean.

At the same time, Michael took a deep breath of the chlorine-tinged air and plunged back into the pool. *This is my world,* he thought, *my new world, and I'm going to make the most of it.* He swam hard, lifting his head out of the water every third stroke to take a quick breath, and felt energy protrude from every pore. He didn't feel tired—though even if he did, he was not about to give in. Michael stopped swimming only when he reached the end of the pool and heard Mr. Blakeley blow his whistle.

Ronan stopped swimming only when he reached the cave and heard the familiar hum. The sound emanated from The Well. It was ordinary-looking, made of thick blocks of curved stone that jutted out from the base of an underwater cave, and was surrounded by nothing except rough sand. From the center of The Well came a light, dull, not especially bright, but enough to bounce off the cave's roof and illuminate the space. This place was a haven, dry and cool, right in the middle of the Atlantic Ocean about a mile northwest and below the shore off the island where Ronan was raised. But it was only a haven, in fact only visible, to those who could hear its call. This was where the ceremony would take place and where Ronan's feeding would end.

This is where everything will begin, Michael thought. He stood next to one of the heated lamps drying himself off with a towel and tried not to put too much weight

on what was about to take place—swim team tryouts—
but today was important. This was another step in his
emancipation from that other life, that life he left behind.
He would feel much less nervous, much more confident,
if Ronan were standing by his side, but unfortunately he
was nowhere to be found.

Ronan knelt before The Well, placing both of his
hands on the rim, and bowed his head. Immediately the
humming grew louder, causing the stones to vibrate and
pulse. The Well recognized Ronan as one of its own de-
scendants. As the light shone with more intensity, the
pulse of The Well invaded Ronan's body to create the
final transformation. Ronan gripped the stone rim even
tighter, eyes closed, his fangs pressing down on his lips,
and felt one continuous wave of energy travel through
his body until he was filled entirely with The Well's
power. Then the final change began.

Slowly and a bit painfully, his fingers and toes elon-
gated, and small, thin pieces of flesh rose out from between each digit to create webbed hands and feet. Eyes
still closed, Ronan smiled despite the pain. Even though
he was by himself in this secluded cave, he was connected to every other vampire like him, to every other
vampire who belonged to his race, and he was reminded
that no matter how lonely he might sometimes feel, he
was hardly alone. The transformation complete, all vibrations stopped. Now The Well of Atlantis would
allow Ronan to finish his feeding.

Ronan bent over The Well, which was half filled with

a clear liquid that was so smooth, its surface appeared solid. It was the essence of his people, the life force that kept them whole and allowed them to exist in a manner that other vampires could only dream of and covet. He leaned over and dipped his hands into the cold liquid, scooping up a handful. He held his now-webbed hands up over his head, careful not to spill a drop, and recited the prayer:

> *Unto The Well I give my life,*
> *my body's blood that makes me whole.*
> *I vow to honor and protect*
> *and ask The Well to house my soul.*

When he was finished, he brought his webbed hands to his mouth and drank. At first, there was no taste, nothing, just a cold sensation until the elixir reached warm blood, then the two liquids, the two individual life forces, united and, as always, the result was intoxicating.

This time when Ronan gripped the side of The Well it was to steady himself. As the two liquids swirled together inside of Ronan to create an even more powerful mixture, he felt he would either faint or float upward. That's how exhilarated he became after a feeding. He knew that his race was shunned by the majority of vampires and that they were considered impure, but he also knew that he couldn't imagine living his life any other way. He also couldn't imagine living his life without

Michael. Now that his feeding was over, it was time to get back to that part of his life.

About thirty seconds before Mr. Blakeley was set to begin tryouts, Ronan bounded into the gym clad in his Speedo, a towel casually thrown over his shoulder, looking more muscular than Michael remembered. Even though Nakano recognized the look and understood that Ronan's muscles had been given a boost since he had just fed, he, like Michael, had to look away to catch his breath. Fritz had no need to take such a pause. "Thought you were gonna chicken out, Captain!"

Ronan smiled and tossed his towel on the bleachers before shouting back, "Just giving the rest of you time to warm up, Fritzie."

Michael noticed some dark black hairs growing in the cleft of Ronan's chest and around the circumference of his deep brown nipples that he hadn't noticed before. Were they new, he thought? He wasn't sure. All he knew was that they made him even more striking.

"Sounding a bit cocky, mate," Fritz said. "Remember we've got an Ameri-*can* who might show you up."

Ronan winked at Michael. "I think the American will do just fine."

Again Nakano had to look away, but this time it was so no one would see him sneer. Fritz just laughed. "Oh, I'm sure you do, Ronan!" He didn't get Ronan's attraction to Michael or to boys in general, but he admired Ronan's athleticism and sportsmanship, so he long ago decided to accept how Ronan felt and not question it.

Anyway, he didn't have time to razz a teammate. Right now he had to concentrate on winning a starting spot on the team.

"The policy here at Double A is that any student who wants to join a sports team must be allowed to do so," Mr. Blakeley explained. "A load of rubbish! If you bloody well stink, I don't want you on my team. But I'm not the headmaster, I'm just a lowly gym teacher."

Under his breath Fritz mumbled, "Lower than low."

"I heard that, Ulrich," Blakeley said. He didn't have to turn to face Fritz to know that the boy's dark complexion turned a few shades closer to white. "By academy rules, I am forced to give each and every one of you a place on my team regardless of your abilities. However, I do not have to make you a starter or even let you dip one mankie toe into my pool."

Michael was completely surprised by this cantankerous speech. He had thought Blakeley, like his previous gym teacher, aimed to instill a sense of pride in his students with positive reinforcement and encouraging words, not intimidate them with threats. So much for thinking he could judge someone's character. His fellow students were about to have the same revelation.

"Hey, where's the Hawkman?" one of the boys shouted. "He's always at tryouts."

Blakeley tried to hide his contempt for his superior, but failed. "Our illustrious leader is M.I.A."

"That's two days in a row," another boy said.

"Maybe he's on a bender," Fritz suggested.

"Hawksbry?" Penry replied. "Hardly. Steady like a hawk and all that."

"Everybody's got a secret," Nakano added. "And all that."

If Ronan weren't so elated from his feeding, he would have understood there was cause for concern. The headmaster was the headmaster for several reasons, most notably, that he was, as Penry suggested, steady and unchanging. He would never disappear for even an hour without telling his assistant where he was. But for the moment, none of that registered for him. And as far as Blakeley was concerned, he would've let the Hawksbry-bashing continue all day, but he had tryouts to oversee. "All right, enough! Within the hour you'll know if I think you're worthy to be on my team or if I think you should be our own personal kettle boy."

Some of the boys chuckled nervously and although Michael had no idea what a kettle boy was, he knew by Blakeley's derogatory tone that it wasn't something he wanted to become. How quickly his confidence disappeared. He felt as inferior as he did in the hallways at Two W. He couldn't shake the feeling until Ronan came up behind him and whispered in his ear, "I wouldn't mind if you were my personal kettle boy." Suddenly the prospect of being a kettle boy didn't seem quite so bad.

Michael playfully tossed his towel over Ronan's head. Just one look at Ronan's face, open and smiling, his hair tousled as if he couldn't be bothered to run a comb through it, and Michael couldn't remember why he had felt anxious only a few seconds earlier. Then Blakeley started shouting again, and he was reminded. "Eaves, Ulrich, Poltke, and Howard, in the pool."

Michael felt his stomach somersault and then heard it growl. He had never tried out for a school sport before and now he was going to do so in front of his boyfriend and an antagonistic coach. He felt queasy from the pressure. "C'mon, Ameri-*can*," Ronan teased, slapping his backside with the towel. "Show us what you got." When Michael took his place at the edge of the pool, he still felt a bit disoriented, but for a completely different reason.

"Swim two laps! As fast as you can! You're being timed!" Just before Blakeley shot his starter gun, he shouted again. "Hold on!" Instantly the four boys broke their starting positions and relaxed, not knowing what to expect next. Ciaran's position was so low and angled he almost fell into the pool before regaining his balance and straightening up. "Poltke!"

"Yes," Penry said.

"Didn't you pass out the other day?"

"Flat on his back," Ulrich replied for him. "After getting Imogene flat on hers."

Despite feeling grand amid the approving cheers of his classmates, Penry knew he had to defend his girlfriend's honor. "Don't be a git, Fritz."

"Did MacCleery say it was okay for you to try out?"

"Yes, sir. He said he couldn't find a thing wrong with me and there was no reason why I couldn't try out for the swim team," Penry said, then quickly added, "He also said that he was quite sure I'd make the starting team."

Blakeley, like Mrs. Radcliff, had honed a special skill over the years and could tell when a student was telling the truth. Penry was. Even the last bit about the doctor's guarantee. But Blakeley had an image to uphold and he couldn't make it appear as if he were swayed by anyone else's opinion, even a doctor's. "Yeah, well, you might have fooled MacCleery, but you still have to convince me."

With no further warning, Blakeley raised his hand, shouted, "Ready, set, go," and pulled the trigger. Even though the gym was large, the blast was earsplitting and Michael could hear it echo from underneath the water after he dove in. The sound rippled over him until it was carried away by the current, and then just for a second, there was silence. Michael lay suspended, not moving, just letting the momentum propel him forward, not hearing anything except his own heartbeat and feeling it vibrate throughout his body. He always liked to swim, but here at Double A he felt that the water was beginning to change him, somehow make him even feel more alive. It was weird, but it was a feeling he was starting to love.

When his head emerged to take a breath, he heard Ronan and the others shouting, urging them to swim faster, faster, faster, and so he did. Kicking his legs vigorously, he used strength in his arms that he didn't know he had. He had no idea what position he was in, he couldn't see anything clearly, but he felt movement all around him and so he decided to do what he thought was best and focus on himself and not on the others. It was a good strategy because if he had heard what Nakano was saying to Ronan, it would have shattered his concentration.

"Do you have any idea what you're getting yourself into?"

Ronan didn't take his eyes off of Michael. "My life is no longer your business."

"Well, if you're not concerned about yourself," Nakano sneered, "think about Michael."

"He's all I *can* think about."

Not the response Nakano wanted to hear. "Then I suggest you be careful, for both your sakes."

It's not that Ronan didn't hear the threat; he just knew that it existed even before Nakano spoke the words. No matter how Ronan responded, he wasn't going to change anything; as long as Ronan was with someone other than Nakano, his ex-boyfriend wasn't going to be happy. But the only way Ronan was going to be happy was with Michael. So he would just have to do everything in his power to keep them both safe. And of course remind Nakano that he wasn't dealing with a novice. "You might want to take your own advice."

Nakano didn't like Ronan's condescending tone. "What's that supposed to mean?"

When Ronan spoke again, it was in such a hushed, low voice that no one around him except Nakano could hear, no one looking at him would even suspect that he was moving his lips. "I'm talking about Penry, you idiot. What the hell were you thinking?"

"I was hungry."

"So what? You know the rules."

How dare he scold me, Nakano thought. *My life is none of his business and he's no better than I am.* "You were about to feast on him yourself! You didn't stop because of the rules, you stopped because you heard me and thought it was your precious Michael. You didn't want him to see you with your mouth on another guy."

Ronan knew Nakano was right, but he would keep that thought to himself. "It doesn't matter why I stopped; it just matters that I did."

"I made a mistake, Ronan; we've all made them before."

For the first time, Ronan looked directly at Nakano. "Some of us having been making a lot more mistakes than others."

"Sorry, chum, I forgot I was talking to Mr. Perfect," Nakano replied, finding it very hard to control his voice so no one other than Ronan could hear. "You and your people think you're so much better than everybody else."

Because we are, Ronan thought. "Whatever you say, Kano," Ronan said. "Now if you don't mind, I'd like to watch my boyfriend win this race."

Contracting into a tight ball, Michael flipped and touched the end of the pool with his feet. He bent his knees and pushed off, twisting his body at the same time so he could resume swimming. When he lifted his head again to breathe, he took a split second to see where he was in relation to the other swimmers. On his right he saw Penry about two arm lengths behind, one lane over and it looked like he was even with Ciaran. On his next breath, he looked to the left and saw that Fritz was about a stroke behind him, but since Fritz was taller, he could probably overtake him in fewer strokes. It was a tight race and Michael wouldn't be satisfied coming in anything other than first.

Surprisingly, his satisfaction grew when Blakeley announced that he tied for first with Fritz. Being knowledgeable in such matters, Michael realized Fritz was less likely to torment him if they were equals. Ciaran, who came in a very close second, realized he was definitely not Michael's equal when he saw Ronan extend his hand to Michael to help pull him out of the pool.

"I knew you'd win."

"A shared victory," Michael corrected, allowing his wet hand to hold on to Ronan's dry one longer than necessary.

"You touched down first," Ronan said. "Trust me, my eyes are much better than Blakeley's."

Michael couldn't tell if he was lying or not, but it didn't matter. He loved the fact that he was saying something to make him feel good. It was his turn to do the same. "Great race, Ciaran."

Oh, how magnanimous is the champion, Ciaran thought. "Thanks. You too."

"Penry!" Blakeley shouted. "How do you feel?"

"Fine, sir," Penry answered honestly. "Only a stroke or two behind."

"Yeah, but you still came in last," Blakeley reminded him.

Undeterred, Penry shrugged his shoulders. "Somebody had to."

The next heat was about to begin. The late morning sun glistened through the windows, making Ronan look even more majestic as he stood, bent forward, shoulders bulging as his arms stretched behind him. Michael didn't think he looked like a swimmer; his muscles were much curvier and not long and lean, his body built more for manual labor than gliding through water. In fact, if he hadn't seen Ronan race previously, he would have thought Nakano would easily win, but he knew better. And he was right.

From the very first stroke, Ronan commanded the lead and never once faltered. Nakano couldn't even hope to surpass him. Of course he had an unfair advantage—even without webbed hands and feet—he was a vampire who had just fed, the perfect combination of life and death, almost invulnerable and definitely unbeatable. But he didn't let any of that spoil his win. He achieved what he wanted to achieve, seeing Michael look at him with an awed expression. "You were incredible."

"Thank you, Michael."

"I guess that's why you're the captain."

Ronan wasn't sure how, but he contained himself and didn't kiss Michael right there in front of everyone. Instead he quipped, "One of many reasons."

"Listen up," Blakeley ordered. "For the second year in a row, Ronan is your team captain." The loud cheers drowned out Fritz's snide comment. "The starting team is Ronan, of course, Nakano, Fritz, and Michael."

He did it; that's all Michael could think of. He actually attempted something and succeeded. Some of the kids, including Penry, patted Michael on his back, but all he could feel was Ronan's hand gripping his neck, rubbing up and down a bit until finally he mischievously slapped him on top of the head. Michael let out a shocked laugh. "I can do whatever I want," Ronan said. "I'm your captain."

Michael whispered back, "I'll keep that in mind later tonight." No one else heard his comment, but Michael didn't even care. He checked off a goal; he had made the swim team. But then he realized that Ciaran didn't.

"Team B," Blakeley announced. "Not as good as Team A, but better than most everybody else, is led by Ciaran, Niles, Alexei, and despite MacCleery's prediction, Penry."

Ronan patted Ciaran on the shoulder and teased his brother. "Congrats, mate, you're better than most everybody else." Ciaran forced a smile. It was only placement on a team; it wasn't like it really meant anything. Except that he wouldn't be practicing alongside Ronan, who was his flesh and blood. He had to once again relinquish that position to Michael. Maybe this was a sign. Maybe it was time to accept his role as second fiddle. Or maybe it was time to take some action.

"Do you have any idea what you're getting yourself into?"

Michael wasn't sure what Ciaran was asking him. "I know I've never been on a swim team before, but if I keep practicing, I'll only get better."

"I'm not talking about the swim team," Ciaran said. "I'm talking about Ronan."

If someone had asked Michael something so personal a few weeks ago, he would have found a way to avoid answering. He would have changed the subject or just remained silent, lived inside his head instead of in the real world. But now, he knew he couldn't run from such questions, and the best way to answer them was directly. "I really like Ronan," Michael said. "And he feels the same way about me."

"So you think that you should act upon those feelings so soon?" Ciaran asked. "I mean you hardly know each other."

"That's why we're going out on a date tonight, to get to know one another. And hopefully after a bunch of dates we'll know each other really, really well."

There was so much Ciaran wanted to say, but he knew there was no way to begin. "Just be careful, Michael, that's all I ask."

Why was this so difficult for him to accept? Michael thought. "And all I ask, Ciaran, is that you give us a chance."

*   *   *

But what chance could Michael possibly have if he wore the wrong outfit? He looked at himself in the mirror, hated what he saw, and wondered if Ronan was having an equally difficult time trying to figure out what to wear. He doubted it. Ronan always had that relaxed air about him that made it look as if he just reached into his closet and put on the first thing that his hands grabbed. And no matter what he wore, he looked sensational. Michael was desperate to look just as perfect. He hadn't yet realized that Ronan didn't care what he wore and probably wouldn't notice anyway. He was much more interested in looking into Michael's eyes and watching the way his mouth moved when he talked.

"This might work." The emerald green V-neck sweater really did accentuate his eyes, and the white T-shirt peeking out underneath made it look more casual and not so formal. His jeans fit well, not too tight and not too loose, and his new black loafers were a better choice than his muddy sneakers. His skin was, thankfully, blemish-free and his hair was simple and loose, the way he thought Ronan liked it. But maybe he should put some gel in it just to give it a lift? No, because if it doesn't look good, then it'll be harder to get it back to normal. Michael sighed at his indecision and realized he was thinking way too hard. He sighed even louder when he realized that Ronan had probably been ready an hour ago. He was wrong.

The second after he put the pomade in his hair, Ronan regretted his decision. He rarely used hair-grooming products, partly because he thought his hair looked fine without cosmetic help, but mainly because he felt inadequate applying the stuff. However, he had wanted to do something special tonight for Michael. He quickly realized he'd made a mistake. Or wait, maybe it was just nerves talking.

He ran his fingers through his hair, then pushed down some unruly strands that were sticking up at the sides and then stopped touching his hair altogether. It actually looked good. His hair, pushed back off his face instead of flopping on his forehead, made him look a bit older, kind of collegiate and studious. He liked it. He also liked the way his thin, light blue sweater fell over his muscles, showing off enough but not too much. And his jeans, well, they were just jeans, which meant they were comfortable, which helped him feel a bit more comfortable. Just as he started wondering what Michael would look like, there was a knock at the door, and he wouldn't have to wonder any longer.

When Ronan opened the door, Michael couldn't believe his eyes. *He actually gets better-looking every time I see him.* "Wow, love your hair," Michael said, cringing at how girly he just sounded.

"Really? I wasn't sure about it."

"Yeah, I'm sure. It really, um, looks great. So do you." Michael tried to stop speaking but couldn't. "I mean, you know, you, uh, you look great." And now he sounded like a girl with a speech impediment.

He's just as nervous as I am, Ronan thought. *That's*

good. "Thank you." Just as Ronan was going to invite Michael to come in, he noticed his backpack. "Planning on getting some studying in tonight?"

"Oh no . . . this contains the contents of our date," Michael said proudly.

Ronan was intrigued. He crossed his arms and leaned against the side of the door. "In that little bag of yours?"

"Well, laddie, you might call it my li'l bag o' tricks."

Ronan laughed and Michael, recognizing a bad pun even when it came out of his mouth, joined in. They only stopped when Ronan gave him a kiss. "Sorry. I've wanted to do that since tryouts."

"Me too." Flustered, Michael desperately tried to think of something to say. "Still can't believe I made the first team."

"Why not? You swam a great race."

"Just hope I can keep up."

"Don't let Fritz make you question yourself," Ronan advised. "Or Ciaran."

"Ciaran? He hasn't said a word," Michael half lied.

"Exactly. When my brother gets pissy, he shuts down. Keeps it all to himself, he does, 'til he explodes."

"I can't picture Ciaran exploding. He's too, I don't know . . . too *Jane Austen* for that."

"Give him time. He can cause a scene that would make Ms. Austen roll over in her grave," Ronan said knowingly. "Now, enough about him. Where are you taking me on our first date?"

"I like the sound of that," Michael said. "Our first date."

Ronan reached up to hold the top of the doorjamb and leaned into Michael, his biceps bulging a bit more underneath the soft material of his sweater. "Then I'll say it again," he said, his lips barely touching Michael's. "Where are you taking me on our first date?"

Ronan had the ability to scare and exhilarate Michael at the same time, but Michael wanted to stand his ground in Ronan's presence, so oddly it helped him find his own courage. When Michael spoke, he didn't pull his lips away but let them rest on Ronan's. "You'll have to follow me to find out."

When they got to The Forest of No Return near where Ronan had found Michael a few days earlier, Michael stopped. "Here."

"Here?" Ronan asked, intrigued, but concerned.

Michael knelt down and began to unzip his backpack. "The weather's a bit like what we Ameri-*cans* call Indian summer, so I thought it might be fun to have a moonlight picnic before it gets too cold to do much of anything outside." So Michael was a romantic, Ronan thought. "You don't think it's stupid, do you?"

"Not at all; it's sweet."

"I was actually going for sophisticated, but I'll take sweet." Michael pulled out a bedsheet that would double as their tablecloth. "Don't worry, I washed it first." Ronan grabbed the other side of the sheet and together they laid it out on the grass. Next Michael pulled out two napkins that he had swiped from St. Martha's, some glasses, and a bottle of grape soda. "I couldn't find any grape juice—you know, underage wine—so I thought this would be the next best thing."

"You've thought of everything, haven't you?"

"Well, if cheese, crackers, and some grapes are everything, then yes, I have," Michael said, feeling silly and, yes, sophisticated at the same time. "Bon appétit."

Kneeling on the bedsheet across from Michael, Ronan realized that there was no turning back now; he was entering into a relationship with Michael. It was the start of something that could very well be, hopefully be, the most important relationship of his life. It could also be the most dangerous and destructive. So many nights he dreamed, he prayed, that his life would change, that he wouldn't feel so isolated and here, kneeling in front of this boy, under the moon's glow, he realized that his prayers had been answered. He felt the strength of The Well course through his veins and knew that, despite his misgivings, The Well was giving him its blessing. It was just the encouragement Ronan needed so he could relax and enjoy Michael's company.

Michael was enjoying himself so much, he didn't even notice that Ronan wasn't eating or drinking. Of course his limited human vision wasn't able to see Ronan's sleight-of-hand tricks as he spilled soda behind his back or tossed the food into The Forest; his eyes didn't pick up such quick movements. Down deep, Michael might suspect that something odd was happening, but without any proof, his suspicions would remain unvoiced. His emotions, however, were a different story.

"No, I didn't have the best childhood," Michael admitted. "Never felt comfortable in Weeping Water."

"I'm sorry to hear that. Mine was just the opposite. I was too comfortable growing up on the island."

"How so?"

Ronan rolled a grape between his fingers. "Never really wanted to leave."

"Must be nice to come from a place you love so much you don't ever want to leave."

"That's a better way of looking at it." When Michael's eyes blinked, Ronan tossed the grape to the side, and a second later it was carried away in a robin's beak. "So what made you so uncomfortable back home?"

"Me," Michael replied. "Didn't like who I was, who I am, so of course I hated everything around me." Michael took another sip of soda and was happy he could speak so openly about himself to Ronan. "It's hard growing up gay in the Midwest. Since I've come here, though, I don't know, I feel differently. Things are a bit easier here."

Ronan knew more than Michael thought, about growing up as a minority, an outsider. "Homosexuality isn't such . . . a scarlet letter."

"Or a love that dares not speak its name."

"Quoting Mr. Wilde now, are you?"

"Well, that one's pretty famous," Michael said. "Even on our side of the pond."

Suddenly, Ronan felt the need to speak without using any words. He reached over and took Michael's glass

out of his hands, placing it on the ground. He brushed
his fingers through Michael's hair and then let his
knuckles caress his cheek; he could tell Michael's mouth
wanted to form words, so he pressed his thumb against
his lips to silence him. Then he gently, but firmly,
pushed him back onto the ground and looked down
into his lovely face. Yes, Ronan reminded himself, there
was no turning back.

Ronan lowered his head and Michael felt his heart
pound and when Ronan stopped half an inch from his
mouth he thought his heart would burst. With one hand
playing with the soft strands of Michael's hair and the
other pressed against his chest, Ronan kissed Michael
softly on the lips. Michael's hand found Ronan's and
their fingers intertwined, rough on soft, just the way
Michael liked it. With his other hand, he found Ronan's
neck, strong and muscular, and took the liberty of em-
bracing it before feeling his back, his shoulders, and
then his waist.

Although their kissing intensified, the tips of their
tongues, curiously, hesitantly, meeting each other, exploring new territory, neither boy had any intention of
getting more intimate. They mutually understood that
they wanted to take things slowly, especially Michael,
who was the less experienced of the two. He wanted to
awaken his body slowly, move to the next level when it
was ready, and not be rushed into anything prematurely.
Instinctively, he knew Ronan would let him take his
time and for that he was thankful.

"This is a perfect first date," Michael whispered, then

added with a laugh, "Not that I have any experience to make a comparison."

Ronan leaned on his side, his head resting in the palm of his hand, his other hand resting on Michael's chest. "I'm not going to lie to you, Michael; I have been on a few first dates before, but this is by far the best."

"You're not just saying that to make me feel good?"

"No," Ronan replied. "I won't ever lie to you."

Something about the seriousness in Ronan's eyes ignited Michael's curiosity and he felt the need to embrace him. Michael sensed that for all of Ronan's muscles and strength and power, he was quite vulnerable. He didn't know what made him that way. It could be nothing; it could be something very traumatic from his past. Regardless, he understood his need to be comforted. So that's what he did.

He leaned forward, pushing Ronan onto the ground, and kissed him deeply. He didn't have the skills yet, but he tried to convey with his kiss that he would always be there for Ronan, always be ready to comfort him when he was saddened, ready to listen when he needed to talk. Michael was successful. Ronan understood what the kiss meant and for the third time today he was grateful. A marvelous feeding, being named captain of the swim team, a beautiful first date. It was a perfect day.

Until he got home to find his mother waiting for him.

"Hello, son," Edwige said. "Why don't you sit down and tell me all about your new boyfriend?"

chapter 14

Edwige Glynn-Rowley was nothing like her son. She wasn't honest, thoughtful, conflicted, or forgiving. Yes, she was a vampire, so they did share the gift of immortality, but other than that, they had little in common. Like the knack for showing up at the most unexpected times.

"Mother?" Ronan said, quickly closing the door behind him. "What are you doing here?"

Edwige stretched her legs and propped her feet up on Ronan's bed, the long, thin heels of her black pumps scrunching up the bedspread a bit. She was sitting at his desk, her arms resting on the sides of the captain's chair, her head leaning against its curved back. She was so pe-tite and the chair so substantial that she looked like a student taking a break from studying. If anyone had seen her, they would have mistaken her for Ronan's girl-friend unless, of course, they knew Ronan, and then they would realize that it was very unlikely that Ronan would ever have a girlfriend. He did, unfortunately, have a mother who was very involved in his life.

"So tell me all about Michael," Edwige said, raising her hand absentmindedly to caress the smooth collar of her pink silk blouse.

The bad feeling Ronan felt earlier in the pit of his stomach once again returned. "How do you know his name?"

Edwige crossed her ankles and smiled. She was about to use her index finger to push some strands of hair be-hind her ear, a sultry gesture she liked to use on any man, but realized at the last moment that just this morning she had her long, straight black hair cut into a short pixie. "And since when are you a blonde?" Ronan asked.

"Doesn't it look so natural?" she asked. Instead of pushing her hair back, Edwige brushed it forward with her nails. "I woke up this morning and realized I had never been a blonde, so I made an appointment with Marcel. He's a genius when it comes to these things. He said if I wanted to dye my hair, I had to go for a whole new look, and you know how I love to experiment. Do you like it?"

Regardless of what Ronan truly felt, he knew from experience there was only one answer to give. "It looks great."

Edwige smiled approvingly. "It truly does, doesn't it?" And it did. It actually suited her much better than long hair since her body was less about curves and more about confidence. She knew she was a woman; she didn't need traditional feminine characteristics to enhance her beauty. Her allure came from within. Such a boyish haircut on another woman would look harsh, androgynous; on Edwige it made her look sexier than ever. And against her skin, which was as pale and unlined as Ronan's, her blond hair made her look tantalizingly fragile. It was a look that would cause most men to want to protect and ravish her, but Ronan saw past the new color and style and into his mother's eyes. They were as manipulative as ever.

"I said, how do you know Michael's name?" Ronan asked, trying not to sound as unsettled as he was.

Edwige stared at her son. *He looks like such a man,* she thought, *but still he's a little boy.* "I'm your mother, Ronan; it's my job to know these things." In one quick movement she sat up in the chair, swung her legs off the bed, and crossed them, her burgundy leather skirt traveling away from her knees and toward her thighs. If she was going to interrogate, she might as well look like an interrogator. "He's quite beautiful," she commented. "He and I have a very similar bone structure. Have you noticed?"

Ronan smoothed out the bedspread, not caring the slightest if it was rumpled or not; he simply needed a moment to reclaim his strength since his mother had the skill, and quite possibly the desire, to steal it from him. When he sat at the foot of the bed, he was a bit more in control. "No, Mother, the comparison escapes me."

"Really?" She made a small circular motion with her foot as if the pointed toe of her shoe were tracing something round in the air. "Because we have the same high cheekbones. Mine are bit more delicate, of course, but his, his are quite remarkable. And of course we're both blondes."

"But he doesn't need to rely on Marcel's genius for a touch-up when his roots start to show." That made Ronan feel good. It wasn't every day he was able to make his mother wince simply by choosing the right words.

Folding her hands in her lap, Edwige changed the subject. "This flaxen mortal is not your usual type. Why the drastic change?"

Now she sounded snippy, almost childish. Ronan was finally starting to feel more comfortable in his mother's presence, which was quite an accomplishment. Sometimes he could be with her for an entire weekend and never once feel at ease, relaxed. He assumed it must be the aftereffects of having such a wonderful day. Whatever the reason, he decided to go with it. He propped up his pillows against the headboard and leaned into them, then he folded his hands, mimicking his mother's pose, before finally speaking. "Haven't you read the school rule book? Parents are allowed on campus only during previously scheduled academy-approved events."

Edwige glowered at her son; she detested obstinacy. "You know I don't share your obsession for literature." It was worse than that, actually; Edwige hated to read. The only exception being her financial statements, which had grown monthly ever since she inherited a fortune from a spinster aunt years ago after convincing her with a lie that she loved her more than her own mother. Her aunt, unmarried and childless, was grateful that one other person on the planet held her in the highest regard and, when she died, left Edwige her entire estate. Financially savvy, Edwige took the money, invested wisely, and attained a state of independent wealth most single mothers could only dream of. Then again, Edwige was hardly like most single mothers.

"This Michael looks nothing like your other boyfriends," Edwige said curtly. "I'm not saying I disapprove. I think the two of you make an attractive couple, but I would like to know how he's drawn you out of your comfort zone."

"I guess I'm just like you," Ronan said with a smirk. "I woke up one morning and realized I never had a blond."

Sometimes a mother has to allow her son some freedom; sometimes she has to allow him to feel that he is winning an argument. Or wandering this earth independently without familial obligation. Edwige did not feel that this was one of those times. "The Well needs fresh blood, Ronan," Edwige reminded her son. "You must take him."

His mother's words slammed into his ears and echoed loudly. *This is all she wants,* Ronan thought. *She doesn't care about my feelings; she doesn't want to know how wonderful Michael makes me feel. Sure, I can have his flesh as long as The Well has his blood.* "I can't," Ronan replied.

"You mean you won't," his mother corrected.

Abruptly Ronan jumped off the bed and flung open the door of his closet, his sudden and random action hardly surprising Edwige, who always found her son to be predictable. *He's a vampire,* she thought lovingly, *but he is a teenager.* "No, I mean I can't," Ronan shouted. Then he added quietly, "Not yet anyway."

Good, he understands; he isn't a complete imbecile. "I didn't mean take him *tonight,*" Edwige said in a soft, motherly tone she had heard other women use, "but soon." She watched her son pace the room, his strides choppy, like a caged animal, like his father, and her mind was filled with unwanted memories. "He does love you, you know."

Ronan stopped moving. "What?"

"I saw it in your face the moment you opened the door. I've only seen you look like that once before, and you know how *he* made you feel."

A spark of pain started to grow within Ronan, moving quickly until it erupted. "I told you never to talk about him!"

Edwige wasn't sure how much more of this tedious

conversation she could take. "You told me never to speak his name aloud," she corrected. "I had to swear on a Bible, of all the most ludicrous things, and I haven't mentioned his name, not once. But the fact remains that he loved you and so does this Michael." Edwige paused just long enough for her words to form meaning in Ronan's brain. "I daresay that Michael loves you even more."

Ronan may have been angry, but his mother was clever. He had no idea that she was saying exactly what she knew he wanted to hear. "Do you really think so?"

Although she was tired and her feet hurt from wearing heels all day, Edwige knew she had to get up to play her role most effectively. She walked over to her son and looked up into his eyes. She forgot to prepare herself and for a moment she became speechless as she was reminded of how beautiful his father was. She hated recalling such details; they were useless to her now. *He's even wearing his hair like him,* Edwige realized. *Must be to impress his new beau.* She reached up to touch his cheek and felt the stubble of his beard. *My boy really is a man,* she thought. "Darling, I say this with absolute certainty. Michael will be the greatest love of your life." She took a step back and held his hands in hers. "And that's why you must offer his blood to The Well."

Ronan looked at Edwige and it was one of those rare moments that he didn't see a manipulative creature or a spiteful woman, but only his mother. "I don't know if I can do that to him," Ronan pleaded. "I don't know if it's what he wants."

"It's what the universe wants," Edwige replied. "It's what The Well wants, so everything else is secondary." Unable to hold her son's gaze any longer, Edwige walked to the other side of the room to gather her jacket and purse. "I don't think I have to remind you that without The Well, we are nothing, and The Well is nothing if we don't continue to replenish it with fresh blood." She looked at herself in the mirror and loved how the bolero jacket, a burgundy, white, and black tweed trimmed in leather the same color as her skirt, gave the illusion that her shoulders were wider than they were. A smart purchase, she told herself, very smart. Then she turned to her son and made one more comment. "Blood bound by love."

His mother may have changed her appearance, but she hadn't changed her tactics. She spoke directly and she spoke the truth and that was one of the reasons that, despite all of her many faults, Ronan continued to love her. "It's what makes us special, isn't it?" he asked.

And although her son looked like a man, he was still her child, a child who desperately clung to sentiment and idealism, which is why, despite all of her many shortcomings, she would always love him. "Yes, it's what makes us special."

She opened her purse and found her lipstick, a new shade of frosted pink that Marcel had demanded she buy, and faced the mirror to apply a fresh coat. *Yes, that man truly is a genius.* She tossed the lipstick back into her purse, snapped it shut, then faced her son. "But remember it's what also makes us vulnerable. So do the

right thing and turn Michael into one of us before someone else beats you to it." An air kiss to each side of
Ronan's cheeks. "Maybe tomorrow when you all go on
your little school trip into town."

She couldn't be serious. "No, that's impossible."

"Eden is filled with narrow, cobblestone streets that
lead to dark alleyways, perfect for a lovers' rendez-
vous."

Without warning, an image popped into Ronan's
mind. He was pressing Michael against the cold stone of
some abandoned building, kissing him deeply in the
shadow of the alley, his body pushing into him, his passion growing, his fangs piercing Michael's hot flesh.
"Mother!" Ronan shouted, stopping Edwige on the
other side of the door. "Why don't you visit Ciaran before you leave? I know he'd love to see you." Ronan
had no idea why he suggested that. The words tumbled
out of his mouth without any thought. Guess it was better than saying what was really on his mind. But one
look at the way his mother's body tensed and he knew
his suggestion would be ignored.

Nervously, Edwige patted her purse against her leg,
never once losing her smile. "How sweet of you to think
of that one." She grabbed her purse with her other hand
and jammed it into her armpit. "But no, I'd rather not."
Ronan could only see the top of her blond short-cropped
hair as she descended the stairs, but he could hear her
final comment. "Remember to do as I say."

For several minutes after he closed the door, Ronan
was paralyzed, still under his mother's control. He leaned

his head against the door, unable to move. He was filled with so much anger that he wanted to ransack his room, he wanted to rip the doors off their hinges, he wanted to take his bed and fling it through the window, but he couldn't find the strength.

When the anger subsided, he was filled with so much sadness, for himself, for Michael, and even for Ciaran, that all he wanted to do was cry, crumble to the floor and sob. But he didn't have the will to do that, either. Edwige took with her all his strength and left him a little child filled with so many strong emotions, but without the ability to express them. She left him just the same way she was. Like mother, like son.

chapter 15

The only thing that got Ronan through the night was thinking about tomorrow. That he would spend the day with Michael and at the end of the day, they would have a shared memory. When he woke up, his mother's instructions were not forgotten, but her hold over him had lifted slightly. And, luckily, by the time he got off the train with Michael, Ciaran, and Fritz and stood before the Apple Tree, the towering bronze sculpture that marked the official entrance to the town of Eden, other people's statements occupied his mind.

"I hope Eve was hot," Fritz announced.

"What?" the three other boys responded in unison.

"She was a dumb bird, you know, eating the apple

and all," Fritz explained. When the three boys continued to stare at him with bemused expressions, he continued speaking in a louder tone. "Creating original sin? Plunging humanity into a world of darkness and conflict for all eternity? She was a right swab and you all know it. I'm just saying I hope she was hot so she could make up for it."

"You know, that's a really insightful analysis," Ciaran said.

"I know," Fritz agreed, not hearing the sarcasm. "I do pay attention in theology, even though Joubert can be a right bore most of the time."

"Well, the next time he prattles on about Genesis," Ciaran said, "I think you should share your thoughts about Eve with the class."

"You think so?" Fritz asked.

"Definitely," Ciaran replied. "But it would be helpful if you brought in some visual aids or maybe a Power-Point presentation to show how you really envision Eve. Is she curvy? Does she have a nice arse? Big knockers!"

Finally, Fritz figured out Ciaran was ragging on him. "All right, wrap it up, Eaves!" Ciaran had wrapped it up, but he couldn't stop laughing and neither could Ronan and Michael. "And that's enough out of you two!"

"Don't look at me," Michael said. "I don't know nothing about no knockers." After this comment, the three boys laughed so hard they couldn't walk. Even Fritz, forgetting how the laughter began, joined in. "You know something, Nebraska?" Fritz said. "Sometimes you're not all that bad."

Ronan leaned into Michael and whispered so close to his ear that Michael shivered from the sensation of his hot breath. "I can't wait to find out just how bad Nebraska can be."

As they continued into the town itself, Michael and Ronan fell back and walked behind Fritz and Ciaran. The temperature had already dipped a few degrees from the other day and it no longer felt like Indian summer; the sky was cloudless and a lovely shade of blue, but it was definitely autumn. A few leaves floated to the ground; occasionally a chilly wind wrapped around their faces, bringing with it the smell of a fireplace burning somewhere in the distance. It was a perfect day for an excursion, crisp, with just the right amount of sunshine.

Michael pretended to be busy looking at the landscape but was actually working up the courage to ask Ronan to be his date to the Archangel Festival next week, so busy pretending that he didn't feel Ronan's fingers until they were entwined with his. He felt his heart beat faster once the realization set in that he was walking down the street in broad daylight holding another boy's hand. It was something he wouldn't dare dream of doing back in Weeping Water; he couldn't believe he was doing it here in Eden. The simple act was so revolutionary to him that he couldn't speak, he couldn't even look at Ronan; he just stared straight ahead, all thoughts of the festival gone, and he barely had the strength to walk. Until they turned a corner and bumped into Penry, Imogene, and Phaedra. Then he quickly let go of

Ronan's hand. In the next instant he turned to face his boyfriend and whispered, "I'm sorry."

"Don't be," Ronan answered back. He wanted to tell Michael that he understood and that they had time for all of that, but he was drowned out by Penry. "Hey, mates! I thought it was just going to be me and the ladies."

"We had to take a later train," Ciaran said. "Fritz changed three times."

"I thought you were late 'cause you forgot your bloody wallet," Ronan said.

"Well, yes," Fritz replied. "I had it in the first pair of pants I put on, but they were a bit wrinkled."

That was odd, Michael thought, Fritz not making a rude comeback.

"I think you made an excellent choice," Phaedra noted. "They look great with your sweater."

Fritz beamed. "Thank you."

Thank you? Everyone's head snapped to look at the uncharacteristically polite Fritz. "It was a birthday present from my mum. I told her I thought I needed some more classic pieces for my wardrobe."

"Well, it's not every guy who can wear yellow and make it work," Phaedra said. "Kudos to both you and your mum."

"Thank you," Fritz said once again. "I'll make sure I tell her when I ring her up later tonight."

Michael looked at Ronan, who looked at Ciaran, who would have looked at Penry except Fritz's statement had sent him into such a state of shock that he couldn't even move his head. It was a well-known fact that Fritz never called his mother. She went so far as to berate him about it in the middle of St. Martha's during the last Parents Day Brunch. Michael didn't know that, but it didn't take a psychic to figure out that Fritz had a crush on Phaedra and was trying to appear reserved and well-mannered to make a good impression. A wise move, Michael thought, but one he hoped wouldn't last too long. He was actually starting to find Fritz's obnoxious behavior a lot less obnoxious and much more palatable.

Fritz made his next move when the group started to walk down Paradise Road, the not-so-subtle name for Eden's main avenue. He brushed past Ciaran and quite smoothly squeezed his way in between Imogene and Phaedra. When Ciaran fell back a few steps, he found himself between Michael and Ronan and, feeling awkward, immediately tried to navigate himself onto the other side of Michael. Before he could get all the way over, Ronan put his hand on his brother's shoulder and said, "You're fine right where you are." Ciaran assumed the gracious comment was meant to impress Michael, but he latched on to it anyway.

Penry, overhearing some of what Ronan said, turned around, not letting go of Imogene's hand of course, and said, "I'm fine too, but yesterday my eyes were so sensitive to the light I felt like Nakano! Thought I was going to have to wear sunglasses today. Isn't that weird?"

Once again Ciaran was speechless, so Ronan spoke. "You're a weird bloke, Penry. What do you expect?"

"That's what I told him," Imogene said, tossing her head around. "I said, 'Pens, you're a right sod weirdo.' "

Penry didn't even hear the jeer, just his nickname, and when Imogene twisted her head back to the front, he informed his friends, "She calls me Pens."

Ciaran forced a smile and when Penry turned back around, he glanced at Ronan. Ronan, however, aware of Michael's presence, didn't acknowledge Ciaran or the fact that Penry had suffered an aftereffect from Nakano's attack that he hadn't anticipated. He took a deep breath, hoping the others would think he was breathing in the country air and not recognize it as a worried sigh, and wondered just what else he had ignored.

The one person he couldn't ignore was Michael. Across the street from the Eden Arms hotel was a small English garden that was still lush despite the lack of colorful flowers that usually filled the ground during the spring and summer months. This time of year the garden was more a cavalcade of greens and browns, not as vibrant but still robust. Ronan and Michael sat together on a bench, and Ronan couldn't decide which was more beautiful, his boyfriend's sweet grin or the majestic weeping willow that was the centerpiece of the garden. Its trunk, surrounded by a pile of fallen leaves, thrust upward about three stories and then exploded into a spray of curved branches that created a domelike effect.

As if he were reading Ronan's mind, Michael looked up and could see slithers of blue peek through the willow's makeshift ceiling. He felt like he was looking at a piece of heaven.

"Catching up on Oscar?" Ronan asked, holding a brand-new copy of *The Picture of Dorian Gray.*

Instinctively, Michael patted the now-empty pocket of his jacket from where the book must have fallen. "You got me." A bit embarrassed that Ronan found out he was reading his favorite novel, Michael looked away and swallowed a mouthful of hot cider until he could think of an excuse. The liquid filled his throat with warmth and the courage to just be honest. "Can you believe I've never read it?"

Ronan examined the cover. A beautiful young man with haunting green eyes stared out at him, and behind the man a portrait of his inner self, decayed and grotesque. Ronan shivered, not because of the chilly air, and leafed through the book as if looking for a specific passage, stopping only when he came to the piece of paper Michael was using as a bookmark. It was Ronan's drawing. "You know," Michael said, "maybe if we put that portrait in the attic I can stay forever youthful?"

I can make you stay forever youthful and beautiful and happy if you just let me. Ronan heard the words so clearly in his head he wasn't sure if he had spoken them aloud. "It could happen?"

Michael's face turned serious. "You're forgetting one thing."

"What?"

"I don't have an attic." Ronan didn't laugh along with Michael right away, but Michael found his comment so funny, he didn't notice. "Hey, maybe there's an attic in the cathedral; we can put my portrait up there! I can be forever youthful *and* holy at the same time." If Michael knew that Ciaran was watching him from across the garden, he probably wouldn't have let his hand linger so long on Ronan's knee when he gave it a little squeeze. But at the moment, he felt like he and Ronan were the only two people in the world. Ronan felt the same way, which was why he was able to push the conversation into more serious territory.

"You laugh, but if the soul is immortal, why not the body?"

But Michael was having too good a time with his boyfriend to be coaxed into having a provocative conversation. "Because if the body were immortal and eternally youthful, there would be no need to ever get a facial, and I'm kind of looking forward to having one when I'm a middle-aged gay man." Michael's silliness was infectious and Ronan found himself chuckling despite the serious thoughts that were embedded in his mind. "So please, Ronan, don't take that dream away from me."

"They really are adorable, aren't they?" Imogene observed.

Penry turned to see who his girlfriend was talking about. "It's nice to see Ronan happy again. He was miserable after that row with Nakano."

Imogene put a spoonful of whipped cream into her

mouth, the crowning glory of her coffee concoction. "I think Michael's perfect for him. When you're the strong, silent type like Ronan, you need a boyfriend who's more gregarious, bit more of an extrovert. Plus, Michael's a lot cuter than Nakano, don't you think, Ciaran?"

Startled because he was only half listening, Ciaran wasn't sure what Imogene was rambling on about. "What?"

"Oh, don't be like that," she chastised. "You don't have to be gay to notice if a bloke's handsome or not, right, Pens?"

Penry shrugged his shoulders. "He's a good-looking chap, I guess. Not as handsome as me, but then again, who is?" Ciaran welcomed the opportunity to laugh, anything to hide how he was truly feeling at the moment. Here he was sitting among his friends and yet he felt very much alone. Imogene and Pens were so smitten with each other, there were moments when Ciaran felt like he had crashed their own private party. A few feet away, Fritz and Phaedra were sharing a bench and that all-important first conversation that was magical because it was filled with both awkwardness and awe. And across from him Ronan and Michael were giggling and talking and touching. He heard a rustling in the trees and looked up to see a bird bouncing from branch to branch as if it were lost and was trying to find its way. *I know just how you feel,* Ciaran silently remarked.

"Imogene," Phaedra called out. "You promised to

help me pick out a dress for the festival when I reached my goal weight."

"Okay, but, um, don't you have five more pounds to go?" Imogene teased.

Feigning outrage while everyone around her laughed, Phaedra tried to keep a straight face. "I am three pounds away! Now come on. I'll buy you something with my mother's credit card."

"Perfect! I wanted to get elbow-length gloves but ran out of money," Imogene replied, then instructed, "Boys, we'll catch up with you in an hour in front of the Apple Tree."

"Sir! Yes, sir!" Penry replied, signing off as if she were a four-star general and he a common private.

"You'll pay for that later, Pens," Imogene shouted as she grabbed Phaedra's arm and the two sauntered off toward the few gift shops that populated Eden.

"I'm counting on it," Penry mumbled to himself.

"And you promised to help me buy some lab supplies at that old apothecary store." At first Ciaran didn't realize Ronan was talking to him. "I have to buy a flow-meter test tube and you're the only person who knows what that is, so come on."

Ciaran heard some chirping and looked up to see that the bird was now settled and sharing a branch with another, more vividly colored bird. "How can I deny my expertise to someone in need?" He looked away before he could see that they flew off in different directions.

"Thank you," Ronan said, and then mouthed the same words to Michael, who nodded and smiled, both unaware that Ciaran witnessed the exchange. Ciaran realized his earlier assumption that Ronan's words were merely meant to impress Michael were true. His hurt only deepened when they were out of earshot from the others and Ronan whispered to him, "And let your big brother buy you some lunch. Lord knows I don't spend any quid on food." His kindness was just a game.

Michael smiled, watching them turn the corner. As much as he enjoyed Ronan's company, he could let him hang out with his brother for an hour. It wasn't like anything exciting was going to happen while they were apart.

"Hawksbry's a poof!" Fritz shouted, pointing down the narrow alley that separated the coffee shop and an antique store that, despite the OPEN FOR BUSINESS sign in its front window, was pitch black inside.

"What are you talking about?" Penry asked. Then he saw. "Oh my God!" It was indeed the headmaster, Alistair Hawksbry, walking down the alleyway arm in arm with another man.

"I knew it!" Fritz declared. "I always knew it! Hawksbry's a homo." Then Fritz remembered he was standing next to Michael. "No offense, mate, but he's always so neat and tidy. It's just not right." *So much for a kinder, gentler Fritz,* Michael thought. "Come on."

Fritz ran across the street toward the alley, and Penry and Michael followed like Pavlovian dogs. They didn't think about what they were doing; they just knew they had to do it. Luckily, they were all wearing sneakers, so they didn't make too much noise on the cobblestones, but if either Hawksbry or his companion turned around, the three of them would have been seen. There was simply nowhere to hide. Halfway down the alley, Michael realized that if the man with his arm wrapped around Hawksbry's waist did turn around, he wouldn't just be seen, he'd be recognized. "That guy's my father's driver," Michael whispered.

"You *and* your father's driver are both gay?" Fritz asked.

"What's that supposed to mean?" Michael asked.

"Nothing," Fritz said. "But you gotta admit, it is a little queer, you know, two gays in one family."

"He's not part of my family!"

"Mates!" Penry interrupted. "Looks like our boys have disappeared."

They all turned to look down the alleyway and saw that Penry was right; it was empty. "Where'd they go?" Fritz asked rhetorically and then started walking down the cobbled path. When they walked a bit farther, they realized the alley led to a dead end. Fritz was astounded. "The poofs just poofed into thin air."

"Or they're on the other side of this door," Michael suggested.

Fritz couldn't be blamed too harshly for missing the door; it was made to blend into the surrounding wall. The only clues that there was a door in the stone wall were a small metal horizontal plate that looked as if it could only be opened from the inside, and two feet below and a few inches to the right was a keyhole without any kind of doorknob. "Bet it's one of those secret gay bars," Fritz surmised.

"In Eden?" Penry asked. "I can't imagine that kind of bar here, you know, in the middle of nowhere."

"Nebraska, what's the code to get in?"

Michael was dumbfounded. First, the headmaster and his father's driver were a couple; second, there was a secret gay bar in an alleyway in this little country town; and third, Fritz thought he knew some secret code that would get them inside. "Fritz, you've lost your mind. I don't know any code."

"I do," Penry announced, and proceeded to knock on the door.

"Have you lost your mind too?" Michael asked. "What if somebody answers?"

What was Michael talking about? Penry thought. "That's the whole point."

When the metal plate slid open, both Michael and Fritz jumped back. Penry was the only one who appeared calm and stood his ground. But once he realized the man behind the door was wearing sunglasses, he became excited and forgot that he was going to ask if they could enter. "Blimey! Is the sun bothering your eyes too? Just yesterday I felt the same way." Penry turned to his friends to ask, "Could something be going around?" By the time he turned back, the metal plate was back in its original position, closed. Immediately, Penry knocked on the door again. "Hey, mister, do you mind letting us in?"

"Do you mind if we got out of here?" Michael asked. "Gay, straight, or whatever, I don't think this is the kind of place for us."

"I'm with Nebraska," Fritz said. "Let's go!"

As they dragged a reluctant Penry away from the door and back to the main street, they had no idea that the people on the other side of the door were as nervous and agitated as they were. "Are you an absolute idiot?! You're not supposed to open the door unless you hear the password!" Brania waited a moment and then slapped the man so hard across his face, his sunglasses were knocked off. "That could've been one of them and not just a bunch of stupid kids from the academy."

Alistair stirred in his chair. "The academy?" When he spoke, his lips barely moved and his eyes remained shut. When Jeremiah pushed his shoulder to remind him to keep quiet, he almost tumbled to the floor, but swayed back at the last second, his head falling backward. If Michael and the others gained entry into the room or saw their headmaster's face outside, they would have been startled, frightened even. Once healthy-looking, vigorous, he now appeared ashen and gray, his skin colored only by the black circles beneath his eyes. The cleft on the left side of his chin was now so pronounced it looked like a groove, a deep etching. He was alive, but only barely.

"Careful, Jeremiah," Brania chided. "Or I'll take back your gift."

Vaughan's driver turned to face the voluptuous girl

who looked so incredibly out of place in such dreary surroundings. "My gift?"

"As a thank-you for handling the situation with Alistair so well." Done with the club's bodyguard, Brania walked over to Jeremiah, her heels clicking loudly on the cement floor and echoing throughout the windowless, tomblike room. "I left it in your apartment upstairs. It's a marble planter filled with the most extraordinary white roses."

"Flowers?" Jeremiah asked, his puzzlement understandable. Even before he became a vampire, Jeremiah was not the kind of man who would receive flowers as a gift.

Brania detested ingrates, but since the gift was from her father and not her, she didn't have the power to take it back. All she could do was gather her patience and explain its worth. "Not flowers, white roses. Keep them watered and protected and they will thrive and bring you nothing but joy."

Jeremiah still didn't understand why Brania was giving him flowers, but he was grateful that someone of her stature felt compelled to give him a gift. "Thank you, Brania, really."

Turning on Jeremiah to address the bodyguard one last time, Brania said, "And I'll thank you to wear your contacts from now on. Do I have to remind everyone that we are trying to blend in?" Suddenly disgusted to be among such fools, Brania decided it was time for her to go. Thanks to the bodyguard's carelessness, she would have to take the long way; she couldn't risk being seen by people who might recognize her. Before she opened the trapdoor that led to an underground passageway, she reminded Jeremiah of his final instructions. "Help him with his feeding and then bring him home. It's time he got back to work."

Jeremiah nodded dutifully and then said, "Thanks again."

But Brania didn't hear him; she was already underground.

At the top of the stairs, Michael watched Ronan leave, his kiss still moist on his lips. What an eventful day. Even though their hand holding was cut short, it was another step in the right direction, a step forward toward the man Michael longed to become and away from the child he was. And then finding out that Alistair and Jeremiah were a couple. That was a shock. The group was split on whether they actually believed it, but Michael did. There was something distrustful about Jeremiah that led Michael to believe he was hiding something; his sexual preference could easily be that something, but Ronan wasn't too sure. "Not everything is always as it seems," he had said. Ciaran seemed to agree with him.

"You never really know what's going on inside a bloke's head," Ciaran remarked, already in his pajamas and sitting on his bed.

"It's not what we saw on the inside, but what was

going on outside," Michael explained. "My father's driver had his arm around Hawksbry's waist, for heaven's sake. They were, like, on a date or something."

Ciaran shrugged and flipped through some celebrity magazine. "I don't know. It's like Ronan. You look at him and think he's like us, but . . ." Ciaran flipped the pages faster and prayed Michael didn't pick up on what he just said, what just slipped past his lips.

"What do you mean 'not like us'?"

"Bloody hell, look how fat she is!" Ciaran turned the magazine so Michael could see a photograph of a once-svelte Hollywood starlet who now looked like she was in desperate need of a fat farm.

"Answer me, Ciaran," Michael demanded. "What do you mean Ronan's not like us?"

Sighing, Ciaran put down the magazine. *Think fast, mate, so it doesn't blow up in your face.* "We're the out-siders, you and I; we have to try and fit in. But Ronan's already at the center of everything. Yet when you look at him, all quiet, pensive, it can look as if he's the one stuck on the outside looking in." Ciaran went back to glancing at the pages of the magazine, hoping what he just said made some sort of sense.

"Do you even know your brother?"

By the incredulous tone of Michael's voice, he guessed that he wasn't buying his explanation. "Feel free to dis-agree with me."

Michael felt his cheeks redden and he couldn't con-trol the impulse to come to his boyfriend's defense. "Are you trying to say that he's acting? That he doesn't feel out of touch, like he doesn't belong? Because if you are, I have to say you really have no idea what you're talking about."

Even though Ciaran knew that he'd made up that story to cover a slip of the tongue and he was still angry with Ronan for his careless actions today, he still didn't like anyone accusing him of not understanding his brother. He understood Ronan better than anyone, at times probably even better than Ronan himself, so he found himself unjustifiably, but vehemently, defending his statement. "You might be his new boyfriend, Michael, but I'm Ronan's brother."

"Why are you so jealous of our relationship?" The words spat out of Michael's mouth so quickly, he couldn't stop them if he'd wanted to.

"I'm not jealous!"

Michael took a few steps closer to Ciaran's bed, his legs shaking slightly. "Yes, you are! You have been since the first night I told you I met him outside the cathedral."

He just couldn't keep his composure any longer, he just couldn't. Ciaran flung the magazine across the room and bounded right up to Michael, his legs quite steady. "I know you think you know everything and I know you're damned pleased with yourself! You swoop into a new school, snag yourself a boyfriend within days, make the bloody swim team! But I'm telling you, Michael, you don't know anything. Ronan is not like you and me! Go ahead and ask him yourself and see what he says!"

Unnerved by Ciaran's outburst, but refusing to back down, Michael shouted back, "Maybe I'll do just that! And then we'll see who Ronan chooses!" Needing to escape, Michael found himself racing down the steps, two at a time, Ciaran shouting something after him, something that he couldn't hear, possibly because his own voice was still screaming in his head.

"Go outside! See if I care!" Ciaran shouted from the top of the stairs. He ran back into his room, slamming the door behind him, but then remembered the promise he'd made to Ronan, to watch after Michael and help keep him safe. Cursing his inability to go back on his word to Ronan, he ran outside into the cold night air to rescue his brother's boyfriend, hoping he wasn't too late.

Just as he rounded past St. Jerome's, Michael thought he heard a cry, muffled, but definitely a cry. He stopped in his tracks and for the first time saw that it was quite dark tonight; the stars seemed to be hiding, the moonlight lost behind the clouds. He listened, but the only thing he could hear was his own breathing, growing more rapid by the second. He turned to head back home and heard the same sound again. This time there was no question, it was a cry. Someone or some thing was in trouble.

He started walking back toward St. Peter's, his body moving in a straight line, but his head frantically moving from side to side to try and take in the entire campus at once. Then he heard a twig snap from the weight of someone stepping on it; at least that's what it sounded like to him.

Slowly he turned around but didn't see anything, even though two people saw him.

Behind him was Ciaran, arms crossed, shaking a bit in his thin pajamas, and in front of him, hidden by the bulk of a dead deer, was Nakano. Unaware that Ciaran was a short distance away, Nakano made a split-second decision and decided to accept this offering from fate. He wiped the deer's blood from his mouth and started walking toward Michael. But Michael couldn't see him because in an instant he was covered by fog.

Not again, Nakano thought. *What the hell is going on?!* The fog moved quickly, encompassing Michael and the surrounding area and stopping only when it reached Nakano's feet. Enraged that once again, this fog, this barrier that had to be the result of some supernatural force, was blocking him, was getting in the way of his taking Michael, he lashed out, punching the fog with his fists. This time the fog was denser and Nakano's hands couldn't even penetrate the mist. He punched, but once they hit the gray smoke, his fist bounced back. It didn't hurt; it was like he was punching a soft, rubbery surface. No matter how many times he hit it, he couldn't pass through.

From where Ciaran was standing, he could see everything. He saw the fog appear out of nowhere, rise, and engulf Michael and then he saw Nakano repeatedly punch the fog, unable to pierce the smoke. None of it made sense, except that to Ciaran in a dark, twisted way, it made perfect sense. "What have you people done now?" he asked the cold night air. And then he simply turned and walked home. Most people who had witnessed something so strange, who knew that a vampire, disgruntled and violent, was only a few yards away, would run at full speed, silently praying that they would make it safely home, but not Ciaran. He wasn't afraid. He had his reasons that to some wouldn't make any sense, but at least he was able to walk back to his dorm without fear. Whatever would happen to Michael was out of his control. But no matter what happened, at least he knew he'd tried to protect him.

Jeremiah was of the same mind. He looked down at Alistair sprawled on the ground before the Archangel Academy gate and gave him a little kick to wake him up. He had done everything Brania had asked him to do and had earned his gift. He made sure Alistair fed, he brought him back home, he even got him cleaned up since the chap was starting to smell, but he drew the line at putting him to bed. He was a driver, not a man-servant. So before he drove off, he simply made sure that Alistair was standing. Whatever happened next was out of his control; he had done everything he could to get the man home safely.

His eyes flickered to adjust to the moonlight after staring into the strong headlights of the sedan. Alistair looked around and for the first time in days he felt safe. He was home. He didn't fully remember where he had been, but he was once again among things that felt familiar. Suddenly, the wind howled and blew through Alistair, carrying his scent into the air and to Nakano. The boy breathed in deeply and was uncertain at first, but then, yes, he recognized the smell. Giving up on trying to break through the fog and reach Michael, he turned and ran toward what he recognized.

When he reached the headmaster's cottage, he saw Alistair in the distance grab hold of the gate and pull it open. He then saw the electric current rip through his body, volt after volt of electricity pulsing through his skin, his body lighting up like a white-hot flame. But what surprised him even more was how gently Alistair closed the gate and continued walking toward his home. He was unhurt, completely unharmed by the burst of electricity that should have rendered him lifeless.

Nakano was in shock. "So they didn't kill you, they just turned you into one of us."

chapter 16

The thunderstorm took both boys by surprise.

When Michael left Professor McLaren's British literature class, the only clouds that spotted the sky were
large and white, hardly ominous-looking. But by the
time he passed St. Jerome's, they had turned dark gray,
the sky behind them murky, shadowy, and not the clear
blue it was just moments earlier. Before the first raindrop fell, thunder clapped from somewhere deep within
the sky to announce the arrival of a sudden storm. And
when Ronan grabbed Michael's arm and pulled him
under the awning behind St. Joshua's, they were both
soaking wet.

"Is everything in this place unexpected?" Michael asked.

"Only the good stuff," Ronan replied with a grin.

The stone canopy over the library's basement entrance was small, only a few feet wide, but large enough to give the boys shelter from the rain, and desolate, so it gave them privacy in the middle of a busy school day. Ronan ran his fingers through his hair, slicking back the loose strands so he looked like he just emerged from the pool. Drenched and alive.

A stream of rain slid down his nose, lingering at the tip to become a drop before falling and bursting onto Michael's lips. Ronan grabbed Michael's neck and felt the heat emanating from the boy despite the chill in the air and pressed his lips to his, not kissing him at first, just tasting the rain, but quickly the rain was forgotten and all Ronan knew was that he was quite unexpectedly alone with his boyfriend and he wanted to take full advantage of the moment.

His other hand found Michael's waist and pushed him closer to him. Michael closed his eyes and did what he did whenever he was this close to Ronan whether in real life or in a dream: He succumbed, he kissed Ronan back, amazed that each time he did, the sensation was the same, yet different. His lips were always full and soft, his body always strong and hard, but today his skin smelled like rain, deliciously cool rain. Michael pulled away, just for an instant, to kiss another drop of rain that had gathered at the tip of Ronan's nose, but Ronan wasn't done; he wanted more.

As the rain pounded all around them, pummeling the grass, bouncing off the stones over their heads, Ronan pushed Michael harder against the door and pressed himself into him. Michael groaned, but the sound was lost as Ronan, unable to control his passion, pushed his tongue into Michael's mouth. The boys kissed deeply and held on to each other, tightly, desperately, unsure where they were going, but unable to stop.

Hips and thighs rose and fell; heads changed position; Michael's hand explored the small of Ronan's back, pressing into it, and found the courage to move his fingers just a little bit lower. What wonderful freedom this was, to express himself, express the passion that burned deep within him and not keep it locked away, ignored, admonished. What a wonderful gift his mother's death brought him.

Michael froze. Why was he thinking of his mother at a time like this? Luckily, Ronan didn't question Michael's thoughts when his movements stopped; he understood passion had its boundaries, especially behind a library in the middle of the day during a rainstorm. "Sorry," Ronan gasped, "but this *is* all your fault, you know."

"My fault?" Michael questioned.

"You're even more handsome wet than you are dry."

Blushing, Michael tried to concentrate on the boy in front of him and not the woman in his mind, but for some reason it was proving difficult. His mother was gone, which was her decision, the way she wanted it. Why was Michael wasting time thinking about her now? He couldn't speak any further, so he embraced Ronan and rested his cheek against his shoulder, wondering if his mother chose to die so he could live. No, he didn't want to contemplate her motives; he wanted to lose himself in his boyfriend's strong arms. "This feels so good, Ronan, so natural."

"It is," Ronan whispered. "And don't let anyone ever make you believe differently."

Not even your mother. Michael shut his eyes tightly. *Stop thinking of her,* he commanded. After a second, he opened them and tried to focus on the long strands of black hair matted down on Ronan's chest, visible beneath his wet white shirt. He was just about to press his lips to them when the thunder roared so loudly he jumped in Ronan's arms. "Is somebody afraid of a little thunder?"

Smiling, but shivering, Michael replied, "No, but honestly, if I don't get inside, I think I might freeze to death."

Ronan's gym towel wrapped around his shoulders, Michael allowed the warmth of the fire to envelop him. The heat felt good and his shivers had subsided. He looked up and for an instant thought Brother Dahey's black eyes staring down at him from the portrait were filled with life, examining him, trying to determine if he was worthy of a place here at the academy. Worthy of such an elite education, such a privileged existence, such a welcomed awakening. *Yes, I am,* Michael thought.

But when he looked back up, the monk's eyes were black but lifeless. "Feeling better?" Ronan asked.

"Yeah, thanks," Michael said, noticing that Ronan had changed into a T-shirt. "You're all dry."

"Bit smelly, though," Ronan said. "I'm not sure how long this shirt's been in my knapsack."

Michael was going to protest, but then took a deep whiff and smelled a stale, musky odor. Not entirely offensive, but definitely not fresh. "I'd say at least a week."

Another wet student sat on the couch next to Michael to reap the benefits of the fireplace, forcing him to inch closer to Ronan. They both shared a conspiratorial grin as their thighs pressed together, their connection igniting almost as much heat as the flames from the fire. Michael looked up and again caught the monk staring at him. He laughed out loud at the thought of Brother Dahey being a witness to his and Ronan's budding romance.

"What's so funny?" Ronan asked.

Michael shook his head. "Nothing." But then he remembered something he had forgotten to share with his boyfriend. "Well, this isn't funny, not really, just weird. Last night I went out for a walk and got lost again." Ronan fought to hide his concern. "Not sure where I got to, but the next thing I knew I was back in front of my dorm." Michael rubbed his hands vigorously in front of the fire and raised his eyebrows. "Maybe you spiked my cider."

Ronan smiled but didn't think anything Michael had

just said was funny. "Why were you walking around last night?"

Looking away, Michael's impulse was to remain quiet, but he then reminded himself that secrets had no place between boyfriends. "I had a . . . well, I had a little fight with Ciaran and ran out. It was dumb, but I got mad and just left."

"What do you mean, a fight?"

"Oh, you know Ciaran," Michael said, patting his damp hair with the towel. "He said something, then I said something. You know how it can be with a roommate; I don't even know exactly . . ."

Ronan grabbed Michael's hand to make him stop. "What did he say?"

"Look, I shouldn't have said anything, I don't want to cause any trouble between you guys. It was nothing, really."

"It was enough to make you storm out."

Michael buried his face in the towel, breathing in Ronan's scent. He couldn't take back what he said, so he leaned in close to Ronan and whispered, "He said . . . you're not like us."

Luckily, a few more kids burst into the anteroom to escape the downpour that continued outside, and distracted Michael so he didn't see fury mask Ronan's face. His porcelain cheeks grew red; his lips clung to each other tightly. *What the hell was Ciaran thinking?* When Michael turned back around, Ronan had regained most of his composure. "Not sure why he'd say such a thing."

Taking a deep breath, Michael said what was on his

mind. "Do you think he could be jealous? I mean not of us, me and you; he's your brother and all. But just that we're together and maybe he's jealous that he doesn't have a boyfriend of his own."

If Ronan weren't so upset at the moment, he would have laughed out loud. "Ciaran isn't gay."

"What?!" Michael shouted so loudly, heads turned.

"My brother isn't gay, Michael, just very British."

Michael thought back to the first time he met Ciaran; he appeared so refined, so guarded. And what about his comment about girls? "If you go for that sort of thing." He thought of his look, his demeanor. "You're kidding me?"

"Trust me, I know my brother. He may not have a girlfriend, never had one really, but no, he's straight."

"Then why in the world would he tell me that you're not like us?"

Ronan knew; he just couldn't explain it. "My brother likes to fit in, to be accepted. Maybe he is a little jealous that I spend more time with you than with him." Ronan didn't know if he was making any sense, so he just kept talking. "He knows you're gay, probably did from the first moment he met you, and so he let you think he was the same and tried to get you to think I'm different." If there was logic in that statement, Michael didn't recognize it; all he heard was that Ronan thought that anyone who looked at him would immediately assume he was gay.

"Oh, so you're saying I can't even pass for a straight guy?"

Ronan smiled. "Michael, there is nothing wrong with appearing on the outside exactly what you are on the inside."

A log in the fireplace twisted and fell, causing the flames to stir and crackle loudly. Michael shrugged. "Unless of course you're Dorian."

Ronan stared into the fire, watching the embers burn, and it reminded him of things that Michael couldn't comprehend and things Ronan hoped Michael would never have to see. "You don't have to worry; your soul is far from black and burning."

There it was again, Michael thought, the melancholy, the sadness that sometimes took over Ronan's eyes. He wished he was back outside with Ronan underneath the tiny stone roof, so he could hold him in his arms and tell him that *he* would protect *him,* that he would help prevent those feelings of sorrow from ever returning. He couldn't do that, but he could make a small gesture. He placed his hand over Ronan's and let his fingers caress his briefly, hoping that his touch conveyed compassion. Michael couldn't tell because Ronan's eyes drifted back to the flames, orangey, red, and some a deep chestnut brown, the color they were just before they turned black and evaporated into smoke. The same exact color as Phaedra's hair.

"What are you doing here?" Michael asked when he noticed the girl standing next to him.

"I picked a fine day to search for a book," Phaedra replied, her normally curly hair plastered down against her face.

Michael handed her Ronan's towel. "Doesn't St. Anne's have its own library?"

Rubbing her head furiously, Phaedra's words shook a bit when she spoke. "Yes, but it's not as complete as yours." She explained that she was writing a paper on the Brontë sisters, and the library on St. Anne's campus didn't have a copy of *Agnes Grey*.

"Which one wrote that?" Michael asked.

"Anne," Ronan answered, staring at Phaedra.

"Impressive," she said, tossing the towel back to Michael and wiping away some remaining drops of water from beneath her eyes. "Not everyone knows there's a third sister."

"There were actually five sisters; two died of tuberculosis at boarding school," Ronan said. "And there was a brother too. Branwell."

"Branwell Brontë?" Michael said. "Sounds like a character from one of their novels."

"His first name was Patrick," Ronan explained. "But he was a bit of a dandy in his day and 'Patrick' lacks luster."

Michael was so happy that his boyfriend and this girl, whom he already considered a friend, had so much in common. He imagined that the three of them could spend hours chatting about the Brontë siblings, Oscar Wilde, and a ton of more unliterary topics. He never imagined that both Ronan and Phaedra were trying to hide their growing suspicions of each other behind innocuous conversation. "Maybe I should get you to help me with my paper. My lit professor wasn't too thrilled with my antifeminist take on Virginia Woolf."

Ronan leaned back, folding his arms against his chest. "I'm sure you're being modest."

Phaedra smiled as the fire roared behind her. "Yeah, just a little. You know us urban snobs; we're perfectionists."

"Well, I'm just a laid-back country boy," Michael joked. "I don't believe in trying too hard."

"Miss Antonides, I have your book," the librarian called out, interrupting them. "And an umbrella that you may borrow."

Phaedra bent forward, her damp hair hanging loose in the space between her and Michael. "Which is code for the girl intruder must now leave the premises." They all laughed, Michael much more than Ronan and Phaedra. Before she disappeared, she said, "See you Saturday night at the festival."

The Archangel Festival! In all the excitement the other day, Michael had forgotten about asking Ronan to be his date. Coinciding with Archangel Day, the annual festival was held in early November and was the only official event that brought together Double A with Saint Anne's on the same turf, the gymnasium at St. Sebastian's. Penry had told Michael that it wasn't as posh as the high school proms Americans were known for, but it was fun, and Fritz could always be relied upon to sneak some alcohol onto the grounds. Penry, of course, was taking Imogene, and rumor had it that Fritz had asked Phaedra. Now it was Michael's turn. "Would you like to be my date?"

"What?" Ronan replied, startled since he was paying more attention to the girl leaving the room than to the boy sitting next to him.

"Oh, I, um, just thought, that we could, maybe go together," Michael stuttered. "But that's okay. We don't have to."

"No, of course we're going together," Ronan declared. "I'd be honored to be your date."

"Excellent!" *Don't get too excited,* Michael reminded himself. *It's just a dumb dance.* "You just sounded, you know, surprised, like it was the last thing you wanted to do."

Best to be honest, Ronan, or as honest as you can possibly be. "I'm not sure if I like her."

"Phaedra?"

"There's something, I don't know what exactly, but I don't trust her."

"Maybe it's because Ciaran's right. You're not gay and you think she's kinda hot."

Despite the fact that they were sitting in a crowded room with a bunch of other students all trying to dry off from getting caught in the sudden downpour, Ronan grabbed Michael's hand and leaned into him so they were a breath away. "You are the only person, Michael, male or female, that I'm attracted to. And that's not going to change. Not ever."

"I have to get to geometry," Michael replied. It wasn't an appropriate response, but it's all Michael could think of. Well, it was the only thing he could think of saying or doing that he had the guts to say or do in public. He would have to wait until later when he and Ronan were again alone to respond the way he wanted to.

But as Michael turned to leave, he noticed that no one was really looking at them. They were all engrossed in their own conversation or drying themselves off, so he grabbed on to impulse and bent forward to give Ronan a quick kiss on the lips. Chaste, but courageous. He left without saying another word, not that one was necessary.

Alone, Ronan was conflicted. He loved the fact that Michael was brave enough to kiss him in public. It meant that his feelings for him were growing, that their relationship was indeed moving forward, perhaps, maybe, toward where Ronan wanted it to end up. But he hated the fact that he had come face-to-face with a liar. Phaedra hadn't come to St. Joshua's searching for a book; she had come searching for them. She obviously didn't know that he, against his mother's wishes, bought an entire collection of first-edition Brontë's and, after reading them, donated them to St. Anne's library. *Agnes Grey* was right there on the shelf, aisle four, third row from the top, if Ronan remembered correctly. It was a clever lie but, like most, not foolproof.

Could Phaedra possibly know the truth about him? Ronan wondered. The simple answer was that he just didn't know. He hated questioning himself. As a vampire, Ronan was physically superior to almost every creature around him, which made it more difficult to admit when he was intellectually stumped. He had no idea what Phaedra was up to and he didn't yet know how to go about uncovering the truth. Ciaran, however, was a different story. He knew exactly how to deal with his brother.

The rain had finally abated and only a few lingering drops still fell to the earth; the sky itself had returned to the beautiful shade of blue it had been that morning before the darkness swooped in unexpectedly to take over. Ronan strode toward St. Albert's, the science library, where he knew he would find Ciaran during his free period, sequestered in one of the back rooms, conducting yet another pointless experiment. He would demand the truth from him and only heaven could protect him if he chose to lie.

St. Albert's was on the other side of campus, tucked away in a secluded enclave with two other buildings that comprised what the students referred to as the Einstein Wing. It normally took ten minutes to walk there from St. Joshua's, but Ronan was in a hurry to confront his brother, so he used his preternatural speed and got there in about five seconds. When he reached the front door, he paused to take several deep breaths; he wanted to maintain the upper hand and couldn't do so if he couldn't control his anger. Out of the corner of his left eye he saw the statue of St. Albert bent and placing a hand on the side of a lamb. The white marble was cold and formidable, but the statue still exuded compassion and illustrated the power of healing. It reminded students that scientific research meant nothing if mankind couldn't benefit from the result. The hell with that, Ronan thought; sometimes research was just the beginning of revenge.

"I'm not going to ask you again, Ciaran. Why did you tell Michael that I'm not like the two of you?" This time when Ronan spoke, his deep voice vibrated throughout the Spartan room. He had found Ciaran where he expected him to be, in his favorite lab, in the farthest corner of the basement of the library. It was a small room with only two lab tables, one on which sat a few microscopes in different sizes and a second where Ciaran spread out his notebooks and stainless steel test tube racks. The only other piece of furniture in the room was a bookshelf that housed both reference books and less important lab paraphernalia. Ciaran loved it for its simplicity; Ronan appreciated it for its seclusion. He pounded the granite tabletop with his fist so hard that Ciaran had to grab the largest microscope to keep it from falling over. "Answer me!"

"Because it's the truth," Ciaran responded quietly. "Doesn't Michael deserve that?"

"I told you that I will tell him everything."

Ciaran squeezed the eyedropper, and a small amount of greenish liquid fell onto the slide. "Of course you will." He covered it precisely with another piece of glass and placed it under the microscope. "In your own time."

Ciaran had not planned on this, he had not planned that his accidental comment to Michael would find its way to Ronan's ears. His words were not deliberate, but they were proving to be fortuitous. The moment Ronan spoke, Ciaran knew that he was being presented with an opportunity to fulfill a dream and he decided to take it. He followed his instinct and could tell it was working, his calm composure, his arrogance, was having its desired effect. Ronan was growing angrier by the second. And when Ronan got angry, he got violent. Ciaran was able to ignore his racing heartbeat, but he knew Ronan would not be able to ignore the familiar tingle in his mouth. "Who gives you the right to decide when Michael should know the truth?!"

"I don't need to be given the right, Ronan. I have the knowledge," Ciaran replied, his eyes looking at the slide through the microscope, "and when you have knowledge, you have power."

Ronan was airborne before Ciaran gasped, and before he took his next breath, he was lying flat on his back, Ronan on top of him, his eyes narrowed and shining against his will. "You don't have any power! You have nothing!"

It was happening just the way he had dreamed. Ciaran swallowed hard, swallowed his desire; he had to keep his longing hidden, make Ronan think he didn't want this to happen. "And what do you have?" he whispered vilely, struggling underneath Ronan, which he hoped his brother would believe was an attempt to break free from his hold. "A virus in your body? An affliction that makes you want to kill, makes you drink blood?"

Slowly, Ronan felt his fangs descend, not hungry, but filled with rage. "I can destroy you right here!" Ronan growled. "Among these stupid tools that you love so much!"

Tears escaped Ciaran's eyes, tears that were always just beneath the surface. They fell down the side of his face to the cold floor below. *Do it, Ronan! Please, God. make him do it!* Ciaran couldn't resist any longer and with his free hand he reached up and grabbed the back of Ronan's neck. He pushed down with all his strength and brought Ronan's mouth closer to his neck. "Take me!" Ciaran begged. "Please, Ronan, make me a real part of our family."

Ciaran closed his eyes and felt the glorious sharpness of Ronan's fangs scrape his neck. It was happening, it was happening to him before it was going to happen to Michael, before it would happen to anyone else. Ronan was going to take him, his brother, and bring him to his rightful place, make it so that he could stand next to him as an equal. End the loneliness, end the solitude, end the pain.

One fang pierced flesh, and Ronan gripped Ciaran's body so tightly he could no longer move no matter how valiantly he struggled. He just closed his eyes and willed Ronan to press into him deeper, harder, until both fangs were plunged in as far as they could go.

But then Ronan opened his eyes.

He saw his reflection in one of the mirrored slides that fell to the floor, he saw his fang beginning to enter his brother, his own flesh and blood, and he saw the tears stream down the sides of Ciaran's face. Then he saw his own eyes, wild, enraged, like an animal's. They were everything he fought so hard not to become. And here after one confrontation with his sibling, whom he loved and whom he hated, he had turned into the kind of creature he loathed.

Frightened and fearful, he pulled himself off of Ciaran, but just as he did, Ciaran reached out, arms scrambling to keep the connection. "No! Do it, Ronan!" Now Ciaran was like an animal and lunged at Ronan, grabbing the back of his head and thrusting it to his neck. A guttural cry erupted from his throat, "Take me!"

Ronan pushed his brother away hard and Ciaran slid across the floor into the wall. Dazed, but only for a few seconds, he shook off the impact and limped toward Ronan, grasping blindly in front of him until he fell to his knees and caught hold of his foot. He tried to pull Ronan closer to him, but Ronan kicked his hand away and Ciaran fell onto his side. Undaunted, he got up and crawled back toward Ronan, unaware that Ronan's fangs had receded, his eyes were once again normal. He was no longer a vampire, but only a brother, and he was heartbroken. "Ciaran, what are you doing?"

The emotions could no longer stay silent; the feelings had to be given a voice. "I DON'T WANT TO BE ALONE ANYMORE!" Ciaran howled. He wanted to continue speaking, but the sobs made it impossible. On all fours, he let his head hang low and wept. Ronan sank back on his haunches and gripped the legs of the table. He felt dizzy and needed to hold on to something or risk passing out. He couldn't believe what he was hearing, he couldn't believe what he was seeing, and he couldn't believe what he had almost done. "You don't mean that. You . . . you don't know what you're saying."

"It's all I ever wanted!" Ciaran cried, his body heaving with each word. Ronan didn't know what to do so he simply watched his brother, raw and exposed. When the sobs ran their course, Ciaran slowly raised his head and looked at Ronan. He lifted himself up so he was now kneeling, but his arms were limp, his eyes stained with tears. "And how would you possibly know this isn't what I want? You've never taken the time to listen to one word I've ever said."

"That's not true," Ronan said, reaching out to help Ciaran stand, but his brother pushed his arm away.

"Leave me alone!" Ciaran shouted, using all the energy he had left to stand. "It's the way you want things. You, our mother, your entire kind, you all wish I would just leave, go some place far away and die."

"No," Ronan protested, "that's not true."

"Stop lying to me!" Ciaran shrieked, his emotions shaking throughout his body. "Go run to Michael, lie to *him,* make him believe that you're his soul mate, his savior, and then do to him what I begged you to do to me." Ciaran looked down at his brother, who still hadn't found the strength to rise. The words tumbled out of his mouth like daggers. "And when you've finished making him in your image, Brother, don't be surprised if he hates you as much as I have always loved you." Ciaran picked up the slides that had fallen to the floor and placed them on the table next to the microscope, which he then turned upright. Walking toward the door, he spoke to Ronan without turning around. "Maybe then you'll realize that no one can take the place of family."

Long after Ciaran left the lab, Ronan stayed on the floor, unable to move. His brother's words stung not because they were harsh, but because they were true. Especially what he said concerning Michael.

On the way back to his dorm room, he was amazed at how complicated his life had become as a result of one simple fact—he was in love with Michael. He wasn't sure if he could admit that to him, he wasn't sure if it was the right thing to do, but it's how he felt. Yes, he was young, but he knew his soul and it was meant to spend eternity with Michael's. Before that could happen, though, he would have to transform him, and despite his belief that The Well condoned his desire, he had doubts that, thanks to Ciaran, were growing. And they were about to grow even stronger.

"Ronan."

Startled, the boy turned to see Hawksbry standing in front of the main building. Ronan had been walking in such deep thought, he didn't even realize where he was. "Yes, sir?" Slowly, apprehension traveled up his spine as Ronan noticed a difference in the headmaster. He looked the same, well, maybe a bit tired, the circles under his eyes a bit more pronounced, but he was a workaholic; everyone knew that. The difference wasn't physical. No, it was something deeper. Maybe he had been blindsided by a relative too.

When Alistair was directly in front of Ronan, he finally spoke. "You disgust me, Ronan. I don't know who you're trying to fool, but you and your kind make me sick. You are not superior. You're all an abomination, a foul plague that needs to be destroyed. And I for one cannot wait for that day to come."

For the second time in less than an hour, Ronan felt as if someone had taken a sledgehammer and slammed it into his stomach. He reeled back and watched the headmaster calmly turn and walk back to his office. As he did, an emotion that was becoming much too common overwhelmed Ronan: fear. He knew! He knew exactly who he was just like MacCleery did, no, more so than the doctor. The doctor just suspected, the headmaster actually knew that he was a vampire. But how could he? It didn't make sense. Once again he felt lightheaded and he gulped down long breaths of air and clenched his fists to regain some strength. He was out in the open and yet he felt like he was trapped inside a small box that was growing smaller still. Uncharacteristically, he let the fear control his body and he didn't fight the urge to run.

When Alistair entered the main building, he started to walk to his office but couldn't move past the huge mirror in the waiting room. The golden archangels looked at him with wide eyes, but when he saw his reflection, half man, half beast, looking back at him, he cringed.

Then when he felt the hunger that was becoming all too familiar rise up within him, he cursed himself because he knew what he had to do.

He entered his office and locked the door behind him and immediately knelt at Brania's feet. "Very good, Alistair," Brania exclaimed. "You remembered all of your lines."

Ashamed, Alistair avoided her eyes and stared at her arm. "May I feed now? Please."

Brania extended her arm and tried to conceal her contempt for the pathetic creature kneeling before her. "Of course you can. I always keep my promises."

As Alistair bit into her arm and sucked the centuries-old blood from her veins, Brania hardly took notice. She was too busy looking out the window, watching Ronan run, run, run from a danger he wasn't even certain of, and she wondered how much longer she'd have to wait before she would have permission to destroy his world completely.

chapter 17

"I can't be your date for the festival," Ronan declared.

"I think it's best if we don't go together," Ronan stated.

"I'm not feeling well," Ronan said. "I, um, don't think I'm up to going."

No! Ronan swiped the air with his fists and paced his room. He ripped off his suit jacket, flung it onto his bed, and yelled at his reflection in the mirror, "You can't do this to him! You can't cancel at the last minute!" He knew that at this very moment Michael was looking in his mirror, wondering if he looked good enough, wondering if he would make Ronan's heart skip a beat. Oh, of course he would, he always did. And Ronan couldn't wait to hold him in his arms, kiss his beautiful mouth, and roughly rip every piece of clothing off of him. But he couldn't, he couldn't continue this charade any longer. "No!" he screamed. "Call it what it is, this lie!" He covered his face with his hands for a few seconds, then calmer, forced himself to face his reflection. "I can't be your boyfriend, Michael. It's over."

The pain that ripped through Ronan's body had nothing to do with his own emotional anguish. It was coming from somewhere else, it was coming from deep within the waters of The Well. Ronan lurched forward, his head crashing into the mirror, fracturing it. Lines like a spiderweb spread across the glass, causing some shards to fall to the floor, followed by Ronan, who could no longer stand.

He pressed his hand down on the hard wood to brace himself and felt a piece of glass pierce his flesh. Crying out in agony, he watched blood seep from the palm of his hand and slowly trickle toward the webbing between his thumb and forefinger. He was changing even though he wasn't near The Well, even though he wouldn't feed for nearly a month. He could feel his feet inside his shoes growing, straining against the leather. He looked up and he saw his true self, multiplied tenfold by the cracks in the glass, and then he saw The Well's message.

Behind him stood Michael. One clear image spread out among all the cracked pieces of the mirror, radiantly handsome, his features never softer, his eyes never brighter, his fangs never sharper. Ronan shuddered, but Michael placed a webbed hand on his shoulder and steadied him. "Don't be afraid, Ronan," Michael said. "This is all meant to be."

He turned around to look at Michael, but there was no one there. When he turned back, the mirror was unbroken, the image gone, and so too was the pain. For the first time in his life, The Well had communicated to him, and Ronan knew instinctively that it was reassuring him that he and Michael were each other's destiny. He watched the cut heal itself, his features retract, and he was filled with a sensation of pure joy because he knew The Well was never wrong. The feeling only grew stronger when he opened his door and saw Michael standing before him.

His blond hair was neatly parted on the side and combed over, the gel he'd used creating a glossy curve. His green eyes were wide, nervous, but very happy. In his narrow-tailored dark blue suit, white shirt, and olive green tie, Michael looked like the perfect gentleman. He acted like one too. "I brought this for you."

Ronan accepted the small, white rose from Michael's slightly shaking hand. "It's beautiful." He tucked it into his lapel to match the one in Michael's. "From outside St. Joshua's?"

"Yes," Michael admitted. "Ciaran told me that most guys pluck a rose from the bushes for their date to bring them luck."

"Michael, you don't need luck," Ronan said, sliding his hand to the back of Michael's neck and bringing him closer so they could share their first kiss of the night. "This is all meant to be."

Michael was amazed that once more Ronan looked handsomer than he did the last time he saw him. His hair was slicked back again to show off his masculine features, his blue tie was almost as bright as his eyes, and his black suit somehow made his muscles seem even more pronounced. Michael caressed the skin of Ronan's earlobe just because he had never touched that part of him before and said, "You must be right because I have never, ever been happier in all my life."

Ronan smiled, his red lips parting to reveal strong white teeth. "And the night hasn't even begun."

Outside the door to St. Sebastian's they could hear the music blasting on the other side, the voices of the kids laughing, in full celebration. It was enough to stop Michael in his tracks. "Everything okay?" Ronan asked.

Michael looked at the doorknob and realized that once he entered with Ronan by his side, he would no longer be able to hide. Up until now, he and Ronan had blended into the crowd. Yes, their close friends knew what was going on between them, but once they entered the gym together, everyone, for better and for worse, would consider them a couple. "This is just a big step for me," Michael replied.

Ronan looked at Michael and thought how wonderful that, decades from now, centuries even, he would look just as beautiful underneath the moonlight. "Take your time," Ronan said. "I'll follow you whenever you're ready."

Michael's laughter shattered his tension. "Do you always say the right thing?"

Rubbing the small of his back, Ronan grinned. "You know me, I probably read it in some book."

What in the world are you waiting for? Michael asked himself. *This is the feeling you've been craving, the feeling that was always out of your grasp, of being connected, being accepted, feeling utterly natural.* "Let's go in."

The noise and color of the crowd washed over them as they entered the gym, not separately but together, shoulder to shoulder. Everywhere they looked, their friends were clustered in groups talking and laughing or dancing on the hardwood floor that now covered the swimming pool. Penry was right; the room wasn't overly decorated like most American high school dances, but like most things at Double A, the décor was tasteful and with a nod to the celestial beings for which the school was named.

From the ceiling hung several rows of clouds that were simply large pieces of Styrofoam with cotton balls glued to them. But in between were more elaborate creations—wings—some small and pure white, some feathery and expansive, others sprinkled with silver glitter so they created sparkles of light as they rotated overhead. Michael looked up and thought it was magical.

On the walls were hung tapestries depicting the various archangels in flight or in action, all powerful and majestic, all woven mainly in deep, masculine colors of burgundy and plum, but with softer, more feminine-colored accents like lilac and chartreuse, which gave the fabrics a brightness they would otherwise lack.

The centerpiece was an immense ice sculpture that was placed in the middle of the wall of windows, a sculpture of St. Michael in his iconic pose, standing about seven feet tall, with his wings spread almost as wide. Michael felt a surge of pride knowing that he was somehow linked to this fearless warrior. For now they were linked in name only, but Michael was certain— how, he couldn't say—that if necessary he would be able to find the same strength and courage within himself to defeat any foe who dared try to harm him or the ones he loved.

Feeding off some of that courage, Michael let his fingers wander closer to Ronan's, but just as they were about to clasp, Ronan shoved his hands into his pant pockets. He saw the headmaster standing at the entrance and was reminded of their last encounter. Alistair, however, didn't seem to remember a thing. "Ronan, Michael, welcome to the Archangel Festival," the headmaster said, extending his hand to greet both boys. Bending his head toward Michael, he whispered as if sharing a secret, "It's our hundred and twenty-second, you know."

"Wow, maybe it'll catch on," Michael teased.

"I hope so, Michael." Alistair laughed. "It is a highlight of our year, isn't that right, Ronan?"

"Yes, sir" was all Ronan could say. The headmaster was looking at him as if he were just another student, not the foul being he cursed at a few days ago. The disgusting creature whom he wanted to watch die, his entire race be annihilated. Ronan thought it might be a game, but when he looked into Hawksbry's eyes, he saw only the usual kindness, not the hatred he saw the other day, not even fear.

"And it might just be coincidence, but this year the festival committee has chosen St. Michael to be our featured archangel."

Now that Michael assumed Hawksbry was having an affair with his father's driver, he felt oddly relaxed in his presence. He was still a figure of authority, somewhat intimidating, but now more of an equal, so Michael was able to joke. "It may not be the humble thing to do, but I'm going to take some credit for that."

Again Hawksbry laughed, confusing Ronan even more. "Well, go enjoy yourselves, boys," he ordered. "The night will be over before you know it."

When they were a few feet away, Ronan turned back to see if the headmaster's expression changed, but he was still smiling, still looking out over the crowd of students as if they were all his children, which to some degree they were. But when Ronan turned back around, Hawksbry's expression did change, not because of Ronan, but because of the man who questioned him.

"So, Alistair, where've you been hiding?" Dr. MacCleery asked, looking less doctorly now that he'd swapped his white lab coat for a brown corduroy jacket, and his shirt was, for once, tucked into his pants.

When Hawksbry turned to face the doctor, benevolence was replaced with contempt. "I don't recall having to answer to you."

Lochlan looked at Alistair as if he were his patient instead of his colleague and he did not like what he saw. He had learned after years of treating uncommunicative teenagers to listen for symptoms concealed behind words, and he heard very loudly that Alistair was in trouble. He didn't know what kind of trouble, but he knew that something, whether it be physical or otherwise, was trying to destroy him. "I wasn't trying to be disrespectful," MacCleery said. "I'm merely concerned."

Alistair saw the look in the doctor's eyes; it was the same look he saw lately when he found the strength to gaze into a mirror. But no matter how often he saw it, he still abhorred pity. "Don't waste your concern on me, Lochlan," Alistair said. "It could be put to better use." On the contrary, his remark only made the doctor's concern deepen.

Not as deep as Ronan's, however, when a while later he saw his mother standing in front of the ice sculpture. He couldn't tell by her expression if she was admiring or objecting to St. Michael's flamboyance. All he knew was that twice in the same week, he had to ask his mother the same question, "What are you doing here?"

"Darling," Edwige demurred, "is that any way to greet your mother? Especially in front of your . . . companion."

Don't flip out, Ronan, she won't do anything here, not in public, not with everyone watching. "Michael, this is my mother, Edwige."

"Mrs. Glynn-Rowley," Michael said, extending his hand, "what a pleasure."

Edwige gripped Michael's hand firmly, not letting go

until she was finished talking. "Lesson number one, call me Edwige. Mrs. Glynn-Rowley only comes alive once a month when I need to sign the back of a check, which thankfully is quite a large one."

Behind his back, Ronan's hands were clasped so tightly his fingers were gnarled. "Mother, why are you here?"

Waving her hand in front of her face so the diamond and ruby bracelet twirled halfway down the sleeve of her black lace dress, Edwige explained that she was here to be a chaperone. "You know how I love a party even if I have to be responsible and make sure things don't get out of control."

"You could have told me you were coming."

"And spoil the surprise? Where would the fun be in that?" she asked. "Isn't that right, Michael?"

This woman was not at all what Michael was expecting. He surmised from what he had heard that Ronan's mother was quite different from his own and not at all matronly, but he never expected her to look quite so . . . sexy. Yes, she was petite and her hair was cut like a boy's, but there was a confidence about her, something Michael guessed some women learned as they got older, a knowledge his mother never acquired. All he knew was that in her long-sleeved backless black lace mini-dress, Edwige looked like no mother he had ever seen. "Absolutely, Mrs. Glynn . . . I mean, Edwige."

"You're a quick learner," Edwige said, smiling approvingly. "I like that." She then turned to Ronan and added, "You've chosen well."

Ronan was going to chastise his mother for making such an inappropriate comment but realized Michael hadn't even heard her. He was too busy staring at the man talking to Hawksbry. "That's my father." If Ronan didn't catch the sound of fear in his voice, he saw Michael's face turn white and knew that he was even unhappier to see his father than Ronan was to see his mother.

"*That's* Vaughan Howard?" Edwige asked.

Michael was so thrown by the unexpected presence of his father that he didn't even question how Edwige knew his name. He just nodded, and then excused himself, telling Ronan that he needed to get some of Fritz's punch. "Don't worry, dear," Edwige said. "I'll handle this." Before Ronan could plead with his mother not to make a scene or say anything that would make Michael even more uncomfortable, she turned to him and remarked, "Oh, and do you realize that the man Michael's father is speaking with is a vampire?"

Alistair Hawksbry. Headmaster. A vampire? "What?! Are you sure?"

The body of a man, but the mind of a child. "I may not be maternal, dear, but my other instincts are finely tuned and I can recognize a vampire half a world away."

Stunned, Ronan watched his mother saunter across the dance floor, ignoring the stares of every heterosexual teenage boy in the room, and wondered just how she knew Hawksbry was a vampire. When Nakano walked over to him, Ronan thought he at least figured out how he had become one. "What the bloody hell did you do to Hawksbry?"

"I didn't do anything to him!" Nakano protested. "And bugger off if that's the way you're going to talk to me."

"Well, if you didn't do it, who did?"

His answer came when the front door opened and Brania walked in arm in arm with her date—Ciaran. Not only were they a surprising couple, they were a poorly matched one as well. Dressed in a royal blue halter dress that highlighted and enhanced every one of her many curves, her hair teased up dramatically and held in place, in part, by an antique sapphire and silver comb, Brania effortlessly eclipsed Ciaran who, in a light gray suit, yellow tie, and dour expression, looked frail and sallow in comparison.

Stunned for the second time in less than a minute, Ronan watched his mother casually turn Michael's father around, his back now facing the gymnasium, so they could greet the latecomers. From where he stood, Ronan saw Brania never lose her smile, but saw her eyes narrow when Alistair nervously looked away from her. She did it. She may not have been the one to pierce his flesh, but she most certainly gave the command. Ronan couldn't believe she was the cause of such change, and for a different reason entirely, neither could Fritz.

"So Ciaran's not a poof after all," Fritz announced.

"Language!" Phaedra scolded, slapping Fritz on the arm.

"Oh, come on, like you didn't think the same thing," he protested. "That Brania lassie must have some special powers."

Phaedra sighed while swooping a loose tendril of hair back behind her ear. "You go to an all-boys school, Fritz. Half the student body is lusting after the other half. It's only normal."

"Which is why Imogene settled for Penry," Nakano quipped snidely. "Slim pickings."

It was Nakano's turn to be slapped in the arm, this time by Imogene. "That is not true, Kano," Imogene declared. "There are a lot of boys who wanted to be in the position Pens finds himself in."

Nakano grinned wickedly. "And what position would that be, *Pens?*"

Although he was still a virgin, Penry loved having his friends think he may have crossed over into more experienced sexual territory, so he just smiled and shrugged his shoulders. Imogene, however, wanted to keep her reputation unblemished. "Get your minds out of the gutter, boys. No one has been assuming any position. And no one will be!" Imogene paused for effect, smoothing out a crease in her little black dress and then pulling up her white gloves so they would rest securely past her elbows, just like she had seen Audrey Hepburn do in an old movie once. "Even if I do partake in another glass of Fritz's really delicious punch. Phaedra, join me?"

Phaedra downed her glass, which was half full of the spiked drink, the same shade of red as her chiffon cocktail dress, then linked arms with her girlfriend and said in her best faux British accent, "Cheers, mates."

Fritz shook his head as he watched Phaedra walk away. "Maybe tonight I'll get as lucky as Ciaran."

Michael had just recently reconciled to the fact that Ciaran wasn't gay; now he was forced to try and consider the idea that he might get lucky with Brania, of all people. It just wasn't something he could imagine. "You really think Ciaran might . . . you know, with *Brania?*"

"Look at her," Fritz said. "I know she doesn't do anything for ya, but trust me, she's giving most of the blokes in here a bloody howler."

Ronan had heard just about all he could handle. "Hey, Fritz, does it look to you like Alexei is trying to hit on Phaedra?"

Fritz turned his head so abruptly it almost made an audible snap. "What? Hey, KGB! Get your own date!"

After Fritz ran off to prevent anyone else from scoring points with his would-be girlfriend, Nakano realized he was the third member of a crowd, a position he refused to remain in. "All this hetero talk is making me thirsty. Later."

Finally alone, Michael and Ronan stared at each other and smiled. The music changed abruptly from some alternative rock song to a lilting waltz. "Will you listen to that, they're playing my favorite song," Ronan joked. Michael laughed, but not completely. He was still unsettled since he knew he couldn't dodge his father all night long. In fact, right at the moment, he felt as if a pair of eyes was staring down his back. He was half right; there were two pair.

"So it's true," Brania announced with Ciaran a few steps behind her. "You two do make an adorable couple." When Michael turned around, he was prepared to thank her and accept the compliment because it was, after all, the truth. Instead he shouted, "Dad!"

"Sorry it took me so long to get over here," Vaughan said. "But I had to make the rounds."

Awkwardly Michael hugged his father, which he thought was the appropriate thing to do until he actually tried to do it, then he felt childish. "Why didn't you tell me you were going to be here?"

"I thought I would surprise you."

"Must be something in the air," Ronan deadpanned, then smiled at his boyfriend's father. "I'm Ronan. Michael's friend."

Vaughan shook his hand and immediately noted the strong grip. When he spoke, he tried to make his the tiniest bit stronger. "Edwige's son. Your mother's a lovely woman."

"Thank you," Ronan said. "However, I take no credit for how she turned out."

Nervous about this father-boyfriend conversation, Michael felt the need to interrupt, so he told Vaughan something that he probably already knew. "And Ciaran's my dorm mate."

"Yes, we've already met," Vaughan said dismissively.

Well, at least he's acknowledged me, Ciaran thought. *My own mother hasn't even said hello.*

"Brania, may I have this dance?" Vaughan asked. "I promised your father I would make sure you danced at least one proper waltz. You don't mind, do you, Ciaran?"

His expression unreadable, Ciaran replied, "Not at all."

After Vaughan led Brania to the dance floor, Ronan turned to his brother. "I'm glad you came." But ignoring the sincerity in his voice, Ciaran walked away without saying a word.

Between Ronan's mother, his father, his dorm mate's surprise date, and Fritz's punch, Michael's head was spinning. "Could we please get out of here for a bit? There's got to be a hidden passageway or an alcove somewhere that we can hide in for just a few minutes."

Ronan smiled mischievously. "I know the perfect place." He looked around quickly to make sure Vaughan wasn't watching them and then grabbed Michael's hand to lead him toward the far end of the gym. Just as they disappeared behind the tapestry depicting Uriel holding a sword engulfed by flames, Brania turned her head in their direction.

"I must admit I'm a bit disappointed you're not Michael's date this evening," Vaughan said.

Closing her eyes to hear the music better, Brania replied, "I don't think I'm your son's type."

"Oh, come now," Vaughan scoffed. "Don't give up so easily."

Regardless of the century, men always think women speak to be contradicted. Will they ever be freed from their own ignorance? she wondered. *And will they ever be capable of just listening to the music? One, two, three. One, two, three.* How she loved the waltz. She let the soft, lingering notes of the violin glide through her and wished she could find a man who could touch her in the same way.

"Brania?"

Grudgingly, she opened her eyes. "Do you think I would have worn this dress if I were a quitter?"

Embarrassed, Vaughan abruptly lifted his gaze from Brania's cleavage to her smirk. "It is, um, quite remarkable."

Well, if she couldn't fully enjoy the music, she might as well enjoy this man. He was, after all, just as handsome as his son. She pressed her body closer to Michael's father and quickly realized someone else was already fully enjoying the moment. "At least one of the Howard men has noticed."

The only thing the other Howard man noticed was how sweet Ronan's lips tasted, thanks to the raspberry punch they had been drinking all night. Ronan had led Michael to a small closet that housed everything from extra gym equipment to towels to cleaning supplies. Standing among volleyballs and bottles of bleach was hardly a romantic setting, but the closet was out-of-the-way and very dark, so the boys could imagine they were kissing anywhere—in front of the cathedral, next to a well in an underground cave, away from a father's disapproving glare.

"I'm sorry to make you go back in the closet," Michael whispered, swaying lazily in Ronan's arms to the rhythm of the waltz.

"I understand," Ronan said, after kissing the palm of Michael's hand. "As long as there's room for the two of us in here, I'm happy."

Michael brought his arms around Ronan. "There'll always be room for you."

The time for dancing was over. Ronan pushed Michael back and covered his lips in a flurry of kisses. The metal bar of the shelf pressed into Michael just below his shoulder blades, but he hardly felt it. His entire body was too busy reacting to Ronan's touch as his strong hands moved up underneath his shirt to stroke his smooth chest. Michael arched his back and rolled his head from left to right, knocking over some bottles, all the while holding on to Ronan's shoulders for support, afraid he would topple over from the excitement these new sensations were causing. Panting slightly, Michael grabbed Ronan's hands and led them behind his back so he could rest a moment, but once Ronan's mouth was close enough to kiss, all thoughts of resting were taken over by desire.

Tugging at Ronan's shirt, Michael followed his instinct and soon found himself groping Ronan's chest. Nothing, absolutely nothing, felt better than cool flesh over rock-hard stone. "My God, you feel so good," Michael whispered.

"So do you, Michael," Ronan said between kisses, his

fingers desperately curious but trying to remain respectful as they played with the elastic band of Michael's underwear. "Spend the night with me. *Please.*"

The darkness prevented Ronan from seeing Michael smile, but he could feel his lips move underneath his. "Well, since you said *please,* how can I say *no?*" Ronan didn't respond verbally, but only kissed Michael deeper, pushing him harder against the shelf, which then collapsed, causing a box of volleyballs to topple on their heads. Cackling loudly, not caring if anyone heard them, Michael embraced his boyfriend and whispered in his ear, "I think it's time for you to take me home."

Back on the other side of Uriel's tapestry, Ronan whispered to Michael to meet him at the front door, but just as he was halfway across the dance floor, his father interrupted him. "What's going on?"

Still reeling from Ronan's passionate embrace, Michael wasn't levelheaded enough to feel frightened. He felt wonderful and he didn't think to hide it from his father. "Ronan and I are leaving."

"You and Ronan are what?" Vaughan noticed his son's untucked shirt and a thought popped into his head, something unacceptable, something that he would not stand for. "I think it's time you and I talked."

Maybe more of St. Michael's courage pulsed through his body or maybe he was just making up for lost time and felt the need to be defiant toward his father—whatever the reason, Michael didn't back down. "We definitely need to talk, but I don't think you're ready to hear what I have to say."

Who the hell does he think he's talking to? Doesn't he know who I am? Vaughan felt the fire rise from the pit of his stomach and scald his throat. "I did not go to all the trouble of bringing you here to lose out to some . . . to lose out to him!"

"I didn't know that I was trouble, Dad," Michael shouted. "I thought I was your son!"

Vaughan reached out to grab Michael by the arm as he stormed off but was sideswiped by some kids who ran onto the dance floor to catch the final chorus of the latest chart topper. He would have raced after his son if someone hadn't grabbed him by the arm, someone who was a lot stronger than she looked. "Vaughan," Edwige said, "I know you were once married to an American, but that's no excuse for acting like one."

She's mighty powerful for a tiny woman. "Do you know what's going on here?"

Edwige pulled Vaughan's arm around her so he could feel the strength and possibility of her back. "I'm a mother, I know everything. Including the fact that no matter how angry you get, how disappointed, it will not change how our sons feel about each other."

Her back felt incredibly solid, warm, nothing like Brania's soft flesh, but enticing nonetheless. Vaughan shook his head. He couldn't let himself get distracted from the problem he had to solve, or could he? If Michael was anything like him when he was a teenager, there was nothing he could say that would prevent his son from acting on his impulse. No matter how inappropriate and unacceptable that impulse might be.

Maybe he should collect his thoughts, figure out a new approach, and in the meantime get to know this woman better. "Maybe you're right," Vaughan said. "Maybe I should leave him alone for tonight."

"That's my boy. Leave the children to explore and perhaps . . . perhaps the grown-ups should do the same." Although Edwige spoke to Vaughan, she didn't take her eyes off of Ronan. She saw him whisper to Nakano and, despite the blaring music, could hear him tell the boy not to come home tonight. Confident that her son was finally going to satisfy the needs of The Well, Edwige turned her sights back to Vaughan and realized she might be able to have her needs satisfied as well.

As the DJ announced that the last song was about to be played, Nakano knew he had no more time left. He rushed over to Brania, who was standing next to, but not talking with, Ciaran. Not that it mattered who was nearby. Brania was his master, so he didn't need to speak; he could think his thoughts and she would be able to hear him. Sometimes being a vampire was so efficient.

Michael is sleeping over at Ronan's tonight. It'll be the perfect time for me to take him.

No. He doesn't want us to act just yet.

Why not?! This is what we've been waiting for.

Brania sighed loudly. Ciaran knew coming to the festival with her was a mistake, but he didn't think she was going to do such a poor job appearing interested. Well, one more dance and the whole foolish night would be over anyway. Ignoring Ciaran, Brania looked straight ahead and spoke telepathically to Nakano. *I don't know why He wants us to wait, but if you ever question Him again, I will kill you.* Done with both the vampire and the teenager, Brania finally spoke to Ciaran. "Before I die of boredom, I'm leaving. I trust you can find your own way home."

Ciaran was too shocked to respond, so Nakano spoke for him, "Looks like you're as successful with the ladies as you are with the boys."

Looking at the vampire, Ciaran was filled with a mixture of jealousy and disgust, but let the latter emotion shape his words. "At least I had a date this evening, which means you're an even bigger loser than I am."

Left alone amid the swirl of noise and activity that signaled the end of the festival, Nakano felt the rage boil within him. Ronan had left him, Brania had turned her back on him yet again, and now this one had insulted him. Did no one know who he was? He deserved better than this, better than watching couples all around him pair off as he, the one who was superior to every single person left in this room, was abandoned, ignored. Well, not for long.

As Alistair watched Nakano walk toward the wall of windows, he thought he was just going outside, near The Forest to take a shortcut back to his dorm. He never thought he was on his way to feed. Still, he felt uneasy.

"Well, Alistair," Sister Mary Elizabeth said, "another successful festival is about to end."

He heard her words but ignored them. "Sister?"

"Yes, Alistair?"

"Please pray for me," the headmaster asked. "Please pray for us all." Long after the front door closed behind him, Sister Mary Elizabeth tried to make sense of his strange request. She really couldn't, but as she watched the students dancing the final dance of the night, she did as he had asked.

At the edge of The Forest, just out of the glow cast by the festival lights, just out of reach of the Sister's prayers, Penry held Imogene in his arms, nervous, still unused to holding something so soft, something that smelled so clean. "I . . ." A lump caught in Penry's throat, causing him to swallow hard. "I think I . . ."

Imogene looked up into her boyfriend's eyes and she knew what he was trying to say; she also knew that he might not find the will to speak the words out loud, but that was okay. She could tell by the quick beating of his heart and the warmth of his breath that he felt the words and for her that was more than enough. She understood.

"I love you," Michael gasped. He didn't mean to say it out loud, but he couldn't stop himself. He had dreamed about being alone with Ronan like this, naked, scared, yet unashamed, and he knew that it would be exquisite, but it had surpassed his expectations. Ronan was powerful and gentle, quick and slow, and above all, loving.

He made Michael feel innocent and worldly all at the same time and he said things to Michael that he never thought another boy would ever whisper to him. And so Michael said the words he felt, the most honest statement he had ever made. "I love you."

Ronan lifted his head from Michael's taut stomach, which he was smothering with kisses, and paused. He needed to make sure Michael was speaking coherently and not as a result of the passion being unleashed within him. "Do you mean that?"

Michael pushed the covers away and sat up, wrapping his legs around Ronan, so it was just the two of them, flesh to flesh, and spoke the words again quietly and with confidence. "I love you, Ronan. I know I'm young, but I also know that I've loved you since the first day I saw you. I think since before I even came here."

I am looking at everything I have ever wanted in another human being. "I love you, Imogene." Penry was almost as surprised as his girlfriend when the words crashed through the air. But Imogene was more surprised when something sharp slashed through her neck.

Nakano moved so quickly, Penry didn't see him approach them, and then when he saw him dig his teeth into his girlfriend's neck, covering her mouth so her screams would be stifled, he didn't understand what was happening. Nakano was acting like an animal. When he tossed Imogene to the ground, Penry got a better look at his face. He looked like one too.

*   *   *

Ronan pushed Michael back on the bed, their passion and excitement completely out of control. In between kisses and groans of delight, Ronan declared, "Michael Howard . . . I am in love with you . . . and I want you to be mine . . . forever."

"Yes," Michael replied, his voice gruff and constricted with so many emotions, "yes, forever and ever."

Ronan buried his face in Michael's neck and felt the warmth of his body penetrate his. He held his life in his hands. All he had to do was let his fangs descend and feast on his heavenly, willing flesh.

His blood tasted heartier than he expected. Penry wasn't virile or an athlete; physically, he was an average specimen. But oh, his blood was something special. Wave after wave of luscious bright red fluid flooded Nakano's mouth. He took more than he needed because he could; he could do anything he wanted because the boy in his arms was merely human and Nakano was much, much more.

When the release came, it surprised Michael. He couldn't believe how thunderous it was, much different from when he was by himself. He clutched Ronan's back and felt the final waves of passion rip through his body as well. He thought he heard him whimper, but then realized his moans were muffled because his mouth was buried in his neck. Michael twitched when he felt the pinch of Ronan's teeth, then smiled because he had received his first love bite.

Ronan shifted so his body was directly on top of Michael's. He was trembling, his face flushed, a bit sweaty, and his eyes were moist. He said exactly what Michael was thinking. "That was beautiful."

Nakano spoke the same words to Penry. They were the last words Penry heard before he fell to the ground and died.

chapter 18

The morning light exposed two sets of bodies, each entangled in an embrace.

Michael's eyes were closed, but he could feel the sunlight spread across his face like a warm hello. He snuggled closer into Ronan so his back was pressing against the boy's chest, and brought his arm around him tighter, making their connection even more secure. Though after last night, Michael had no doubts; their connection was unbreakable.

Ronan stirred and nuzzled his cheek against Michael's, his stubble rubbing against Michael's smooth skin roughly, but so very pleasantly. Ronan moved his leg so his muscular thigh rested on top of Michael's hip.

The boy couldn't move, but that was perfectly fine because there was nowhere else he wanted to go.

Imogene's arm was wrapped around Penry, her head lying on his chest. The sun's warmth felt good, but when a breeze, sudden and cool, floated over her, she held Penry tighter, rubbing his arm with her hand. *This is strange,* she thought. *I don't remember falling asleep with Penry last night.* Stranger still, her ear was pressed against his chest and yet she didn't hear any beating.

Unable to remain still, Michael rolled over, struggling a bit underneath Ronan's weight, until he was face-to-face with his boyfriend. Ronan kept his eyes closed and tried to pretend to be asleep, relishing the fact that he was being admired by this boy whom he loved like no other, but he couldn't resist; he had to see how beautiful he looked first thing in the morning. "I was right."

"About what?" Michael asked.

"You're cuter in the morning sun," Ronan replied.

Michael laughed and thought, *Ronan must be in love; my hair's a mess, little bits of crust are still in my eyes, and my breath, oh God.* But he understood because he felt the same way. Ronan was still the muscular young man he had first seen bathed in moonlight in front of the cathedral, but here, brightened by the sun, he looked even more delectable. His hair falling every which way, his eyes half open, he looked like a little boy, impish and full of life, who needed to be watched at all times. Michael was more than willing to take on that duty.

Softly, Ronan kissed Michael on the lips. "Thank you for last night."

"It was fun," Michael said, blushing through his smile. "I loved every second of it." He kissed Ronan back, then kissed his cheek, and his ear, before rolling on top of him and hugging him tightly. Ronan felt wonderful, not so much because of Michael's kisses, but because he could see that his neck had no marks on it. He had resisted. He wanted their first night together to be only about making love and nothing more. His mother wouldn't be happy, but right now her happiness was the furthest thing from his mind.

Ronan brushed Michael's hair back off his face. "Fancy taking a shower with me?"

The water felt cool, very refreshing, and it helped revive Imogene, pull her out from her deep sleep. She pressed her ear against Penry's chest and while she could hear the raindrops plop down onto the grass, she still couldn't hear his heart beating. She felt his wrist, and nothing.

"Penry . . . Penry, wake up," she urged.

Fighting the panic she felt gaining speed inside of her, she tugged at the tips of her gloves. Maybe she couldn't feel his pulse because of the material? That had to be it. Yanking her right glove off, she threw it onto the ground and wrapped her fingers around Penry's wrist. She waited for the familiar pulses, indication that blood was pumping through his veins and into his heart, but she felt nothing.

She wiped the rainwater out of her eyes, smearing her

mascara, the black ink mixing with the bloodstains on her glove. *Bloodstains? Why are there bloodstains on my glove?* She looked all around her and for the first time fully realized she was outside in The Forest. *Why in the world am I here?* She could see through the windows of St. Sebastian's that the festival decorations were still hanging from the ceiling, but the ice sculpture was half melted; St. Michael was almost gone. Who would protect them? Who would heal Penry's wounds? The rain had washed away the dried blood to reveal two gaping holes that Imogene knew shouldn't be there. Her scream blared in her head before echoing through the air.

Michael didn't think about sighing; the sound just formed on its own. That's what he loved so much about being with Ronan. He was feeling more than thinking; he was allowing his body to do what it naturally wanted to do without being prohibited by his fears or the world's ignorance. He knew his actions last night had upset his father. He couldn't imagine how upset he'd be if he knew what he was doing right now, if he knew that Ronan was behind him, his arms wrapped around him, the warm shower water drenching their bodies. But right now his father had no say and no place in his world. His world was made up of just two people, him and Ronan. And whoever was knocking on the bathroom door.

Through the steam Michael could tell Ronan was not pleased. "Nakano!"

"No . . . it's me."

Agitated, Ronan fumed to Michael, "*Now* Ciaran wants to talk to me."

"Ronan, I need to see you," Ciaran shouted. "It's . . . it's an emergency."

Leaning his head against the tiles, Ronan wished he and Michael could go some place far, far away where they wouldn't be disturbed, but then Michael said something that made him realize that no such place truly existed. "Maybe it has something to do with your mother."

Dripping wet, a towel hugging his waist, Ronan opened the door with such force it startled Ciaran. He jumped back as Ronan closed the door behind him, but not before he saw Michael's silhouette behind the sliding glass shower door. "I wouldn't have interrupted the two of you if this wasn't important."

Since he didn't believe his brother, he ignored the comment. "What do you want? Last night you didn't have the guts to tell me to sod off and this morning you're banging down my door."

"I thought you'd want to know Penry's been attacked."

A memory flashed through Ronan's mind, a vision of Penry lying on the ground, two holes in his neck, Nakano watching in the distance. "Where's Nakano?"

"You think it's him?"

Ronan wiped some of the shower water off his face with his hand, a few drops falling to the floor. "Who else could it be?"

"Nakano wasn't the only vampire at the festival last night."

Furious, Ronan pushed Ciaran in the chest, making his brother stumble backward and fall onto the unmade bed. When he spoke, it sounded like a hiss. "You think I had something to do with this?"

Refusing to back down, Ciaran fought back and kicked his brother as hard as he could. Not expecting any physical response from Ciaran, Ronan was caught unawares and staggered back from the impact, knocking into the bathroom door. "Why do you always think the worst of me?!" Ciaran didn't wait for an answer because he knew none would come, so he just explained what he had meant. "I was thinking of Brania."

"What about Brania?" Michael asked, opening the bathroom door.

Once again Ciaran lied to Michael's face. "Penry and Imogene were attacked in The Forest last night and I was concerned for Brania's safety. She left the festival by herself." This time his lie sounded a lot more convincing because it consisted mainly of fact. The only untruth in the statement was Ciaran's concern for Brania. He didn't care what happened to the girl, but Michael needn't know that.

"Oh God, not again!" Michael shouted, unconsciously grabbing Ronan's arm. "Are they all right?"

It must be nice to take a morning shower with another person, Ciaran thought, forcing his eyes to look elsewhere other than at the two wet boys standing in front of him. "They're both with MacCleery," Ciaran said. "I think Imogene's okay, but . . . I'm not sure about Penry."

"We have to go see him," Michael said, rushing past Ciaran to put his clothes back on.

"You may want to wear something else," Ciaran suggested. "You'll look a little obvious in your suit."

With only one pant leg on, Michael realized Ciaran was right. He wasn't embarrassed, but there was no need to advertise to the entire academy that he spent the night with Ronan, especially under the circumstances. "I have some sweatpants that should fit you," Ronan said. "Third drawer from the top."

"I'll wait downstairs," Ciaran announced. "But don't take too long getting dressed."

The waiting room at St. Luke's was unusually crowded. The last time Penry was attacked, only Ronan and Michael knew about it at first, but this time thanks to Imogene's shrieks, which rang through the air like the morning church bells, half the academy was trying to get inside to find out what was going on. But since it was Sunday, all the students should have been walking over to the cathedral for mass, attendance at which was mandatory. "You have five minutes to make nine o'clock mass," Mrs. Radcliff reminded everyone. "I don't think Headmaster Hawksbry will tolerate your absence."

Collectively, the group griped. They knew she was right, but they also knew something was wrong with their friends. "Can't you tell us what's going on?" one student bellowed over the crowd.

No, she thought, *I cannot tell you what's going on because I will not be able to handle the mass hysteria.* "Imogene and Penry are being treated by Dr. Mac-Cleery," she stated. "By the time mass is over, we should have a better idea of their prognosis." She hated lying, but she hated disobeying the doctor's orders even more. She only hoped that her voice was calm and that it didn't reveal how distraught she actually was.

When nearly all the students had left the building, MacCleery emerged from his examining room. "Ronan," he bellowed. "I want to talk to you."

The silence that followed the doctor's statement was thick with blame and suspicion. Everyone could feel it. Typically, Ronan was wary in the doctor's presence, but this time he had his nerves under control. He had nothing to do with the attack, and for once he had an alibi. "Yes, sir."

"Come with me."

Ronan hesitated, alibi or not. He wasn't fond of confined spaces. "Anything you want to ask me, you can do in front of them."

MacCleery looked at the students who refused to leave—Ciaran, Fritz, Phaedra, and the American student, whatever his name was. Then he looked at Ronan. The boy wanted to make a scene, that was fine with him. "Imogene remembers being attacked from behind just as the festival ended. Where were you at that time?"

What a brazen accusation, Ronan thought, *but at least my instincts are on target. He really does believe I'm dangerous.* Which Ronan did have to admit was true, but only when he was provoked. "I left the festival shortly before it ended. At the time of the attack, I would have been in my room. Sir."

"Can your dorm mate confirm that?"

Ronan felt like he was on trial. Everyone in the room was looking at him, wondering how he was going to respond, and the most curious juror appeared to be Phaedra. "No, sir, he can't."

For some reason, MacCleery felt sweat spread across his palms; he was nervous, his throat dry, but he didn't understand why. Once again he was afraid to be in this boy's presence, but it didn't make sense. He was just a kid, nothing more. "So you, um, just want us to accept that what you're telling us is the truth?"

"It is, sir," Michael said, his voice clear and firm. "I left the festival with Ronan and I was with him all night."

Well, well, well, boys will be boys, won't they? "There's no need to lie for your friend," MacCleery advised.

Anxious, but still amused by the situation, Fritz chuckled. "Ronan's more than just his friend, sir."

That's right, Michael thought, *it's time we all spoke the truth.* "I've been with him since we left last night. If you want proof, ask Ciaran. He saw me there this morning when he told us what happened."

Dammit! Why do they always work in a pack? One

always ready to take a bullet for the other. "Is that true, Ciaran?!"

"Yes, sir, it is."

"What about Nakano?" Phaedra asked the question so quietly, it almost went unheard. But as its implications set in, MacCleery thought it made sense. He never noticed anything out of the ordinary with Nakano, not like with Ronan, but they were very close, dorm mates, so maybe, maybe there was some sort of connection.

"Mrs. Radcliff," MacCleery shouted. "Get Nakano in here. Now!"

Before the nurse could make a move, Ciaran spoke. "That won't be necessary, sir. Nakano was with me all night."

Ronan's cry concealed the doctor's "What?!"

Calmly, Ciaran told another lie. "Since Michael was spending the night with Ronan, Nakano had no place to sleep. Michael's empty bed seemed like the perfect solution."

The doctor ripped his glasses off his face and wiped them vigorously with his shirttail. He didn't know who to believe anymore, but he knew that no matter how many more questions he asked, he wouldn't be told the truth. Maybe he should just retire, live out the rest of his days away from youth and illness. Unfortunately, before he could make any life-changing decisions, there was a dead boy lying on a table in the other room, who had to be dealt with. "Tell Hawksbry to call Penry's parents," the doctor ordered. "Then call the morgue."

"No!" This time, Phaedra's word shook the room.

Worn out, the doctor retreated back to his office. "Imogene will be fine, but Penry was dead before he got here."

At the same time, Michael and Fritz rushed to Phaedra's side, separating to sit on opposite sides of her to offer comfort. "I couldn't protect them," she cried, her words muffled by her sobs. "I should have, but I couldn't."

"No one could have prevented this," Michael said, moving his hand away so Fritz's arm alone could ease her shaking body. When Fritz saw Michael's own tears fall down his cheeks, the boy gave his shoulder a squeeze. A simple yet effective gesture from one friend to another.

While Mrs. Radcliff was busy making her phone calls, Ronan grabbed Ciaran by the arm as he was about to leave. "I know what you're trying to do, and you have to stop it."

Ciaran shook his arm free from his brother's hold. He swallowed his anger so when he spoke, he merely sounded patronizing. "Please don't worry about me, Ronan, not when you have a boyfriend to console." After Ciaran left, that's just what Ronan did. He sat next to Michael and put his arm around his shoulder. Michael and Ronan, Phaedra and Fritz, just two couples overcome with grief over the death of their friend. Ronan was thankful, however, no one was looking at him, because he was no longer able to hide his fear. He was just as scared as every mortal in the room.

Within the hour, the whole campus was buzzing with

the news that Penry was killed and Imogene, though she survived, had been left for dead. As a result, a mandatory curfew was placed on both Double A and St. Anne's. No student was allowed outside without an adult after sundown. But since Hawksbry refused to make a formal statement—an act that made many students question his leadership skills—all that was left was rumor, and according to gossip, the couple had been attacked by an animal, maybe a bear, although no one could ever recall seeing a bear wandering through The Forest. Whatever it was, whatever committed this heinous act, it was bloodthirsty, because Penry had lost more than half his blood. And though Imogene for some reason hadn't been severely injured, she had been taken to the trauma center in Carlisle to be examined more thoroughly and, of course, questioned by the police. Thanks to Ciaran's alibi, Nakano wasn't worried in the slightest.

But Ronan was. He didn't want to believe that Ciaran would willingly protect Nakano, but he had been right there, had heard his brother lie to protect him. Ciaran was hardly friendly with Kano, plus he knew that he was capable of committing such a vicious act. As frightening as it was to Ronan, it all made perfect sense. First begging Ronan to turn him into a vampire, then cozying up to Brania, and now protecting Nakano, Ciaran was not making intelligent choices unless . . . *God, could that really be it?* If he wouldn't turn him into a vampire, Ciaran would find someone who would. But he couldn't possibly be desperate enough to become one of Them, could he? As much as Ciaran infuriated Ronan at times, he was still his brother. And it was time he reminded his mother of that fact.

A few minutes later, he was standing in the living room of her London flat, surrounded by a collection of shabby chic furnishings and accessories in every shade of white imaginable. Since she didn't initiate the conversation, Edwige was trying her best to ignore Ronan, but he wouldn't stand for it. The topic was far too important. "You didn't even say two words to him at the festival!" Ronan shouted.

"I nodded when he looked my way," Edwige said, focusing all her concentration on applying her aubergine nail polish with a smooth, even brushstroke.

"He will do anything to become a vampire! He practically forced me to transform him. Doesn't that concern you?"

Blowing a steady stream of air onto her nails, Edwige didn't seem concerned at all. "No, dear, because if you remember, I told you that I would destroy you if you ever gave your brother the gift of immortality." Ronan flinched at the memory, knowing that his mother meant what she had said. "He does not deserve to be given our life, not after what his father did."

"I know," Ronan said quietly. "And that's why I refused him."

Finally, Edwige smiled at her favorite child. "No, you refused him because you're a loyal son. Loyal to your mother and loyal to The Well." Edwige got up, not to walk toward her son but to stand in front of a large painting that covered most of her living room wall. "Do you like it?"

Ronan's eyes glossed over the artwork. "It's fine."

"Fine!? I paid sixty thousand pounds for this painting," Edwige declared. "It's by a fledgling artist, someone who I predict will be the darling of the art scene one day. And this is, by far, his greatest achievement to date."

On the wall in a flat, distressed frame the color of an acorn was an oil painting of two men swimming in the ocean at night. Their bodies, touching so they almost appeared to be conjoined, could be seen above and below a sea that was a beautiful blend of azure, cobalt, and cerulean, deep colors, thickly painted and rich in texture. It was obvious why his mother was attracted to the painting, Ronan thought, but he hadn't come here to discuss art.

"Mother, that doesn't mean Ciaran won't look elsewhere to satisfy his craving. To someone like Brania or Nakano. Those people are immoral. They've killed Penry!"

"And if he does something so incredibly stupid, then he will prove what I have always known, that he is his father's son!" Edwige replied, uncharacteristically losing her temper. "It will be his punishment!"

Stunned by his mother's outburst, Ronan didn't choose his next words very wisely. "Do you hate him so much because he reminds you of what happened to Saxon?"

Edwige slowly turned away from the painting to ex-

354 Michael Griffo

amine her son. "You are very lucky I just did my nails. Otherwise I would slap your face. And we both know that my appearance belies my strength."

Suddenly exhausted, Ronan roughly brushed the tears from his eyes. Why did every conversation with her have to be a battle? Why couldn't she be like a normal mother? Why couldn't he and Michael just run away somewhere and never have to see her or anyone else again?

"Speaking of Michael," Edwige said, reading her son's thoughts, "you let an opportunity pass. Why?" Ronan tried to push the images of Michael from his mind so his mother wouldn't become witness to their intimacy, but it was too late and she was too strong. "The Well wants this coupling, Ronan. It recognizes, as I do, that you and Michael are just like The First and The Other."

Why must she always talk in riddles? "What are you saying?"

"You know exactly what I'm saying," Edwige said, turning back to the painting. "You know the legend, you know our beginning."

"Of course I know all about that! I just . . . I just want to wait for the right moment."

"The right moment is now! You know that you are The First and Michael is The Other. If you would stop fighting it, you would see that it really is that simple."

And Ronan had to admit that it was. He knew the history of his people and he knew that he and Michael were poised to become part of the next generation. He couldn't explain it, but it was as if his ancestors were speaking about the two of them when they told the story of their genesis. Maybe it was just another romantic notion, but something had to explain why Ronan had felt so connected to Michael the moment he saw him.

He thought back to when he was a little boy, when he was still human and his father and grandfather told him how their race originated. Then like now, Ronan didn't fully comprehend the words, but emotionally he was connected to them.

Centuries ago, hidden from mortal eyes, their race was created when a vampire fell in love with a stranger, a woman who was different, who lived beneath the ocean in the city of Atlantis. Sworn enemies, the two species never had any interaction that didn't end in bloodshed, until The First met The Other and their love changed history.

The First's vampiric race did everything in its power short of killing him to prevent him from consorting with The Other. At the same time, her people imprisoned her, tortured her, anything to separate her from this creature whom they considered vile and evil. But to no avail. They loved each other, no matter how unnatural everyone around them felt their connection to be. Their love, deep and never-ending, created The Well in the center of Atlantis, and from its waters a new race was born, a hybrid vampire who could walk from out of the darkness and break through the water's surface, no longer having to fear the sun. A race that had webbed feet and hands that made swimming to the floor of the ocean possible, and lungs that could breathe underwater as easily as above. And a race that would only have to feed once a month as long as they drank from The Well. All they were required to do was create new vampires, not out of hunger or malice or rage, but out of love.

"You and Michael are from different worlds, you're both perceived as unnatural by the majority of your people, and you're both in love," Edwige said. "There should be no hesitation."

"I'm not hesitating. I know The Well approves, but I would like his permission first before changing him forever."

Try to remain calm, Edwige, he is still young. "His love is his permission."

Clenching his fists, Ronan started to pace his mother's room. "I know you think our race is superior. I do too, but there are others who disagree. Not everyone admires us water vamps!"

Such a disgusting word. "Because they're jealous."

"Yes, I know that! And I know their jealousy is wrong, but right and wrong have nothing to do with it. The reality is that there are more of Them than us. How can I bring Michael into a world where he will be reviled by so many? Where so many will wish he would just burn up and die?!"

Edwige turned on her son viciously. "Because we have two choices! Either we increase our race or we allow Them to destroy us and all those whom we love.

And I have seen too much destruction in my lifetime!" She turned away to look out the window. High, high above, a vulture was circling, waiting for the right moment to pounce. She knew the scavenger would wait two minutes or two centuries, but when the time was right, it would pounce to destroy what was left on the ground. "And I will tell you for the last time, if you don't act on your love and bring Michael over to our side, someone else will act on their hatred and create him in their own image."

Ronan sank into a chair and he felt his heart break at the thought of that happening. He stared up at the painting, at the two men who were captured in one moment of a lifetime, and he imagined how many glorious moments he and Michael could share over an immortal lifetime. The Well was right, his mother right. He knew he couldn't wait any longer.

What Ronan didn't know was that there were others who had also decided it was time to take action. "I've spoken to Him," Brania said. "And He has given His consent for you to take Michael."

It was as if a burst of energy flooded Nakano's brain. The feeling was almost as fantastic as when Penry's blood spilled down his throat. "Perfect! I can't believe He's going to let me do it!"

She wouldn't admit it, but Brania shared his belief. "He finds poetry in having another student do the deed. You."

"I know that He doesn't have to explain Himself, but did He give any reason why He changed His mind?"

She would be so happy when she would never have to see this one again. She was forced to accept unintelligence, but she detested disrespect. "He didn't change His mind," Brania explained in as calm a voice as she was capable. "Now that Ronan and Michael have made love, the separation, the violation, will be that much more painful."

"Of course," Nakano said. "That makes total sense. Except . . ."

Her patience was gone. "What!?"

"Why is Michael so important?" Nakano asked. "He's just a mortal, a kid from Nebraska, of all places."

His arrogance was appalling, but so too was his insight, not that she would commend him for it. "You have exceeded your allotted number of questions for one day," Brania said. "Now please get to work."

As Nakano was about to enter the underground passageway that would lead him away from the center of Eden, he remembered something. "I just hope the fog doesn't get in the way this time."

Again with the fog. "You're a vampire! How can a fog prevent you from fulfilling your duty?"

He really was so happy he was gay. No matter how hard they tried, girls just couldn't help being stupid. "I've told you, Brania, it's not an ordinary fog. It's a protection, it's as if someone is deliberately interfering so that no one can get to Michael except Ronan."

That's it. Who's a born protector? Women, not men.

And no one is more protective than a mother. "It's Edwige," Brania declared. "She's the source of the fog."

Maybe, Nakano thought. *She is powerful, that one.* "How do you know?"

"Because a boy's mother will do anything to help her son."

"Wow," Nakano gushed. "I guess women aren't that stupid after all."

No, they're not, Brania thought. They're far more intelligent and resourceful than any man she had ever known. Except of course for Him. Because no matter how contradictory or indecipherable His actions might appear, she always knew He had a plan, and that's why He was the only man she had ever respected. Yes, she considered herself the luckiest woman in the world to have Him as her father.

chapter 19

The Beginning of an End

Outside, the earth was dying.

Patches of dry, brown grass blotted the area outside Archangel Cathedral as if Penry's sudden death had taken life from the land. Trees stood leafless, stark, their branches like jagged edges, lonely, dangerous. But even on the cusp of tragedy, beauty could still be found.

The interior of the cathedral was even more breathtaking than its façade. How a group of monks in the fifteenth century could ever have built such a structure, Michael had no idea, but he was grateful. The combination of elaborate religious imagery and simple manmade woodworking was comforting, especially at this time of mourning.

Penry's coffin had already been carried out, loaded onto a hearse, and was on its way to his family's cemetery in Sheffield. Gone were his parents, weary with sorrow; his twin sister, Ruby, whose hair was an even brighter shade of red than Penry's, his grandparents, weathered but sturdy. They were all gone and they took Penry's body with them. They left behind students who were deeply saddened and also deeply worried because even though very few knew exactly how Penry had died, everyone knew that what had happened to him could just as easily happen to them. Sitting in a pew in the back of the church, Michael clutched Ronan's hand tighter, closed his eyes, and prayed, "Please, God, keep us safe; our lives are just beginning."

When he opened his eyes the cathedral was bursting with light. It was as if God had responded to his plea. The huge circle of yellow stained glass acted like a portal through which the sun's light could enter, and when it hit, as it did now, a perfect cylinder of golden sunshine beamed through the glass and illuminated the altar. Michael knew that the effect was nothing more than the result of clouds moving past the face of the sun, but he didn't want a logical explanation; he wanted something more miraculous. So that's what he believed. To him it looked like a pathway bringing a little bit of heaven to earth. He wanted to reach out and touch it, feel heavenly splendor, but as Ronan's hand moved underneath his, he realized he already was.

He hated feeling so joyful at such a terrible time, but he couldn't berate himself; he wouldn't. Too many years spent loathing life in Weeping Water, too many years wishing it would just be over; now that his life was beginning, he refused to ignore his happiness, even though someone he considered a friend was no longer with them. He looked up at the huge wooden crucifix suspended from an arch and hanging over the altar—different in that Jesus's body wasn't nailed to the cross, but only drops of blood, crimson and thick, were painted where his hands and feet would be—and he hoped that Penry was at peace. That whatever horror he witnessed just before his death was now a distant memory, its image replaced with the mercy and serenity of eternal peace. It was his wish for his friend and he hoped it would be fulfilled.

Michael's eyes moved from the crucifix to the large group assembled near the altar. Classes were canceled today and the front of the cathedral was filled with students, most of them talking to Father Fazio and a few other priests who were counseling them, helping them cope with the grief they were experiencing from this unexpected tragedy. The back of the church, however, was nearly empty. Other than an elderly priest lighting a candle at a statue of St. John the Baptist, it was just the two of them. "I can't believe Penry's really gone," Michael whispered to Ronan.

"It didn't have to happen," Ronan said.

"It *shouldn't* have happened," Michael corrected. "It doesn't make any sense."

"It's death, Michael. As much as we don't want to accept it, it makes perfect sense."

The clouds must have returned; the ray of light was gone, the altar and tabernacle once again drenched in shadow. "But so soon? Penry's life is over before it's even begun."

Ronan was searching for the right words. He needed to hear what was in Michael's mind, what lay in his heart, but he didn't want to frighten him or make Michael think he was losing his grip with reality. He was given a reprieve, some time to collect his thoughts when Fritz, followed by Phaedra, somber and subdued, approached their pew.

As he genuflected hastily, Fritz's hand was a blur as it made the sign of the cross, his knees never bending. He didn't enter the pew to join the boys but remained standing in the aisle, Phaedra beside him, head down, her hands dug deep into the pockets of her sweater. Michael thought she looked older, tired, which made sense since she had most likely spent the night crying. Penry's death and the attack on Imogene had affected her deeply. Surprisingly, it had a similar effect on Fritz as well.

"He was a right fine mate," Fritz said with quiet respect.

"Yeah, he was," Michael agreed. "I wish I knew him longer."

Fritz nodded in understanding. Phaedra's eyes remained focused on the hard wood of the floor. During the ensuing silence, Michael didn't notice Phaedra shift her gaze to Ronan. However, Fritz did. He didn't know what to make of it; he really didn't know what to make of this girl except that she was different from all the other girls he knew. She was high-spirited, then quiet, aloof, then interested. She sparked new feelings in him, adult and unexpected, but she always seemed to be looking at another boy and not at him.

"Do you guys want to sit with us?" Michael asked.

"No," Fritz answered for them both. "I'm going to walk Phaedra back to St. Anne's. Light of day or not, there's a bloody killer out there."

Phaedra's stare didn't waver. Ronan felt her looking at him, but he pretended to be very interested in watching the elderly priest who was now lovingly dusting off the statue of St. John with a very tattered cloth. Even when he heard her ask Michael if he would be all right, he didn't turn, he didn't flinch although he knew exactly why she was asking. She, like Dr. MacCleery, didn't trust him and suspected he had something to do with Penry's death. Luckily, Michael knew otherwise.

"Of course I'll be fine," he replied, squeezing Ronan's hand gently. "I'm not alone."

"Neither are you, Phaedra," Fritz mumbled, but his words got lost among the notes of the soft organ music that began playing in the cathedral's choir space. For a few moments, all that mattered was the music, the rich melody, filled with vibrations. Achingly hopeful, it commanded their attention, swirled around and between them and then floated above, ascending to the cathedral's huge space overhead. The music ended as abruptly as it began, just a few moments, just a brief passage of time, just like Penry's life.

Tentatively, Fritz took hold of Phaedra's elbow. "See you later, mates." As she was led toward the front door, Phaedra moved so fluidly with him that Fritz had no idea she wanted to stay, that she wanted to curl up on one of the pews and fall asleep under the crucifix, and awake bathed in beams of sunshine. But that wasn't going to happen. She couldn't think about her own needs, not now when she was needed elsewhere, at Fritz's side, even if that wasn't the place she wanted to be.

When they were once again alone, Ronan couldn't wait any longer. He didn't have the patience to be subtle; he had to know Michael's answer. "If you had the choice, would you choose to be immortal?"

Someone was finding it difficult to let go of Penry's death, Michael guessed. "Like Dorian?"

"I'm serious, Michael," Ronan said. "If the choice were presented to you, what would you do?"

Michael studied Ronan's face. *He is serious; he isn't asking hypothetically or in terms of fantasy. Oh, don't be ridiculous; of course he is; he has to be.* And yet there was something in his eyes, something that made Michael believe Ronan really was asking a serious question. *That is one of the reasons I love him,* Michael thought. *He's so completely different, so unpredictable. Filled with romantic notions and unusual concepts, his mind is just as attractive as the rest of him.*

"Would you accept such a gift?" Ronan asked, pressing him further.

For many reasons, some understood, some unknown,

Michael was compelled to give an honest answer. He took a moment, not that he needed one. He knew the answer before he was even asked the question. "If it meant I could spend every day with you," Michael replied, "then yes." The idea, the absolutely incredible idea, filled Michael with unspeakable joy. "Yes, Ronan, I would embrace immortality with my heart and soul."

Once again the cathedral was flooded with sunshine, glorious sunshine that announced a new day, a new beginning. Ronan had the answer he was looking for. "Then so be it."

His face, awash with the glow of the sun and his own happiness, looked from one statue to another of saint and archangel and deity, and silently Ronan told them that soon they would be able to add one more to their group. Michael was lost in his own thoughts, trying to imagine what it would be like to spend eternity with Ronan. In one of the small inlays built into the side of the cathedral, he saw a statute of St. Michael. In his mind he called out to him, *What's it like to never die?* A few hours later, Michael was asking much less complicated questions.

"Are you sure they're okay with this?"

Walking past Michael with a box of Nakano's personal things, Ronan kissed him quickly on his cheek. "They both agreed. You and Nakano should switch rooms so we can be together."

Still a bit doubtful, Michael hesitated to start unpacking the suitcase he had plopped onto Ronan's bed. "And Nakano really doesn't mind moving in with Ciaran?"

Ronan grabbed Michael's hand and made him sit next to him on the bed. Looking at him now, beautiful and breathless, Ronan couldn't wait for tonight. "Believe it or not, it was Nakano's idea. He can be a wise laddie when he wants to be, and he figured you'd be spending a lot more nights here so he decided the practical thing was for you and him to switch rooms."

Living with my boyfriend, life couldn't really get any more perfect, any more different from what it used to be, Michael thought, *unless it was somehow against the rules.* "What if Hawksbry finds out? Doesn't the academy have a rule against this sort of thing?"

Despite the recent tragedy, laughter came so easily now, now that he'd made the decision for them. "You mean this sort of thing?" Ronan knocked Michael over onto his side and then crawled on top of him, ravishing his lips and neck with kisses, tickling the sides of his stomach. "Fraternization among the students." Squirming underneath Ronan, Michael was giggling so hard he could hardly catch his breath, let alone speak.

Soon laughter turned into passion, so Michael gave up trying to protest, trying to explain himself more fully, knowing it was no use. He wanted to be here on Ronan's bed, in Ronan's room, in Ronan's life, just as much as Ronan wanted him to be. Maybe it was Penry's sudden death, affirmation that the future was unreliable, that made them want to be together as much as possible. Michael didn't really know, but he wasn't going to fight it.

After their need to kiss waned, they silently shifted

position so they were spooning, Ronan behind Michael, their legs bent, hands clasped, Ronan's arm underneath Michael's head, his biceps doubling as a pillow. Breathing in Ronan's scent, Michael realized he no longer needed dreams; his had come true. Just before he fell asleep in his boyfriend's arms, he made special thanks to Nakano for understanding that Michael and Ronan were meant to be and that he would have to move on.

Michael had no idea that moving on was the furthest thing from Nakano's mind.

Brania's heels clicked against the damp concrete floor as she paced, every few steps or so turning to study the boy. She could not believe that he had triumphed where she had failed. He had come up with a solution, a good one in fact, for this pesky fog nuisance, before she even had any ideas. She was not pleased with herself. She had gotten too caught up with the thought of dealing with Edwige head-on instead of the problem itself, but her father was pleased and therefore so was she. She would give recompense where it was due, learn from this mistake, and reap the benefits from its successful implementation. It was, in the words of today's crass younger set, all good.

For once, Nakano waited patiently for her to speak. He didn't try to interrupt her thoughts or barrage her with questions; he remained quiet and waited for the praise that was sure to come.

"I'm impressed," Brania declared. "Yesterday I thought

you were a complete idiot, but today you show promise."

Just what I thought, but then Nakano heard the full meaning of her words. "Hey, wait a minute."

Interrupting him, Brania continued, "This really is an excellent plan. Allow them to live together, allow them to think that you support their cohabitation, their coming together, and give them a false sense of security."

"Why did you think I was an idiot?!"

It was as if Nakano never spoke. Brania just kept pacing and thinking out loud. "This fog you mentioned has only appeared outside. Now that you've given up your home so Michael and Ronan can have their own little love nest, they have no reason to meet outdoors. The fog should no longer be a factor." Abruptly stopping, Brania pointed her finger at Nakano. "You need to remember this day."

Nakano couldn't resist. "For what? Not being an idiot?"

For the first time in quite a while, Brania laughed. The booming sound bounced off the stone walls and echoed throughout the room. She reminded herself that she should try and stop being so harsh with the underlings; yesterday she loathed his words, today they amused her. What a godsend that her immortality was still capable of being filled with new lessons. "It's the day you made Father forever grateful."

Unable to feel humility, Nakano thought it was about time that someone, even someone as powerful as Brania's father, recognized his superiority. "Sounds like we should celebrate," Nakano suggested.

By the time she crossed the room, Brania had let her emerald green cashmere sweater fall to the floor, revealing her soft white arms, the veins underneath her skin so pronounced and blue they looked like a tattoo of intertwining strings of barbed wire. When she reached Nakano, she could see the hungry look in his eyes. They were black and glistening. His fangs, driven by instinct, were already hanging over his lips; at the end of one, a small bubble of saliva had formed, which burst when it grew too big.

"A gift from me to you," Brania said, as Nakano knelt before her. "Once you make Michael one of my Father's disciples, my blood will always be yours."

Savagely, Nakano bit into Brania's flesh. Torrents of pain coursed up her arm, past her shoulder, and ripped through her brain. "Slowly!!" Pitching forward, Brania grabbed on to Nakano's shoulder to prevent herself from toppling over, which only resulted in the boy gnawing deeper into her skin. Commanding all her strength, Brania stood erect, her eyes focused only on the stone wall in front of her. *It's almost over,* she told herself. She would allow the boy to feed; the pain was worth it if he could carry out her father's wishes. But if he failed, then she would never allow his disgusting mouth to ever touch her again.

As Nakano drank more and more of Brania's blood, Alistair felt pangs of jealousy, sharp and poisonous, pierce his heart. Or where his heart used to be. He had no idea if he still had one. He knew that he was no longer human, he couldn't be, not after the things that he'd done, so the chances of his still having a heart were slim. Then again he just wasn't sure. He wasn't sure about anything since the night they came into his office and dragged him away, stripped him of his clothes, his dignity, and tossed him in the trunk of that car. What happened to him that night and in the following days, he couldn't say, but instinctively, he knew those days were best forgotten. What he did know was that he was no longer the same man. He was no longer a man even, but a thing, a monster who craved blood and death. He was constantly afraid of them, of himself, of what else could possibly happen to him, and he didn't know how much longer he could live with this fear.

He knelt before Penry's makeshift memorial, before the mound of flowers and notes the students had left their friend, and he bowed his head to pray. "Our Father" was all Alistair could get out before his throat burned, a surge of acid swirling up from his stomach. "Our Father . . . Who art in heaven!" He felt another burst of heat scorch the roof of his mouth and his tongue. It felt like the inside of his mouth was charred. Falling to the ground he dug at the earth, ripping out handfuls of dirt, dry and yellow-brown, and said the words silently, fearfully, as the acid continued to burn away at his mouth. *What in heaven's name is happening to me?!*

He thought he was going to pass out from the pain right there among Penry's farewell flowers until he smelled salvation. Like the skilled predator he was becoming, he froze and slowly turned his head toward the scent. He saw the rabbit before it saw him, its white fur standing out like a beacon among the greens and browns of The Forest. Sprinting toward it with the speed of a gazelle, Alistair pounced on it before it could even choose a direction in which to flee. In the next moment, his fangs had pierced the flesh that was hidden by the snow-white fur and finally a warm stream of blood cooled his burning throat. Sitting on his haunches, he leaned back, holding the animal in his hands, and sucked down the blood until there was none left to drink. When he was finished he placed the rabbit gently on a dried patch of dead grass, its fur now pink in places, and he wept. One animal for another.

This was what it feels like to be swept away by passion, to give in to basic animal instinct. Michael could not believe how crazy, how incredibly wild, Ronan was making him feel. There wasn't a part of his body that Ronan hadn't touched or tasted, not an inch of his imagination that he hadn't ignited with his words—some rough, most tender—and not a piece of his heart that he hadn't embraced with the love that he so easily offered him.

"This is amazing," Michael said, breathing heavily. Ronan lifted his head from the cleft in Michael's chest. "And this is just the beginning."

Outside their window, Nakano watched. Brania had suggested he give Michael and Ronan a night to get settled, to become complacent, but Nakano never liked taking orders from a girl. Girls think, guys act. So for the past hour, he had been watching, and finally the time had come. He knew what was happening. He knew how Ronan smelled when he was excited; he had smelled it many times before. Well, once or twice, and never as pungent, never as strong as it was now. As much as he didn't want to admit it, Michael obviously stirred a fire that lay deep within Ronan, a place Nakano never touched, never even knew existed. For a moment, he weakened, remembering how much he enjoyed being held by Ronan, being where Michael was right now. But no. *That was the past and this is my future. My future is not with Ronan; he has made that perfectly clear. My future is with Them, my kind. And as soon as I destroy your future, Ronan, mine will begin.*

Before he lifted one foot, however, Nakano saw it coming. The fog, soft and gray, materialized out of nowhere. "No! Not again!"

The small cloud of gray mist swirled in front of the door of St. Florian's, moving almost in slow motion, teasing Nakano with its laconic approach. But as expected, it quickly expanded, fanning out toward the sides of the building and up toward the sky, gaining momentum with every second until the lower half of the building was engulfed by the thick gray fog. Nakano thought his head was going to explode. *This is not happening to me again! Not when I am so close to showing everyone what I'm capable of!*

Using all his preternatural speed, Nakano raced toward the fog, determined to break through it this time, crash through this aberrant barrier, this abnormal obstruction, and enter the fog so he could pull Michael away from Ronan before he could start the transformation. But when he hit the cloud, it was as if he hit a brick wall. He heard the bone snap a few seconds before he fell to the ground.

His left arm went limp as he tried to push himself off the ground, and once again he was facedown in the grass. For a moment he thought he could circumvent the fog by crawling under it, but it appeared to tunnel down into the earth. The fist that he could still use, he slammed into the ground, burrowing a hole a few inches deep. "What the hell is going on?!" He looked up just in time to see Ronan's window vanish as the fog continued its rise, not stopping until the whole of St. Florian's disappeared into the night.

Eyes half closed, Michael didn't notice that moonlight was replaced by shadow. All he noticed was that it had been several minutes since he had kissed Ronan's mouth. He grabbed a handful of hair and brought Ronan's head to his so he could set things right; he needed to taste him. He also needed him to make a vow. "Promise me this will never end," Michael panted. "Promise me it'll be like this forever."

Ronan felt the familiar tingle in his mouth. "Is that what you want, Michael?"

His eyes are so bright, it's like they're shining, Michael thought. "Yes! Yes!" Closing his own eyes he continued to explore Ronan's body in the darkness, knowing that release was so close, so near.

"I will not let you win!" Nakano bellowed at the fog that stood between himself and his destiny. He grabbed his left wrist and twisted his arm, bones creaking loudly, then he twisted it in the opposite direction. He clenched his fist and bent his elbow, good as new.

Running a few yards back until he reached the sprawling oak tree, he made another sprint toward the mist. This time, however, instead of trying to break through, he jumped up, hoping that the top of the fog would be easier to penetrate. He was wrong.

When he was a foot above the fog's highest point, he leapt forward, but instead of falling through the cloud, he found that the top was just as dense as the section below. Standing on top of the fog, he knew Ronan and Michael were less than ten feet below. Incensed by the unexplained phenomenon, Nakano howled into the night with the force of a banshee because he knew that he was too late.

Filled with the pureness of love, Ronan held the back of Michael's head tightly and followed The Well's command, followed the command of their own hearts, and plunged his fangs into Michael's neck. Michael's eyes opened wide as he gasped in ecstasy, clawing at Ronan's back, his shoulders, as a violent burst of passion ripped through his body and odd visions flooded his brain.

Image after image passed over his mind's eye. He was standing naked before an ocean; he was diving deeper, deeper, deeper until the blue water was almost black; he was drinking from a well, kissing Ronan, pressing his hand against his. What was wrong with his hand? It didn't look normal.

In Ronan's mind, however, everything looked perfectly natural, even though the images were new, never before seen. Michael walking down a hallway in Two W by himself, Michael sitting next to an old man in a pickup truck, Michael alone in his bedroom in Weeping Water, Michael looking out the window at the flooded path that separated him from his destiny. Then the sun shining intensely, the path dry and clear, Michael walking, walking, walking toward something, his eyes bright, his mouth smiling, parting to reveal chiseled fangs, stopping only to embrace Ronan, to pierce the smooth white flesh of his neck.

Another shock wave flooded Michael's body. He couldn't believe the power of the sensation. And neither could Ronan. The blood tasted sweeter and more intoxicating than any he had ever tasted. Warm, free-flowing, and exquisite. Because he wasn't just tasting Michael's blood, he wasn't just feeding, he was acquiring his essence, all the emotions, all the history, every intangible quality that made Michael special, so he could offer it to The Well. He was tasting Michael's soul.

When it was over, the boys shivered in each other's arms. Neither one knew how to express what he was feeling, so they just held on to each other, both wondering how in the world they ever got so lucky to wind up in each other's embrace. Their sleep came quickly and was deep and uninterrupted.

But when Michael opened his eyes to the morning light, he felt them burn, and then his body started to convulse, and he knew something was terribly, terribly wrong.

chapter 20

"Ronan."

The name escaped Michael's lips like a plea. He tried again to open his eyes, but the second they met a piece of light, they burned like they were on fire. "Ronan!"

Hearing the fear before the words, Ronan woke up and instantly knew what to do. He shut the blinds, blocking out the sun's rays, cursing himself for not doing it last night in preparation for this morning, but he had forgotten. It was just that last night was so thrilling, so unexpected even for him, the connection between him and Michael so strong, that it truly was more powerful than anything he had ever felt before, and he forgot to make the proper preparations. But their night of passion was behind them and today there was work to be done.

Frightened, Michael tried to sit up in bed but felt weak. It was as if the room, with him in it, was spinning downward, spiraling down a well, to some place where it was dark and cool. "Ronan, I think I'm sick," Michael said, barely able to get out the words, his throat so dry. "Take me . . . take me to the infirmary."

Rushing to his side, Ronan clutched Michael's hands, his beautiful, immortal hands, and told him he wasn't sick; this was all part of the transformation. *What did he say?* Michael couldn't quite hear him. "No . . . no, I'm not right." He paused so he could gain the strength to speak further. "My eyes . . . and my throat."

"Don't be afraid," Ronan said, wiping a bit of sweat from Michael's brow. "It's completely natural." Rummaging through a drawer of his dresser, Ronan found his sunglasses, the same pair he wore when he was first converted, and placed them on Michael's face. "There, that'll help your eyes." He kissed Michael's cold cheek but could feel the fire just beneath his skin. "It'll be over soon, trust me."

The sunglasses did help. He felt the burn leave his eyes, but sunglasses? Why did he need to wear sunglasses in November? Wait . . . this wasn't the first time. Where else had he seen people wearing sunglasses? Nakano! Yes, Nakano wore them for a few days, said he had an eye infection from his contacts, but there was someone else. Michael felt something being pulled down over his head, something soft. Ronan was dressing him. His hands felt so good. "You need to stay warm," Ronan told him.

Michael felt his leg being lifted, sweatpants being tied around his waist. *How sweet; he's taking such good care of me.* "I am warm," Michael said. "Inside."

"You need to feel warm on the outside too. Believe me, this feeling is only for a little while. It won't last very long."

I believe anything you say, Michael thought, *because I love you.* "I love you, Ronan."

Kneeling next to the bed, Ronan held Michael's hand, tears of pride filling his eyes. "I love you too, Michael, more than you can imagine." *You are my mate, my soul mate, and together we will explore the ends of the earth for eternity.* He couldn't wait to begin their journey, but for it to start, he first had to get Michael to The Well. "I just need to get dressed," Ronan told him.

The man in that club wore sunglasses too. That was it! The man behind the metal plate was wearing sunglasses . . . that was why Penry got so excited . . . *oh, Penry, I'm so sorry.* Penry's face flashed in front of Michael's eyes, but it wasn't the Penry he remembered. He was different, altered. His hair was so long. Why was his hair so long? He always wore it so short. "Ronan?"

"I'll be right there, Michael."

"Why is Penry's hair so long?" No, it wasn't hair

wrapped around his neck, it was blood. Blood gushing out of his neck, rushing over his shoulder. "Oh, Penry, no!"

"No, don't think of that," Ronan ordered, shoving a leg into a pair of jeans.

When Michael wiped the tears from his eyes, the sunglasses fell onto the bed, but with the blinds shut tight and sunlight barred from the room, there was nothing to burn his eyes. *Oh, that feels much better,* Michael told himself. He swung his legs over the side of the bed and realized he probably had a touch of the flu. Served him right for sleeping naked with his boyfriend two nights in a row, but it just wouldn't feel as good if he wore his pajamas.

Michael was able to stand for only a few seconds before he fell to the floor. It wasn't that he was weak, he was terrified. He had seen his image in the mirror. Repulsed, Michael crawled backward until he slammed into the wall and couldn't crawl any farther. "My eyes! My God, what's wrong with them?"

Half dressed, Ronan ran to Michael and knelt in front of him to block his reflection. "It's only temporary," he said. "Once you drink from The Well, they'll go back to normal. Like mine."

The Well? What the hell was he talking about? Michael pushed Ronan to the side so he could see into the mirror. His eyes were like two black holes that burrowed into his skull. *Am I blind? Am I imagining this?* Michael wasn't sure; he needed a closer look. On his hands and knees he moved toward the mirror, forcing Ronan out of his way when he tried to stop him. "They're like Nakano's eyes," Michael said in amazement. "It's what I saw . . . in St. Martha's . . . when his sunglasses slipped." His eyes were as black as a starless sky and yet they shone brightly. How could that be? How could any of this be? He turned to Ronan and was, for some reason, compelled to ask him a question. A question he was utterly afraid to hear the response to. "What did you do to me?"

"Only what you wanted."

This?! This is what I wanted? "What do you mean what I wanted?" Michael bellowed. "I didn't ask for this."

Stay calm, Ronan, you have to stay calm for his sake. Remember what it was like for you. "You asked for immortality," Ronan replied.

What was he talking about? Michael racked his brain and finally stopped when he remembered the conversation they had in the cathedral, the conversation Michael had assumed, ultimately, was hypothetical. But now, looking at Ronan, he realized his instinct had been correct. Ronan was serious. He had been talking about the possibility, the real possibility of becoming immortal. Like Dorian, but without a portrait in his attic. That was fiction; this, no, this couldn't be fact.

Once again his head started to spin. He reached out his hand to grab the side of the bed, but in his mind, behind the blackness of his eyes, he saw something completely different. He saw his hand, distorted, enlarged. What was that between his fingers? Webbing? Then he saw his hand clutch the side of stone, curved, damp stone, and felt a pain roar through his body. "Don't touch me!" Michael screamed when Ronan tried to help him off the floor.

"Please, Michael," Ronan begged. "I need to help you."

Riddled with fear and pain, Michael didn't know what to think. He loved this boy in front of him, loved him more than he thought possible, but something had changed. "Something has changed," Ronan said, understanding his thoughts. "You're like me now, you're immortal."

Pulling himself back onto the bed, Michael searched for the sunglasses and put them on. He couldn't bear the thought of Ronan seeing him with his eyes looking so grotesque. Not that anything about Michael's appearance seemed to frighten him. He wasn't running away; on the contrary, he kept telling him that he was going to help him, bring him to this well. "Why do you keep talking about a well?" Michael murmured. "I dreamed of one."

Ronan grabbed Michael by the arms, enthusiasm overriding fear. "Because it's our destiny."

You are my destiny, Michael thought. *I felt it the moment I saw you because I dreamed of you back home in Weeping Water; you're the boy from the ocean, the dark-haired boy who loved me. Who loves me even now, like this.* "No! I have a fever . . . I must, I'm hallucinating," Michael protested, trying to break free from Ronan's hold. "Please, Ronan . . . bring me to Dr. Mac-Cleery . . . so he can help me."

Sternly, Ronan told Michael that Dr. MacCleery didn't have the knowledge or the power to help him right now. Only he did. "I need to bring you to The Well off the island where I was born so I can offer it your blood and you can drink from it. Then the transformation will be complete and you won't feel sick. You'll be healthier and stronger than you've ever been in your entire life."

Ronan spoke so calmly, his words spilled out of his mouth so effortlessly, that they were almost soothing, like a prayer, but Michael couldn't shake the spasm of fear that clung to his brain. "My . . . *blood?*"

"Yes, your blood must be offered to The Well for you to become one of us."

Now his brain was slowly, but surely, being devoured by fear. When he started to speak, he couldn't stop his voice from shaking, but with each new word, he seemed to be reclaiming his strength. "Ronan . . . I need you . . . to get me to a doctor . . . or get the hell out of my way, because something is really, really wrong!"

"No! Everything is perfect," Ronan said, his eyes bright like a child's. "This is all meant to be. You said so yourself."

"I love you, Ronan, I really do, but right now you're scaring the hell out of me." Michael broke free from his boyfriend's hold and flew off the bed. His legs were shaky, but sheer determination kept them from collapsing underneath him. He was only able to keep the door open for a few seconds before Ronan slammed it shut.

"Don't be scared," Ronan pleaded, his hands pressed against Michael's shoulders making it impossible for him to move. "It's because of our love that I was able to create you in my image." Tenderly, Ronan removed Michael's sunglasses and he wasn't offended by the two dark tunnels staring back at him. If anything, they made him love Michael even more because they meant that he had begun to shed his mortal trappings and was on his way to becoming a far superior being.

Although Michael could see tenderness etched into Ronan's face, he couldn't feel it. All he felt was dread. "You *created* me."

"Yes." Ronan nodded. "You're like me now. You're a vampire."

Following a tense pause, the room was filled with the roar of Michael's laughter, incredulous, loud, and relieving. Chords of laughter flowed so freely from Michael's body that he almost forgot about the pain. "You're a vampire?"

"Yes," Ronan answered quietly, his hands once again pressing against Michael's shoulders.

"Then where's your coffin?" Michael asked, trying to do so without laughing, but unable. "And how come the sun hasn't burnt you to a crisp?"

Ronan felt his breath quicken. He had thought this would be so easy; he thought Michael would embrace his new life, not fight it at every turn. "Because I'm different; I'm a hybrid."

If his laughter wouldn't keep making him light-headed, Michael would have continued, but he needed to steady himself, he needed his mind to be clear. "A hybrid? Ronan, you're incredibly sexy, so very sexy, but you're no comedian. Now seriously, I need to see Mac-Cleery."

"Michael, listen to me, I need you to understand. No doctor can help you now because there's nothing wrong with you. You're simply crossing over from what you used to be to what you've become, a vampire like me."

"This isn't funny, Ronan!" Michael shouted, quickly losing patience with his boyfriend. "I'm not Dracula, for God's sake, I'm sick!"

Michael turned and reached for the doorknob, but Ronan grabbed his hand before he could make contact. Using strength he didn't know he had, Michael brought his elbow up and slammed it into Ronan's chin, the force of which made Ronan stumble backward into his dresser. Ronan realized he wasn't going to convince Michael by using words, so just as he was about to open the door, Ronan showed him his true self. "Look at me!"

It was like watching a horror film unspool and bleed out into the room, the unimaginable coming to life. His boyfriend, his absolutely beautiful boyfriend, was changing right in front of his eyes. His hands and his feet were growing, spreading out, the spaces between each finger and toe being filled in by the same kind of webbing that Michael had seen on his own hand in his vision just minutes earlier. His eyes that were so blue— Michael knew for sure that they were blue—were now like white-hot flashes of light, and his fangs, dear God, he had fangs, sharp, smooth, deadly. Michael couldn't move. If he was breathing, he was doing so only because his body remembered how. His mind had forgotten everything, everything except what Ronan had said. He was a vampire. And if that was true, then so was he.

"Ro . . . Ronan . . . what . . . has happened to you?"

"Don't be afraid," Ronan said. "Please don't be afraid." He slowly moved toward Michael, who involuntarily cowered. "No, no, I would never hurt you."

Michael closed his eyes. He wanted to run from the room, run as far as he could, back to the safety of his old bedroom, but he had no strength, so he shut his eyes and chattered like a child. "This isn't real, this isn't real, this is make-believe."

"No, Michael," Ronan said. "This is our reality. We are a special breed of vampire. We can walk in the sun, we can live normally, and we are immortal. You and I will be together, in love, forever."

He couldn't take it any longer. The fear, the anger, the betrayal couldn't be concealed and controlled, so Michael allowed them to be unleashed. He kicked Ronan squarely in the stomach and sent him flying across the room, smashing into the wall. The stones shook and a spray of dust hit the air. Before Ronan hit the floor, Michael scrambled to his feet, grabbing the sunglasses that were lying next to the bed, and bolted out of the room. He didn't know where he was running to, but he had to get away from that thing that pretended to be his boyfriend. Maybe if he ran far enough and fast enough, the horror of the morning would turn into a harmless memory, and his life would go back to being what it was just the other day. But the farther he ran, the farther he knew his life had already changed and not for the better.

Just as he entered The Forest of No Return, he heard Ronan running behind him. He was gaining speed. He knew The Forest better than he did, and Michael was sure he wouldn't be able to outrun him here.

But Michael didn't realize he had a protector.

"Michael, wait!" Ronan called out, his bare feet hardly touching the stones and ground beneath him, and Michael stopped, not because he was obeying Ronan's command, but because he saw the fog.

The mist encircled Michael and for a split second he remembered something: He had been here before, lost, walking into fog, then when he woke, he thought he was being attacked by an animal with long fangs and white lights for eyes, an animal that turned out to be Ronan. "Oh my God, it's all true," he murmured. "It's always been true."

As the fog rose all around him, Michael turned to see Ronan standing only a few yards away, his chest covered in sweat and heaving, his face distraught. Gone were the fangs and the distorted hands. He was back to being the Ronan he knew and loved. And then suddenly all he could see all around him was gray smoke. He pressed against it, but it was hard as cement, impenetrable. "Ronan!" he cried, but the sound just echoed within his tomb. Falling to the ground, Michael cried out again, but this time his cry was devoid of any love and was filled with hatred. "Damn you!!"

On the other side of the fog, Ronan pounded against the barrier, but just as Nakano had come to realize, Ronan knew that it couldn't be penetrated. Whoever was responsible for creating this protection made sure that its detainee was secure. Ronan understood how charms worked and why they were used, and he knew this one's purpose was to separate him and Michael. He would leave for now and allow it to win, but he would be back to take his place at Michael's side where he belonged. First, however, he needed to get advice from someone who was far more experienced dealing with the unknown.

"Why would someone want to prevent me from helping Michael?" Ronan asked.

"There are countless reasons, dear," Edwige said. "Too numerous to mention."

"I'm only asking for one!" Ronan's voice bellowed throughout his mother's apartment with such force, the painting on the wall shook, the waves moving as if alive. Edwige didn't chastise her son for his outburst; she understood that he was distraught. His lover's blood and soul were pulsating through his veins and what he thought would be a glorious morning spent offering himself and his betrothed to The Well had turned into a nightmare. But Edwige knew from experience that every nightmare, no matter how horrific, had an ending.

"Has this fog ever separated the two of you before?"

"No."

"Has Michael ever mentioned it to you?"

"No, Mother, never!" Ronan rose from his chair and started to pace the room, the untied laces of his sneakers failing about at his feet. But before he reached the other end, he stopped. "Yes! Once, once he mentioned a fog."

"Think," Edwige ordered. "Think clearly and tell me what he said."

Ronan closed his eyes and looked into his memory before conveying what Michael had told him. "He was lost; he was walking on campus at night looking for me and he got lost. I found him the next morning in The Forest. He said he had no idea how he got there, but he remembered seeing a fog and then getting very tired."

Edwige glanced at her painting, which loomed heavily in the room. "He was out searching for you?"

"Yes, he was on his way to my dorm but lost his way," Ronan said.

At another time, when matters weren't so serious, Edwige might not have said what was on her mind, but this was no time for caution. "It sounds like Brania's work. It appears as if They are desperate to prevent you and Michael from coupling."

For once his mother was wrong. "No, that's not it."

Turning to face her son, she said, "I know you would prefer it be something else."

"It is something else! That was the night Penry was

first attacked . . . by Nakano. And Michael was only a few yards away. I never understood why Nakano didn't attack him as well, but now I know Michael was being protected. Trust me, if I couldn't break through that fog, there's no way Nakano could."

Her son made sense. If They didn't want Ronan to transform Michael, why would They create an obstruction to stop Nakano from getting there first? However, They were a hideous race and their intentions were rarely compassionate. "Something isn't right," Edwige declared. "There's a piece missing."

"The fog is protecting Michael, but not from *me*. If it were, I would never have been able to transform him last night." Edwige almost had to look away when she saw the veil of sadness cover her son's face. "But now he's out there alone. He has no idea what's happening to his body and he thinks . . . he thinks I've tried to hurt him." A mother never wants to see her child cry, even a mother as unskilled as Edwige. "Doesn't he know how much I love him? Doesn't he know that I can't live without him?"

The last time Edwige cradled her son in her arms was when she told him his father had been killed, destroyed by their enemies. That was also the last time she felt tears sting her own eyes. She could sense that the pain Ronan was feeling now cut just as deeply as the pain she had felt that night. "I need to find him," Ronan said, his voice cracking. "I need to bring him to The Well so he can feed before it's too late."

Edwige hated giving in to such human frailty, but

maybe it was time to let go of some of the pain, some of the rage. "You have time, Ronan. You have until your next feeding."

When Ronan looked up at his mother, it was almost too much for her to bear. She wanted to look away, she started to, but she compelled herself to look into the eyes of her son, just as she had compelled herself to look into the eyes of Saxon before he left this earth. "But what if he doesn't want me? What if he hates me for what I've done and I've lost him forever?"

Edwige understood the need to ask such questions. She also understood that it was a complete waste of time because she had been asking her own useless questions for years. What if someone comes into your house in the middle of the night and takes your husband from you and your children? What if the last time you see the man that you love, love more than you thought you were capable of loving another being, human or otherwise, he is surrounded by a mob carrying torches, tied to a stake, covered in gasoline, begging for his life? What if you could erase all that from your past? "That will not happen." Edwige cried. "Not again."

She bowed her head and rested it against her son's, fighting to let go of the image of one man, the first to set her husband on fire. The man who shouted, *"Death to all water vamps!"* into the cold night air and whose ugly blue eyes filled with sheer joy when her beloved Saxon started to scream, to shriek in absolute agony, and whose voice erupted into cheers of triumph when

Saxon's body was gone and in its place lay black ash and embers. *But enough! Enough of the past, enough of the memories. Our future is all that matters.* "Come now," Edwige said. "Let go of me." Ronan stood up, not as tall as usual, but at least he stood. "I need to get Michael back for you."

The first stop she made was at St. Peter's Dorm. Ciaran was surprised to see them, but relieved to see Ronan. "You and Michael weren't in class today. Is everything all right?"

Pushing her way into his room, Edwige sat Ronan down on the bed. "Your brother isn't in the mood to talk. Stay with him until he's well enough to leave."

Ronan looked like he had been crying. And if Ciaran didn't know his mother better, he would have suspected the same thing of her. "What's going on?"

"I need you to take care of your brother! Can you do that?"

Sure, Mother, Ciaran thought, *I'll be part of the family now that it's convenient for you.* "I'm sorry, Mother, it's just such a rare occasion when you need my help."

There were those blue eyes again, the eyes that still haunted her. At the moment they contained no joy, they were not lit up by torchlight, nor were they about to shine with the glory of triumph, but they were still as haunting as ever. And Edwige hated them. She didn't care if they were possessed by the father or by the son, those eyes, thanks to the memories they sparked, would never, ever know her kindness.

"Trust me, I wouldn't be here if Ronan wasn't desperate."

When they were alone, Ciaran looked at his brother and knew that whatever was troubling him, whatever made him look so lost and defeated, had to do with Michael. Sitting next to Ronan, Ciaran almost laughed at the irony. The last time they were together, he was begging Ronan to turn him into a vampire and now it seemed that his brother needed a simple human connection. Knowing how it felt to be empty and discarded, Ciaran couldn't deny Ronan his touch although he wished he could. How he wished he had the strength to exist alone, isolated, separated from everyone and everything. But that was just a pipe dream. So, resigned, he put his arm around his brother and let Ronan rest his head against his shoulder. However, neither brother said anything they would later regret.

Edwige's next stop was to a town house in London a mile or so from where she lived, to see a man. "Vaughan." Edwige beamed. "Your assistant told me you'd be working out of your home today."

Surprised, but pleasantly, Vaughan let his favorite new acquaintance into his home. "Edwige, I didn't expect to see you so soon after the festival."

"Quite frankly, neither did I." Quickly she surveyed his home and ascertained, quite accurately, that she was slightly wealthier than he was. "I'm sorry that I had to attend to a business crisis after the festival and we couldn't . . . finalize our relationship."

Vaughan was relieved Edwige hadn't feigned a headache but made up a business crisis to escape spending the night with him. It was much more original. "I must confess I have spent a moment or two thinking about what could have occurred."

Edwige was crestfallen. "Just a moment?"

"Or two."

That was better. Despite the urgency of the current matter she needed to attend to, it made her feel better to know she hadn't lost her feminine charms. "Well, you should be happy to know that it is a personal matter that brings me here. One I believe you can help me with."

"I am at your service," Vaughan said, sitting down on the chocolate-brown leather couch, patting the seat next to him in lieu of a verbal invite. As she walked over to take her seat, Edwige bent down to admire a gorgeous bouquet of white roses in a black marble planter, much too modern for her taste but, from what she could tell, expensive. "Please be careful!"

Before Edwige could even breathe in the roses' fragrant aroma, Vaughan stood and brought the planter to the other side of the room, placing it on top of the granite kitchen countertop that separated the two rooms. "I'm sorry, roses are so delicate, you know," he explained. "And they were a gift."

Lying, Edwige replied, "I understand."

Much less relaxed than he was a minute ago, Vaughan sat on the opposite side of the couch and crossed his legs like a proper English gentleman. And like a proper English gentleman, he concealed his emotion behind a courteous tone of voice. "I assume this visit has something to do with our children."

"You assume correctly," Edwige replied in the same tone. "It seems they've had a misunderstanding."

Vaughan held back a sigh of relief and merely said, "Why, that's too bad." Unfortunately for Vaughan, Edwige had had a rough morning, so her allotted time period for remaining pleasant had already run out.

"We both know you don't mean that. And inside that little brain of yours, you're celebrating or doing whatever a man does when he thinks he's won a battle, but I can assure you that this battle is far from over." Edwige took a quick breath to continue before Vaughan could interrupt. "You see, my son and your son are destined to be together, so it behooves us all to give them a little push so they can find their way back to each other." It didn't matter how many breaths she took this time because Vaughan was speechless. "Now, have you heard from Michael lately?"

After a moment he found his voice. "I can't say that I have. I've been meaning to call him. I have some news for him."

"News?"

"From back home, Nebraska," Vaughan replied. "But I must circle back to your comment about destiny. I hardly think, well, in fact I know, our teenaged sons are not, not at all each other's destiny."

Knowing when to make an exit is one of a woman's best traits, so having done what she came here to do—plant a seed; hope Vaughan takes action so he can lead her to Michael—Edwige collected her things and began to leave. "Vaughan, your thoughts are immaterial because they are the thoughts of a wise and successful man, not those of a teenaged boy. When teenagers are distraught, they tend to ignore their studies. And I know that a man as successful and driven as yourself has his son's future all planned out."

When Vaughan stood up, he was over a foot taller than Edwige. Looking down at her, he didn't know if he wanted to crush her or ravish her right there on his couch. "You're right, I do have his future planned out," he said. "Meticulously."

"Then tell Michael to speak to Ronan to clear up their misunderstanding so they can both get their minds back on their schoolwork and have the bright, promising futures their parents have worked so hard to set in motion."

Vaughan was on the verge of being just as forthright and telling Edwige that he had no intention of advising his son to make up with hers, not when it looked like he may have come to his senses. Instead he chose a craftier tactic. "I will do that. I know how difficult and confusing relationships can be at that age."

"At any age," Edwige said, adding a coquettish laugh to, hopefully, soften her harsh approach.

Standing in the doorway, her mission complete, Edwige was overwhelmed with a feeling of distrust for this man. Then again, she didn't trust any man, so she couldn't put too much credence in that feeling. And even though he was quite handsome and would probably make an enjoyable and enthusiastic playmate, there was something about him that made her regret the fact that their families would, in one way or another, forever be linked. "Please ring me once you speak with Michael," Edwige said. "I do so want to put this matter in the past."

"I couldn't agree with you more." But since Vaughan had learned in business to never fully shut a door, he gave Edwige a kiss on her lips that left her the way he had planned, and the way she hardly ever found herself, speechless.

Minutes later, while he waited for Michael to pick up his phone, Vaughan wondered why women always thought they were in control. Men have the real power, well, men like him, who knew how to use it properly. After the recording, Vaughan left a message for his son. "Michael, this is your father. I'm sorry about the other night. I guess I'm still learning how to do this parent thing properly." Vaughan breathed in deeply, the fragrance of the roses enveloping him. He touched a petal, so soft, so smooth. "I hate leaving this information on a message, but your grandmother died the other day. Please ring me and I can give you all the details." Was there anything he forgot to say? "I, um, I hope all is well with you."

*   *   *

It wasn't. Long after the fog had lifted, Michael still couldn't find the strength to move. He lay shivering on the ground, bothered by the cold but grateful that the sun had set because, even with the sunglasses, his eyes were still irritated by its light. He wished he had never come to this place. The pain of Two W and his home life were nothing compared to what he was going through now. He was physically and emotionally exhausted. And he couldn't believe that it was all because of Ronan, the person he thought was going to be his savior.

When he opened his eyes, he realized that his hand was moving; he was lazily drawing in the dirt. Round and round and round his finger went, creating a circle in the earth. He knew it was a well, that thing Ronan talked about, that thing that was so vital to his existence, that thing he wished he had never heard about. *No, no, no!* He rubbed at the dirt furiously, making the circle disappear, and begged God to do the same thing to him. Just open up the ground and swallow him whole. Because if he couldn't go on living in His image, then he didn't want to go on living at all. But the ground didn't open and he wasn't swallowed up by the dirt, maybe because even unnatural things were created in God's image.

A hybrid vampire! The idea was absurd. It couldn't possibly be true, and yet he believed it, he believed that Ronan was telling him the truth and he was no longer human. When he thought of the implications, the real consequences, he clutched the dirt and screamed in fear, but there was no sound. He opened his mouth, but the sob, the terror, strangled his throat. His body shook uncontrollably.

And when he felt the hand on his shoulder, he actually jumped.

"Don't be afraid," Nakano said. "I'm here to help you."

chapter 21

Somewhere down there was The Well.

Thirty thousand feet below, beneath the Atlantic Ocean, was this well that Ronan had spoken about. This mysterious place that was supposed to grant him eternal life, untold power, and the chance to be an equal to his immortal partner. Michael had no idea if it really existed; he didn't know anything any longer. His life, once again, was a mystery just when it was starting to be under his control. Just when his life was starting to mirror his dreams. Just when his life was about to begin, it ended.

He looked out the window of the plane and it was

like looking into a crystal ball to see his future—he saw nothing but darkness. He couldn't believe he was flying back to Weeping Water and he couldn't believe he was sitting next to Nakano. Nothing was right, nothing was the way he wanted it to be. And it was all Ronan's fault.

"Michael! Thank God you're all right." There was relief in Ronan's voice that was unmistakable, but it wasn't enough to make Michael want to look at him. "Please don't leave. There's so much more I need to explain to you, so much more we need to do." Pleading wouldn't make him look up either.

Snapping his suitcase shut, Michael looked out the window. He thought he heard a meadowlark singing, he thought he heard the familiar song he loved so much. But no, there was no lilting sound, nothing, only silence. "My grandmother died," he said quietly. "I'm going back home for the funeral."

"I'm so sorry to hear that," Ronan said, moving in front of the door so Michael had no choice but to pause and let Ronan take one last look at him. His heart ached knowing that he caused the pain on Michael's face, he was the reason his skin looked so ashen, his eyes so bleak. "I'll go with you," Ronan said. "I'd love to see where you grew up."

"He already has a traveling companion."

Startled, Ronan didn't even know there was someone in the bathroom. *This is only because Michael is scared. He's angry with me right now and he needs some space*

*away from me, but that will change. In time, he'll know
I acted out of love and I did what I did so our love
could only grow and never die.* "Michael." He didn't respond, but he did finally look at Ronan. "You won't be
away very long, will you?"

*Will I ever be able to look at you again without anger
and resentment and confusion?* Michael wondered. "Only
a day or two."

"Good," Ronan replied. "I'll be waiting for you."

If Michael had anything more to say, Ronan wasn't
going to hear it because Nakano ushered him out the
door. "C'mon, mate, we've got a plane to catch. And it's
not every day I get to fly first class, thank you very
much, Father Howard."

Just before Nakano left the room, Ronan grabbed his
arm, his fingers pressing deeply into his thin bicep, and
he used every ounce of restraint he had not to cry in
front of his rival. "You take good care of him, Kano,
you protect him."

Nakano pried Ronan's fingers off of his arm and
smiled, unmoved by the quiver in Ronan's voice. "Don't
worry, Ro, I'll do a much better job than you did."

That had been this afternoon. Now flying through the
night toward his past, Michael had no idea if he had
made the right decision to leave Ronan behind. There
were so many unanswered questions, so many words
swirling inside his head, banging against his brain. He
wanted to strangle Ronan, punch him, grab his neck

and pull him closer so he could kiss him. No! Not that. No more kisses. How could he even think of wanting to do that?

Michael looked over to the boy sitting next to him, stretched out and reclining in his seat, a blanket tucked under his chin, wearing silver satin eyeshades like some experienced world traveler. *Well, he's a lot more experienced than I am.* And he's a vampire too. Not the same kind as Ronan, or so he said, just your regular run-of-the-mill vampire, which was not exactly how he described himself after he took Michael out of The Forest and brought him to an abandoned house with a cold cement floor. The place felt familiar, but Michael couldn't remember ever being there before.

"Ronan is different, part of a minority among our people, and not a particularly celebrated group, if you really want to know the truth," Nakano explained. "For right now, you're just like him."

"What do you mean *for right now?*" Michael asked, suddenly aware that he was ravenously hungry.

"Well, we can get into all of that later," Nakano cautiously replied, "but just know you have a choice how you'd like to spend your eternity."

"A choice," Michael spat. "All my choices have been taken away!"

That's right, Nakano had silently urged, *keep getting angry; get ticked off at what Ronan did to you.* However, when he spoke, it was in a much more empathetic voice. "That's not entirely true. You can choose to live among a band of half-breed renegades or alongside the people who really control all the power."

So not only were there vampires, but there were different types of vampires? Michael was wrong. The earth had opened up and he was swallowed whole and had fallen into some alternate reality. He couldn't think straight. It wasn't so much the gibberish coming out of Nakano's mouth, it was his own body. It was throbbing. He had never been so hungry in all his life.

Nakano recognized the signs. "But all that can wait. I have the feeling that right now you're hungry."

It was at that moment that Michael realized what his fangs were for. They were for feeding, taking blood from another human being, and the thought of it made him nauseous. He rolled over onto his side clutching himself; he felt the steel bars that supported the thin mattress of the cot he was lying on press into his shoulder and he remembered being in the closet with Ronan, feeling the shelf press into his back as Ronan held his face and kissed him. The faint taste of raspberry still clung to his lips. But now he craved another taste, and the thought of it was making him sick.

Out of the corner of his eye he saw Nakano roll up his sleeve to expose a pale, thin forearm accented with dark blue veins. Michael could feel his head throb and his mouth tingle. He could feel his fangs descend against his will and rest against his lips. The smell of blood consumed him. Two days ago he wouldn't have known what blood smelled like, but today he recognized the aroma, the thick scent. A mix of ripe berries and cold metal flooded his senses. He was disgusted and aroused at the same time. All he wanted to do was plunge his fangs into Nakano's arm to see if the blood tasted as magnificent as it smelled.

"Aim for a vein," Nakano instructed. "That'll make it easier for you to drink."

Nakano helped Michael sit up on the cot and he sat behind him, straddling his legs around him the way Ronan had once done. He placed his bare arm underneath Michael's nose, and Michael thought he would faint. "Go ahead," Nakano said. "I taste pretty good, if I do say so myself."

As if he were watching himself in a dream, Michael saw his hands grip Nakano's arm, one hand wrapped around his wrist, the other clutching his elbow. The veins in Nakano's arm throbbed as it was brought closer to Michael's waiting mouth as if the arm was just as eager to be bitten as Michael was to feed. All he had to do was open his mouth and bite down, and the hunger would be quenched, the pain that had spread through his entire body would cease. It was unconscionable what he was thinking of doing, biting into the flesh of another human being, but he was about to do it. And he would have if Nakano had not spoken. "Just imagine that it's Ronan."

That name brought him back to reality. A reality that he simply couldn't deal with, that he simply couldn't comprehend. A reality he didn't want to make worse. "I can't," Michael said, his fangs disappearing. "I can't do it."

Think before you speak, Kano; everything you say needs to create trust, a bond between you and this unsuspecting pawn. "I understand," Nakano lied. "You need time. Why don't you try and sleep?" And so Michael did. Unfortunately, when he woke, the hunger still clung to him as it did now, but so too did an idea. As long as he could remain strong, like St. Michael perhaps, stronger than the hunger, and not feed, maybe he could change back to what he was, human, mortal, and not become this creature like the one sitting next to him now.

Michael looked over at Nakano sleeping so peacefully, looking so innocent. The irony of the situation made him laugh out loud.

"What's so funny?" Nakano asked, rousing from his nap.

"Nothing," Michael said, shaking his head.

Pulling his eyeshades off, Nakano pressed him further. "Fess up, Michael. You haven't cracked a smile since we left home."

Michael gazed out the window and searched for a response. "I swore I'd never go back to Weeping Water and yet here I am."

"Don't sweat it, mate, you just have to remember not to limit yourself," Nakano said, with one eye following the handsome male flight attendant as he walked down the aisle. "Because guess what. You no longer have limitations."

There it was again, that pain. "Speaking of limitations," Michael said, "how long does it take to get used to these contacts? They're not the most comfortable things in the world, you know."

It was Nakano's turn to laugh. "You can blame your father for that."

"My father? What's he have to do with anything?"

"They're a product of Howard Industries," Nakano blurted out, now fully focusing on the flight attendant whose outfit was obviously designed to show off his fantastic physique.

"Nakano," Michael said, raising his voice to gain his attention. "Why would my father's company be making contacts for vampires?"

Backpedal, Nakano. Don't let this newbie screw up your last chance to impress Brania and her old man. "Did I *say* that? One of your father's companies makes tinted contacts, a novelty item, that's all. Our people were positively gobsmacked when they discovered the contacts could perfectly conceal our eyes without losing any of our enhanced vision." *Now, where did that hot attendant get to?*

Now my father's company is involved? It's just one complication after another, isn't it? "They block out the sun's rays too, right?" Michael asked. "That's why you can walk outside during the day."

Don't say too much, Kano, just keep it simple. "You

catch on quick." *No need to tell him that we can only walk in the sun on Archangel ground. Best to reveal that bit of information after he decides to become part of our race.* Nakano glanced at his watch. Local time was 5:25 A.M.; sunrise was in less than an hour. "Let's go over some ground rules before we land," Nakano said. "I don't do funerals; never liked them before and now I find them extraneous." As a member of the immortal world, Nakano considered death a means to an end, a necessity, not something that should be celebrated or honored in any way. But once again, he kept his thoughts to himself and merely smiled. "Extraneous. How's that for a vocabulary word? Betcha McLaren would be impressed."

Michael understood Nakano's aversion to funerals. This would be his third in the past six months and he still wasn't getting used to them. "Not a problem; you can stay at my house all day."

With the windows shut and the shades completely drawn, Nakano added to himself. "Sounds like a plan, mate."

Michael never thought Nakano would consider him a mate. And he never thought he'd relish returning to the simplicity of Weeping Water, even if it was just for a few days. Even if it was just to see his grandmother buried.

He remembered the last time he saw her, the night he left to fly to London. She didn't say much, she never did, but he felt that when she said good-bye to him, she was saying good-bye to a piece of her life, a piece that she would never get back. Hopefully, she's with his mother now and they're saying the things to each other they never got to say while they were alive. He wondered what he would say to them when his time came. Would he rush into their arms as he hadn't done since he was a young boy or would he just wave to them from the other side of a stream as they each went their separate ways? Or would he never get the chance to see them again because as a vampire he would not have an afterlife?

Alarmed by such a disquieting question, Michael pressed his forehead against the window; the cold began to temper his fear. He closed his eyes and pushed such philosophical thoughts from his mind. He wanted to deal with something much more tangible. Like land. When he opened his eyes, he saw that land was getting closer. It looked like he could jump out and easily set foot on top of one of the buildings, and who knows, maybe he could. Nakano said he'd be amazed by how powerful and agile his body would become. Imperious and almost invulnerable. There they were, philosophical thoughts again, inconceivable notions just like the ones that filled his conversations with Ronan. Ronan. *Why did you do this to me? And why aren't you sitting by my side?*

Finally! Nakano smiled back at the flight attendant and unbuckled his seat belt. " 'Scuse me, mate. Before the tires hit the runway, I'd like to become a member of the mile high club." Standing in the aisle, he leaned over to Michael, not noticing his eyes were about to spill over with tears. "Always been a little fantasy of mine."

These days, Inishtrahull Island was like a fantasy land. Barren, unpopulated, windswept. Ronan remembered how different it was when he was a child growing up here with his family and, of course, the others. He knew they were different, undeniably special, and he knew that someday when someone loved him strongly enough, he would be altered so he could become just like them. Until that time, he had to be satisfied being human among the undying. And he was.

He climbed the mountains, played on the beach, swam in the ocean, and waited for his chance to drink from The Well. When that time came nearly three years ago, he was overjoyed. His family had suffered such pain when his father was taken from them that he was thrilled he could give them, especially his mother, a reason for celebration. One hand placed on the rim of The Well, the other holding the hand of the man he thought would be his soul mate, was, up until that time, the happiest day of Ronan's life. He had no idea that man would ultimately betray him and his people. And he had no idea he would be given a second chance at eternal happiness. Until he met Michael.

"Michael." Ronan closed his eyes and whispered, hoping the wind would carry his voice across the ocean to Michael's ears. "Please come back to me."

"If it's truly meant to be, he will."

Ronan heard the girl's voice but didn't recognize it. He did, however, recognize the face. "Phaedra?"

"Hello, Ronan."

Involuntarily, he looked all around the beach, not really sure what he was expecting to see and in fact he saw nothing. They were the only two people on the island. What was she doing here? In his homeland. His bewilderment was evident. "You vampires think you're the only nonhumans roaming this earth."

He knew it. He knew this young girl who fit in effortlessly with their crowd, the girl with the unblinking stare, wasn't to be trusted. "What do you want?"

She smiled as a cool breeze rustled through her curls, her toes digging into the sand. "Relax. I can't hurt you. But I can help you."

For the first time Ronan noticed that her eyes were not quite blue, more blue-gray, like fog. "Like you've helped Michael?"

Phaedra smiled at Ronan. Gay, straight, human, whatever, he really was an extraordinary-looking creature. Then she sighed. Human emotion, whether it be crying over Penry's death or feeling pangs of desire over a handsome face, was something she never thought she'd experience. Life really was the way she was told it would be, filled with surprises. "I've done what I could."

A wave crashed, drops of salt water landing inches from their feet. "I knew there was something about you. Why have you been protecting him? Who are you?"

Phaedra heard Ronan's questions but seemed more

interested in drawing curlicues in the sand with a sea reed. "That's not your concern, Ronan."

"Michael's my concern! I love him!"

"I know you do," Phaedra replied. "And that's why I didn't have to protect him from you."

"But you did!" Ronan shouted, his voice louder than the crash of the waves. "You prevented me from seeing him when he needed me the most, when he was devastated and confused!"

Phaedra marveled at Ronan. Even these water vamps who breed out of love could still be aggressive when they became passionate. "Because at that moment, you would only have caused him greater devastation and greater confusion. He needed to be alone; he needed to be separated from you briefly to decide if he wants to return to you permanently."

"If? If he wants to return to me?" Ronan looked at the majestic ocean before him and breathed in its calm, but the familiar smell of sea salt, the strong line of the horizon, nothing helped. "I don't know what I'll do if . . . if he chooses not to come back to me."

Her hand felt so light on top of Ronan's, like air. "Have faith, Ronan. The Well has never been wrong yet."

Who is this girl? She knows about The Well, she knows everything about me and Michael. She definitely isn't one of us, nor is she one of Them. "Who are you?" But she was gone. He looked all around him, scoured the beach, the mountains behind him, even the ocean, and nothing. It was as if she had disappeared into the water's mist. *At least she gave me hope,* Ronan thought, hope that Michael would soon return and their life could begin.

Edwige had the same thought as she sat and stared at her painting. She had put her life on hold since Saxon's death, no, since his brutal murder, but perhaps it was time to test herself, see if her heart, once so loving and eager, could be reopened by another man. Edwige hesitated, uncharacteristically unsure of herself. *Can I actually do this?* She started to dial Vaughan's number but then set the phone back down onto its cradle.

Why was she so unsure about him? He was handsome, wealthy, successful, but for some reason he gave her cause for concern. Maybe it was simply because he disapproved of Ronan and Michael's relationship, though she thought she noticed a softening where that was concerned. Maybe if she were as honest with herself as she liked to be with other people, she would recognize that it was because, since losing her husband, she had only used men for her own physical needs and never once contemplated allowing them to touch her emotionally. She rolled her eyes at her reflection in the mirror, turning her back on it when she could no longer stand looking at how distorted her image had become since she was made a widow.

Walking through a cloud of very fragrant and very expensive perfume, she said, "Edwige, it's time to stop acting like a woman on the prowl and start acting like a

woman on the verge of irreversible loneliness." It was
time to learn from her son, learn from his full heart and
courageous spirit, and take action. As she left her flat,
she made a silent plea to her dead husband. *Forgive me,
Saxon, for I really don't know what the hell I'm about
to do.*

Now that he was back in Weeping Water, Michael felt
the same way: He had no idea what he was supposed to
do. It wasn't that the town had changed. It was exactly
the same, not a road, not a store, not a branch out of
place. It was he; he had changed, changed inextricably.
Even if he hadn't come back as a vampire, he still would
have felt the difference and so would the people around
him.

"You've grown up, Mike." R.J. was the last person
Michael expected to see at his grandmother's funeral,
but here he was. It was like stumbling onto a lost photograph from the past. A flutter of nerves erupted in Michael's stomach, joining the hunger pains that had yet to
go away. But distance and time had changed R.J.'s appearance. Michael had never noticed the lines at the
edges of his eyes—too many hours spent in the sun perhaps—the way his lips never spread out to create a full
smile. "Looks like that school over there's been good for
ya."

"Kind of," Michael said. "It's changed my life in lots
of ways."

R.J. looked around the cemetery grounds. "Your father didn't come with you?"

"No, just Nakano," Michael said, then noticed R.J.'s quizzical stare. "A friend from school. But he, um, he stayed back at the house."

Wind whistled between the two of them, interrupting their shared silence. "Must be a really good friend to travel all this way with you."

This was nothing, Michael thought. *You have no idea how far I've traveled since I left this town.* "Kano's always looking for an excuse to get out of school." *Just like I was always looking for an excuse to stare at you.* Michael was amazed that he was talking to this boy, this guy he had spent so many nights dreaming about, but his mind was so restless, his body so anxious, he didn't even realize R.J. was nervous himself in his presence, and, yes, even flirting a bit. Perhaps it was all for the best. The time for flirting with humans was probably a thing of his past. "It's, um, nice that you came."

R.J. shrugged his shoulders. "Least I could do." He glanced over to the quiet woman's final resting place, a place Michael couldn't bear to look at. "Your grandmother was . . . she was always good to me. Treated me nice, kindly, like you used to."

Michael couldn't help but think how unkindly R.J. would treat him if he knew what he had become. He was so wrapped up in his own anguish, he didn't even realize R.J. was still talking when he spoke. "Thanks for coming, but I should be getting back now."

Startled, R.J. swallowed the rest of his words. Michael probably didn't want to hear how good he thought he looked anyway, how nice it was to see his face again, not at his grandmother's funeral. So R.J. kept silent.

Just like his grandfather. He didn't think there was any need to talk on the drive home while the stench of death clung to his truck, while he sat next to this stranger. No need to fill the Bronco with unnecessary conversation; just wait until you get home, have a beer, unwind, then you can say what's on your mind. "You're different," he announced. "You haven't been gone that long and it's like I don't even know you. Not really sure that I like what I see, either."

Holding a coffee cup that his grandmother had washed hundreds, probably thousands of times before, Michael was instantly reminded of why he hated it here. The constant criticisms, the uncanny ability to point out flaws and never convey a kindness. Luckily, Michael wasn't that scared, awkward boy he was when he grew up here. No, he hadn't yet found his voice, not fully anyway, and yes, he was not at ease with his current state, but he knew that he no longer had to take crap from his grandfather. "It's not like you ever took the time to know me when I was living under your roof," Michael said. "I don't really see what the problem is."

Across the table, Nakano smiled. This old man made his own father look downright cultured. Michael was lucky that this one was the only remaining relative he had left in this dumb cesspool of a town. If the rest of them were like him, growing up here must have been unbearable.

"You watch your tone with me, young man!" his

grandfather bellowed. "This is my roof you're sittin' under."

"And it was my mother's money that paid off the mortgage," Michael retorted, watching the coffee twirl as he swirled his cup, coffee that he would never be able to taste again.

"Listen here! Just 'cause you're goin' to some fancy school don't mean you can talk to me like you own me. I am your grandfather, you remember that!"

The chair creaked loudly when Michael pushed it back to stand; louder still was the whir from the pipes when he turned on the hot water to wash his cup. Michael had no idea where his future was headed, but he knew that it would not contain parts of his past. "You forgot a long time ago that I was your grandson, so do not expect me to get all sentimental now that you're alone."

His grandfather wanted to speak, he felt the need to, but he was dealing with so many unexpected emotions, he didn't know which word to choose first, so he chose none. His wife of the past forty-two years was now in a coffin, buried in the ground next to his daughter. His grandson was here with some stranger, acting and talking like he had never seen him do before. He was alone for the first time in his life and he didn't like it. He also didn't like Michael's defiant attitude or the smug look on the Oriental he brought into his house. Maybe if he cracked open another beer, he'd find the right words to say.

"That's it, have another beer. That's your solution for everything," Michael said. "C'mon, Nakano, I need some air."

"Sounds good to me," Nakano said. "My fun stopped once the plane landed."

Throwing on a jacket, Michael announced, "Oh, and my father arranged for us to take an earlier flight and fly directly into Eden instead of London, so this is probably the last time you'll ever see me again." Standing in the archway of the front door, Michael turned to his grandfather. "Any final words?"

His grandfather didn't know what feeling was the strongest, fear, regret, anger. But how dare his grandson talk to him that way, like he was nothing? Waving his beer bottle at Michael, bubbles pouring out of the bottle, spilling onto his shaking hand, he shouted, "You go to hell!"

Michael smirked. "Oddly enough, that's not going to happen."

Walking through the flat, deserted streets of Weeping Water, next to a silent Michael, Nakano kept wondering when something would happen. He was ready for anything, good or bad, just to replace the boredom he was feeling. He almost cursed himself for agreeing to Brania's request, not that he really had much of a choice in the matter. Since he didn't get to Michael before Ronan transformed him, Brania and her father were forced to come up with a Plan B. Nakano was to see to it that Michael remained Ronan's spurned lover and use that to work against him. As Brania had pointed out while Nakano was still biting into her flesh, it might even turn out to be a better plan. If Michael joined forces with them willingly, Ronan wouldn't be able to blame them for taking him away; he could only blame himself. Maybe she wasn't so stupid after all. Still, how much longer was he going to have to walk the desolate streets of this dumbass town with Michael before he got to see some excitement? As they turned a corner that led into Michael's old high school, he got his wish.

"Howard! I figured you'd come back to say good-bye to your grandma, but I didn't think you'd have balls enough to bring along your boyfriend."

Mauro looked pretty much the same, still overweight, his hair could still use a trim, he had a few more pimples around his mouth and on his forehead, but otherwise it was the same loudmouthed jerk Michael remembered. "What's the problem? Gay cat got your tongue!"

Doubling over with laughter, Mauro didn't see Michael seethe. He had struggled so hard to make the taunting in his ears stop ringing, make his mind stop replaying the countless incidents he had suffered at the hands of this boy, this stupid, fat boy who stood before him laughing his head off, and with one quick comment, all Michael's hard work was for naught. He felt it was the first day of third grade on the playground when Mauro decided to single him out from the crowd and degrade him for the next decade, abuse him until he couldn't take it any longer. Michael thought he had put an end to his hatefulness before he left Two W, but clearly he hadn't made enough of an impression. He'd have to try harder.

Mauro wasn't sure if Michael hit him with his knee or his foot, but whichever it was, it hurt. Lying on his back on the grass, Mauro shook his head and got up. He hadn't had a good fight in weeks and even if Michael had gotten a bit stronger since he left town and even if he had the help of his skinny, fairy boyfriend, he was still no match for Mauro.

"Come on, faggot! I never got a chance to say goodbye," Mauro shouted. "My way!"

This is more like it, Nakano thought as he crouched down and folded his hands, letting his arms rest on his knees. *Michael can test his new vampire skills and I'll get a show.*

When Michael saw Mauro race toward him, it was as if all the anger he felt against Ronan and his grandfather boiled to the surface. Unable to contain his rage any longer and unable to direct it at the people he really wanted to punish, he unleashed it against Mauro. He saw a tooth fly out of his mouth as he punched him in the jaw, and as he watched Mauro careen sideways for a few seconds and then fall onto the grass, he didn't feel sorry for the boy at all. In fact, he felt quite good.

"Get up!" Michael ordered, but he didn't recognize the voice; it was deeper, gruffer. "I said get up!"

As he struggled to right himself, Mauro spat on the ground and Michael felt himself get dizzy. Mauro spat again, a mixture of blood and saliva that was absolutely tantalizing. Nakano smelled it too, and he left the sidelines to get closer to the action.

"I lost a tooth," Mauro whined. "You're gonna pay for that, faggot!"

Before he could fully stand, Michael kicked him in the stomach so hard that when he hit the ground a few feet away, he continued to roll until he crashed into the fence that surrounded the high school track. Mauro clutched his side and knew that something wasn't right. This wasn't the Michael he remembered; he had to get the hell away from him.

He reached up, his fingers struggling to grab on to the cold metal of the fence. When he finally had a solid grip, he pulled himself up so he was kneeling. But before he could pull himself up farther, he heard some dried leaves crunching and knew that Michael and his Jap boyfriend were getting closer. *Just let me get over the fence, then maybe I can run to the football shed and lock myself in; there's a spare key at the end of the bleachers.* It was a good plan, but Michael was too quick.

Just as Mauro threw a leg over the fence, Michael grabbed him by the back of the neck. "Where you goin', fat boy?" He flicked his wrist and Mauro flew backward, landing at Nakano's feet. When he rolled over, the smell of blood flooded Michael's throat. Mauro's mouth was still bleeding and so too was his forehead. Drawn to the scent, Michael found himself on his hands and knees next to Mauro, his fangs exposed, curving over his lips. It had been almost forty-eight hours since he was transformed into a vampire, since the hunger began, and Michael didn't care about fighting this new-found desire, prolonging the inevitable. He wanted to drink blood. And he wanted to drink it now.

"Who sounds like a girl now?!" Michael asked, his fangs pressing into his lips, making speech a bit difficult. Which was okay since Michael was more interested in feeding than speaking.

Valiantly, Mauro tried to free himself from Michael's grip, but to no avail. And even if he got away, Nakano was hovering close by, sort of Michael's tag team part-ner. "Help me! Somebody help me!"

The anger of a lifetime bleeding out of his body, Michael gripped Mauro by the shoulders and brought his face inches from his own, "Now you know what it feels like to be helpless!" Flung back toward the ground, Mauro's body bounced twice before lying still, his head conveniently tilting to the side, exposing his sweaty, fleshy neck.

"Go ahead, Michael," Nakano hissed from behind. "Enjoy your first kill."

Kill? Is that what he said? This is what I've become? Michael thought. *Not only a vampire, but a murderer too?* Looking into Mauro's eyes, he couldn't find one reason to offer him a reprieve, to extend to him any compassion, but he couldn't find one reason to kill him either. And so he let him go.

"Get out of here," Michael muttered. "Go! Before I change my mind."

Unsure if this was a trick like the kind he used to play

on him, Mauro hesitated until he saw Michael staring blankly ahead, his face back to the way it was. He had absolutely no idea what kind of game he was playing, what kind of sick game he had learned at that new school of his, but he wasn't going to wait to find out. Scrambling to his feet, Mauro stumbled off toward the school, one quick look back to make sure no one was chasing him, and then he was off as fast as his shaking legs could run.

"Are you out of your mind!?" Nakano screamed.

"I'm not a killer," Michael said.

They're always so sanctimonious in the beginning, Nakano thought. "Oh, really? Guess again!"

When Michael turned around, Nakano was nowhere to be found. In the shadow of Two W, he was once again consumed by a feeling of lonesomeness. But the feeling wasn't long-lasting because within a matter of seconds Nakano returned, dragging Mauro by the arm, his body scraping the ground. When the boy landed at Michael's feet, he saw the bloody gash on his neck and knew that he had about ten more seconds to live.

"Now eat," Nakano ordered. "Before your dinner gets cold."

Half a world away, Edwige felt the same way Michael did at that very moment—horrified. When she had arrived at Vaughan's door, she noticed it had been left ajar. She thought perhaps that she and Vaughan were psychically connected and he left the door open as an invitation so she wouldn't feel as if she was intruding. Now, standing in the room, she saw that Vaughan already had a female intruder.

Lying on his couch was Vaughan. Kneeling beside him was Brania. Edwige was repulsed because she knew the blood that dripped from her fangs was most definitely his.

As Michael bent down to shut Mauro's eyes, he felt the same feeling of revulsion because he simply couldn't bring himself to suck the blood out of the dead boy's neck. He had no way of knowing that while he was unable to become a predator, his father had just become prey.

chapter 22

Home. Michael didn't know where home was any longer. It was supposed to be a place that offered comfort, protection, a place where he could breathe easily. But he didn't know where on earth he'd be able to find any of that. None of it could be found in Weeping Water; his mother was gone from there; so was his grandmother. The only thing the town held for him now was an angry, spiteful grandfather, and a makeshift grave that contained the body of a bully. No, that town was lost to him forever.

Unfortunately, Archangel Academy, a place he had grown to love, didn't offer him much more. There was no comfort knowing this was the place where his life ended, and no protection since he had no idea what else might happen to him here. And breathing? Was that what he was doing? Did vampires even breathe? He could hardly believe that vampires were real and that he was one of them. God, could that really be possible?! He felt like he was sleepwalking, like he was reading a book and suddenly the words had ripped themselves off the pages and infected his life. He had become Dorian, except that he had become an immortal unwittingly, a victim unknowingly. He felt so incredibly lost, so willing to shut out the world and hope that he would fade from it that he fell asleep seconds after he felt the softness of the pillow cradle his head. He vaguely remembered hearing Nakano ask Ciaran to watch over him while he slept. "I guess that makes me Double A's resident babysitter," Ciaran had said. "First Ronan and now Michael."

Ronan. That name still made Michael ache with longing, pleasure, pain. But what was Ronan to him? Was he his boyfriend? His lover? A liar? Or just a fellow vampire? There's that insane word again, that piece of fiction that was now, impossibly, fact. No, better not to think about it or him, better not to question at all. Just dream.

The rain was coming down in straight lines from the sky; there was no accompanying wind, no thunder, just long vertical rows of rain. Ronan was standing in front of the cathedral, the moonlight illuminating him from behind to create a glow around his face, an aura that made him look like an angel, like his face should be a carving on the cathedral itself. His black hair was plastered down in bangs, his white T-shirt so wet it looked as if it was sealed to his skin. He looked like a statue, unreal. But then he spoke. "Welcome home, Michael."

"This isn't my home!" Michael shouted, tears sliding down his face alongside streaks of rain. "You destroyed everything we had! Everything that could have been!"

"No," Ronan gently corrected, rain dripping from his bangs onto his eyelashes, down to his unshaven chin, "I've made everything possible."

Tossing in bed, Michael mumbled his name. He felt a hand on his shoulder, but even asleep he knew it was someone else's touch. That was all right. Maybe dreaming was the only way he'd be able to be with Ronan again after what he'd done to him. So in his dream, Michael gave in to his passion and kissed Ronan. His lips tasted so sweet, wet with rain and rich with desire. It was only a few days since he had really kissed Ronan, but it felt like a lifetime. Underneath his T-shirt his skin was slick with rainwater, his body as hard as ever, and Michael felt like a warrior returning home to his lover after a long journey. Their passion intensified by their separation, their kisses a mere hint of the love they would share later on in the privacy of their own bedroom. If only this could be real, then yes, yes, there was no doubt in his mind that he would live his life with Ronan whether his life lasted for a day or for an eternity. But outside of his dream he just didn't know if he could live his life as a vampire.

When he heard the voices, he knew they weren't coming from inside his head. He was no longer alone. But he was too weak—physically and emotionally—to answer questions or speak with anyone, so he kept his eyes closed and listened.

"Thank you for calling me," Ronan said, his voice quiet and scared.

"You don't have much time," Ciaran replied. "Kano won't stay away much longer."

Michael felt two strong arms lift him off the bed and he knew his head was resting on Ronan's shoulder. His breath warmed his face, Ronan's beautiful lips mere inches from his. He was taking him somewhere, maybe to that well, maybe somewhere far, far from here. It didn't matter. Wherever Ronan was taking him, Michael couldn't resist, so he decided not to open his eyes until they got there. Before they left the room, however, Michael felt Ronan pause.

"I don't think I'll ever understand you, Ciaran," Ronan said.

"Does one brother ever fully understand the other?" Ciaran replied. Michael couldn't see, but he sensed Ciaran had more to say. "I just ask . . . that no matter what happens from now on, no matter what happens to me, you continue to try."

Tension spread throughout Ronan's arms, his grip on Michael tightened, and Michael could feel Ronan nod his head hesitantly. "I promise."

When they stopped moving, Michael opened his eyes and didn't see a well; he didn't see some exotic landscape. They were back in Ronan's dorm room. They were back on the bed where they had first made love, where Ronan had taken his life. Desperately, Michael tried to cling to the memories of being ravished, but all he grabbed on to were the memories of being destroyed. If he had more strength, he would have hurled questions, accusations at Ronan, but what would that do? What would that change? Nothing, absolutely nothing. There was no way to erase what was already done, so he remained silent.

Ronan desperately wanted to explain his actions to Michael, but words were useless now. He knew that Michael didn't want to hear that they were bound by love, bound by destiny and the wisdom of The Well. He didn't want to hear Ronan admit that he was scared to tell Michael the truth, the real truth about his being a vampire, because he was too afraid of losing him, too afraid of Michael turning away from him forever. And Michael definitely didn't want to hear Ronan confess that Michael made him forget he had ever been hurt and betrayed and that he reminded him eternal love was possible. No, nothing Ronan could say would change what he had done. He was completely aware that very soon they would both have to find a way to live with the consequences of his actions, but for now he, like Michael, chose to live in silence.

Surrounded by quiet, the two boys sat on the bed, a small, but impenetrable space between them. It was as if the fog had returned and created a physical barrier. But even though they didn't touch, even though soft never made contact with rough, their eyes never left each other. *His eyes are still so beautiful,* Michael thought, looking at them, into them, fully aware that Ronan was doing the same to him. Their gazes unencumbered by words, Michael embraced the tranquility. How wonderful to be silent after all the chaos, the upheaval, the unsettling events at Weeping Water. It was nice to have a moment not filled. But even though the room was silent, it was full.

Beauty, ugliness, love, outrage all were embodied in the silence, each finding a home there. For now they shared the space equally, but Michael and Ronan both knew that soon the balance would be broken and one would become the stronger. Which one would prevail, neither boy could guess.

Outside, the wind stirred, rattling the window, a reminder that movement was inevitable. Ronan realized he could say nothing to explain away his actions or beg for forgiveness. He was certain that Michael had agreed to give his heart and soul to him when he thought they were both human; he only prayed he would give them to him now when they were not. But the decision had to be Michael's alone.

Quietly, he got off the bed and, with one more look at the boy he loved but without a word, left the room. Left before Michael could see the sadness engulf his body, left Michael behind to decide if love would consume the space that existed between them or if outrage would win out. After the door closed, Michael waited. He waited for the silence to be replaced with a moment of clarity, a moment that would give him direction. But none came. The quiet was replaced, however, by music.

Getting off the bed, Michael held on to the end table and then the dresser to steady himself before picking up his cell phone. "Hello?"

"Michael, it's your father. How was the funeral?"

Blunt as ever. "Depressing, final, like most funerals."

Still rebellious, Vaughan noticed. *I guess this insolent, teenaged thing is going to last a while longer.* "Well, I'm glad that you were able to say good-bye. I'm just sorry I wasn't able to be there with you."

"No, you're not." Aimlessly, Michael started to walk around the room. "You never liked Grandma and you never liked spending time with me."

Taken aback by his son's bitterness, Vaughan stopped pacing the floor of his own bedroom. "That isn't true."

"Oh, come off it! I've seen you twice since you made me move here."

Why, the ungrateful punk! "Made you? May I remind you that you wanted to come to England? You jumped at the chance."

"To be with you! To find out what it's like to have a father!" Michael shouted. Standing in the center of the room, Michael was so furious he didn't realize his legs had stopped shaking, his stance was firm, stronger than ever. "But you've done nothing but treat me like somebody on your payroll!"

Vaughan ran his fingers through his hair, stopping only to hit himself in the forehead several times for being unable to control his son. "I'm sorry you feel that way, Michael. I'm doing the best I can."

Howling with laughter, Michael reached for the bathroom doorjamb with his free hand. "Seriously?! Well, I
got a newsflash for ya, Dad. Your best really sucks."

"What did you say to me?"

Still laughing, Michael replied, "You might be a brilliant businessman, but as a father you totally suck."
Michael turned off his cell phone and paced the room
again, mentally adding his father to the list of people
who were gone from his life, not that he was ever really
in his life to begin with. When Michael thought about
it, examined their relationship, he found it hard to keep
laughing. Vaughan never wanted to be a father. Getting
Michael out of Nebraska, away from his mother's family, was merely a business coup, something that made
him feel like he won a deal. No, for better or worse,
Michael had no family. For the rest of his life, he could
very well be alone. For the rest of his life—or in other
words—for infinity.

"Damn it!!!" Michael roared, flinging his cell phone
across the room in frustration. He grabbed the bedspread and yanked it off the bed. It floated to the floor
slowly and by the time it fell in a clump next to
Michael's feet, he was already finished kicking the end
table. He didn't stop because he was tired or because his
aggravation was quelled; he stopped because he saw
something familiar.

Bending down, Michael picked up the drawings, vari-
ations of the ones Ronan had made of Michael months
earlier. They had fallen out of a book that had been hid-

den underneath some other papers in a drawer of the end table. Pushing the drawer to the side, Michael realized the papers had fallen out of the oversize red book that contained page after page of Ronan's unmistakable handwriting. It was Ronan's journal.

Sitting on the floor amid the debris, his back against the bed, Michael began to read, and slowly his anger and frustration were replaced with a kind of peace.

No such luck for Vaughan. He tried but was unable to find peace with his son, himself, or his current situation. Failure was becoming an all-too-common occurrence in his life. He had failed at his marriage, he had failed at being a parent, he had even failed in his attempt to secure his own future by uniting Michael with Brania, the daughter of the most powerful man he knew. "My son, it seems, is quite cross with me."

"Sons usually are," Brania said, zipping up her skirt. "The relationship between a father and daughter is much more satisfying."

Vaughan grabbed the zipper and started to unzip it. "So too is the relationship between a father and the daughter of his business associate."

Slapping his hand away, Brania slipped her feet into her black patent leather pumps. "I have a headache."

"Oh, come on!" Vaughan protested. "You can come up with a much better excuse than that."

No, he definitely wasn't as handsome as his son. Or as interesting. "Of course I could, but I don't feel like making the effort."

Vaughan slammed the door shut before Brania could leave. "Don't be such a cheek. You know how much fun we have together."

Suddenly, Brania found this man standing in front of her, blocking her exit, revolting, and most important, no longer useful. "Michael is now a water vamp, Vaughan, and probably at this very moment locked in a sweaty, passionate embrace with Ronan, his boyfriend and creator," Brania goaded. "You have alienated your son and as a result he wants nothing to do with you. So therefore, neither do I."

"Brania, wait!"

On the other side of the doorway, she paused and turned back to face this arrogant lackey. "You really should have chosen Edwige. She's far more desperate to have a man in her life than I am."

This was unfathomable, losing twice—first Michael and now Brania—no! That was absolutely unacceptable. "After everything I've done for you and your father, you can't just walk out on me."

Brania sighed. It was time to take a short vacation from the opposite sex. "If you don't want *le petit* Edwige, perhaps you should call my father. I know he's quite grateful for everything you've done." Buttoning a button that had come undone on her silk blouse, Brania added with a lascivious grin, "And He fancies the company of both genders." When the door slammed behind her, it only made Brania chuckle even louder.

*   *   *

Nakano found nothing funny about Brania's comment. He might be a vampire, immortal, preternaturally
powerful, but he was still sixteen, surly, and very serious. "What do you mean Michael's not here?!" Nakano
shouted, though Ciaran didn't even flinch. "Where the
hell did he go?!"

"Ronan took him."

This human was really getting on his nerves. "You
mean you *let* Ronan take him."

Unhurried, Ciaran finished the paragraph from his
chemistry textbook, then placed a bookmark between
the pages. When he looked up, his face was calm. "And
what was I, a mere mortal, supposed to do to prevent
one vampire from leaving this room with another?"

"You're resourceful, Ciaran! You could've thought of
something."

And then the calmness disappeared. "I'm always
thinking of something!" Ciaran bellowed, losing control. "I gave you an alibi so no one would find out the
truth, that you killed Penry."

Like I needed your alibi, Nakano thought. *What can
the police possibly do to me?* "I don't care about that
and I never asked you to lie for me! What I want to
know is why'd you let Ronan take Michael away from
here?"

It was hard to believe that Nakano, thinner and
shorter than Ciaran, was so much more powerful, but
that was the truth. Luckily, Ciaran was more cunning
than he was strong. "What would it have mattered?
Even if I could have prevented Ronan from taking

Michael, it would only have prolonged the inevitable," Ciaran said while walking toward Nakano. "He would have come back tonight or tomorrow or the next day and eventually Michael would be in his arms again just as he is right now."

Pushing that image from his mind, Nakano focused on the boy in front of him. He wasn't nearly as handsome as Ronan. Well, he was completely different, but he was better-looking than Penry. And Penry had really good-tasting blood, so Ciaran's had to be that much more delicious. His mouth watered as Ciaran got closer. "The only way I can really help you, Kano, is if I had more power," Ciaran said slowly. "If I was more like you."

Standing an inch away, Ciaran ran his fingers down Nakano's arms, his soft nails gliding over even softer skin. He tilted his head and lengthened his neck so it was within reach of Nakano's mouth. All Kano had to do was allow his fangs to descend and bite down. "I thought you weren't interested in boys?" Nakano asked, a bit out of breath.

Pressing Kano to his body, Ciaran whispered in his ear, "I'm interested in power." He didn't even try to slow down his racing heartbeat. He wanted Kano to feel it thump, thump, thump, and for him to imagine his blood flowing through his veins. It was working. Ciaran felt Kano's body pulse with desire and his fangs graze his neck. Finally, finally he was going to join his family. He may not become exactly like his mother or Ronan, but it was close enough. It would have to do.

Unfortunately, it was not to be.

Stop! The word thundered in Nakano's brain and involuntarily his fangs throbbed in protest. *Do not take Ciaran. Father says he is worth more to us as a mortal.* He wanted to betray Brania's command, he wanted to take Ciaran from humanity to satisfy his own hunger and to spite Ronan, but he couldn't. He heard something in Brania's voice, a tone he had never heard before, and he knew that if he went against her wishes again, he would be destroyed. He hated caution, but he had no desire to die.

"Do it," Ciaran pleaded, cringing at the sound of desperation in his voice. He pushed his neck into Nakano's mouth, but all he felt were lips, dry, uninterested, like Ronan's. "Take me!"

"I can't!" Nakano cried, pushing Ciaran away from him.

Reaching out like a blind man about to fall, Ciaran's fingers sought out Nakano's flesh. He felt his shoulder, then his neck, and pulled him closer to him so once again Nakano's mouth was against his neck. "Do it! Do it now!"

Against his will his fangs descended, instinctively searching out the human flesh that was coated in a thin layer of sweat. Nakano's arms clutched Ciaran around the shoulders and waist, his mind desperately trying to override his craving. He couldn't do this, he couldn't, but how could he ignore this boy who was giving himself so willingly?

"I SAID NO!" Brania's voice was so loud, so unyielding, it transcended space and even stung Ciaran's ears. Nakano pushed Ciaran away from him brutally, a fang scraping the skin of his neck, and fled the room.

As he crashed into the headboard, Ciaran heard the door slam shut. "Not again!" Livid, Ciaran knelt on the bed and banged his fist into the headboard several times, shaking the bed frame. His body heaving, he grabbed his textbook, held it over his head, and let out a guttural cry as he slammed it against a lamp, smashing it to the floor. He kept slamming the book onto the end table over and over again until the fury, the despair, that clung to his body was released.

Exhausted he collapsed onto his bed too tired to even cry when a shard from the lightbulb pierced the palm of his hand. As he pulled the sharp remnant of glass from his flesh, he saw his blood spill out, the blood no one wanted. Quickly the bleeding stopped, producing only a small puddle of the red liquid, but enough to taste. He cupped his hand and brought the blood to his mouth and drank it, the taste intoxicating, even if it was his own. His free hand shook slightly, so he reached out to steady it, resting on the surface of his chemistry book. Tracing the sturdy, reliable edges of the book with his fingers, he suddenly knew what he had to do. What he had done practically his entire life, rely on himself. If Ronan and Nakano wouldn't create him in their images, he would have to take matters into his own hands.

"And when I succeed," Ciaran said, the taste of his own blood still fresh on his tongue, "I'll make the both of you pay."

* * *

Revenge didn't only fill the space of Ciaran's room, it hung over Penry's memorial. Imogene gazed down at the flowers, wilted, lifeless, like Penry's body must now look in his coffin, and her blank stare hid her outrage. She had been hiding it for days. She didn't share it with anyone at the trauma center in Carlisle or with the police; she kept it to herself. Now standing on the soil where Penry took his final breath, she was no longer able to keep it contained and felt the rage bubble to the surface.

Her scream was so loud the birds high above in the trees flew from their nests, frightened. She covered her mouth with her hands, her wails spilling out through her fingers. *Why?! Why was Penry taken from me? Why did his life end so violently?* She didn't know why, but she thought she knew how.

There was no way he was killed by an animal; it was the act of a man. Her boyfriend was murdered. She knew it instinctively, just as she knew there was something wrong with the headmaster when she saw him walk toward her from the other side of the brush. His stare was blank, empty, the line on the left side of his face so deep it was like a scar, and when she called out to him, he didn't respond. He was just staring at her, but not at her face; he was fixated on something else.

"Professor Hawksbry," Imogene said. "Wha . . . what's wrong with you?"

Alistair almost laughed in the girl's face. *There's so much wrong with me, so much inconceivably wrong, I don't know where to begin.* He wanted to leave her, return to his office and close the door, shut the blinds and be alone, the way he'd spent most of his days since the festival. But even a monster will seek company when isolation becomes too unbearable.

And even a reluctant vampire will seek blood. In one clean rip, Alistair pulled the bandage off of Imogene's neck, exposing the two small puncture wounds. Imogene tried to scream again, but this time she was too frightened because she saw a vision of that face, the face she had seen right after Penry told her that he loved her. It was only a flash. She saw it only in shadows, out of the corner of her eye, but she would never forget it. The face was long, the teeth huge, and the eyes the same empty black color as the headmaster's. She wasn't sure if it was a hallucination or if she was seeing a ghost, but the last thing she saw before she fainted was Penry's face. He looked the same way he did the last time she saw him alive. He looked terrified.

When Alistair placed the girl on the table, however, Brania wasn't terrified; she was simply appalled. "Why the hell did you bring her here?"

"I didn't know what else to do," Alistair said meekly. "Please, she needs help." He went on to explain how he had found her and why she had fainted.

Although she was disgusted by Imogene's presence, Brania did love the way her scent mixed in with the dampness of the room. A virgin's blood always smelled better in the dark, entombed by stone. "I know you're struggling with your new existence, Alistair, but you need to be more careful. You can't reveal your true self to humans willy-nilly."

God, how he loathed being here among these . . . things. He hated them almost as much as he hated himself. "Just help her."

"You mean help ourselves," Jeremiah said, his fangs already descended.

Pushing him away from Imogene, Alistair cried out, "Get away from her!"

"You touch me again and that'll be the last thing you do!" Jeremiah growled.

"Boys!" Brania shouted. "There's no need to squabble." She stood over Imogene and admired the girl's youthful beauty. She bent down and inhaled deeply, sniffing the entire length of her body, then she stood upright and placed a hand gently on the girl's foot. "I'm sorry, Alistair, she is far too scrumptious to receive clemency. Her time has come."

His knees buckled under the cruel simplicity of her words; he wanted to help the girl and he had brought her to slaughter. Devastated, Alistair could only watch as Jeremiah threw Imogene over his shoulder and walked toward the stairs that led up to his apartment. "I want to take this one in private."

"You're becoming quite the gentleman, Jeremiah," Brania remarked. "If your restraint permits, however, leave a few drops for me. It's been quite a while since I've tasted untainted blood."

* * *

One drop, two drops, three drops, four. These were the words from the poem Michael heard in his dream when he was still living in Weeping Water, when he was still human. They were also the words he was reading in Ronan's journal. The similarities were mind-boggling. Ronan had written about things Michael had dreamed of, imagined, long before they met. He wrote about a beautiful blond-haired boy from another land who lived far from the sea, a boy who took his breath away. A boy who was surrounded by people, by family, but who had no real friend. He had written about Michael.

One drop, two drops, three drops, four. That's all Jeremiah wanted. Well, that's all he wanted for a start. He sniffed at the dried wounds on Imogene's neck like a wild dog would sniff at a corpse to see if the meat had spoiled. He licked his lips when he confirmed that the girl was still fresh and her flesh ripe for the taking.

Floodgates open, the waters pour. Michael couldn't believe what he was reading; word for word it's what he had heard in his dream. *How long have I been dreaming about him?* Before he left Weeping Water, when he was dreaming of a new life, dreaming of spending it with one special person, he had been dreaming of Ronan. Not figuratively but, somehow, literally. The dark-haired boy who looked like Phineas from *A Separate Peace* but spoke with a British accent when he told him he could jump safely from the tree, that was Ronan. The boy who swam with him naked in the ocean, just the two of them while his mother committed suicide, that was also Ronan. He had been with him in his dreams before he entered his life. What more proof did he need that he and Ronan were destined to be soul mates? He felt his heart swell; he was overcome with a feeling so powerful it was undeniable. Regardless of what Ronan had done, his actions and their connection were inevitable. Their love was quite simply meant to be.

Cool and warm and clear and red. That's what this little bitch was going to taste like, Jeremiah knew, the saliva dripping from his mouth. Her blood would be cool and warm, melded together to create something new, something beyond intoxicating, and she would give herself to him freely.

But Imogene had other plans.

She had no idea where she was; she had no idea who this man on top of her was, but she knew that if she didn't make a move instantly, her life would be over. As Jeremiah arched his back to unbuckle his belt, Imogene brought her knee up into his groin, hard and fast. The pain, amazingly intense and unexpected, spread out from his center and by the time it reached his brain, it was almost intolerable. When she kicked him again in the same place, Jeremiah wished he were dead.

Standing in front of the mirror that took up most of the waiting room outside his office, Alistair felt the same way. He looked at the faces of the archangels Gabriel, Uriel, Zachariel, Michael, all of them, and pleaded with them, "Why have you abandoned me?" Silence. The only sound was Alistair's belabored breathing as he looked at his distorted image in the mirror. Something that grotesque didn't deserve to be alive.

Am I alive? A few days ago Michael wasn't sure of the answer, but now reading Ronan's words, the words that came from Ronan's mind and heart, he knew the answer was yes. The moment of clarity, of understanding that he prayed for, had come. *This is the boy I've been dreaming of; this is my destiny. I was brought here not by chance but for a reason. To find a new home.*
And that home was Ronan.

Am I alive? Jeremiah wasn't sure; the pain was that intense. He stumbled backward and Imogene took full advantage of his disorientation. She reached for the first thing she could find, the black marble planter filled with white roses. "NO!" Jeremiah shouted, but it was too late. The roses were already in the air, hurtling toward him.

Am I alive? Alistair didn't believe he was. He died a symbolic death the day they took him and made him into something monstrous.
It was time he made that death final.

Or am I dead? "Yes, Ronan, without you, I am," Michael said, the words in the journal growing blurry from the tears in his eyes. Everything was so clear now.

He didn't want to be alone; he definitely didn't want to be among Nakano and his kind. He wanted to be with the boy he had always loved.

All that was left was for him to tell Ronan he had made a decision.

Or am I dead? The decision was made for Jeremiah. He tried to grab the planter before it hit the floor, but Imogene lunged forward, clawing at his eyes, and he missed. He looked down and saw the roses, uprooted, covered in brown dirt and black marble.

And then he saw the girl trying to run out the door.

Or am I dead? The piece of wood in Alistair's hand shook so violently he had to press it against his leg to steady it. He had never conceived of taking his own life, but he had no choice. If today was an example of what his life had become, it was no longer worth living.

He only prayed that God would understand.

No prayers filled Jeremiah's heart when he grabbed Imogene and pulled her toward him, only the desire to kill. Screaming and kicking, Imogene was able to wrench herself free and push Jeremiah back, his foot slipping on the bedsheet that had fallen to the floor. When he fell, it took him a second to realize that he had been impaled through the heart by the wooden stake that was used to keep the roses in place. But it took only another second for his body to be consumed by flames.

Imogene covered her face in horror and disbelief as she watched Jeremiah disappear in the fire.

Alistair didn't see the same fiery image in the mirror because he had shut his eyes before ramming the stake through his own heart.

Closing Ronan's journal, Michael pressed it to his chest and for the first time in days felt complete.

He had no idea death was hovering so nearby. He could only feel himself being reborn.

chapter 23

It was dark when Michael woke up. He had thought he would just close his eyes for a few moments, think of the perfect way to tell Ronan that he was ready to share eternity with him, imagine how happy he would look, how relieved and ecstatic, but his body had given in to the exhaustion.

Now, his eyes fluttering to adjust to the absence of light, he remained still; he needed to wait a while longer before he would be strong enough to move. Until then he hugged Ronan's journal tighter to his chest, wishing it were the boy himself, and called out his name. There was no answer; he was alone. Michael wasn't afraid, but he knew intuitively that he had to find Ronan soon. His time was running out.

When he finally felt his energy return he slowly rose, fully aware of the pains that traversed throughout his body. There was the throbbing in his head, sharp twinges of heat pulsating in his hands and feet, his throat was rough and incredibly dry, his eyes were sore, and the stabbing pains that had plagued his stomach for the past few days had melded together to become one agonizing ache. He felt as if his entire body were being mangled, crushed from the inside, and he knew the only way to end the pain was to find Ronan. But where was he?

Outside St. Florian's, he was vaguely aware of the chill. It didn't cause him to shiver. On the contrary, it roused him, the cold bringing down his temperature by a few degrees, the wind pushing him forward. Then he smelled something. He inhaled what he thought was a familiar scent; could just be the earth, but it could also be Ronan, so without a clear path to pursue he followed its trail. He walked east past St. Joshua's, past the white roses that were still in full bloom despite the late month and the inhospitable weather, past St. Martha's, where the pungent aroma of beef stew and boiled potatoes seasoned in rosemary infiltrated the air. Michael paused only for a second when he realized the smell no longer made him hungry; in fact, it no longer had any connection to his new world. He took it as yet another sign that such basic human needs were part of his past and that he needed to move toward his fate, toward Ronan.

Breathing in deeply once more, he didn't know who the smell belonged to, but he was certain it was human. Ever since becoming a vampire, even when he refused to believe the possibility truly existed, Michael had noticed a change in his senses. They were gradually becoming heightened just as Ronan and even Nakano had said they would. His vision, his hearing, his sense of smell, were all vastly improved. And when he touched things, simple things like a coffee cup, fabric, his own skin, the sensations were intense. He couldn't wait to be alone with Ronan again to find out how much more intense those sensations could become. But for now he needed to focus on the sounds he heard in the distance.

Just beyond the entrance to The Forest he heard a twig break, then a few seconds later, he heard someone stumble on a rock. There were two people out here along with him even though all of Double A was under curfew. Michael walked toward the sounds and reminded himself that a student could be out after dark if accompanied by an adult so perhaps that accounted for the separate noises. But when he saw who was making them, he realized he was wrong.

Imogene was running blindly, and several yards behind her was Fritz. Even this far away, Michael could hear the girl's panting, her quick breathing, and he knew she was frightened. When she turned her head around for a quick look behind her, he saw that her face was pale, her bangs wet with sweat, her eyes wide. Why in the world would she be so afraid of Fritz?

Unless he was trying to hurt her.

* * *

"Imogene, wait up!" Fritz cried out, his voice thick and commanding. Imogene's vision was so blurred by her sweat and tears, her ears still ringing with Jeremiah's screams behind the crackling of flames, that she didn't recognize Fritz's voice; she didn't know it was her friend running behind her. She only knew that she was being chased. She thought she would be able to hide in The Forest, lose this stalker, but it was a stupid decision; she was alone now in the woods, and whoever was behind her was gaining speed. Every time she opened her mouth to scream, to call for help, she felt her throat constrict, her lungs battle to find air. Fear was suffocating her, making her limbs feel like heavy steel. She had witnessed such unexplainable horror today, she knew that if she didn't move faster, if she didn't get help soon, something unspeakable was going to happen to her too. She was sure of it.

"Imogene!" Fritz called out. "Where are you going?!" *Why the hell is she running away from me?* Fritz had lost track of time and left St. Sebastian's just after the sun set. He went there to swim some laps alone to try and clear his mind of all the crazy things that had been happening. First Penry gets killed, then Michael's missing in action for a couple of days, and Phaedra, no matter how many times he tried to comfort her, just kept saying she wanted to be alone. "That bloody well suits me just fine," Fritz had told her, not that he meant it. He wanted to hold her, feel her soft shoulders relax under his arms, and say all the words to her that were jumbled inside his head. Make a bit of sense out of the confusion he was feeling.

That's why he sought refuge in the pool. He needed life for a few moments to be just about him and the invigorating water. Swimming in the narrow lane of the pool, he could make sense of things, he understood what he needed to do. Put his right arm over his head, then his left, then lift his head to breathe. It was a simple rhythm, a known routine, nothing at all like life outside the pool. Everything outside the water was royally screwed up and getting worse by the second.

Why won't she just stop so I can help her back to St. Anne's? Fritz thought. She couldn't walk all the way over there by herself, not with the curfew, not with whatever or whoever killed Penry still on the loose. He stopped abruptly when he heard the growl. It was low and deliberate. "Who's there?" *Stupid question, Fritz, like an animal's going to respond.* But it did. With an even louder growl, this time with a cracking sound at the end of it like a jaw breaking or expanding. Fritz looked in front of him and saw Imogene just as she disappeared into the woods. When he turned back around, all he saw was fog.

"What the . . . ?" he muttered. He couldn't see anything in front of him except a thick gray mist hovering a few feet away. He held his breath, his ears searching the grounds for a sound, any sound that would indicate the beast was getting closer, but he didn't hear a thing. Then he noticed something odd: He wasn't afraid. He should be; there was something out there, something very close by, but he felt, no, he knew that somehow he would be unharmed. But just to be safe, he turned and began to sprint and didn't stop running until he heard the front door to St. Peter's Dormitory lock behind him.

Michael couldn't believe those sounds had come from him. When he thought Fritz might be trying to harm Imogene, something clicked in his brain and he wanted to use his newfound power to protect her. Fritz was no longer his friend, but an enemy who had to be stopped, an enemy whose sweet blood was pumping furiously through his veins. Michael felt his fangs descend and the pain in his stomach swirl into something even more cruel. It had become need. He needed to taste Fritz's blood, he needed to devour him, not only so he could prevent him from attacking Imogene but so he could feed his own body, which was so close to collapse. As he leapt into the air, he envisioned killing him the same way Nakano had killed Mauro, quickly and unmercifully. And he would have if it wasn't for the fog.

But where had it come from? And why was it now evaporating as suddenly as it appeared? The fog began to condense, becoming more vertical than horizontal, but instead of continuing to rise, instead of disappearing into the black sky above, it curved from its highest point and sped toward Michael like a giant gray snake.

Michael found the courage to stand firm. He couldn't run from this thing that had been plaguing him; he had to find out what it was. He didn't flinch when it landed a foot from him, the gray smoke shrinking and spinning until it was no higher than Michael himself, until it was no longer fog and had turned into something else.

"Phaedra?" Michael asked in disbelief.

"Hello, Michael."

Astonished, he was going to ask her how this was possible, how she could possibly be this fog. But then he realized that was a foolish question. He knew better; anything was possible. And yet this was unbelievable.

"For someone who's been stripped of his mortality," Phaedra said, "you look a bit surprised."

Michael couldn't erase the shocked expression from his face, and then her comment registered. "You know?"

"Since the moment it happened," she said gently.

He felt his body waver but couldn't do anything to prevent it. Phaedra grabbed his arm to stop him from falling, and Michael barely felt her touch. "You're like air."

Sitting next to Michael on the grass, she corrected him. "Like an efemera."

Maybe it was the dizzying sensation that was still making his brain jumbled, but he had no idea what she just said. "Like a what?"

"An efemera," Phaedra repeated. "That's what I am."

Michael clutched his head and the spinning actually felt like it was slowing down, it was coming to an end. His confusion, however, was not. "I have no idea what you're talking about."

Smiling, Phaedra wrapped her arms around her knees; she looked like a teenager, innocent, human. She wasn't any of those things. "We're not as well known as vampires, but we do have a following," she began. "Efemeras are protectors, spirits who are called upon to watch over humans who are in danger."

The dizziness threatened to return. "But I didn't call upon any spirit to be protected."

"No, you can't ask to be protected. We don't hear those requests," Phaedra explained. "We're called upon to protect a loved one."

Of course! "Ronan asked you to look after me."

The love between these two is so strong, Phaedra admired. "No, he does love you fully and completely, but it wasn't his call I responded to," she said. "It was your mother's."

Tears stung his eyes and he felt his body slump as if someone had reached inside him to steal his breath. "My mother?"

"Before she died, moments before, she begged for us to watch over you," Phaedra said, her eyes searching out the stars in the night to give Michael some privacy. "And when we hear a call from a dying soul that is filled with the purity of love, we have no choice but to respond."

"I don't understand," Michael said, ignoring the tears that now fell freely down his face and the anger that swelled in his chest. "She committed suicide. She didn't care about me or anybody else! Why would she ask you . . . anyone to watch over me when she couldn't be bothered to do it herself?"

Pointing to their left, Phaedra said, "Why don't you ask her yourself?"

Standing in a clearing, some newly fallen leaves
twirling at her feet, was Michael's mother. Grace looked
different; her face was softer, the lines from years of
worry, anxiety, regret were smoothed away, her eyes
were no longer cautious but eager to take in all they
could see, especially her son.

Like a child taking his first steps, Michael walked toward his mother. Unsteady and unsure that he would
reach her, but filled with joy for the opportunity. When
he stood before her, when he saw her face again, which
he never thought he would, all the anger he felt toward
her for choosing to leave him floated off of him and was
carried away by the breeze. "Mom?"

Grace's voice was quiet, but strong. "Yes, Michael,
it's me."

This is my mother, Michael thought, *back from the
dead.* Yet another unthinkable possibility come true.
Michael threw his arms around his mother and
breathed in her warmth. He no longer judged her for
her actions; he didn't care why she chose to leave him,
he was simply grateful that she had returned. "I've
missed you so much," Michael cried.

Grace held her son tighter, his touch truly a gift. "I'm
so sorry," she whispered. "I never meant to hurt you."

"Me either," Michael said, which was the last thing
Grace ever expected to hear.

She pushed Michael away gently and looked at him,
her unbeating heart breaking at the sight. "Why would
you ever think that you hurt me?"

Dig deep, Michael. Find the courage to tell her; you may never get another chance. "Because of what I am," Michael said, his voice hushed with shame.

For a moment Grace didn't understand what Michael meant, but then understood that he was talking about his sexuality. And then she was the one who was consumed with shame. "No. No, Michael, you have nothing to apologize for. You have never hurt me," Grace said. She didn't think she would be able to cry any longer, but she was wrong. "I'm the one who hurt you. I let you down in so many ways." Fervent for another touch, Grace grabbed Michael's hands in hers and held them against her face, wishing she had taken the opportunity to comfort her son like this when she was alive. "I should have told you that it didn't matter to me. I was never upset or ashamed that you're gay," she said, looking directly into her son's eyes. "I'm sorry that I wasn't brave enough to tell you how I felt. But you need to know that I always loved you."

Unable to resist, Michael had to ask. "Then why did you leave me?"

Wind fluttered past Grace, and her body vibrated. She was out of focus, then clear once again. "I don't have much time, Michael, and none of that matters."

"It matters to me," Michael protested.

Scared, Grace looked to Phaedra, but she no longer had any control over the situation. "What matters is that I was able to protect you."

"From what?" Michael asked impatiently. "Were you trying to protect me from Ronan?"

Just hearing that name gave her strength. "No, not him," Grace replied honestly. "I called upon Phaedra to make sure that nothing prevented the two of you from coming together." Grace beamed. "He's the one you're meant to share your life with."

There was no wind, but Grace's body shimmered as if behind an opaque curtain. No, he couldn't lose her, not so soon. "Wait, please! There's so much I want to ask you!"

"You don't need anything more from me," Grace said. "I've done everything I had to do." She was a mere shadow now and when Michael reached out to her, his hands moved through her like she was the ghost that she was.

"Please, Mom! Don't go!" Michael begged, his voice parched and cracking.

Grace reached out to him, her hand now only a flickering patch of light. "Never forget, Michael, you are who you were born to be." Those were the last words Michael heard his mother say before she disappeared into the night.

"No! Come back!" Lost and so very tired, Michael fell to his knees, sobbing, his face buried in his hands. He was more distraught now then when his mother first died.

Phaedra wished she could allow him time to grieve, but she couldn't. "Michael, you have to find Ronan," Phaedra ordered. "You need to go with him and offer yourself to The Well or risk being like Nakano and his kind for all eternity."

Michael nodded; he understood. "I will. I just need some time."

Phaedra lifted his chin so he could see the seriousness in her face. "You don't have any more time."

The same thing, unfortunately, could be said about Imogene.

Somehow she made it to her dorm room at St. Anne's. While she was locking the door, breathless but relieved, she called out for Phaedra, but her dorm mate didn't answer. So when she turned around, she was stunned to see that she wasn't alone.

"What are you doing here?"

"You came to visit one of my homes. I thought I would return the favor." Imogene didn't really know Brania, but she didn't like her. She was far too flirtatious and conceited. She had no idea that she was also deadly.

"What do you mean I visited one of your homes?" Imogene asked. "I don't even know where you live."

Brania admired the girl's tenacity. She had survived not one, but two attempts on her life. Nakano obviously didn't do a very good job cleaning up his mess; he merely wounded her when he should have left her as lifeless as the other one, her boyfriend, so she was simply lucky to survive that attack. But she had proved her mettle against Jeremiah. Sadly, she would have to pay for that.

"Really?" Brania asked, stretching out on the bed, her head cradled in her hand, her hair falling free. "How quickly we forget."

Adrenaline was still pumping through Imogene's veins and acted as an antidote to her fear, so when she spoke, it was with an indignant tone. "I hardly know you; what makes you think I was at your house?"

"You don't remember the cold, dark basement?" A chill enveloped Imogene's heart. "What about the apartment upstairs? Small, but smartly decorated." No, that was impossible. She couldn't possibly have anything to do with that man who burst into flames. "Those beautiful roses you destroyed were a gift from me to Jeremiah."

Behind her back, Imogene was trying to unlock the door. "You need to leave here, now!" she demanded, her bold tone at odds with the panic she was feeling. When she turned to open the door and run from the room, she was amazed to find Brania blocking her exit. "What the hell?"

With one hand Brania relocked the door; with the other she fondled Imogene's hair. "I could never wear bangs. I just don't have the face for them."

Involuntarily, Imogene stepped back. When she spoke, her tone was infinitely less bold. "I told you to leave."

"Sweetheart, I think you've already realized that I don't take orders."

Standing still, Imogene tried to survey the situation. For the second time in just a few hours, her life was in danger, but she succeeded in getting away once. She could do it again. *There's a window in the bathroom,* she reminded herself, but before she could make it to the bathroom door, Brania blocked the entrance, once again foiling her plan. "And I always get what I want."

"Not always, darling."

Blinking her eyes several times, Imogene still wasn't sure if she truly was seeing another person in her room or if she was hallucinating. "Mrs. Glynn-Rowley?" Imogene asked incredulously.

"How many times must I ask you children? Please, call me Edwige."

Imogene knew less about Ronan's mother than she did about Brania, but with one glance at Brania, who was now seething, she could tell they were not friends. She figured she had about three seconds to decide where to lay her trust. "Edwige?"

"Yes, dear."

"It's, um, very nice to see you again," Imogene stuttered. "But, um, what are you doing here?"

Smiling, Edwige pulled her black leather gloves off, one finger at a time, before tossing them into her purse. "I've come to thwart Brania's plan to kill you."

"Oh, well, that's really nice to hear," Imogene replied. *Wait a second! What did she say?* "Kill me?!"

Brania lunged at Imogene, but before she could grab the girl's arm, Edwige's purse struck Brania in the face. The force of it knocked her backward and Brania fell into the bathroom, hitting the back of her head on the sink. Seeing Brania crumble to the floor, Imogene ran to the front door, but just as she turned the doorknob, Edwige gripped her hand so tightly she couldn't move it any farther.

"What are you doing?!" Imogene screamed. "We have to get out of here."

Edwige didn't look like she was exerting any energy and yet Imogene couldn't turn the doorknob an inch or release her hand from this woman's grip. "Darling, you misunderstood me," Edwige said calmly. "I'm not going to let Brania kill you because I want that honor all for myself."

Finally the terror that Imogene had been feeling all day rose to the surface and she screamed. Edwige cut the bloodcurdling sound short with a harsh slap to her face that sent Imogene sprawling on the floor. Scrambling to get to her feet, Imogene saw Edwige standing over her, her face changing right before her eyes. Frantic, she grabbed whatever she could and threw it at her, shoes, books, a chair, but all her effort only made Edwige laugh wildly. Until Brania jumped on Edwige's back and knocked her to the ground.

"This one is mine!" Brania shrieked, grabbing the back of Edwige's head and ramming her face into the hardwood floor. Before she could do it a second time, however, Edwige flipped around and grabbed a fistful of Brania's hair. "Let go of me!" Brania screamed. Naturally, Edwige didn't comply but simply pulled harder, causing Brania to tumble over onto her side and crash onto the floor. Straddling her, Edwige grabbed Brania's wrists and pressed them to the floor. "She's mine!" Brania shouted, gasping for breath. "She killed one of my most trusted men!"

Edwige's eyes were filled with such uncontrollable hatred that for a moment she lost herself. She released the pressure she was exerting on Brania and leaned forward so her face was less than an inch away from hers. "And you took Vaughan from me!"

That's what this is about? Rallying all her strength, Brania cocked her head forward and banged it into Edwige's forehead. Lurching backward, Edwige fell onto the bed, and before her eyes could focus, she felt Brania's hands violently squeezing her throat. In one quick move, Brania stood up and held Edwige high over her head. "So it's revenge that you want?!" Brania cried. "You're jealous because I got to that fool before you did?"

Edwige kicked Brania in the chest with the heel of her shoe, and Brania was thrown back into the window. Edwige fell to the floor, her feet firmly planted, and stood over her nemesis. "Damned right I am! And now I'm going to kill this one before you can bring her over to your side."

But the one she was talking about was almost out the door. Once again, Brania was impressed with Imogene's moxie, but there was no way she was letting her escape, and there was no way she was letting Edwige get to her first. Like a flash of silent lightning, Brania yanked Imogene away from the front door and held her in front of her. Imogene's feet dangled a few inches above the floor while her hands tried to pry away Brania's arm, which was tucked underneath her neck. It was no use. Imogene was kicking and flailing as much as she could, but Brania's hold was like a vice. She tried to scream, but no sound could penetrate through the hand that was covering her mouth. Imogene was filled with despair when she felt something scrape against her neck just like it had the night in The Forest, the night Penry was killed.

Brania smiled triumphantly. "Once again, Edwige, you lose."

Not so fast! Scurrying across the floor like a rat running from a flood, Edwige's fangs ripped through Imogene's thigh before Brania's could pierce the girl's neck. Stunned at Edwige's speed, and furious at being outsmarted, Brania loosened her grip for just a second, but it gave Edwige enough time to pull Imogene away from her and drag her across the floor. Sitting in a corner, Imogene lying limp in her lap, Edwige raised her head and purred, "No, Brania, this time I win."

If she weren't so incensed, Brania might have felt some pity for this girl who put up such a valiant fight to live. Instead she watched in disgust and loathing as Edwige plunged her fangs into her neck, and blood was transferred from one body to another.

While Imogene's life on earth had come to an end, Michael's was about to begin its next phase. The fourth time Michael whispered Ronan's name, Ronan appeared. Leaning against a tree in front of Archangel Cathedral, Michael looked like he was sleeping. "Thank God," Ronan muttered. How he would love to cradle him in his arms and let him sleep through his exhaustion, but the time had come.

"Michael . . . please, we have to go to The Well,"

Ronan said. He then added with more than a little hope, "Will you come with me?"

Looking up at Ronan, Michael's eyes filled with the glow of the moon. "I love you, Ronan."

If only that were enough. "I love you too," Ronan said. "But time is running out; you've gotten too weak."

Michael nodded his head. "I know, but I'm not scared any longer. I've made a decision and I've chosen you."

A lone drop of rain fell from the sky, landing somewhere between the boys. Ronan's heart had never been fuller and he extended his hand to Michael. "Does that mean you trust me?"

Without hesitation Michael placed his hand in Ronan's. "Yes."

chapter 24

"I can believe anything, provided that it is quite incredible."

The words were written by Oscar Wilde in *Dorian Gray*, but it was Michael who spoke them aloud. "My life," Michael continued, "since I met you, Ronan, has been nothing but incredible.'"

Ronan leaned in and kissed his boyfriend on the mouth. "And after today it's going to get even more magical."

The waves crashed hard on the sand, their sound thunderous, as if to remind them that there was still work to do, while cold sea foam cavorted over their feet, making Michael's naked body tremble slightly.

Ronan rubbed Michael's shoulders briskly to create some heat. "Are you ready to enter my world?"

I've been ready since before I met you. "Yes," Michael whispered, his voice clear but almost lost amid the rough noise of the waves. One final kiss above land and then . . . Michael wasn't exactly sure what would happen next, but he trusted Ronan with his heart, his soul, and his life, so he simply held his hand and followed him into the water.

Knee-deep in the ocean, Ronan stopped and looked at Michael, his expression both fatherly and passionate, and took a deep breath and exhaled, so Michael did too. He repeated the action and Michael once again followed. All around them was activity. Gray clouds traveled in a swift, horizontal path across the navy blue sky, the cool air swirled to create an insistent wind, the ocean undulated wildly so that their bodies were covered in a smooth layer of salt water. But the boys remained still, their breath now slow and even, their eyes locked in an embrace. What was happening around them had no consequence; all that mattered was what was happening between them.

Nodding slightly, Ronan squeezed Michael's hand. Before he could imagine where Ronan was taking him, he felt his body dive into the water. Michael glided effortlessly, his body steered by Ronan's strength. They swam farther and farther away from the beach, moving on a diagonal so they were also swimming deeper into the depths of the ocean. He could feel the water above him churn with more force and he could see it growing darker. How much lower would they go? How much longer could he hold his breath?

Burrowing deeper, Michael felt a pain creep into his lungs and he tugged at Ronan's hand. When he looked at him, he couldn't hide his fear. But Ronan was as calm as the water that now enveloped them. As Michael's legs nervously treaded water, his free arm creating a small whirlpool around his hand, Ronan seemed to float, his body relaxed, suspended. Michael watched as Ronan opened his mouth and breathed underwater, easily, as if he were born to perform such an inhuman act, as if somehow he was born of the water. Didn't Ronan mention something about being able to breathe underwater? Or was that a dream? Michael laughed a little, some bubbles escaping from his mouth. What did that matter? Hadn't he come to learn that his dreams were mere visions of reality?

His trust for Ronan outweighing his fear of the unknown, Michael opened his mouth and felt the cool rush of water fill him; his body tensed involuntarily and Ronan grabbed his free hand to steady him. Michael kicked his feet and tried to pull away, to race toward the surface of the water, toward air, but suddenly realized he wasn't choking, he wasn't rejecting the water, he was, quite impossibly, breathing. Astonished, he smiled at Ronan, and wondered what other wonders lay ahead. He wouldn't have to wait much longer to find out.

Ronan pointed downward and led Michael deeper and deeper into the ocean, so deep that there was hardly any light and it looked as if they were swimming in the darkness of the night sky. Instead of stars twinkling, iridescent light emanated from the eyes and skin of fish that inhabited the ocean floor. Michael felt like an explorer entering a world he always knew existed but had never seen before with his own eyes. And when he stood before The Well of Atlantis, the feeling only grew stronger.

It looked just like it did in his visions: the underwater clearing, the curved stone, the serene and quiet beauty filling the space all around it. Letting go of Ronan's hand, Michael walked toward The Well, his legs confident, his stride full of purpose, the simple truth clear in his mind. All his dreams, all his prayers, had led him to this point, had led him to stand before this altar with his equal by his side. Without turning to look, Michael reached out his hand and Ronan's was there to take hold, just as he knew it would be. They may have started their journeys separately, but from now on they would continue together.

Standing before The Well, Michael peered over its edge and saw the shimmery silver liquid, its surface like ice, solid and strong, and saw their reflections look back at him. Michael and Ronan. How he loved the sound of that, how he loved this boy next to him. It no longer mattered how he had reached this point, it no longer mattered that he was no longer human, but a vampire. All that mattered was that he would spend the rest of eternity looking into his beautiful blue eyes, feeling the strength of his body next to his, his love always just a breath away. *How far have I come?* Michael thought. *How far from the lonely, unsure person I was. Someone who never thought he'd have a future, and now I'm someone whose future will never end. My life is truly just beginning.* But for there to be a beginning, there must be an end, and it was time for Michael to put an end to his mortal life and offer himself to The Well.

Ronan stood behind Michael, his warm flesh pressing into him, and he placed his hands on the rim of The Well. As soon as he did, Michael felt its power; a current, like electricity, flashed through his body, the sensation not entirely painless, but Michael understood he couldn't let go and so he held on to The Well even tighter.

Slowly the pain grew; every inch of his body was touched by it, and it couldn't be ignored. He would have shouted out in agony, but his fangs prevented him from making any sound. The sharp, white fangs throbbed more intensely than before, craving the blood they had so far been denied, and Michael felt them twitch when Ronan reached in front of him and held out his arm.

The blue veins looked so inviting underneath the smooth, alabaster flesh that Michael felt faint. Ronan had already offered his body to Michael and now he was offering his blood. It was a gift he could no longer resist.

Gripping the side of The Well even harder, Michael gave in to his desire and bit into Ronan's skin. His blood flowed easily and willingly, and Michael couldn't imagine that two beings had ever been closer than he and Ronan were at this moment. So close that it was overwhelming and he felt as if his spirit was leaving his body, that his mind was going to burst. This time, however, his mind wasn't bombarded by images; he didn't see visions that were previously known only to Ronan. All he saw was the icy water of The Well begin to swirl.

Firmly, Ronan held Michael's body close to him and gently pulled his arm away from his mouth. Michael watched as Ronan held his arm out over the center of The Well so his blood would pour into it, the blood that was a mixture of his and Michael's. As Ronan spoke the ancient prayer, Michael found himself mouthing the words. How he knew them he didn't know, but they were a part of him as surely as Ronan was.

> Unto The Well I give our life
> our bodies' blood that makes us whole.
> We vow to honor and protect
> and ask The Well to house our souls.

When the last drop of blood fell from Ronan's arm, he placed his hands on top of Michael's, which were still holding on to the side of The Well, and noticed that they were starting to develop webbing between each finger. Michael bent his knees and arched his back as he felt the same painful sensation in his feet, and when he scooped up the cold liquid from The Well, he needed Ronan's help to steady his shaking hands. Ronan let go when his hands grew still so Michael could place his webbed hands to his mouth and drink. At first Michael's throat encountered cold, then a taste that he couldn't describe, but one that he knew he could no longer live without.

Together they watched the swirling water of The Well

begin to steam, become a mist that rose almost to the roof of the cave. It didn't touch them, but Michael could feel a presence, a welcoming presence that enveloped him. It was warm and comforting and loving, and Michael felt as if his mother was once again wrapping her arms around him. It felt like home.

And so it was completed. Michael was now a part of Ronan's race, a vampire with ties to Atlantis, a descendant of The First and The Other. Ronan kissed Michael softly on the temple, a kiss filled with love, pride, and even surprise; he had seen and felt this transformation once before, but this time was different, this time the connection was stronger. He pressed his cheek into Michael's and he didn't know if the words came from him or from The Well, but he heard them clearly all the same. "This union will last forever."

When the mist disappeared, there was another change. The smooth silver surface didn't return as Ronan expected; in its place was a sight that filled Ronan and Michael with awe, a sight that made them understand how undeniable their destiny was. They saw their individual souls meld together to create a bond that could never be broken. They saw their souls and themselves become one.

Miles away as he walked across St. Anne's campus, Fritz hoped Phaedra would want to create a similar bond. He didn't understand his feelings, but he knew he was changing, and it was all because of this girl. Until he met her, he was content with being a smart-ass, the guy who cared more about sports and making fun of others than someone who wanted to have a girlfriend, someone who wanted to have a relationship. Part of him still wanted to take that familiar, safe route, but lately, since Penry's death maybe, Fritz wanted more. He longed to be with Phaedra and not just to kiss her or see if he could score, but to be in her presence, talk to her, get to know her better, and as a result get to learn more about himself. When he saw her packing her clothes in her room, he thought he would never get the chance.

"These aren't my things," Phaedra said. "They're Imogene's."

Greatly relieved, Fritz was speechless for a few seconds. "So, um, I guess the rumors are true. She's not coming back."

Phaedra tenderly folded one of Imogene's favorite T-shirts, black with a white stick figure whose head was in the shape of a heart. It made her smile as she lied. "No, it seems that she ran away from the trauma center in Carlisle. The police still haven't found her."

What? That was news to Fritz. "Her parents must be out of their bloody minds."

Don't cry, Phaedra; you can't protect everyone. "Yes, they must be."

"Do they have any idea where she went?"

Phaedra shook her head. "No, but I . . . I get the sense that she's going to be all right." Suddenly, Phaedra was more interested in what Fritz was holding. "Is that for me?"

"Um, oh yeah," Fritz stuttered. "I, um, thought . . . I

just . . . I just wanted to get you something." Exhaling, Fritz sat down on the bed next to Phaedra. Normally he'd make fun of a girl with such hair, always kind of unruly and disheveled, but he liked that she wasn't perfect; it made it easier to look at her.

"I see that you wrapped it yourself," Phaedra said, smiling at the thin, rectangular box that was covered in three different types of paper held together by thick strips of masking tape.

Blushing, Fritz explained, "I kind of ran out of supplies."

Phaedra looked at this boy, his smooth dark skin and lovely light brown eyes, and had no idea what she was doing or feeling, but decided to take advantage of his kindness. "Thank you, this is very sweet."

Score one for Fritz! Well, not *score,* he chastised himself, more like *congratulations.* "I know you have a sweet tooth."

No one had ever given Phaedra a box of chocolates before; in fact, no boy had ever given her a gift. She liked how it made her feel. "Thank you, Fritz, this is really . . . really thoughtful."

And Fritz liked how Phaedra's comment made him feel. He hoped the answer to his next question would make him feel even better. "There's another rumor going around campus too."

Mmmm, chocolate-covered cherries truly are delicious. "What's that?"

"That, um, that you're leaving school too," Fritz said. "Is that true?"

Maybe it was the hope in Fritz's eyes or the feeling that her work here was not yet done, but Phaedra was certain. "No, I'm not going anywhere."

Beaming, Fritz couldn't contain himself and kissed Phaedra quickly, but sweetly. "I'm glad to hear that." Phaedra didn't trust herself to say anything more, so she simply held the boy's hand. Once again, Fritz was relieved. Her hand felt a little heavier than before, like it really was going to stay and not disappear. Not like some others.

"Hawksbry!"

Out of respect, Dr. MacCleery waited for a response, but none came. He knocked on the headmaster's door once more and called out, "Hawksbry, are you in there?!" How he loathed this room. It always made him feel inferior, like he was waiting to be summoned by some higher authority. Ideal to remind the students who was in charge, but annoying to those who already know their power is limited. What he hated most was the faces of those damn archangels staring down at him, condemning him for being a mere human. As a scientist he didn't believe in their existence, but still, did they have to look so angry? "Hawksbry, I'm coming in."

When he entered the room, he didn't see the headmaster sprawled out on the floor as he had feared nor did he see him sitting quietly at his desk reading as he had hoped. He saw no one. He looked around for signs of an intrusion, but again found nothing. He opened the doors to his private bathroom, his closet, both empty.

476 Michael Griffo

"Where the hell did you get to this time?" But just as he was about to leave, he saw something that caught his eye. On the otherwise uncluttered desk was a folded piece of paper, propped up and looking like a tent. When Lochlan read the handwritten scrawl, he felt the eyes of the archangels peering at him, reading over his shoulder. He knew the handwriting was Alistair's, though the words seemed to be written fast and without his usual flair. The message, however, was succinct. *Evil walks among the angels. The children must be protected.*

What?! MacCleery looked around the room, convinced someone was playing a trick on him. But then he read the note again and then he remembered how Alistair looked the last time he saw him and that he had disappeared for a few days once before, and the doctor quickly became convinced that something was wrong. He had no idea what was going on. He wasn't sure if he really believed the words on the paper, but he felt certain that Alistair believed them. And when it came to the children, Alistair was rarely wrong.

The doctor was so deep in thought when he walked past the mirror and the haunted faces of the archangels, he didn't even notice that he stepped in a small pile of ash.

The mahogany box was hardly ever noticed by anyone even though Edwige kept it out in full view, placed on top of a small table carved from the same wood. There was nothing fancy about the box or the table; the lines were smooth and neither was embellished with carving or adornment. They were both simply sturdy and strong. Just like Saxon was.

Edwige opened the box, the smell of the burnt ash now faint like a rarely spoken memory. But even unspoken memories never completely die. "Forgive me, Saxon," Edwige said. "I faltered. I grew weak and thought I needed the love of another man." Her eyes filled with tears, but her voice was steady when she vowed, "I will never make that mistake again."

That was the thought that filled Ciaran's brain when he entered St. Albert's. When he entered the lab, he didn't know what to think.

"Hello, Ciaran," Brania said. "We've been waiting for you."

Act normal, Ciaran, these people can't possibly know what's inside your head. "I thought I'd seen the last of you after the festival," Ciaran said, placing his books down on the counter. "Didn't think you'd want to be in my presence again and, you know, risk dropping dead of boredom."

Brania looked at Nakano and laughed. "Now, if only you could learn to be as witty as our friend here, maybe I wouldn't have to constantly request that you keep your mouth closed." Nakano looked like he wanted to respond in a not-so-witty manner, but he did indeed keep his mouth closed. Ciaran accurately assumed he was only doing so for fear of being reprimanded. Something intriguing was going on, he had to admit, but he knew better than to admit it to them, so he continued to set up his lab as if he didn't have any visitors. "Aren't you the least bit curious why we're here?"

Pulling a tray of specimens from out of the freezer underneath the counter, Ciaran answered without looking at either vampire. "No."

Nakano opened his mouth to speak, unable to remain civil, but Brania dug her nails into his thigh before he could utter a sound. "I understand your apathy," Brania began. "But I think once you hear our proposal, it will be displaced by great interest."

"I'm not interested in anything you might have to propose," Ciaran said firmly.

"Even if the proposal comes from my father?" Brania asked. When she saw Ciaran's hand hesitate, linger in the air for a split second before placing the glass plate on the microscope, she knew she had succeeded. Ciaran had taken the first step toward entering her lair.

Looking at the sample of blood through the microscope, Ciaran tried but was unable to focus. Her father? This was not what he had expected. He knew it could be a trap, he knew he could be setting himself up for false hope like all the other times, but it could also be the opportunity of a lifetime. "Your father has a proposal for me?"

"One that will change your destiny." Not wanting to appear too eager or too desperate, Brania started to leave, Nakano close behind her. She only stopped when Ciaran spoke.

"If your father wants to do business, he knows where he can find me."

When Brania smiled, she tried not to look too victorious. After all, she may have lost a few small battles, but winning the war was all that mattered. "Yes, He does, Ciaran." She was impressed with how intensely the boy pretended to be working and how he so admirably tried to hide his interest. Luckily, she knew his true desires. "Don't worry, Ciaran, He'll be in touch."

For a long time after Brania and Nakano left, Ciaran didn't move, he didn't speak, he hardly breathed. He was thrilled and he was disgusted. He didn't want to bargain with Them; he didn't want to work with Brania's father. But most of all, he didn't want to be alone.

Feeling Ronan's arms around him, Michael knew he would never be alone again. They sat, Michael leaning into Ronan, their faces warmed by the first rays of dawn, and listened to the sounds of the earth. The earth that was as immortal as they were. The waves were now rolling onto the shores of Inishtrahull Island, no longer crashing forcefully onto the beach, their vigor replaced with contentment. There was no wind, just a placid breeze that ebbed and flowed with the movement of the tide, bringing with it the smell of salt and a gesture of peace.

Michael smiled when he heard the meadowlark's song; the soothing notes sounded like an old friend as they wafted over him. It was the same song he followed from

Weeping Water, from his other life that brought him here where he was born to be. Into the arms and the heart of Ronan.

And Ronan's heart was never so full. He looked at Michael and was overcome with joy. *He really will be forever beautiful and forever mine.* Softly, they kissed, parting only when the first lazy drops of rain fell from the sky. Ronan smiled as Michael bent his head back, allowing the rain to anoint his face. "Should we find shelter?" he whispered.

"No," Michael replied in a strong, confident voice as he pulled Ronan's arms tighter around him. "This is the most natural feeling in the world."

Dear Reader,

Now that you've read *Unnatural* and have gotten to know Michael, Ronan, Brania, and the rest of the students at Archangel Academy, I thought I'd share with you some of the exciting stuff that's set to come as their journey continues in *Unwelcome*, the next book in the series.

Change is in the air this semester at Double A. Just because Michael is now a vampire doesn't mean his world is suddenly perfect—far from it. He may have gone through a physical transformation, but emotionally he still has a lot going on—starting with his relationship with Ronan. He's never been someone's boyfriend before and suddenly he finds himself connected to Ronan in a way he never imagined. It doesn't matter that he loves Ronan more than he ever thought possible—a relationship needs more than love to survive. He also has to deal with the lingering feelings of his mother's death, plus his father, who's distant and not what you could call accepting of the fact that his son is gay. Just wait until Michael finds out his father's not only a vampire but one of Brania's creations!

As Michael struggles to come to terms with the young man he is becoming—physically, emotionally, and sexually—Ronan struggles to let go of the demons of his past. This is not his first relationship, but he's desperate for it to last an eternity. His fear that it will end like all the others causes him to make questionable decisions and could endanger his destiny. He also decides to follow some of Edwige's advice, and you just know that isn't a smart thing to do.

There are lots of other new relationships too. Phaedra and Fritz are growing closer, but will they ever be close enough for Phaedra to confess that she isn't even human? And Ciaran, tired of being lonely and an outsider, makes a bold choice—to join forces with Brania by doing some scientific experiments on the water vamps for none other than her father. It's a choice that will have deadly consequences.

Meanwhile, two new characters arrive on the hallowed grounds of Archangel Academy, creating even more mystery. Ronan's younger sister, Saoirse, comes to Eden harboring a secret that only a handful of people know about and one that has made her a legend among water vamps. And then there's the new headmaster, the enigmatic David Zachary, who has come to the school to lead the students into a new era. But as you know, nothing at this school is what it seems.

All the action and all the stories culminate and explode at the end of the school year at The Carnival for the Black Sun. It's David's brainchild to celebrate a solar eclipse when the sun disappears and for a few moments the world is without any light.

Will Michael and Ronan overcome one obstacle after another to remain forever beautiful and forever together? Will Ciaran side with the enemy? Who will cause more pain—Brania or Edwige? And will an evil plot be thwarted or will Archangel Academy be plunged into a new era of darkness? You'll just have to read *Unwelcome* to find out.

Thanks for reading—and enjoy!

Michael Griffo

one drop
two drops
three drops
four

water is mixed
with blood once more.

shadows and light
on a crimson stain

will the sun prevail?
or will darkness reign?

prologue

Outside, the earth was cold.

The New Year brought with it an early frost, burying the past, at least temporarily, beneath a thick layer of snow. Archangel Academy was practically empty, most of the students spending their holiday break with family, so the campus was a sea of white, an enormous unsoiled blanket with only a few patches of brownish-green grass, bruised yet resilient, peeking out every hundred yards or so as a reminder of what was and what will be again. Tomorrow when classes resume, the sprawling blank canvas will be tarnished with footsteps, the imprints of students making their claims on the land, their own private piece of the world. Looking out from his dorm room window at the wintry landscape, a landscape that would soon be altered, Michael was once again amazed at how quickly everything can change.

Only a few months ago, Michael was looking out a different window at an entirely different landscape, wondering when his life would begin, when it would change. And now here he was, half a world away, his life transformed in more ways than he could ever have imagined or even thought possible. Sometimes he didn't know what was more incredible: the fact that he was a vampire or that he had a boyfriend. He looked over at Ronan sleeping in the bed that they shared, the moonlight making his skin look almost translucent, his thick black hair tousled like a little boy's, a faint smile on his full red lips, and Michael's breath caught in his chest, for he was fully aware that Ronan and everything else that had happened to him since he left Weeping Water, Nebraska, were the answers to his dreams. It was just that everything had happened so quickly.

He didn't hear the sound until a few seconds after it began, a sound like teeth, sharp and strong, clicking, chattering. It had started to rain and the raindrops, more ice than water, were hitting the window, striking it, as a welcome, a warning. That's why Michael loved the rain; it could be so many things. It could cleanse, destroy, interrupt, change. The first time he saw Ronan, it had rained. The memory of rainwater riding down Ronan's cheeks, clinging to his lips, still stirred feelings within the pit of Michael's stomach, still made him feel nervous and excited and passionate, still made him feel

incredibly alive, even though, well, even though technically he wasn't.

He watched two drops of rainwater travel down the
window. One moved swiftly in a straight course from
the top to the bottom, never slowing down, never hesitating, bubbling at the bottom of the window until it
could no longer hold its shape, then bursting into the air
to continue its journey elsewhere, maybe fall into the
snow-covered earth below and wait for the rest of the
world around it to melt. Or perhaps become something
completely new, a glade of ice, hard, silver, and sleek.

The other drop of rain moved with caution, traipsing
slowly to the left, then the right, pausing a moment almost as if to ask Michael in which direction it should
travel. But Michael had no advice, so the raindrop was
forced to make its own decision. Slowly it continued to
move down the window on a slight angle, hugging desperately to the glass so it wouldn't fall, so it wouldn't
stray too far and too quickly from what it knew, moving
in its own time. Finally, it reached the base of the window long after the other raindrop had disappeared, and
made the decision to stay, content in its travel, content
to allow life to continue to move around it as it stayed
unchanged, a simple drop of rain, nothing more, nothing less. For a moment Michael felt regret, just for a moment, but the presence of the emotion, no matter how
fleeting, was profound, because he was beginning to realize that nothing in his life would ever be simple again.
Not even his reflection.

In the window, through the crisscrossing currents of

rain, among the grayish-black shadows of the moonlight, he was reminded once again that his image was
forever changed. Changed by a drop of red, one tiny
drop of red blood that clung to his lip.

Before he came here to Double A, before he met
Ronan, he would have thought a spot of blood would
spoil his image, ruin it, but now he knew that it enhanced his reflection and gave him strength and courage
and power that he had yet to fully comprehend and em-
ploy. He flicked the dash of red, the stubborn blood
drop, with his tongue, and savored the taste, the taste
that reminded him of his monthly feeding earlier in the
day, the taste that reminded him of Ronan and of himself. And he couldn't help but smile. Michael thought
how fascinating it was that something like the bitter
taste of blood, someone else's blood, that a few months
ago would have been repulsive, was now a vital aspect
of his life. And it was all because of Ronan.

Before Michael could turn to look at Ronan, a
thunderclap roared somewhere far above him, somewhere out of reach but somehow right next to him, and
his gaze remained with the rain, with the cold, with his
grotesque face. Because the rain, falling with more intensity now, had altered his reflection. He saw that he
wasn't the Michael he remembered, the Michael he was
still trying to hold on to; he was something different,
something much, much different from who he was
when he began his journey to this new place.

It was as if each drop of rain latched on to the window, sliding in a multitude of directions to create dark, watery veins that sprawled across Michael's face like sins as they begin to etch into a soul. His image, torn and dissected, heightened and distorted, looked back at him as if to announce *This is who I am now; that other Michael is no more.* But strangely he wasn't afraid. He didn't know exactly how he felt, but he knew that this harsh truth didn't frighten him. Maybe it was because he was stronger now or because he was learning to accept the unacceptable. Or maybe it was simply because he knew he was no longer alone.

There was no more time to ponder his misshapen reflection or how his present was so vastly different from his past because he heard his name. Ronan's husky whisper never failed to arouse Michael, never failed to remind him how lucky he was, how grateful that he was exactly where he was born to be.

"Michael," Ronan said, his eyes still half closed with sleep, "where are you?" Michael didn't move, but he smiled. *His first thought is about me, the first word he speaks is my name.* It filled Michael with joy and, yes, pride. "Michael!"

"I'm right here."

The two boys stared at each other, Michael framed by the first determined rays of the sun that demanded to be seen through the dark gray rain clouds and Ronan sitting up in bed, his bared flesh almost as white as the rumpled sheets, his black hair a stark contrast. Reaching out his hand to Michael, he said, "Come back to bed." And Michael did because he missed Ronan's touch just as much as Ronan missed his.

Silently, the boys melded together as one, Ronan behind Michael, his strong, powerful arm wrapped around him, their hands finding one another, their fingers intertwining. A soft kiss on Michael's neck, a shiver down his spine, bodies moving even closer together, then Ronan's even breathing, a gentle rush of air every few seconds passing by Michael's ear, reminding him that he isn't alone and that he won't be, not for the rest of eternity. A comforting feeling and one that Michael had begged for but never imagined would come. It had come so quickly that sometimes, like now, his mind was so filled with thoughts and emotions, powerful and conflicting, that it was hard to fall asleep. So instead of sleeping peacefully, he simply held Ronan tighter around him and listened to him breathe.

chapter 1

After the Ending

Michael was being watched. He liked how it felt and so he kept his eyes closed even though he wasn't sleeping, hadn't been sleeping since he crawled back into bed a few hours before. He could feel the sunlight on his face, not strong, but enough to remind him it was morning, and he could smell the fresh chill of rain that lingered in the air. January was colder than the locals had predicted—snow had already made several appearances—so Michael, like most sixteen-year-olds, preferred to stay in bed on a Monday morning rather than be up and about, getting ready for class. Especially since he had an audience.

Ronan loved watching Michael. It didn't matter if he

was talking to friends, swimming, reading a book, or, as he was now, pretending to be asleep, he cherished the view. And even though Michael's attempt to get a few more moments under the covers would result in his being annoyed when he'd ultimately have to scramble to get dressed and get to class on time, Ronan smiled at the boyish trick. He then decided one boyish game deserved another.

Leaning over Michael, Ronan let his tie dangle an inch over his boyfriend's face, swaying in the air like a benign pendulum, casting a thin horizontal shadow across Michael's cheek. Michael lay still. He could feel Ronan's presence, he knew what was coming, but he didn't move, because that would ruin the game.

As he bent over even farther, Ronan's tie scraped the tip of Michael's nose, but Michael still didn't respond, he didn't move until the endpoint of the tie brushed against his lips, then he smiled. He felt the silky material glide over his lips, his chin, his cheek, as if to say hello, good morning, it's time to get up. Then the tie began to fold and bunch up as Ronan lowered himself and brought his face closer to Michael's. Both boys were smiling mischievously now, knowing how their game would end, but Michael kept his eyes closed. He knew the rules.

"Who's there?" Michael said, purposefully adding a nervous tremor to his question.

Ronan lowered his voice as low as he could and growled, "It's the big bad vampire."

Michael opened his eyes and feigned a look of fear, but forced himself not to laugh. "Oh no, not again."

In one fluid movement, Ronan whipped off the blanket and sheets and jumped on top of Michael, his naked body now practically hidden by Ronan's larger frame. Then he did his best Dracula impersonation. "I've come to suck your blood." Instead of inciting fear in Michael, Ronan's imitation of the legendary vampire made him laugh out loud, which it always did, so Ronan continued to speak like the count. "You are not afraid of me? You do not fear my power?"

Ronan was many things, Michael thought, but a mimic was not one of them. "Not when your accent sounds more Jewish than Transylvanian."

It was Ronan's turn to laugh, hearty and buoyant, and he kept laughing while kissing Michael, wishing they could stay in bed all day exploring and enjoying each other's bodies, but they had to get to class, couldn't start the new semester off by being late for first period. Before he could drag Michael out of bed and make him get ready, however, he noticed something in his eyes, resistance perhaps. Could it be sadness, disappointment? "You're not still upset about your father, are you?" Ronan asked quietly.

Michael looked surprised and shook his head before he spoke. "No. I didn't expect him to call on Christmas, not after I told him I didn't want to spend the holidays with him in Tokyo." As usual, Michael's father changed their plans at the last minute and informed him a few days before Christmas that he had to go out of town on a business trip to oversee yet another crisis at one of his factories. Far from being upset, Michael was relieved.

He was not looking forward to spending his break with Vaughan, not after the endless series of arguments and disagreements they'd been having lately. He was much happier spending every moment with Ronan. But Michael was bothered by something and he found it curious that he was actually still a bit disappointed by his grandfather's inaction. "You know, I kind of convinced myself that he would call either on Christmas or New Year's Eve," Michael confessed. "I am the only family he has left."

"Age doesn't make people wiser, Michael," Ronan said, brushing the smooth side of his tie against Michael's cheek, "just makes them old."

Luckily, age was not something Michael and Ronan were going to have to worry about. And for that matter, Michael thought, neither should education. "I know! Why don't we go see Germany today instead of hearing a lecture about it? Or what the hell, why not Tokyo?" Michael suggested. "I'm sure it's really exciting even if, you know, my father's there."

Oh, I can't wait to travel the globe with you, Ronan thought, *country by country, but those kinds of adventures will have to wait.* "We have forever for me to show you the world," Ronan said. "First we have to learn about it."

Underneath Ronan, Michael sank deeper into his pillow, one hand pressing into the back of Ronan's neck, the other into the small of his waist. "That's 'cause you have a crush on Old Man Willows."

Taking the bait, Ronan pushed his body closer into

Michael's, making the mattress bend even farther under their weight. "No, but McLaren's bloody hot."

"I knew it!" Michael cried out in mock jealousy, slapping Ronan on the shoulder. "That's the only reason you like to read!"

"And if you want to read past a tenth-grade level, you need to get up now and get dressed," Ronan declared. "You've world history in fifteen minutes."

Thanks to his preternatural speed, thirty seconds later, Michael was completely dressed, his clothes a bit unkempt yet presentable, and ready to leave, but still he was without his usual enthusiasm for education. "Seriously, Ronan, why do I need to go to school anymore?" Michael moaned.

The question surprised Ronan. "I thought you loved school."

"I did, but that was, you know, before, and, well, now . . ." Michael stuttered, then announced, "I'm a vampire."

"Um, so am I, mate."

"And you're also a student, which just doesn't make any sense."

Tucking Michael's shirttail into his pants, Ronan looked knowingly at his boyfriend. He understood his questions, his desire to be an active part of the world and not just read about it in a textbook, but he also understood that outside of Archangel Academy, the world was different. It wasn't as safe, it wasn't as receptive to their kind, and so, for now, this was where they needed to remain so they could learn and prepare themselves for the world beyond the academy's borders. "We may be immortal, Michael, but we're not infallible," Ronan said, aware that his tone was dangerously close to patronizing. "If we want to prosper and lead, we can't be ignorant prats; we have to study, learn everything we can."

"You can teach me everything I need to know," Michael said.

Ronan blushed and thought how wonderful it was to have someone need him so much, someone who revered him, but no, he was forced to acknowledge that even he had limitations. "About being a vampire, yes, but Double A will teach you how to become educated." Michael couldn't stop his eyes from rolling. "And trust me," Ronan whispered, his lips a breath away from Michael's, "there is nothing sexier than an educated vampire."